WIDOWER, 48, SEEKS HUSBAND

Raymond Luczak

Rattling Good Yarns Press
33490 Date Palm Drive 3065
Cathedral City CA 92235
USA
www.rattlinggoodyarns.com

Cover Design: Raymond Luczak

Library of Congress Control Number: 2023930958
ISBN: 978-1-955826-31-0

First Edition

Also by Raymond Luczak

Fiction
Compassion, Michigan
Flannelwood
The Last Deaf Club in America
The Kinda Fella I Am
Men with Their Hands

Poetry
Chlorophyll
Lunafly
once upon a twin
Bokeh Focus
A Babble of Objects
The Kiss of Walt Whitman Still on My Lips
How to Kill Poetry
Road Work Ahead
Mute
This Way to the Acorns
St. Michael's Fall

Nonfiction
A Quiet Foghorn: More Notes from a Deaf Gay Life
From Heart into Art: Interviews with Deaf and Hard of Hearing Artists and Their Allies
Notes of a Deaf Gay Writer: 20 Years Later
Assembly Required: Notes from a Deaf Gay Life
Silence is a Four-Letter Word: On Art & Deafness

Drama
Whispers of a Savage Sort and Other Plays about the Deaf American Experience
Snooty: A Comedy

In Gratitude

Writing a novel, especially steeped in a history that hasn't always been recorded, often feels like taking a voyage without a map. One never knows where the raft is going, but these people have provided moments of clarity or suggestions for my many questions—historical, religious, technical, geographical, medical, editorial, and otherwise—in the last fourteen years prior to its publication: Richard K. Adler, Ph.D., CCC, SLP, Speech-Language Pathologist; Jim Aune (*in memoriam*); Meir Bargeron; Glenn D. Bottomly, Ph.D.; Tim Campbell (*in memoriam*); David Cummer (*in memoriam*); David Ellis Farnham (*in memoriam*); Will Farr; Stuart Friedman; John Gerard, M.D.; Jill Hartman; Harvey Hertz (*in memoriam*); John Kowalczyk (*in memoriam*); Daniel J. Langholtz; Heather B. Lawton; Alex Leffers; Steve Munsinger; Tony Santos (*in memoriam*); Tom Steele; Shannon Todd (*in memoriam*); Russell J. Toscano; Jean-Nikolaus Tretter; Stewart Van Cleve; Matthew Vigé; Phillip Ward; Jim Wardlow; and John Whyte, M.D. And of course, I'm most grateful to Ian Henzel and St. Sukie de la Croix for bringing my novel to the finish line!

Two books in particular have helped me ground my story in historical reality: David Carter's seminal text *Stonewall: The Riots That Sparked the Gay Revolution* (St. Martin's Press) proved to be invaluable in correcting my many misconceptions about "the hairpin drop heard around the world." The reader is advised that I've taken a small but important dramatic liberty with the first Stonewall Inn riot as well as the events leading up to a notorious incident involving Anita Bryant. Steve Endean's memoir of his early days as a gay activist in Minneapolis and St. Paul, *Bringing Lesbian and Gay Rights into the Mainstream: Twenty Years of Progress* (Harrington Park Press), lent invaluable insights into the burgeoning gay politics scene in Minneapolis during the 1970s. The Jean-Nikolaus Tretter Collection at the University of Minnesota Library is a true godsend for those interested in LGBTQ history.

"Judge not, that ye be not judged."
~Mark 4:24, The King James Bible

for
Joseph L. Cumer

1
Timm

Timm Gay Johnson was an unrepentant nudist. He didn't care whether anyone saw him naked. In fact, if anyone appeared at the front door, he never bothered to put anything on. "Just in case the Jehovah's Witnesses pay a visit," he always said. Likewise, when guests came over for dinner, he never put on his clothes. "My birthday suit's my best outfit."

The size of his endowment had given him the nerve and courage to go naked. He was the school sissy all his life until he turned fourteen. The bullies always targeted him because he was short and smooth like a girl, leaving him bruises to remember. But finally, when they saw him naked in the locker room, they turned silent. They left him alone. Girls heard whispers about his equipment, but he said he wasn't ready for dating.

The day after he graduated from high school in 1976, he gathered up his graduation gift money and took his car to Minneapolis, a four-hour trip southeast. He had no interest in college. A married traveling salesman with whom he once had furtive sex in a rank public restroom told him all about the wicked charms of the city banked on the Mississippi River. He never told anyone where he'd gone. He had gotten tired of working on the farm and having his older brothers, who were buddies with those bullies, always teasing him that he had to *milk* those cows again. Men and women still talked about him at class reunions and wondered if he would show up. He never returned. They had no idea that after living a few months in Minneapolis, he'd changed his name from Timothy Neil Johanssen to Timm Gay Johnson. He had added an extra "m" to his first name for effect. If he felt the need to remind a stranger that he was indeed of the fairy persuasion, he pronounced his first name "Tim*mmm* Gay Johnson." His new middle and last names were an inspired reference to his legendary appendage.

On that afternoon, after arriving in Minneapolis for the first time, Timm found a room at a boardinghouse on the corner of West 22nd Street and Bryant Avenue South. An hour later, he strolled into Antonio's Floral Shop, a few blocks away on Hennepin Avenue, and said, "May I please speak to the manager?"

Timm was secretly thrilled to see that Antonio was just as nelly as he was. He had greased his hair so much that his sides looked like dried paintbrushes, and he wore polyester plaid pants that left little to the imagination. They sat together in the cluttered office. They talked about everything except flowers and sex. Thirty minutes later, Timm had found himself a job. He'd managed to convince Antonio that he was a quick study. And he indeed was. Antonio was surprised by how much Timm had mastered the art of maintaining and arranging flowers after studying the flowers photographed for Antonio's shop portfolio. Timm borrowed one pile of books after another from the public library downtown and devoured them all during his lunch breaks and late at night before going to bed.

Three months later, nearly all the straight people who worked at the shop were horrified to learn that Antonio was a homosexual. "But you look so ... *normal.*"

"Honey," Antonio deadpanned, "if I wanted to look normal, I wouldn't look like this."

Most of the straight people quit. Timm found it hilarious that these poor folks hadn't been able to figure Antonio out.

Antonio and Timm advertised for men blessed with flair and a love of flowers. They either had it, or they didn't. Prospective employees had to have a lilt, a soft sway, or a telltale mannerism; if they'd done drag at the Sandbox Bar in the 1960s, or hung out at Sutton's or the Gay 90s, even better. The few remaining straight employees felt embarrassed to overhear men treat each other with endearments such as "Girl, if I wanted to make my flowers scream, I'd have used *fuck*-shia." But their floral arrangements, getting more elaborate and outrageous, often warranted copy in the local magazines and newspapers, and scored flocks of curiosity seekers who became customers.

It wasn't long before Timm moved into a one-bedroom apartment at the end of Bryant and Franklin Avenues. His new best friend, Queen Betsy York, lived upstairs. She was christened *the* wittiest emcee for the drag shows performed at the Gay 90s when it was recently transformed with go-go boys after having employed female strippers for decades. Timm had chosen the apartment because it was closer to Loring Park, where he could have sex on the way home from the baths downtown. He loved the feeling of having that option.

He hadn't cared for puffs of cologne in his hair and dabs of moisturizer around his eyes. But then he read in a New York City gay newspaper that effeminate men made it harder for gays to progress in being "assimilated." Assimilation was the very last thing Timm wanted. Emboldened by Queen Betsy's example, Timm felt it was his duty to live the life of a stereotypical queen. It was true that he never cared for Judy Garland, Barbra Streisand, or Liza Minnelli. But right there and then he decided that he would change the way he lived. Although he hadn't cared for wearing pumps and bandanas before, he wanted to now. Betsy taught him how to apply foundation, mascara, and eye shadow. After all, Betsy worked as an embalmer by day, so she was quite an expert on makeup.

The next morning, he walked to work as usual. He'd seen pictures of Quentin Crisp, who had written a most charming autobiography that was turned into a great film. He couldn't get over the fact that the film was shown on the BBC in England! In deference to Mr. Crisp, Timm donned a gaudy fedora hat and a garish yellow-and-brown ascot. He carried an ivory-handled cane even though he didn't need it at all. He would welcome any and all hisses that would surely be tossed his way.

Cars stopped.

Drivers honked and yelled epithets at him.

Male dogwalkers tried to sic their dogs on him, but the dogs only wagged their tails happily.

Timm gently kissed the tips of his fingers and blew them away. He'd kill them all with love and affection. He'd show just how strong he was.

In the shop, Antonio stood speechless. "What the hell are you doing looking like that?"

"I don't want anyone to think I'm normal."

"Timm, you're lisping."

"I'm a queen who likes to suck dick and fuck men's holes. So, what's on today's clipboard?"

Timm leafed through the sheaf of orders and plucked out the more complicated ones. He sauntered over to the greenhouse, which had wide windows right on the sidewalk on Hennepin Avenue. Passersby could see the rows of houseplants and the wide table in the back. Timm brought vases of flowers and plants to the table, arranging a bewildering array that matched a wedding's color scheme. He hadn't realized that as he put one finished bouquet after another onto a delivery cart, people were stopping to gawk at him through the windows. An hour later, Antonio beckoned him to his office in the back.

"You have to change the way you dress. Right now."

"Right now?"

"Yes. We've got people standing outside the greenhouse."

"They're out there? Looking at me?"

"Yes."

"Darling, that's so wonderful."

"But this here is *my* goddamn business."

"I'm good at what I do, aren't I?"

"You're the best. You were born to arrange flowers."

"Then screw 'em."

"You can't. They're my customers."

"Then fire me."

"You know I can't. You're too good."

Timm glanced around Antonio's office. He picked up a roll of paper and a magic marker and left.

Antonio followed.

Timm entered the greenhouse and saw the gawkers waiting for him. He smiled, blew them a kiss, and unrolled the paper. He wrote "A <u>REAL</u> FAIRY— COME LOOK!!!" and taped it to the window right in front of the gawkers. Startled, they moved away when Timm kissed his fingertips and placed them against the glass. "Mwah!"

He had begun preparing himself for a life of faggotry back in high school when he insisted on taking home economics instead of mechanical drafting. The principal and everyone else were up in arms over the idea of a *boy* learning how to cook with a class of girls, but Timm asked to see the handbook of class requirements and looked up the page for those who could take home economics. "It doesn't say anything about girls in here," Timm told the principal. True to form, he became the best student Mrs. Avery ever had. Even with his chocolate chip cookies, she was stunned by his perfectionism. The chips had to be dispersed evenly. If he knew what the class was going to make next, he read through his mother's cookbooks and tried the recipes a few different ways at home. Of course, his attempts were the hit of his household and his class. His father took him aside one afternoon and said, "Don't tell your ma, but you cook a hell of a lot better than she does." He joined his mother in the kitchen and made meals for their family. He didn't mind. Cooking was a way out of his otherwise dreary life as a farm boy. His brothers picked on him a bit less. One day he would leave and never come back.

The next day at work, he wore a tiara, a wig, a dress, and a pair of fuck-me pumps. Betsy said, "You know, you got more balls than the rest of us put together!" Then, using a cheap plastic camera, she snapped pictures of him standing proudly outside as if he was a bride on her wedding day.

By the end of that day at Antonio's Floral Shop, so many people had clustered around the window to watch Timm that the police eventually had to shoo them away. Timm was all gowned up with a tiara, putting together his flowers. He didn't change anything for them, nor did he try to camp it up. He simply put together his arrangements, cutting and pruning. Sometimes he turned around and presented his latest creation. Flashbulbs went off.

At first, Antonio objected to the crowds, but the notoriety brought in more customers than ever. Even the local TV station broadcast a short bit about a "militant homosexual florist," which in turn generated publicity for Antonio's Floral Shop. Of course, the shop was deluged with hate mail, boxes of JESUS WILL SAVE YOU brochures, a box of someone's turds wrapped up in Sunday comics, and lots of prank calls. Antonio was bemused when giggly brides-to-be insisted on talking flowers with Timm and no one else. They didn't know his name, so they simply called him "the fairy florist."

Nights, though, Timm had a vastly different reputation once he showed up at The Locker Room on North First Avenue on the edge of downtown. At the baths, he never had a shortage of tricks. It was so different from his high school days when no one knew what to do with him, and he loved every minute of it. He felt like a god sent down from the heavens amidst the swirl of dry ice and disco music. He felt his goal was to make every man gay. He would show them how much pleasure could be had from being with another man. There was absolutely nothing to be afraid of except homophobia itself. Some men stuffed cash into his hands when they saw how gloriously he could impale them. Timm found the idea of being paid for sex outrageous because he'd have done anyone for free! Nevertheless, he never objected when someone offered him cash. He squirreled away the fives, the tens, and the twenties in a tin can in a secret place in his closet. He was rarely in his apartment. Some nights he stayed over with tricks and spent only thirty minutes at home showering and changing into a fresh set of clothes. The whistling and name-calling eventually lessened when everyone in the neighborhood knew him as *that* fairy florist.

Then, that October, Antonio had a heart attack. Apparently, a daily diet of burgers and fries, combined with a heavy nicotine habit, hadn't done much for him. Timm showed up at his hospital room. "Darling, are you alright?"

"No, but I've been doing some thinking."

"Lord, what now?"

"I want you to buy me out."

Timm didn't have enough saved up in his tin, but he and Antonio worked out a deal. When Antonio returned to the shop two weeks later, he was flabbergasted to see the awning changed from ANTONIO'S FLORAL SHOP to THE FAIRY FLORISTS. "You can't do that!"

"Yes, I can. I'm the new owner, remember?"

Timm came up with the now-classic tagline that ran in all their ads: BECAUSE FAIRIES KNOW FLOWERS BETTER THAN ANYONE. His shop scored a prominent writeup in *Minnesota Bride*, which Timm sent straight to national industry periodicals like *Flora* and *Florists' Review* for another round of writeups. Gay magazines like *The Advocate* published glowing articles about The Fairy Florists. The name alone was an instant article hook. Then porn magazines like *Honcho* and *Inches* ran pictures of his floral arrangements. "How the hell can my flowers compete with this gorgeous hunk?" he kept saying when he showed the opposite page facing the writeup to his employees. They all laughed when one of them said, "What do you expect? He's got the most beautiful rosebud."

Then, out of the blue, a legendary editor named Bill Whitehead gave Timm a call from New York City. He wanted to know if Timm would be interested in doing a coffee table book featuring his floral arrangements. For the cover Timm posed in a glittery red dress, a bouffant wig, and a ton of pancake makeup with a look of shock at the over-the-top floral arrangements crowding around him as if they were monsters from a cheap and cheesy horror flick. A year later, *My, My, What Fairies and Flowers Everywhere!* became one of the biggest selling floral titles. He was surprised and disappointed that no one from his family tracked him down. He often talked about doing a sequel to his first book, but nothing came out of it. Then Bill died of AIDS in 1987, so that was the end of that.

But for all his activism, Timm was most proud of the gay community a decade earlier, in the days when Anita Bryant, then the spokesperson for the Florida Citrus Commission, ruled the airwaves, constantly misinforming everyone, insisting that homosexuals recruited children, and other nonsense. Everyone was horrified to learn that he *loved* her. "But why?"

"Look at what she's done for us. We've finally gotten our faces out of each other's crotches to see what the hell's going on out there!"

He had Betsy embroider a T-shirt with sequins that said SQUEEZE ME, I'M A FRUIT. He wore tight jeans that outlined his cock, donning a wig that looked like Anita's and putting on makeup that matched hers, right down to the exact lipstick color. He had relied on the homosexual network and managed to track down Anita's own makeup artist, who was gay, of course. Some of Timm's customers were put off by his appearance and left in a huff. Then he asked Betsy for a new T-shirt that announced NOBODY RECRUITED ME.

Everyone hid their looks of shock when they saw him prance down the winding Nicollet Mall in downtown Minneapolis. He did this on his days off, particularly if there was a lot of lunch-hour foot traffic. Eventually, his T-shirt's proclamation caught on, and quite a few men wore similar T-shirts during the Gay Freedom March 1977 down Hennepin Avenue that June. The night before, at the Gay 90s, he participated in an Anita look-alike contest with Queen Betsy as the emcee; there were five judges. He chose Anita's bland cover of "Till There Was You" from the musical *The Music Man* for his lip-sync number. It had taken him a few months and a lot of favors at the local Channel 4 TV station to track down video footage of Anita singing that song and watch it on their monitor. It was terribly important that he get her mannerisms and the tilts of her head right. He also listened to her talk on the radio in his apartment and imitated her accent while Betsy tried to hide her guffaws at his initial attempts. Seeing the eleven other Anitas, most badly done, milling about offstage made him laugh and not care whether he won or not. Touted as Anita Number 666, he did his number to great applause. Later, when he won the $200 prize, he said all of the money would go toward the Minnesota Committee for Gay Rights. He felt so bathed in love when the audience stood up and cheered his announcement. "I love you all, because Minnesota—not Florida!—has the best fruit. We're so juicy!" Then he turned to the other Anitas and asked them to join him in the march the next day. "What could be more heartwarming than an army of angry Anitas?"

The next day 37 Anitas showed up carrying signs that said things like: I WAS WRONG. HATRED IS DEVIANT. GOD DOESN'T CARE WHICH FRUIT I SQUEEZE. A DAY WITHOUT HUMAN RIGHTS IS A DAY WITHOUT SUNSHINE. Even though there were only a thousand onlookers, the Anitas got more press than anything else in the march. Everyone on the sidewalks along Hennepin Avenue cheered and guffawed when they grasped the irony of Timm's Anita lip-syncing to "Till There Was You" in a gay parade. Decades later, Timm was very tickled to hear that with over 125,000 packing the sidewalks of Hennepin, the Gay Pride March proved easily the most popular parade in Minneapolis. Of course, he never missed a single march. He insisted that all his employees wear hot pink T-shirts that weekend which proclaimed I'M A PANSY FROM THE FAIRY FLORISTS and mingle along the festival crowds and pass out postcards featuring a handsome discount. Interacting with strangers who initially laughed at their T-shirts turned them into potential customers; as far as Timm was concerned, the extra weekend pay for them was well worth it.

But more importantly, after Timm won the Anita look-alike contest that night, he'd gotten to know Thom Higgins, a militant activist, better over some drinks. They'd met earlier at a protest against Anita when she sang a few songs at the grand opening of the Bergin Fruit Produce Wholesaler plant in May 1977. Then, as part of their self-proclaimed National Fruit Day, they joined the 750 protesters who lined both sides of Kasota Avenue to welcome Anita and her entourage. When it began raining, they chanted, "Rain makes fruit grow." As one of the Fruit Marshals, Timm had been there to ensure the crowds stayed orderly.

Over the next few months, Thom stopped by frequently at Timm's apartment. Over dinner with Betsy, the three vented their frustrations over Anita and the rise of the Far Right. Ms. Bryant was still getting press and protesters, but it seemed like the same old thing. One night, when Timm served a banana cream pie for dessert, Thom poked at his piece with his fork. "So creamy and sticky."

"Doesn't that sound like an orgasm, dear?" Betsy quipped.

Thom picked up his fork and shook it once. The pie didn't come off.

"What are you doing?"

Thom looked at them. "Anita's gonna be in Des Moines next month. She'll probably do a press conference. I wanna throw a pie in her face."

Timm and Betsy gasped.

"Darling, that's brilliant!"

"But we have to keep this a secret."

"*I'll* make the pie."

It was their delicious secret, and they couldn't stop tittering every time they ran into each other. But they knew better to say nothing.

Being the perfectionist that he was, Timm experimented with his banana cream pie recipe for maximum stickiness. He wanted the pie to stick in *clumps*. Even Betsy had to say no when Timm brought yet another partially-nibbled pie up to her apartment. Then he brought the test pies to his shop, where everyone devoured them in mere minutes. That was how Timm developed the habit of bringing in a fresh pie to celebrate each employee's birthday.

But Betsy was furious when she learned that Thom had taken the initiative of asking a few people from the Channel 4 news station to accompany them on the trip to Des Moines. She had done her part to keep the pie a secret, so why couldn't Thom? She refused to join them. Timm got into the van anyway. He had to make sure that his pie was safe inside its ice-filled cooler.

On that day, Thom and Timm wore suits and ties in order to pass for straight. Thom trimmed his beard, and Timm had his long blond bangs hacked off for a crew cut. The new hairstyle didn't look right on him, but no matter. Thom even practiced lifting the pie up from the shopping bag so it would be quick and smooth. He also practiced carrying the pie with one hand while walking briskly around Timm's apartment. Nothing would be left to chance.

The two men shadowed their Channel 4 comrades into the building. Thom carried the pie in a shopping bag and stood quietly with Timm as the newscaster and cameraman set up their equipment. Then in came Anita and her husband, Bob Green. Timm was struck by how tiny she truly was. How was it possible that someone so evil seemed so small? She looked exactly what he'd thought she would look like: the puffy curls, the perfect cheekbones, those fucking immaculate teeth.

Then Anita and Bob sat down at a long table lined with microphones.

Lights went on. Bob tapped on the microphones to ensure that they were working.

Anita Bryant began her all-too-familiar spiel against homosexuals. Her husband nodded, having heard all this before.

Timm suddenly felt Thom thrust the handles of his empty shopping bag into his hand.

Anita didn't see him coming as she continued. "We are going to go on a crusade across the nation trying to do away with the homosexuals. And, um, every ..."

Timm watched the pie hold steady in Thom's hand as if in slow motion, but his friend didn't hesitate. Thom walked simply past the lights and cameras right up to the table and pied her. It couldn't have been more perfect.

Anita was absolutely stunned.

Timm was so proud of how the pie had clumped to her face. All that tinkering with his recipe had been worth it.

The atmosphere turned absolutely electric. "Security agents! Security agents!"

"No. No. Let him stay."

She said, "No."

Someone else said, "Let him stay."

Timm jumped further back when he saw the camera switch from her to Thom, who was already holding up his hands and licking his thumbs clean. He was surprised to hear the best thing Anita had ever said: "Well, at least it's a fruit pie! Huh!" With that witty remark, she made Timm think for a split second that he and Anita would've made good friends in a different time and place.

Then the camera panned back to Anita. "Father, I wanna ask that you forgive him."

Her husband added, "And that we love him."

She repeated, "And that we love him." Her voice cracked as she tried to continue. "And that we are praying for him ... to be delivered from his deviant lifestyle, Father. And I just ..." She broke into sobs. She looked so pathetic.

Timm said nothing. That pie represented a lifetime of being picked on. It was the most just dessert he had ever served anyone, and who better to lick it than the bitch herself?

A few hours later, the video clip of Anita being "pied," suddenly an acceptable verb, had played on all three television networks. The image became branded on the nation's consciousness. That night gay people in bars everywhere in America cheered and toasted the act of humiliation. When Timm heard about that, he knew it wouldn't be right to tell everyone that he'd made the pie. It was important that every closeted person *see* Anita get pied and gain hope that they too would fight back. By the time Thom died of hepatitis C in 1994, it was as if time had forgotten the pie that upstaged Anita. Ten years later, Timm felt enormously heartened to see that someone had remembered the infamous clip and posted it on YouTube. Thom would've been so proud because it was Thom's finest hour as activist.

In 2007, Timm was made the Grand Marshal of the Ashley Rukes GLBT Pride Parade. But he wasn't interested in sitting in an open convertible and waving to the crowds like a lame dame on her last legs. He was a fit 48! In honor of the 30 years since Anita had unwittingly galvanized the gay civil rights movement, he decided to dress up as her once again. Behind him on the truck was a picture of a just-pied Anita blown up with his favorite quote of hers below: "As a mother, I know that homosexuals cannot biologically reproduce children; therefore, they must recruit our children." —ANITA BRYANT, 1977. He'd managed to find his original sequined T-shirt from thirty years before and wore it tightly over his Anita dress: NOBODY RECRUITED ME. He thought it a complete hoot to wear long-sleeved gloves and that ratty wig. This time, when he lip-synced to "Till There Was You," he made expressions of shock whenever he saw yet another lesbian or gay couple kissing each other. He loved it when the crowds took his cue and made out in front of him as others cheered them on. He acted as if he was having one heart attack after another while lip-syncing. This meant that for a few minutes, the widely divergent community could laugh and be together as *one*. Anita had been their second Stonewall moment. Of course, he got a great deal of pleasure from monitoring Anita's drawn-out fall from grace with divorce, bankruptcies, and lawsuits.

Despite Timm's blatant activism and his political signs brandishing the front windows of his shop, the customers never stopped coming. He continued to score a string of extremely high-profile weddings and shocked everyone when he showed up in a suit and tie at the church and reception hall. Not with a tiara, not even in a dress. He knew that when he went out there for clients, he was on *their* turf, and he was never to upstage the bride.

Less than a year after taking over the shop, he soon tired of dressing up and putting on makeup, so one morning, he wore a T-shirt and jeans. Everyone was confused. Where was the Fairy Florist? Customers had expected to see fairies look like, well, *fairies*. "What's your problem, darling?"

They couldn't articulate their profound disappointment. But the men continued to buy bouquets for their girlfriends, wives, and mistresses. Timm was secretly pleased when he saw how some of these straight men repeatedly glanced at the outline of his cock inside his tight jeans. He couldn't wait to see them show up at the bars and the baths, as they eventually would. Then he'd perform the sweetest recruitment possible.

Timm realized that it was far more radical to dress like everyone else in a place called The Fairy Florists. After all, homosexuals were just like everyone else.

Antonio lived another four years before his second heart attack finally killed him. By then, a mysterious epidemic had killed off nearly half the staff. But in the halcyon summer of 1979, no one had a clue of such black clouds to come. By then, Timm was already living with his husband.

2
Howie

When Howard Dwight Taft accepted his high school diploma from the principal in June 1978, he heard two people in the audience clap. It was his parents. As children of the Great Depression, they had played it very safe all their lives, rarely going away on vacations, and if they did, they slept nights in their car instead of checking into a motel. In winter, they turned down the heat at night to exactly three degrees above when the pipes might freeze. In summer, when the breeze died down, they did not use a fan. They opened the windows and waited for the wind to return. They watched every single penny and put the money they'd saved from their grocery shopping into their savings accounts. His father fixed watches for a living, and his mother was a housecleaner who also worked as a motel maid. They never talked much. They rarely cracked a smile. And they didn't care for the entertainment on their TV. Newspapers left behind by their customers were more than sufficient.

When Howard saw how emotional strangers on the street could be, he realized that perhaps his parents weren't normal. He hung out with the boys in the neighborhood, but he sensed that he was different. He couldn't figure out how or in what way. Not until the night he happened to look through his bedroom window and caught Jimmy Jenkins, a tall senior from his school, scooping up Vera Lind into his arms and sticking his tongue down her throat in the alleyway behind his house. There, in the gleam of streetlight and shadow, he felt a flare of desire and embarrassment. He wanted to be Vera in Jimmy's arms, but not dressed up like her, of course. He had heard some talk about faggots and sissies, but he never felt that applied to him. He was just different. He didn't know where that feeling came from. At twelve years old, he just was.

After seeing Jimmy in the alleyway, he observed how each boy his age carried himself. Then there were the men who mowed the lawns, harvested the crops, policed the streets, and fixed flat tires. He felt as if each one of them became a tiny ray of light seeping into his dull life. He didn't know the word for his condition, but he sensed that it was not to be talked about, much like his parents at the dinner table. If they spoke, it was always about how much money they'd saved that day. Sometimes one of them was pleased with the grades on Howard's report card, but compliments were seen as indulgent, rather like saffron and filet mignon.

His changing body stirred in ways no one warned him about. At first he was frightened at the fur that seemed to grow out of nowhere; he felt as if he were turning into a chimpanzee. Then, when he had his first wet dream, he felt intense pangs of pleasure and guilt. He couldn't believe what a mess he had made inside his underwear. No one must ever know! His mother was a fanatic about keeping the house clean. The hardwood floors gleamed in the dimmed lights. The few figurines that lined the shelves in the dining room were dusted once a week. The pots and pans were at least forty years old. The toilet bowl exuded a whiff of lemon-scented disinfectant every morning.

It was before the toilet that Howard learned to relieve himself, and often, but he had to be quick about it. They were concerned about paying for the water each time someone flushed the toilet. His parents did not approve of leisurely tasks and staying too long in the bathroom was one of them. Life was hard, so why be lazy about it?

His parents watched only the news on the television, and then turned it off. They weren't into watching entertainment of any kind. They reread the Bible. Howard sneaked Tom Swift and Hardy Boys novels from the school library and read them in secret. He mowed neighboring lawns for cash. When Howard saw how his parents insisted on taking his earnings and putting them into a savings account in his name, he felt something snap inside him. He knew he wasn't supposed to feel this way, but he realized he *hated* his parents. They were too unforgiving, too rigid. Come on, it was the 1970s! Once away from his house, he could hear and see how the world was changing. He loved that Sylvers song "Boogie Fever." Whenever he heard it on the radio, he always stopped to listen. It made him so happy whenever he heard it. He wanted to save up for a record player and buy that song, but he knew his parents wouldn't allow it. Howard dreamed of the day when he would be far away from home and when he could play that song as loud as he wanted.

He began counting out the remaining months of his high school years. He couldn't wait for June 1978. Homework was easy, but he couldn't spend so much time alone in his bedroom reading forbidden novels. His parents might get suspicious. The problem was, he wasn't interested in sports. So he signed up for the yearbook staff, the next best thing. They gave him the least popular job, and that was to be responsible for the money. Everyone had to raise funds to help defray the cost of printing the yearbook, so every month he sat at the table where cheerleaders, bosomed and lipsticked, stood while they sold cupcakes and cookies. They handed the money to him, scarcely looking him in the face. They were more interested in catching up with their friends on the other side of the table.

Nevertheless, Howard kept a meticulous list of monies earned and deposited them at the bank five blocks away. He had the unpopular task of figuring out just how much students had to pay for their copies of the yearbook. He asked their yearbook advisor, Mrs. Erna Galway, to break the news. He was grateful that she understood why he didn't want to be the bearer of bad news. Everyone was aghast at how much it was going to cost.

The yearbook staff doubled their efforts to raise more money. Car washes came and went. The Lemon-Day was a huge success. One Saturday, the bank was willing to allow the students to run a lemonade stand between the bank's drive-by lane and Vinnie's Car Wash. All in all, the students only had to pay two dollars less than originally announced. Howard was in the center of all this. He knew where each penny went. He didn't mind. It made him feel rather important. Someone said that he had the look of a banker.

Later that night, when he looked at himself in the mirror, he had to concede. He wore glasses. He combed his hair to the side. He shaved every day. He wore khaki slacks. He always buttoned up his shirts, leaving the last one open to reveal the white undershirt underneath. He felt strange when he saw how the hairs on his forearms began to take on a darker color. He was relieved that his white undershirt hid the fur creeping all over his chest. He changed to wearing long sleeves at all times. This was another reason why he wasn't interested in doing sports. He was afraid of being called names. He knew that he was the only uncut boy in his class. He knew that he had the body of a man, but in no way did he feel like one. Men were never put down or called names. He didn't know what he wanted out of life, but he knew he had to get out of Luverne, a town of not much distinction in southwestern Minnesota. Its saving grace was its proximity to Freeway 90, which ran east and west between Wisconsin and South Dakota, places that promised more than what existed in his hometown. He couldn't wait to become a senior. In the fall of 1977, he applied for college up north in Minneapolis, which seemed as far away as the moon, but he didn't tell his parents, not at first. He knew how they'd react. He went to the public library and pored over studies that proved that those with college degrees tended to earn at least twice what their non-educated peers earned. He copied down the title, the call number, and the page number for each study, carefully assembling them into columns on a sheet of legal-sized paper. Then he read up on the most promising fields filled with high-paying jobs and wrote these down, again noting where the data could be found.

One night he felt ready. He placed the three sheets of paper on the table in front of his parents without saying a word.

"What's this?"

"I want to go to college."

"We can't afford it."

Howard explained what he'd learned. It was the most he'd ever talked to his parents on a single occasion. After five minutes of nonstop talking, he felt as if he had become long-winded like Reverend Källqvist at church. He said that he was now awaiting word on his application from the University of Minnesota. His guidance counselor said that he had an excellent chance of getting in.

His parents said nothing.

He left the sheets on the table.

Later that night, he thought about how he'd run away to Minneapolis and find a job there to help pay for tuition. It might take him a lot longer to get a degree, but that was okay. He needed to get out of Luverne.

The next morning his parents told him, "We'll make an exception."

He was stunned.

He was even more so when the acceptance letter arrived that April.

His parents finally smiled.

He stared at them. He wanted to get a camera and take a shot of their smiles—just in case he'd forgotten how they actually loosened their facial muscles.

Later that August, his parents went north with him to Minneapolis. They had never been there, so when they went off the frighteningly fast freeway toward the campus, they kept quiet when they saw young people dressing a bit more loosely than back home. Women were wearing shorts and platform shoes that accentuated their curves, and men were wearing their blow-dried hair long. His parents cast questioning glances at Howard.

"I'm not going to dress like that."

He had always rotated his seven shirts, one for each day of the week. He would've liked a few more for variety's sake, but his parents were adamant about not needing another shirt. He thought about the pathetic clothes in his suitcase and felt a deep blush of shame. If he had been ignored like wallpaper in high school, he would surely stand out here! This was not good.

Nevertheless, his parents did not say much as they surveyed his dorm room and met his roommate. They had insisted on waiting until his new roommate showed up. They tried to hide their twitches of shock when Gene, who'd let his puffy curls turn into a frayed Afro, said, "Hey, what's up, man?" They hid their shock at the waiflike quality of his arms and his threadbare cutoffs. But they didn't insist on Howard moving out or changing roommates. Because they had saved up so much money, they already paid for one year's tuition in advance. They didn't think it was possible to ask for a refund.

He didn't expect his parents to hug him goodbye.

They didn't. They said, "Good luck, and write us every week."

He was startled when his mother handed him an envelope containing stamps.

Later that night, after Gene hung rock-and-roll posters on his side of the room, Howard didn't know what to do. He didn't even have a book to read. So, while the record player played The Sweet, he lay on his bed and watched Gene, who basically carried on a one-sided conversation with him. Howard was stunned when he heard their single "Love is Like Oxygen." It was nothing like the Sylvers.

Gene turned and gave him a puzzled look.

"What?"

"Can I ask you something?"

"Uh, sure."

"You been watching me." Gene sat down on the bed opposite him. "You gay?"

"Excuse me?"

"You don't know that word?"

"It means 'happy,' right?"

Gene chortled. "You're *really* a small-town boy, aren'tcha. Look, it's cool if you are."

"I don't know what you're talking about. I'm not gay."

"Sorry. I thought you were."

"I mean, I'm not happy."

Gene burst out laughing. "I get it, I get it. You're a homosexual."

He stared agape at him.

"Like I said before, it's cool. I got a lesbian sister, so it's cool. If you want, I can introduce you to some people."

"No, no. I'm not gay that way."

"Hey. It's cool, man."

Later that night, when Gene took off his clothes for bed, Howard found himself absolutely rigid. No one had been naked in such close proximity! He couldn't sleep at all that night.

On campus, he listened carefully for these overheard words: "pansy," "queer," "faggot," "sissy," and all the other words that signified *homosexual*. He attended all of his five classes that semester and turned in his homework like clockwork. He didn't want to let his parents down. He ate his three meals a day dutifully in the campus cafeteria and learned to look busy with his textbooks as he ate. The students there didn't know his name, and they didn't seem to care. As in high school, he just wasn't cool enough. He hesitated about growing his hair long, but he didn't have any friends to encourage him to loosen up. And he had no clue about what clothes he should buy to replace his wardrobe.

He began taking long walks across the Mississippi River and explored downtown Minneapolis. He loved it there. The buildings were tall and imposing. They were nothing like the low-slung skyline of downtown Luverne. Each evening, as the chill of fall brittled into winter, he walked more and more until he reached Loring Park and its two connected ponds. In those days, the park was a riot of groves and shrubs that made it easy for men to have anonymous encounters in the shadows. Along West 15th Street were a row of parked cars where strangers could slip inside and service each other. No streetlamps overlooked these parked cars. Howard didn't know any of this yet, but as he walked around the larger pond, he noticed how intently men of all sizes and shapes bored their eyes into his face. This made him feel queasy. He had seen the sleazy movie theaters and seedy bars that lined Hennepin Avenue between Sixth and Ninth Streets, but he avoided them. He was afraid of getting mugged in those places. But here in Loring Park, what could these men possibly want?

He felt too hot inside his coat, so hot that he had to sit down on a bench. He wasn't looking at anyone or anything in particular.

"You okay?"

He looked up to see a short blond fellow wearing a full-length fur coat. Now, even though Howard wasn't sure what homosexuals were supposed to look like, this guy *had* to be a homosexual.

"I've been watching you. It's your first time, hm?"

Howard didn't say anything. He wasn't used to having a stranger talk to him in that weirdly familiar way.

"Come with me."

"I don't know you."

"But I do."

"No."

"Darling, out here's a pack of wolves who'd eat you alive. What am I? A lamb in a mink coat. Baa-ha!" He laughed.

Howard couldn't help laughing either.

He followed Timm home to his apartment on Bryant Avenue. Howard was aghast at how intricately decorated Timm's place was with feather boas, saloon lamps, and red walls. The place screamed FAIRY.

"I'm sorry, but this isn't—"

Timm closed the door, pulled him into his arms, and rubbed him gently down there. Howard creamed his own pants.

"Oh, dear."

"Sorry, I didn't mean to—"

"No, no. This is wonderful."

"What? This? I made a mess."

"So? Let me take care of you tonight."

Completely naked with Timm on the bed, Howard couldn't believe how delicious lovemaking could be. Every so often, he had to curl his toes. He had never felt *this* good. He couldn't get enough of Timm's body. Whoever said that all this was unnatural had never experienced such joys!

Afterwards, Howard sighed deeply. He put his hands behind his head on the bed. Timm snuggled up to him. Their bodies fit together like two puzzle pieces.

They talked.

Howard had never laughed so much, or so hard, in his life. By the time he left Timm's apartment the next morning, he knew he was in love. Who cared about all those things that had made Timm a flaming queen? He was truly a wonderful human being.

They met again and again.

One evening Timm made Howard a meal of veal scaloppini, green beans, and potato au gratin, and served him a glass of Chardonnay.

"Oh, this tastes *wonderful*. Can I marry you?"

"Now?"

"Sure."

They took off their clothes and stood right there in the dining room.

"I, Timm Gay Johnson, agree to marry you, Howard Dwight Taft. I agree never to judge you and love you as exactly as you are."

Howard repeated the vow.

When they kissed again, they ended up never finishing their meal.

The next day Howard came out to his roommate, who said, "Hey, it's all cool, man." He moved out of his dorm room and moved in with Timm; as long as he was a college student, he didn't have to help pay the rent. On Timm's days off, he followed his husband around the thrift shops in the area, and discovered new clothes for himself. He allowed his hair to grow long, but Timm insisted that he wear his hair short. "I have to be the nelly one, not you." He loved Timm for that. Timm was completely opposite his parents, and he was a constant breath of fresh air. He even adopted Timm's suggestion that he stop calling himself Howard and use Howie instead. "Makes you sound a little less stuffy."

When his freshman year ended, Howie never went back to school. He had found a bookkeeping job at Smith & Keeler, a wholesale florist company that specialized in selling fresh cuts, bouquets, and supplies to florists all over the Upper Midwest. A friend of Timm's who worked there as a customer service representative had told Timm about the position. It wasn't exciting to be working at a desk with such a tiny window overlooking East Hennepin, but Howie was content. It meant that he'd have more time to be with Timm instead of taking classes and doing homework. All he cared about was that he had Timm, and all the cut flowers that no one wanted at his floral shop. Sure, the flowers lasted only one or two days more, but he never complained. His parents would've appreciated the gesture too.

His parents seemed increasingly distant each time Howie visited them. He knew them well enough to know that bringing Timm along would kill them. Finally, it seemed pointless to see them in person if their conversations weren't much. It seemed easier to pick up the phone and have very short calls since they were still worried about the ticking meter of long-distance.

In January 1979, when his parents died in a car accident off an icy patch of road, he felt nothing. He was hardly surprised by the obscene amount of money in their savings account. That was how Howie was able to put down a sizable down payment on a huge house off the corner of Aldrich Avenue and West 22nd Street. The deal was, that Howie would *fix* things and Timm would *decorate* things. The arrangement worked out very well. Howie didn't mind the gaudy spectacle of everything around him. Maybe it felt like too much at times, but that was Timm. Who was he to tell Timm how to live?

Eventually, once they put up a higher fence around their backyard, Timm took to sunbathing in the nude. He was proud of the fact that he had no tan line. For his part, Howie felt a bit odd being naked outside. He felt so pale in spite of his fur.

"You shouldn't be naked."

"What? Look at you."

"You're the straight one. I like you better when you're formal. Makes you hotter in bed."

"Really?" Howie found that he could attract someone as desirable as Timm hard to comprehend, but he went along. Whatever Timm wanted was fine by him. After all, he was a happily married man.

3
Howie

Over the years, Howie would often wonder why Timm had chosen to marry him. Once, when he was at the Gay 90s during the Pride 1979 weekend, a heavyset man standing next to Howie whispered, "You know that guy over there?"

His eyes followed the stranger's finger pointing at his husband. Timm was laughing and carrying on. As always, he was flamboyant with his movements, but that didn't seem to faze the men with trimmed beards, leather pants, and impressive bulges. Between sips of beer, they laughed right along with him. "Yeah. I know him."

"I heard he's horse-hung. Is it true?"

"No, I don't think so."

The man nodded slowly. "Thanks for telling me."

He was not surprised when the stranger left. The gay community, he felt, had too many size queens. The funny thing was, Howie never cared about size. Yes, at first, he was surprised by Timm's equipment, but he was so in love with Timm by that point that he never obsessed on its size. They had glorious sex, and that was it.

One night Howie surprised himself by going down alone to the Locker Room. Timm had talked about going to the bathhouse a number of times, so he was curious. He didn't tell his husband that he was going there. He found the whole experience rather unsettling. Was he supposed to take off his clothes and wrap a white towel, which wasn't really long enough to fit around his waist? Yes. And right there in the changing room where some men were taking their sweet time disrobing and waiting to see what Howie had between his legs? Yes. Even then, he felt vulnerable in exposing his densely furred chest.

"Fuck."

Howie shot up to see who'd said that. It was a thin man with a mullet. He suddenly felt fat even though he wasn't overweight. He knew he had a stocky body, but still, seeing how thin and tan most of the men were, he felt ashamed by how sweaty and sticky his body was. He left the changing room and saw a dimly lit corridor of doors. The walls were painted a shiny black; there was a black light near the end of the hall. The loudspeakers were playing Donna Summer's newest song. The men leaning against the walls struck him like statues in repose. Their white towels and the whiteness of their bodies practically jumped out in the dark. For some reason, he thought of panthers when he caught the whiteness of their eyes. He felt odd walking barefoot up and down the corridors. He could hear moans and cries through the din of plywood walls and music that pulsated through the air.

As his eyes eventually adjusted to the dimness, he started to recognize some of the customers he'd seen at Timm's shop and nodded. He didn't know their names. But he began to notice that some men were slowly following him. He couldn't imagine why. Was it because he had a furry body? That couldn't be. He hated having all that fur. Sometimes the dense hairs in his asscrack clotted around his hole, and that truly hurt when he sat down on the toilet.

After he'd scoped out the corridors and the rooms, he felt more confident. He saw how some men left the doors open to their rooms. They either lay on their backs, showing off their cocks, or on their stomachs to show their asses. He surmised that had to be how they'd advertised what they wanted. However, he wasn't sure what he was in the mood for. He had just never had anonymous sex before. Still, he felt obligated to try it once for himself.

Around the corner, he saw a strikingly tall man. His acne-scarred face wasn't great to look at, but Howie liked the rest of his body. He had well-defined pectorals and a washboard stomach. The stranger locked his eyes on Howie's.

Howie couldn't believe his luck. He started to feel erect underneath his towel. But he wasn't sure what the protocols were for this sort of thing.

The stranger approached him.

Nearby were a few men leaning against the walls between doors. They seemed slightly bored with stroking themselves through their towels. Even though it was dimly lit in the hallway, Howie still felt exposed and self-conscious. He knew everyone was there for the same thing, but still, he couldn't shake his discomfort. He looked up into the stranger's eyes.

No expression whatsoever.

Howie smiled slightly. Maybe that would get him to react a little.

The stranger leaned forward and slipped his hand between the folds of Howie's towel.

Howie gasped. He wasn't expecting that at all!

The stranger fondled him briefly and walked away.

Howie was so surprised that he didn't know what to think. The other men, having seen the stranger's reaction, moved away.

He felt a rash of humiliation itch throughout his entire body. It was the most unpleasant sensation. These guys knew that he wasn't hung. Nobody was going to want him now. Fuck.

He debated leaving the place right then and there, but he thought about the money he'd spent on the admission.

He resumed walking slowly. The nameless men looked more and more familiar.

Then he heard Timm's voice cut through the music: "Oh, man! Yeah! YEAH."

He followed the direction of his voice urging someone on.

A small crowd clustered around an opened door.

Howie went around their backs and caught a glimpse of the tall stranger going down on Timm. That was it. He wasn't going to come back.

At that moment, Timm looked up and caught sight of Howie turning away.

Howie put on his clothes so fast in the changing room that no one could see what he had between his legs. He didn't care. He stormed down the steps and walked briskly along Hennepin Avenue, cutting through Loring Park for home. He felt wordless in how he'd felt. Unattractive. Ugly. Unsuckable.

He was already in bed when Timm showed up. "Hey. I looked around for you, and you were already gone."

Howie said nothing.

"What happened?"

"The guy I wanted didn't want me. He groped my dick, and I wasn't big enough. Then I found him sucking *you* off."

Timm rolled his eyes and sat down. "I don't know what to say."

"I'm not going back. I don't want to know anything about that awful place."

"You can't let one guy ruin everything for you."

"I thought I'd get as much fun as you, but I guess that's not gonna happen."

"Oh, Howie. You know I still love you."

"You don't get it, do you?"

"I do."

"Really? Why do you have to go out there? I thought we had great sex. Am I that boring to you?"

"Come here." Timm opened his arms for a hug.

"What?"

"Please."

"*I* have to come over just for you? Just like all those guys who want your big dick, huh? How about *you* coming over here?"

Timm walked around their bed and embraced him. "I don't want to live with anyone else but you."

"Yeah, right. But everyone gets to have you, and ..."

"Oh, Howie."

"Don't 'oh, Howie' me. It's not the first time I've gotten dismissed."

Timm said nothing.

"Cat caught your cock?"

"That was ..."

"Fine. You go sleep in the other room, then."

"No. No. I'll cut back on going to the baths."

"Right."

"I'm serious. You'll see."

"You don't get it, do you? I do so much for you around the house, and you never say a single word of thanks. Tonight you sleep in the other room."

It was the first time in their living together that they didn't sleep in the same bed. The wall that divided their rooms felt impermeable. Neither man did not sleep at all. They lay there, looking up at the ceiling and wondering about having a future apart from each other.

A few moments before Howie's alarm clock was about to ring in the morning, Howie heard Timm knocking on their bedroom door.

"What?" Howie's voice was low.

"Can I come in?"

A beat. He sat up a bit in the bed and crossed his arms. "Okay." Timm entered the bedroom and took a deep breath. "I've been doing a lot of thinking. You're right, absolutely right. I don't appreciate you enough." In a torrential rush of gratitude, he thanked Howie for everything that Howie did: keeping their cluttered house clean and always without being prompted; scrubbing bathtubs and using an old toothbrush to remove mildew from the grout between tiles; for balancing their checking accounts and filing their income taxes; for liking everything Timm cooked, even when Timm felt it wasn't up to his own standards; for so often holding Timm's hand at the table when they ate their meals. "Howie, I've never had anyone love me like you do." He pulled down the blankets to expose the rest of Howie's naked body and leaned down to fellate him.

"No. Don't."

"What? I thought you loved my blowjobs."

"I'm not a pity fuck." Howie pulled the blankets back up to cover himself.

Timm said nothing.

"Don't act like you're surprised. You made me sound like a damn housewife. I'm not! You need to remind everyone that you have a *husband*. Me!"

"Howie. You're different from everyone else I know. You're the only man who's made me feel like I'm much more than my cock. That's why, if we could get legally married, I'd marry you all over again."

"Really?"

"Yes. I'd still choose you over a thousand guys."

"Oh, yeah?" Howie pushed the blankets off himself and smiled. "Then act like it."

They ended up running late for work that morning, but Howie was too happy not to care when he strode into his office for the day.

The first few weeks felt like a regeneration. It helped that Timm didn't have a lot of commitments in the evening.

But with the onslaught of new orders from brides for their weddings and receptions from late spring to early fall, Timm had to stay later in the shop. It was that time of year. Howie was used to seeing Timm come home, practically wiped out.

Eventually, their relationship fell back into its old and familiar groove. Howie kept wondering if he'd made a mistake in staying with Timm. But then again, who would want him?

As the years went by, Howie felt more and more inadequate. He saw how easily extremely masculine men flocked to Timm, begging to have sex with him even though Timm didn't reduce his nelly mannerisms. He felt more and more envious at how Timm didn't seem to appreciate their beauty. All he had to do was to unzip his trousers and let it flop out. But himself? He wasn't hung. He was average. Not even thick. Just average. His balls didn't hang low. He tried shaving his balls to make them look larger, but Timm said, "Why? You're fine just the way you are."

As Howie grew older, he began to gain weight. He knew it was because of Timm's rich cooking, but he was also not the type of guy to enjoy running around as much as Timm did. Howie sat all day at his desk where he ran a spreadsheet program called SuperCalc on an expensive IBM personal computer. At first, his weight gain was a slight belly flab that made itself felt when he sat down at his desk. It didn't seem so bad because once he stood up, the flab disappeared. He drove straight home from work and watched the TV news while waiting for Timm to appear in the doorway with, "Dinner's ready." Sometimes Timm arrived a bit late, so Howie ordered takeout for the two of them. Howie and Timm rarely went out during the week; they simply sat home and watched movies on VHS tapes they'd rented. Sometimes they went out to an AIDS fundraiser, but after a certain point, they had to stop. Too many of their friends had died.

They began hearing stories of gayborhoods like Greenwich Village and the Castro, much like their own Lowry Hill East neighborhood, changing from a carefree spirit into a ghost of paranoia. "You have it?" their gazes passing by always asked. They saw this in every major city they visited in those days. Timm always visited New York once a year to absorb the latest trends in decoration and design, so Howie tagged along. Howie wasn't interested in spending entire days listening to Timm talk nonstop about flowers and techniques for floral arrangements with shopkeepers, so he walked around the West Village. Even though Howie knew he could have sex with anyone, he never did. It didn't feel right; it just didn't. He understood that being gay should mean that one didn't need to follow all the heterosexual norms and expectations for a long-term relationship.

Nevertheless, Howie didn't feel right. He was a monogamous creature at heart, but he hadn't tried to stop Timm from having sex after they got married. In fact, he understood. He, too, wouldn't have turned down offers to have sex with the hottest men if he himself had a tool that was the stuff of legend.

Once, in the days before AIDS changed everything, Timm insisted that Howie try doing a threesome with him. The third guy turned out to be a well-built man with aquiline features; he was a novice go-go dancer at the Gay 90s. But the minute the guy saw Timm's tool, he forgot about Howie being there. Timm caught the look of hurt on Howie's face, but the guy going down on him was apparently so good—no gag reflex whatsoever!—that he didn't stop when Howie got up and left the bedroom.

That night, after the guy left, Howie and Timm had their second quarrel that night. If they had a few petty arguments before, this was nuclear.

"I don't even know why I'm staying with you. It's like I'm an afterthought to everything that you do!"

"I'm sorry, Howie. I do love you."

"Really? You didn't even stop the guy when you saw me. I thought I was supposed to be included."

"The guy's a jerk."

"So? You didn't tell him to stop." He surprised himself when he gave Timm the finger.

That night Timm slept on the sofa in the living room.

The morning after Timm made lemon-ricotta hotcakes, Howie's favorite.

Howie ate glumly and didn't say 'thank you' as was his custom. He got up and left.

Timm called in sick.

When Howie came home, Timm was sitting on the sofa. "Please. Sit down."

"What?"

"We need to talk."

"Okay. So, talk."

"When we do threesomes again, he'll have to make you come first."

"No, you don't get it. They'll only have sex with me because of *you*, but not because of *me*. The ordinary and boring Howie."

Howie got up and left the house. He had been steaming mad and hurt all day at work. He was surprised how well he was still able to focus and not make any mistakes with the numbers. Months of hitting the keypad enabled him not to look at the keypad itself. He was grateful that his boss Elaine was out that day, so he was pretty much alone all day. He experienced moments when he wanted to kick his desk. Why did he marry someone like Timm? There was no way in hell he could compete with Timm on the basis of anything. He had to wonder if Timm had wanted him so he could feel superior.

Howie walked quickly toward downtown and cut through Loring Park. He paid no attention to the men loitering and sitting aimlessly on benches with their legs open. He knew where he wanted to eat, and that was Gary's Restaurant. He was in the mood for orange roughy broiled with scalloped potatoes; it was his favorite dish there. On Hennepin Avenue between Sixth and Seventh Streets, the place was tucked away in the seediest part of downtown, though; two Shinder's newsstands bookended the block and sold mostly porn. Rand Hotel and McDonald's huddled between Moby Dick's ("A Whale of a Drink"), easily the seediest bar in the city, and Brady's Pub. As he sat in Gary's Restaurant and surveyed the other gay customers talking and laughing among themselves, he felt more desolate. The orange roughy didn't taste so good after all. He thought about tricking with a stranger at the Locker Room a few blocks away.

He decided against the bathhouse and walked west to the Hotel Amsterdam. It was a bit seedy, but at least it was gay-owned. He paid for a room and lay down on the bed. He tried to sleep, but he couldn't. Stale cigarette smoke from the hallway seeped into his room. He turned on the TV and watched. The flicker and the hum of Hennepin Avenue below eventually lulled him to sleep. He found himself aching to touch Timm's body, so he pulled the other pillow to his own chest.

The next morning, he took a bus back to his neighborhood. He went into their house and took a shower. He listened for Timm, but he didn't seem to be anywhere. Which was just fine. He was probably fucking some hot guy. Howie put on his boxers, shirt, tie, and suit. He was the only one out of eighty-two employees at Smith & Keeler, who felt compelled to dress up in a suit for work. The suit was a uniform that made him feel serious and focused. It had nothing to do with sex, even though Timm kept insisting that he looked unbelievably hot in a suit. Thanks to that hot traveling salesman in his youth, Timm had developed a major weakness for well-dressed businessmen.

He was surprised to find Timm waiting outside in Howie's car. "What do you want?"

"I've been doing a lot of thinking. I think I see your point. Many guys are very shallow, and I was wrong to take advantage of that. So, I'm not going to sleep around. You can sleep around, but I won't."

"Oh, Timm. I don't need to be with a lot of guys to feel good. You're more than enough for me."

"Well, I'm going to be a good boy. Just you wait and see."

As it turned out, Timm's decision was a most fortuitous timing. Some of their friends were starting to come down with strange purple lesions and hacking coughs. Then their friend Bruce Brockway, an aspiring concert pianist, became a poster boy of sorts as the first Minnesotan to be diagnosed with the new disease, and died in 1984. He was the one who begged for Timm's help in bringing his friends around to support the fledgling Minnesota AIDS Medical Project, later known as Minnesota AIDS Project. As the 1980s wore on, Timm found himself far more grateful than ever for being monogamous, even though he found the porn on videotapes to be a bit tired after repeated viewings.

Then Timm had a most unexpected quickie with a young man at his shop. He had come in for an interview, but with the two of them alone at the end of day, the young man merely opened his legs. His thighs had the sexiest plumpness to them. That was more than enough to push Timm over the edge. "You do realize that if we do this, I can't hire you, right?"

The young man groaned. "Oh, yeah."

Afterwards, Timm felt a huge weight lift off his shoulders. He'd forgotten how good it was to taste another man's body for the first time. That the young man wore a condom, which tasted a bit powdery in the mouth, didn't matter. It was the freshness of a man's unfamiliar touch. As he walked home, he felt the shadow of guilt overtake him. Should he tell? Or keep quiet?

Howie sat there, as always, watching the news. He was so predictable, and that, Timm had to admit, was part of his charm. He was almost like a dog, loyal and true no matter what happened. "Something wrong?"

"What? What are you talking about?"

"I can smell you."

Timm sniffed his own armpits. "I've been working hard all day. So?"

"No, it's a different kind of smell."

"So? Our bodies are all different."

"You had sex."

Timm hesitated.

"How long has this been going on?"

"Just once. Just now."

"Why can't I trust you? Now I'm gonna think that I'll get *it* from you. Fuck." He got up and left the living room.

"Howie! Please don't leave me." He ran after Howie and gripped his arm on the stairs. "Please. Don't make me beg."

Howie looked deep into Timm's eyes. "You want me to stay?"

"Yes. God, more than anything."

"Okay. You and I will never have sex again. Life goes on as before. Okay?"

Afterwards, Howie rarely allowed him to cuddle in bed, even on winter nights.

As much as Timm hated the deal, he understood where Howie was coming from. Of all the men he could have, he discovered that he wanted Howie the most. It didn't matter that they used to have sex often; they were sexually compatible and understood what pushed each other's buttons.

But Howie was resolute. If he was determined about something, nothing could sway him. Timm used to resent that about him, but in time, he came to see that was part of the deal. Once Howie decided he would commit to Timm for life, that was it. There was no hesitation or quavering about it. How many men could be like that? Not many. In the late 1970s, the temptation of easy sex with other men was much too strong. Some of Timm's friends thought that Timm was crazy to have such a dullard in his life when he could share his magnificent body with the world.

Nevertheless, some of Timm's friends got wind of the tension between the couple, and they told him to dump the bastard and move on. His dick still worked, didn't it? They didn't see a problem. In the weeks that followed, Timm turned quiet. He didn't laugh as much. He felt as if something had died. He knew he'd taken Howie for granted way too long. He had to make things right, but how?

As winter faded into spring, their house warmed up again. The sun lingered longer in the living room. One day he stepped out of the shower on the second floor and realized that he'd forgotten to stock up the bathroom with a batch of fresh towels, which were waiting next to the dryer downstairs. Annoyed, he walked shiveringly naked and picked up those damn towels. He left behind wet footprints as he went down the stairs. Howie was pouring himself a cup of coffee when Timm went through the kitchen.

"What are you looking at?"

"Nothing."

"The towels. I forgot them." Timm went down into the basement and took a towel. He immediately dried himself. He thought about the startled look on Howie's face as he did so. He wondered if Howie had betrayed a bit of lust in his eyes. Timm dried his private parts more thoroughly. Excited by the hope of having sex with Howie again, Timm climbed the stairs. It felt so good to let the air swirl around his body. He should be naked more often. Timm went into the dining room where Howie was eating a doughnut and reading the *Star Tribune*. Without another word, Timm bobbed his erection onto Howie's forearm.

Howie looked up slowly into his husband's eyes. He was surprised to see Timm holding back his tears.

"Please. I love you so much."

Within seconds Timm was all over Howie, tearing off his clothes. Timm insisted on showing Howie just how much he loved him. They were stunned by how they'd ejaculated not just once but *three* times within the space of an hour!

From that day on, Timm stayed naked at all times in the house. He relished the idea that he was being admired by the man he loved the most. He took to working out again. He had to be more buff than ever. He didn't care if Howie had some extra padding. What mattered was how Howie still loved him, and how they made love. It was nothing like the frenzied encounters he had with strangers years ago. Afterwards, he loved to wrap his arms around Howie and listen to his sighs as he fell into slumber. That's why he didn't mind Howie's weight. Hell, he'd been responsible for most of that! Timm felt safe. The more he heard from his friends how hard it was to find someone willing to commit to a long-term relationship, the more he knew just how lucky he was. Howie was a truly fine husband.

4
Howie

The 1990s came and went in a blur. The number of their friends dying from AIDS-related complications slowed down to a trickle. Everyone felt relieved. There was talk among gay men about how they weren't dead yet, and how they were going to resurrect sex as a recreational sport, just like in the 1970s. They had been filled with memories of these good old days, and they wanted them back in some form. It didn't matter if they were already pushing their 40s and 50s. It didn't matter if they couldn't always get hard as quickly as before. They were *gay*, dammit. So many gay bathhouses all over America had closed, but in the first decade of the twenty-first century, they had discovered the biggest bathhouse available: the Internet.

Howie had first bought a computer from FirstTech on Hennepin Avenue. At first, he browsed profiles online. The wide and wild variety bewildered him. It was as if each person had become something one could pick off the shelf for a while. Some of their nude shots were hot, but so many of them were badly taken, or they revealed too much of their backsides. He became much more interested in looking at their faces and reading the stories between the lines of what they wrote. Some he recognized around town and in bars, but most he didn't. That was fine. He was sure that many of them had sex with Timm, who'd posted a simple picture of his ready-to-impale erection. Timm didn't need to post a face pic at all. He was always getting emails filled with hot men showing off their equipment. Sometimes Howie was a bit disgruntled when he saw how much time Timm was spending online, so he insisted that Timm get a computer of his own. Howie often had to tell him to come to the living room and watch a movie with him. He felt that it was essential to have a *life* offline, and together.

Even though Timm had assured him that he'd never leave him for another man, Howie wasn't going to take any chances. He insisted that Timm introduce each trick to him in the living room before he and Timm, who always met him naked at the door, went up to their guest room. This, he felt, would unnerve the guy because he knew full well that Timm's partner was *downstairs*, reading a newspaper or watching the news. He felt very much like the father who was concerned about keeping his daughter pure and innocent.

Many of those guys never returned.

Timm seemed never to have noticed this, but Howie did. He knew he shouldn't feel this way, but he felt quite glad about how things had turned out.

Then came a guy who begged to serve both Timm and Howie. He was a pretty blue-eyed blond blessed with a pout; he wore a thick parka with moon boots. Already on his knees in the foyer, he swore to them that he had absolutely no limits whatsoever. He would do anything, and everything asked of him without question. Timm and Howie traded glances. Howie was surprised when Timm ordered the sub to fellate Howie.

The sub didn't hesitate.

As energetic as the sub was, Howie felt unable to stay hard. This didn't feel right. He pulled out and zipped himself up. "Sorry. I can't."

"Howie?"

The sub threw himself at Howie's feet and wept for mercy. He wanted to be kicked. To be flogged. To be punished. He deserved it for giving a substandard blow job.

Howie looked at Timm and shook his head.

"Get up," Timm said.

"Yes, sir."

"Go home."

"Please, sir, I'll make it up to—"

"Go home."

The man left.

"Howie, I'm sorry that didn't work out."

"Threesomes can be fun to watch on TV, but threesomes don't feel right to me, okay?"

"I thought maybe ..."

"Ask me next time before you invite someone, okay?"

"I thought you'd appreciate something different."

"Well, I guess I'm boring."

"No, you're not," Timm said automatically.

"Well, yes I am."

Timm watched him go up the stairs and felt an overwhelming burst of tenderness. Howie was really the kind of husband that everyone had dreamed of. Loyal, faithful, and sensible. Granted, he wasn't always the most interesting conversationalist, but he excelled at listening. Timm loved to talk, and there was no better listener than Howie.

Then came the most awful day in the spring of 2008. Early one morning, Timm complained of intense pains in his chest, found himself short on breath, and felt jolts of sluggishness in his legs. Howie took Timm promptly to Urgent Care at Southdale Medical Center. The X-ray and chest electrocardiogram prompted the doctor to run a duplex ultrasound on his legs and then venograms on his legs. "Well, it appears you have a pulmonary embolism in the anterior section of the inferior lobe of your right lung and it's possible that it was caused by the other clots we have detected in your right leg. We'll continue to run tests to verify our preliminary diagnosis of deep-vein thrombosis and to determine if there could be any other underlying conditions responsible for your condition."

"Plain English, please?" Timm clutched onto Howie's hand.

"Looks like you have two blood clots in your left leg, and a big one in the lower lobe of your right lung. That's why you couldn't breathe. A blood clot's travelled up from your leg right into your lung. You have to stay here for at least a few days. We have to monitor the clots. We'll put you on some blood thinners and anti-inflammatory drugs."

"Uhm," Howie spoke up. "What's the medical name for his condition again?"

"It's called deep-vein thrombosis. He's got a pulmonary embolism."

An hour later, they were up in Timm's room. His roommate was an older fat woman who kept moaning every other minute. Her daughter sat with her face averted in embarrassment. Howie pulled the pale blue curtain around Timm's bed.

The woman kept saying, "Oh, this hurts!"

"Ma, I know that. You have to be patient."

"But—oh!"

"Doctor Shannon gave you the maximum dosage."

"Oh! My back hurts."

Timm leaned forward and whispered, "I'm going to shut her up." He fell backwards and spoke in a louder voice. "Darling, do tell me about the last time I got fucked. I really, *really* enjoyed having your cock up my ass."

There was an absolute silence from the other side of the room. The woman wasn't moaning anymore.

Timm and Howie had to stop looking at each other because if they did, they'd have burst out laughing.

Thirty minutes later, the woman was moved to another room.

Once she was gone, Timm and Howie couldn't stop laughing for a good 20 minutes. Then the pains in his chest flared up again.

In those fleeting days when Timm had to rest in bed, he listened to Madonna's latest record *Hard Candy* nonstop on his iPod to take his mind off the pain and the boredom. When Howie was away from the hospital, he took one of his nurses aside and whispered, "Tell me the truth. Are blood clots fatal?"

"They can be."

After she left, Timm thought about how Howie was going to live without him. They had never talked about the eventuality. Of course, they had wills made out to each other back in the 1980s when no one knew anything about the "gay cancer" as it was first known, but death was never a topic of conversation. Timm knew that many men wouldn't be interested in Howie once they saw his pudgy body. He thought about whom among his friends might be interested in dating him.

Alan Hewson popped into his mind. Alan was an orchid fiend who kept his entire basement's temperature and humidity precisely controlled so he could grow his rare and expensive flowers. Living not too far from the Mall of America in Bloomington, Alan always wore white undershirts underneath his short-sleeved shirts, an army belt, tan khakis, and a pair of cheap shoes from Payless.

There was also another reason why Alan couldn't seem to find a partner. At just over five feet, he was very short. He also had some acne-scarred tissue on his face. If Howie had been a dweeb in high school, Alan was a major dweeb by comparison. Even though Timm found dweebs of a certain age to be sexy, he'd never found Alan hot. Maybe Howie would find Alan interesting enough.

Once Timm had been home after a week, he called up Alan and asked him to come to their house. He had enough energy to cook together a simple meal of vegetables, pasta, and wine for the three of them. In the dining room, they talked. Timm, who was fully clothed for a change, was relieved to see that Alan and Howie seemed to get along with each other. Maybe there was hope for Howie after all. When Alan left, Timm closed the front door and looked at Howie. "What do you think?"

"Think about what?"

"Him. Alan."

"Oh, he's all right. How are you feeling?"

"This is not about me. This is about you."

"What are you talking about?"

"Do you find Alan sexy?"

"What? Are you crazy?"

"Howie. You're going to need someone after I go."

"I don't want leftovers. Fuck you." Howie stormed up the stairs.

In the bedroom, Timm lay down beside Howie, who then moved himself over closer to his edge of their bed.

"Howie."

"I can't believe that you think I deserve someone like him. Nice guy and all, but he's ... I don't know. Not my type."

"What's your type?"

"You."

"Oh, Howie. You're so sweet."

"You're not going to die, okay?" He turned to Timm. "Come here." They snuggled together. Howie kissed him on the forehead before turning out the lights.

Then suddenly, one June morning, Timm found himself gasping for breath. The pain was in his left lung. Howie took him to the Southdale Medical Center.

Timm didn't argue when the doctor suggested that he stay the night in a private room in case he suddenly developed another clot. The one in his left lung had suddenly mushroomed out of nowhere. Timm gripped Howie's hand while he tried to breathe. "Darling, I don't think I'm going to make it."

"Don't say that." Howie had spent the entire day with him.

"Please. Listen to me."

"Anything." Howie searched his face. "Anything!"

"People know me as the fucking florist. I don't want any fucking flowers at my service."

"But ..."

"They'll be telling each other how nice the flowers are. Well, if I could do my own flowers, I would, and they would blow everyone else out of the water. You know it too."

"Well."

"Please. No flowers."

Howie turned to him. "I'll do what you want, but I do want one thing."

"What?"

"I'm going to pick the very best red rose I can find and put it in a vase and leave it on top of your ..." Howie didn't want to say the word "coffin." It sounded too final.

"Oh, my God, that's so brilliant!" Timm broke into a wail. "I don't wanna go!"

Howie lay down beside him on the bed, which squeaked from his weight. "I love you."

Timm stopped and looked up at him.

"What's so funny?"

"You know, I think that's the first time in 30 years that I've heard you say that."

"I never thought I was supposed to say it. That's just for the movies. This, here, is real." He gripped Timm's hand.

"Oh, Howie." He tried to reach up to kiss Howie on the lips, but he was a bit weak.

Howie kissed him and stroked his chin. "Everything will be okay."

"You know what's so amazing about you? I never needed to hear those three words from you. You're the world's greatest husband. I've been so horrible to you. Please forgive me. Oh, I'm so worried about you."

"Hush."

"I can't hush up. Look at me. I'm sticks and bones in an ugly gown. Whoever designed these hospital gowns with this horrid print should be shot. They're so ugly!"

Howie broke into a chuckle.

Timm took Howie's hand and kissed it. "Whoever designed you is a genius. You are perfect."

"Me? I don't think so."

"Oh, yes. Someone wonderful will truly love you as much as I have."

"I hate it when you talk like that."

"I'm dying, okay?" Timm looked quietly at his husband and then glanced at the door. "Can you lock the room for a few minutes?"

"Sure." Howie got off the bed and locked it.

"Strip."

"What?"

"I'm so ugly in this gown, and I need to see the most beautiful man in the whole world naked."

"But …"

"A few minutes. Please."

"Okay." Howie felt surreal as he pushed off his shoes, unbuttoned his shirt, unzipped his trousers, and took everything off. "You happy now?"

"Please. Don't be so angry with me. Turn around slowly."

"I can't. I'm so fat."

"Oh, that's where you're wrong. You're perfect. All that fur. All that meat on your bones. That foreskin! Oh, turn around slowly. I want to see you like this forever when I'm in heaven." Howie blinked his tears. He was grateful that his back was facing Timm at that moment. "Darling, I'd still marry you even if you were over 400 pounds. That's how perfect you are."

Howie finally turned. He was shocked to see Timm's erection tenting underneath his gown. He lifted the gown to see. "I used to hate this part of you so much."

"Shhh." Timm pulled him close for an intense kiss. "One more for the road."

They had never grieved so much for each other as they hungrily devoured each other's body and went through their favorite positions. They didn't care if anyone heard them from the hallway. They moaned hurt and ecstasy from the pits of their guts. They ignored the persistent knocks at the door. Even Timm took out the oxygen tube out of his nose. Each time they kissed, they burst into sobs, but they weren't going to stop fucking now. They had known each other so well that they knew how to time and prolong the moment of inevitable release. When they finally ejaculated simultaneously, they broke into sharp fits of giggle. The reek of sex and orgasm was pungent. The laughter didn't stop at all, not even when Timm pulled down his gown and covered himself. Howie put his clothes back on and kissed him on the lips. "Thanks."

"Darling, that's the best sex I've ever had," Timm whispered, "and that's saying a lot."

Howie chuckled and unlocked the door.

Outside were a few orderlies and nurses who looked as if they were in a state of permanent shock. They had been apparently listening.

Howie said, "Sorry. Were you looking for something?"

Timm cracked up.

When the visiting hours drew to a close that evening, Timm pleaded with the night nurse to allow Howie to stay the night in his bed. He was afraid of dying alone. The door finally closed, and Howie undressed, leaving on his boxers and undershirt. There wasn't really enough room for the two of them to sleep on the bed.

"Gee, this is like camping," Timm said.

"I don't care. I'm gonna stay right here. Come here."

Timm snuggled up to Howie. "Oh, this is so nice," he said as he rubbed his hand all over Howie's chest. He was finding it harder to breathe.

"Hush. You need to rest."

"No. I don't want to sleep because if I do, I'll never get to say good-bye."

"Then say your good-bye just in case."

Timm tried not to sob.

"You're tougher than thorns. That's what you always said. That's why you had to be the Fairy Florist."

He suddenly gasped and let out a chortle.

"What's so funny?"

"You know, if you were really into flowers, we should've gone into business together as 'The Hairy Fairy Florists'."

"I don't look good in a dress."

"You were the worst drag queen in the history of Minneapolis. Remember?"

They chuckled at the memory of Howie wiping the lipstick off on the sleeve of his white dress the instant he saw in the mirror how flaming red his lips were. Then Timm found a wide-brimmed white bonnet and tied it onto Howie's head. When he saw himself as the Little Bo Peep in the mirror, he wanted to bolt. Timm had poured some stiff drinks into Howie's glass and then they took a taxi to the Gay 90s. It was Halloween, of course, so the place was jumping and jiving with men in all sorts of costumes. That year Donna Summer inspired the most popular look with black Jeri-loaded tresses, black lingerie dresses, and very long eyelashes. So being Little Bo Peep made Howie stand out even more in a sea of men who tried to look like hookers. He felt apprehensive about going out in public like that, but once he saw how everyone broke out into helpless laughter at the sight of a hairy-chested man wearing blond tresses and a white sleeve smeared with lipstick. He was aghast when he was called to the stage. He had won two hundred bucks as the first place winner for best costume. Flashbulbs went off like crazy. Later that night, when Howie, feeling quite drunk, straggled out of the bar, he caught a new look on Timm's face while they waited for a taxi on Hennepin Avenue. "What are you lookin' at?"

"Oh, God. What can I say? I love you more than ever."

Two weeks later, he found a picture of himself in that dress in the pages of *Gay & Lesbian Times*, a new local magazine. He was angry at first, but he had to remind himself that it was nothing compared to what Timm went through, dressing up in drag every day for work.

When they finally stopped laughing at the recollection, they turned to each other. "I dare say we've had one hell of a ride. Thirty fucking years."

"Yeah," Howie said.

"And you never wore a dress again."

"No." Then something occurred to Howie. "Here's what I'm going to do for you. I'm going to require everyone to wear a dress and a hat for your service."

"You—you're going to wear a dress?" Timm gasped.

"Well, I'm not going to wear pumps. My back would kill me."

"Darling, you'd do that for me? I can't leave you now. I have to stick around and see that."

"My point exactly."

They whispered and chuckled into the wee hours at their ideas for his drag memorial service. Sometimes they nodded off into sleep, but one of them always jolted awake.

Howie said, "You there?"

"More alive than ever," he always replied.

When the morning nurse entered the room early after sunrise, he found Howie fast asleep with Timm dead in his arms. The date was June 15, 2008.

5
Howie

Before Howie notified anyone about Timm's passing, he called St. Mark's Episcopal Cathedral, which overlooked Loring Park at the corner of Hennepin Avenue and Oak Grove Street, and booked it for the Monday evening of June 23, 2008. Then he called Betsy to organize the service. "Timm specifically asked that everyone wear their best dresses, and be *on time.* I quote Timm here, 'If you're late, you're not coming into my house in Heaven! No more banana cream pies for you, bitch.' Oh, one more thing. Everyone must wear a hat. No ifs, ands, or buts about it."

Betsy agreed and went straight to work; she had done this many times before because so many of her friends died back in the 1980s. Timm's iconic signature as part of his drag ensemble was always a spectacular hat. And while she enlisted a few of her friends to bake twenty-four banana cream pies using his recipe, a most delicious thought occurred to her. What if she asked Anita Bryant to show up? But she decided against it, though, because that would've upstaged the focus on Timm. Still, surely that would have awakened Timm from the dead!

Then the emails went out. The local media picked up on it and ran long pieces extolling the many accomplishments of Timm Gay Johnson, the legendary "Fairy Florist." The buzz seemed to get more intense by the day. A former mayor of Minneapolis announced that he would attend in a dress. There were whispers of ghosts returning from the past when Timm hosted fundraisers for gay politicians on the rise. Allan Spear, the second legislator who came out while still in office as a state senator in 1974 and would work for 20 years to get the 1993 Minnesota Human Rights Act passed, would make a rare public appearance. He had retired eight years earlier. Even Jack Baker and Michael McConnell, the first couple to file a lawsuit to get their marriage legally recognized in 1970, would attend. Ann DeGroot, the charismatic woman who had helped turn OutFront Minnesota into a formidable political powerhouse, planned to wear a baseball cap lined with sequins. Then it was rumored that Tim Campbell, the publisher of gay newspapers like *GLC Voice* and *Positively Gay*, would make a surprise appearance after having moved back to Houston a decade before. It was clear that Timm's service would be a once-in-a-lifetime gathering of local legends who sometimes fought with each other and yet remained friends with the same man who had united them all.

Howie was flattered that so many dignitaries were coming. Still, he couldn't wait for the memorial service to be over with. Expectations were so high that he was afraid that people would be disappointed.

The night of June 23rd came quickly enough.

Afraid that there wouldn't be enough parking spaces, Howie decided to walk the entire way from his house to the cathedral. This was something that Timm would've done. Timm felt if you were going to spend hours putting on makeup, you might as well get out there and get appreciation. Even an epithet hurled at you was better than nothing.

Howie was genuinely stunned by the spectacle outside the cathedral overlooking Loring Park. It seemed that everyone, with the exception of cameramen and newscasters, was wearing makeup, wigs, dresses, and hats. Everyone was laughing and pointing at the unbelievable variety of all the hats while everyone posed for pictures and swapped their digital cameras for still more snapshots. Howie felt rather dull and matronly with his green dress and pearls, the kind of outfit that an older woman might wear to a formal party. But still, it was much better than being Little Bo Peep. He decided against wearing pancake makeup, although he allowed himself some lipstick and a wig that was reminiscent of Louise Brooks's helmet haircut in the silent film *Pandora's Box*. He didn't want Betsy to help out with the makeup.

When Betsy recognized him from atop the steps, she yelled, "Stop! Everyone, stop! We have here the most important man in Timm's life!"

The ones who knew him personally went into a tizzy and gave him air kisses.

As Howie walked up the steps to meet Betsy at the front doors, he felt his knees start to go weak. To say the least, it had been a stressful week, taking care of the endless paperwork and calls and emails. Timm was no longer there with him; Timm, now the object of obituary and memory, had somehow become something he scarcely knew.

Once inside the cathedral, he nearly faltered again when he saw how packed the pews were. He recognized some of Timm's straight friends. They were all wearing outrageous hats even though some didn't wear dresses. He felt a bit disappointed, but at least you had to give them credit for trying. They were heterosexual, after all.

"You look great! Timm would've been so proud of you."

It had been a while since he'd seen Betsy, who looked positively regal in her red dress and feather boa. In fact, she did look a bit like Queen Elizabeth II, her namesake. Even though she had to be at least 60, she still looked great. She'd miraculously aged little from the time he'd first met her thirty years before in the hallway outside Timm's apartment. "Thank you for doing all this, Betsy."

"Oh, you know I'd do anything for Timm. He did so much for all of us. You think you can lead us down the aisle?"

He looked at the expectant faces in the pews. Then he saw the coffin in the distance. He'd told Betsy to pick one out; he didn't really care. Betsy insisted on paying for it wholesale.

He sighed. "Let's just get it over with."

"Your seat's right in the middle. Front row. You'll see your name there. The show starts in five."

Betsy went outside and clapped. "Everybody inside!"

He didn't know what to think. He had been so busy, never been busier, that he was too tired to notice that there was no one next to him when he fell into instant slumber every night. Time felt slippery all that week. People wanted to call him and share their Timm stories.

As more and more queens gathered around him, he scarcely heard their voices. He so wanted the evening to end immediately.

Then the music started with a Madonna song. Timm had insisted on "Give It 2 Me," a bouncy tune that opened with a question: "What are you waiting for?"

Betsy nodded to Howie.

It was time.

He felt embarrassed about his low heels when all those glamorous queens had high heels, but no, he would do this for Timm. He knew he wasn't a dancer, so he would walk simply in a straight line down that aisle. He only wished that it was to marry Timm and not bury him. He was sure that everyone else behind him would dance and dazzle the crowds. Howie walked slowly. He was afraid to turn around and look.

Behind him, all the drag queens strode down the aisles and grooved to the song. They even vogued. Flashbulbs went into overdrive. People cheered.

When Howie arrived at his seat, he turned around. What he saw astonished him. In the muted lighting, it seemed as if everyone's hats in the pews looked like flowers of all kinds and colors in a field full of breezes and joy. He was amused by the way the drag queens seemed to be competing for attention among the pews, but Betsy flitted among them, nudging them along to the front pews. "Zip along, ladies," she cajoled.

When the song ended, everyone gave a standing ovation. Howie didn't clap. He was mesmerized by how lovingly and perfectly lit the single red rose in a crystal vase on Timm's closed casket was. Timm had insisted on a closed coffin. That and the absence of flowers felt absolutely right.

Betsy went up to the pulpit and adjusted the microphone. "Hello, everyone. We're here to have a party, so please don't cry. As Timm would say, crocodile tears are as disgusting as sewage."

Everyone laughed.

Howie sat there, not quite listening to one speaker after another sharing stories. He heard waves of laughter and applause. He kept looking at just how crimson the rose was. He had picked it out from his backyard earlier that afternoon and gave it to Betsy when she stopped by. He hadn't realized how beautiful roses could be.

Then he heard Betsy on the microphone. "Howie? I have a surprise for you. When Timm thought he was going to die, he called me and asked me to do a very special favor. He made a special recording for everyone here tonight. It uses some colorful language, so you are forewarned." She nodded to someone offstage. The lights dimmed again when Timm's voice spoke.

Howie's heart jumped. He had no idea how much he missed hearing that voice! Timm suddenly sounded everywhere, cocooning Howie's body.

"I don't want people to remember my Dick of Death, because I don't want to be that shallow. I don't want people to remember me because I have a successful business, because that's shallow too. I don't want people to remember me because I gave away money to charity and politicians. I don't care about that. But I do want everyone to remember Howard Dwight Taft, my husband of 30 years. He's turned out to be the best thing in my life. He's the world's greatest husband. He never complained about my cooking. He never complained about my tastes in music. He was always home and took care of me. Dead people don't care about being remembered, but living people do. My darling Howie is alive. So please remember him. If it hadn't been for Howie, I'd have been just another tired old self-centered queen with an oversized dick and nothing else to show for his life. Howie, you gave me courage to stay true to myself. No matter what I did, you loved me anyway. I was a cowardly lion, but you were a true lion. Roar on, Howie. Roar." Then he gave a hilarious rendition of Eartha Kitt's infamous growl.

Howie didn't know what to think. This was so unexpected.

The applause was instantaneous.

People chanted, "Howie! Howie! Howie!"

Betsy spoke into the microphone. "Would you like to say something?"

Howie's knees felt like putty, but he inhaled. Finally, he got to his feet. He'd forgotten that he was wearing a dress and a hat. He hesitated at first, but he walked to the casket, touched it for a moment, and thought of how much he'd rather have had Timm up there doing all the talking for him.

He went up the steps to the lectern. "Honestly, I don't know what to say. I'm just an ordinary man. I'm not really anybody special. I miss Timm. I wish he were home with me. That's all I have to say. Uh, thank you for coming."

The applause was tender, almost loving.

When Howie sat down, Betsy said, "There's one more thing. It's not on the program. Timm's requested a special song for you, Howie." She turned to the front pews. "Ladies?"

Howie turned around to watch an army of drag queens file out of the pews and take their places onstage. They seemed so much taller and quite formidable onstage. It was as if the cathedral couldn't contain them all!

"Ready, ladies?"

The opening notes of an old Connie Francis song washed over Howie as the drag queens lip-synced with grand gestures: "Where the boys are, someone waits for me / A smilin' face, a warm embrace, two arms to hold me tenderly ..." After the first stanza, the queens parted like the Red Sea before Moses and allowed men to come through from behind. In any drag venue, these men would've been Muscle Marys in Speedos, but here, the men were middle-aged. Some of them were portly, tall, short, and not muscular; they wore ties and glasses. They looked dorky and self-conscious, not knowing whether they should dance or watch the queens get wrapped up in the song's sentiments.

Watching their faces twitching from embarrassment, Howie felt their awkward pain. He wanted all of them to get offstage right now. He understood what Timm was trying to do, but he wished that Timm had checked with him on this! This was too humiliating. He didn't want to be offered up like a sacrificial lamb.

Afterwards, at the reception downstairs in the church, some of these men introduced themselves to Howie. It turned out that Timm had given a list of his single friends to Betsy, who then asked them to participate.

"I'm so sorry that you had to humiliate yourself like that," Howie said to each of the men who approached him.

"Oh, no. It's okay. I don't get to be in show business much," one of them said before coughing into a handkerchief. "Sorry."

Another said, "Do you like train sets? I collect them. My entire basement has seven train lines that can run for an hour without crashing."

"I live with my mother," another said. "You'd like her. She makes the best pies."

It felt like the longest night of his life. Still, it was great to see old acquaintances and familiar faces, even if how they had aged was somewhat jarring.

Timm had cooked meals for them at their house over the years, and sometimes they appeared at fundraisers that Timm and Howie attended. Howie had truly forgotten about all these people. Nearing fifty, he suddenly felt old. Where did all those years go?

When Howie got home, he sank onto the sofa in the living room. He was so tired. But it was the first time he allowed himself to think about the absence in his bedroom. He just couldn't go in there now, looking like the morose matron that he was. He took off his wig and pearls, and fell asleep on the sofa.

6
Nick

One of the single men who didn't appear onstage during the "Where the Boys Are" routine was Nick Clayton, who'd gotten Howie his job at Smith & Keeler.

He never forgot the first time he met Howie, then a 19-year-old college dropout, on his first day on the job. Tall and stocky, Howie looked a little shy but appealing in his three-piece suit. He watched Elaine Witzel, the company president, introduce Howie to the entire sales department where Nick worked. "They're the ones who work with our clients and make sure that they get everything they've ordered." He couldn't believe that Howie was still wearing a suit and tie when everyone else wore long-sleeved shirts and jeans. Hadn't he seen what the madhouse was like when he came in for his interview? It was hard for anyone to be formal when there were over 12,000 square feet of cooler rooms containing cut flowers from all over the world. Some salespeople had to wear a jacket when culling flowers onto their carts before delivery to their customers.

Nick took Howie out to lunch across the street. "That suit—your tie—well, that should go. Nobody dresses up at Smith & Keller."

"Well, I don't feel right. I work in the office. I have to look presentable in case our customers show up."

"Most of them work with flowers and dirt all day long. They're not gonna care what you look like."

"My parents said that having a job is a privilege."

Nick stared agape at him when he listened to Howie explaining how important it was to show respect for his job, no matter how low paying it might be. It was his first real job, after all. By the end of his first week at Smith & Keeler, Howie acquired the nickname "Mr. Taft." No one but Nick ever called him by his first name. Sometimes, when Howie walked over to the sales department to compare a certain invoice against a salesperson's records, customers were a bit startled to see someone so immaculate and quiet in their midst. They moved aside for him and gazed at him. They had no idea what everyone else in the sales and finance departments knew: He was absolutely precise and reliable, especially in the days before online package tracking. He could look at invoice numbers only once and recall seeing one of them pass through his desk. Howie had a photographic memory when it came to numbers, and he liked to organize receipts, bills, invoices, and checks. He turned into a bloodhound when numbers didn't match between his master company's books and the sales department's records.

It was also clear that Howie wasn't all that comfortable about using four-letter words and talking about sex, not even in the privacy of Howie's office. Howie was surprisingly a bit strait-laced for someone who wasn't even twenty years old. Nick found that so peculiar because Timm was completely the opposite, but then again, he knew that old adage: Opposites attract. When Nick wondered out loud to Timm whether Howie was truly gay a few weeks later after Howie began working there, he was surprised to hear: "Still waters run very deep. He's absolutely insatiable. You have no idea!"

Nevertheless, Nick and Howie got along very well. If it hadn't been for the fact that they worked together, Nick felt that they probably wouldn't have been friends. He knew he was almost as different as Timm; he too liked the thrill of anonymous encounters in parks and elsewhere. It was almost a compulsion. He had to have a variety of sexual partners to feel satisfied, but a most curious thing happened as he hit his 40s. Howie had hit 30 a few months before, which meant that he and Timm had been together for twelve years. He found the notion amazing. He couldn't imagine being with the same person for that long. He was a bit disappointed in Timm because he thought that Timm would be one of those people who'd shatter the whole idea of gay people having to follow the monogamous heterosexual ideal, but then again, the AIDS thing threw quite a monkey wrench into such hopes. The mid-1980s were hard on him. It wasn't just the friends he lost; it was the fact that so many men had become too afraid to have casual sex. He watched porn on his VCR until the tapes wore out. He knew that some people would say that he was just an oversexed guy, but he couldn't help his high sex drive, which continued right into his 40s.

As time passed, the better he got to know Howie, the more Nick had to wonder if he himself was missing out on something. He was touched by how business-like Howie remained even though they had known each other for over a decade. Early on, when Nick discovered a dark and dank bar, which was a fly-by-night operation and therefore illegal, in the Fawkes Building's basement off Loring Park, he had experienced what he thought was love, only to be dumped a few weeks later. He berated himself for such foolishness and swore never to fall for anyone again. He never did, and he was very proud of this fact. He could go home and not have to apologize to anyone about what he'd been doing out there. Later, when he explored the endless ocean of profiles online, he was happy that he didn't have to apologize for recycling his personal ad over and over again. He was just a very sexual guy, and that was that. He knew that some people might call him a sexual compulsive, but he didn't care.

Then he started to notice that once he turned 59 in January that year, his erections were not as stiff, or as quick to spring to life. He fretted, constantly checking himself in the mirror. He couldn't be old, could he? He had always worked out at the Y downtown, so he knew he was in good shape. He had nice muscle tone. Some men raved about his bubble butt. He trimmed his pubes, armpits, and chest hair. He always wore a tank top, tight-fitting 501 jeans, and boots. His body always got appreciative glances from men half his age.

His body was another reason why he couldn't afford to be in a long-term relationship. He had seen this happen to almost everyone who was in a committed relationship: It was almost as if by magic that they started to gain weight. They didn't seem to work so hard on their looks. They weren't interested in hitting the bars and clubs on weekends. He knew that his body would go to seed if he had to share a life with the same person. He couldn't afford to let that happen!

Going to Dr. Benz for his annual physical was a ritual that Nick relished. Every single time Dr. Benz checked off the list of vitals and asked the same old questions, all of which Nick happily answered in the negative. And no STIs, either!

But this visit was going to be different. How was he going to explain that his body—the favorite part of his body—had begun to fail? He had heard whispers among older gay men that their erections weren't what they used to be, but he laughed them all off. His erections had never failed to give him not only the pleasure of fucking but also the self-satisfying knowledge that he had full possession of his own virility. His lovers were always taken aback by the volume of his ejaculate and the force of its motility.

Nick had known Dr. Benz for over thirty years. He'd chosen the doctor simply because his clinic happened to be only five blocks away from where Nick worked. Early on, when they first met, Nick told him upfront that he was homosexual and that he didn't believe in marriage.

Dr. Benz glanced up from his chair at the small desk next to Nick. "Really? What do you believe in, then?"

Nick pointed down to his own groin.

"Ah. As long as you play safely, well … more power to ya." He went back to his checklist. "Where were we? Oh. Have you …" It was just another question.

Nick was surprised by how unfazed he had seemed, and this was back in the 1970s! After that, they never talked again about the particulars of each other's sex life.

With each visit, Nick slowly accumulated a few personal details of Dr. Benz's life. He was, by all accounts, a happily married father with three children; his wife worked as a podiatrist elsewhere in the hospital. He wasn't one to offer details without being asked; just a quiet and lanky man with a distinctive walrus mustache that he waxed every morning. The only thing that changed over time was the creep of gray, then white, in his mustache.

This time Nick felt skittish in his own skin while awaiting Dr. Benz. He didn't want to be sitting in this same old room where a chair and computer sat in the corner; it seemed that the room had never once changed in all the years he'd visited. He wasn't sure if they had fake plants along the windowsill, but there were no plants now. Maybe the computer was upgraded now and then, but that was pretty much it. *He* had changed. How was he going to explain to Dr. Benz?

"Hey there, Nick." Dr. Benz strode in with a smile and closed the door. "Good to see you again."

They shook hands as usual.

Nick tried to muster a smile as he watched Dr. Benz sit in the chair at his computer and enter his password. He watched the doctor move his mouse and type a few keys.

"Okay. So, how're you doing?"

"I'm doing all right," Nick said. "I guess."

The doctor turned to look at him. "What's wrong?"

"Nothing."

"There's a new tone in your voice that I haven't heard before. Something's not right."

Nick stared at the shiny squares of linoleum and mumbled, "I can't get it up."

"Nick."

He was absolutely terrified of looking up at Dr. Benz's face, but he did so. Nick was surprised to find a softness in the doctor's face. "It'll be all right. Why don't we go through the checklist, and we can figure out what we can do. Okay?"

After Dr. Benz finished the physical, he smiled. "Good news. Looks like you don't have any heart issues. I'll be right back." He returned with a small box. "Here's a sample of the infamous blue pills. Everyone reacts differently, so start small and see how your penis reacts. You should use a pill cutter in the beginning. But do take detailed notes for each dosage, like the time of day, how long it took to get to full erection. Email me in a week or so, and I'll prescribe the correct dosage."

After he got home and ate his dinner, he popped a halved blue pill into his mouth and downed it with some water. He wrote down the date, time, and amount taken on a blank index card. He didn't know what else he was supposed to do, so he sat down in the living room and pressed his DVD remote. Two naked men, both beautiful and buff, were graceful like gazelles interlocked in sexual positions that shifted all over again after a while, but he didn't feel a twinge of arousal even when he massaged himself.

Nothing.

Then, some twenty minutes later, he looked down on himself. He wasn't stiffly erect like before, but he was hard!

It was then he noticed how slightly feverish he felt; he didn't feel sick, but he wasn't used to this slight rise in body heat.

Oh, how I've missed you! He thought as he looked down on himself.

As he gripped himself, he watched the men fuck on the TV.

But there was something else he hadn't quite anticipated: the penis he was stroking—his own penis!—didn't feel quite attached to his own body. He saw that yes, it was clearly a part of him, but at the same time, it did not feel like it was a part of him. How was this possible?

Nevertheless, he continued stroking.

The men on the screen were now in that familiar frenzy toward their climaxes.

His erection stayed the same. There was no buildup of tension toward his own climax.

The men grunted and fell into each other's arms on the bed afterward.

Nick looked down on himself. Yes, he was hard, but his body felt as if it had no desire to ejaculate. It was somehow disjointed from the core of his being. The erection felt like an add-on now.

He picked up his remote and pressed the button to scroll through the DVD's menu. He found a scene featuring an older man with a younger man. Maybe that would help.

A well-built older man with powerful biceps that popped out of his polo shirt opened the door to find a young delivery man with a package. It was not long before their flimsy dialogue was dispensed with, and they bared themselves to each other. Their passion all over the sofa seemed genuine.

Nick watched the scene all the way through, but there was no discernible change in his erection. Just no excitement whatsoever.

He turned off the TV and went straight to bed, where he continued to massage himself until he fell soft, all the while staring up at the ceiling in the dark. Maybe, he thought, if I were with a guy, my dick would feel differently. It took him a long time to fall asleep.

Two nights later, a hookup from Craigslist showed up at Nick's door. David was a gym rat in his 20s from out of town. The pictures he'd emailed Nick did not do the man justice, especially when David immediately kicked off his sneakers, pulled down his jeans and briefs right there with his erection bobbing free for a hello. David stood proudly with his hands behind his head and said, "Hi." It was the first word David had ever said to Nick!

The stranger's confidence both intoxicated and intimidated Nick's own.

This time Nick had popped a full pill a good hour before David's appearance, so he felt fairly confident that he'd become reasonably hard. He just didn't like the sensation of feeling a bit overheated.

Yet when he groped David's erection, he felt a sudden pang of—what?—loss, perhaps. But the loss of what? The pang evaporated just as quickly when the two fell into a comfortable choreography of kisses and gropes as they navigated from foyer to bedroom.

Nick worried that David would notice the not-so-stiffness quality of his own erection, but he said nothing. It still felt slightly disjointed from his own body.

Then came the ultimate test when David fell back on the bed and lifted his legs. Would Nick be able to ... He unrolled the condom onto himself as if it was an act of prayer.

Yes, he soon discovered to his own joy, he could! It wasn't quite the same as before, but as long as David didn't complain, he figured it was all good as long as he thrusted away.

It was not long before David ejaculated.

But Nick felt strangely unable to ... "Sorry," he mumbled as he pulled out of the young man and pulled the condom off himself.

"Hey. Want me to go down on you?"

"No, no, it's okay."

"You sure? You got a nice sausage there."

"Thanks, but ..."

"Seriously, I enjoy going down on daddies."

That word. *Daddy*. He was not old, dammit! "No, it's okay. I'm glad you had a good time."

"You sure? I seek to please." David was already on his knees, his mouth open. "Please?"

He felt another pang of loss. He finally understood what it was: He could no longer count on his own dick to deliver like before.

In an earlier time, he would've thrust into David's eager mouth without hesitation, but not tonight. Just ... no. No more embarrassments. Not in front of such a hot man.

When David finally left, Nick felt as if a huge weight had fallen off his shoulders. He felt empty as a bottle when he lay there in the darkness.

With each hookup every few days, he gauged each new dosage and eventually realized that the blue pill didn't always enable him to ejaculate. His erections still felt disjointed from his own body. He had to content himself with just fucking. Being a shadow of his former self was better than nothing.

Yet, with the fourth guy, he found himself squirting so much that he broke down in a fit of ecstatic tears that fell all over their bodies.

The guy kept asking, "What's wrong? You okay?"

"I'm okay. Thank you!" How could he explain to such a young man?

After Nick had used up all the sample pills, he emailed Dr. Benz his notes.

He was startled to hear Dr. Benz's voice on his phone a few minutes later. "Hey, Nick. I got your notes. Very helpful, but before I write up your scrip, I have a question."

"Sure. What?"

"Do you care about any of the guys that you meet up with?"

No one had ever asked him such a question. It was completely understood among gay men in the habit of hooking up that an emotional connection wasn't necessary for a good time. "What do you mean?"

"Do you *care* about them like people you know, or ..."

"Oh. Not really."

"Well, for some people, sex is better when the heart's involved."

With time, though, Nick discovered that the more he used the blue pills, the more he began to experience its side effects. His vision began to strobe, and his eyes felt dilated. It seemed like his body began to get overheated too often. He had read online what the potential side effects were, but he never thought they'd happen to him too. He emailed Dr. Benz about the growing side effects.

Dr. Benz wrote back, "Come in. I know someone who can help you."

Two weeks later, Nick found himself sitting on a plush sofa opposite a short and wide-shouldered younger man with an unusually large nose and a prominent Adam's apple sitting at a computer near Nick's end of the sofa. Dr. Richmond wore a pale blue button shirt and navy blue suit jacket but with no tie. He seemed to be in his late thirties.

"So, Nick, would you like to talk about why you're here?"

"Well …"

"ED is nothing to be ashamed about. Anything you say today won't shock me. Believe me, I've heard it all. My goal here is to find a safe way to make you hard and happy."

Nick burst out laughing. "Okay."

"Before we start, you can call me Les."

"Okay, Les."

"I'm going to ask you lots of personal questions. Don't be shy with your four-letter words. You can say words like 'dick' or 'cock.' I won't be offended."

As Nick answered Les's barrage of questions, he began to wonder about Les. Was he gay?

Then the questioning became more specific, more personal.

Nick hesitated. He didn't want to utter out loud those feelings of inadequacy. As he began to look right through Les, he felt as if he was talking dispassionately about someone else's penis, as if he was no longer quite there. The pronoun "my" felt like a mistake on his tongue. How does one tell the story of a penis, let alone his own? Nick enumerated in great detail its many failures of late, as well as the disorienting side effects of those pills. He was surprised that Les had not interrupted him at all. He simply tapped away on his keyboard, nodding now and then.

As Nick blathered on, he felt as if he was looking at Les for the first time, even though they'd met only fifteen minutes before. Dr. Richmond did not betray a single look of shock or roll his eyes; in fact, his brusque face was oddly full of compassion. Seeing so much compassion right there on his face made him feel that unfamiliar swell of possibility, of desire … of love? *Yes.* He could love this stranger easily. He felt his entire body undergo an unexpected tsunami of emotion cascading from all directions. He felt helpless and so alone—as if cast off on a raft without an oar? He needed to be with a man who would not laugh at him. He knew that now.

A split second later, he found himself breaking into sobs of shame and looked away from Les. As the deep wracks of his body finally subsided, Nick stared at the floor in front of him. "Sorry."

"I'm so sorry that you're hurting over this," Les whispered, "but the good news is, it *is* treatable. Let me explain how Trimix works."

Nick sat quietly as Les went into his well-worn spiel about its pros and cons of the mixture, which would be injected into the side of his penis.

"What? I have to inject something into my dick just to ...?"

"The pain is really minimal. Some men feel nothing. It's different for everyone."

"Oh ..."

"Many diabetics used to feel the same way about insulin injections, but they get used to the needle."

"But I don't know if I ..."

"It's okay if you're not comfortable with the idea right now. But I assure you, the main reason why it's *so* effective is because it's localized. It's only right there in your penis, so you don't get the side effects that you get all over your body from the pills. If you want, I can inject it in your penis and see how it reacts."

"What if it doesn't get hard?"

Les chuckled. "Oh, it *will* get hard. We just need to see how stiff it becomes. Every man is different, so it can be tricky at first."

"Are you going to, um ... watch?"

"Yes."

"But what if ...?"

"I've injected into men in their 80s," he chuckled. "Boy, they're like teenagers again! But it's really up to you. We can do a test injection if you like."

Nick looked away from Les's face. "I just can't." Then he turned to Les. "Why do we have to get old? Why?"

"Ah! The eternally impossible question. I know this can be very scary because you love your penis very much and you don't want to hurt it."

Nick dared himself to stare into Les's eyes. "Are you gay?"

"No. I'm sorry."

"Then what the hell are you doing here?" He felt the intense need to leave. *Right now.* But he felt glued to the sofa.

"My job is to make *all* of my patients happy with their own penises."

"I bet you laugh at all of them because you don't have a problem with your dick." Nick felt as if looking more at Les would make him sicker.

"Why do you think I'm so good at what I do? I *understand.*"

"You? But how's that possible? You're like half my age!" Nick dug his fingers into the sofa's cushion. *No, no, no—*

"ED affects men of *all* ages. Even some guys in their 20s have ED. You'd be surprised."

Nick waved Les aside. "I'm sorry. I gotta go." He grabbed his hat and jacket off the sofa. He hurried out so fast of the clinic he didn't hear the receptionist calling out after him.

Once back in the safety of his car, he went straight home. He felt as if he was no longer himself. Yes, he was still Nicholas Charles Clayton, but his body didn't feel like his anymore. He tried to eat a microwaved burrito, but he lost any desire to eat anything. He tried to watch Helen Mirren play DCI Jane Tennison in *Prime Suspect,* but the show's gritty atmosphere depressed him more. He tried to fall asleep, but he drifted in and out of dreams not entirely his. He saw the ghost of his younger—and randy—self prance about like a satyr in a lush forest graced with bursts of sunlight where smooth-chested young men equally horny as him loitered against trees. They all looked at him with desire underlining their coyness. How he'd missed being wanted like that, like in those days and nights he'd spent inside the labyrinth of the Locker Room! Then he caught sight of flickering shadows so oddly familiar. He wondered if they were the dead friends and acquaintances and tricks he'd once known back in the days before AIDS appeared, but no, that wasn't quite it. They were all the same size. After a while, he realized that they were really all him. But why shadows? He wasn't dead; he was very much still alive. Nothing ever made sense anymore.

Nick couldn't sleep at all that night. He wasn't going to end up like those people at work who got bloated from being in a relationship! Then he thought about Timm, and how impossibly slender he still was. Maybe he was wrong after all about how relationships fattened people up. Thinking about Timm always reminded him of a problem he'd never shared with anyone.

After working 29 years with him, Nick came to develop peculiar feelings for Howie. He often wondered how that could possibly be. The man was hirsute, a physical attribute that Nick did not like. He had also gotten, for the lack of a kinder word, fat. Still, he appreciated how predictable Howie was. He had seen way too much drama in the bars where he hung out when not online. Howie was like a breath of fresh air. It was that quality that made Nick wonder about those feelings.

It was strange, sometimes, how he tried to fall asleep when he fretted again over how he was losing his erections. He had proudly declared himself a top online. He wasn't as hung as Timm, but then again, who else in the Twin Cities was? He had one thing going for him, and that was pure stamina. He felt completely masculine when he didn't let up—even when the bottom begged for mercy. But now? He couldn't sleep. What would his stable of fuck buddies think of him if they sensed him going soft now and then? He knew he wasn't getting any younger, but he couldn't admit that he was getting older. He knew he was, but he just wasn't ready to say so. He knew guys his age were still going at it, and they didn't need those damn pills. Why him? What had he done wrong to deserve such a letdown? He had no other diseases. Hell, given how much sex he had, he was always amazed to find his test results for STIs turning up negative every single time. Of course, he always used condoms, but still, he felt divinely blessed whenever his doctor said the magic word: "Negative." It meant that he was very much free to do what he had been doing all along. Drug-and-Disease-Free or not, he was finding it harder and harder to fall asleep. He tried watching more porn. He tried chatting with strangers online. He tried reading a dull textbook. Nothing. He kept looking up at the ceiling. Sometimes he tried to masturbate, but he couldn't get aroused.

Then he tried something that he hadn't done in years. He wrapped his arms around a pillow. That felt somehow better. It occurred to him in that moment how things had truly changed. Before the Internet came along, if a guy met someone at a bar and took him home, he usually stayed the night. It didn't matter if they exchanged phone numbers in the morning or if they never met again. They didn't just have sex; they also spent the night together. Maybe that was why he remembered these guys more than the guys he'd met online and invited to his condo. These online guys were usually gone within 30 minutes. If there was genuine chemistry, they stayed two hours maximum. Sometimes they wanted to talk afterwards, but most of them lied when they said, "I'll keep in touch." But Nick knew he couldn't take all of that personally.

The more he clung to his pillow that night, the better he felt and yet more depressed at the same time. He was getting satisfaction from holding a fucking pillow? He pulled another pillow out of the closet and added it to the one he had. The pillows, squeezed together, felt even better. He didn't think of a particular guy; he just needed to feel his arms around *someone*. The plumpness of the pillows made him think of Howie—how nice it would be to hold someone like that. He still didn't care for fat or hairy guys, but someone as solid as Howie for the night would be so nice. A second later, he was shocked at the very idea of wanting to snuggle up to a teddy bear like Howie. He was a colleague who smiled now and then, and never told a bawdy joke. The most he had ever seen of Howie's body were his furry forearms and shins when he walked around with Timm one Pride weekend. Even then, he'd thought how much better Howie would look like if all that fur could be shaved. By then, Nick had become aware of the growing bear community who gathered at Trikkx, a gay bar in downtown St. Paul, and he avoided them. He just couldn't imagine how overweight guys with scruffy facial fur could be attracted to each other. All those bellies rubbing against each other? Disgusting!

But Howie was different. He was fastidiously neat. He shaved his face every day. He trimmed his fingernails. He never left behind empty soda cans. He was like a cat who constantly groomed himself. As he held those pillows, he realized why Timm had refused to take Nick's advice to leave Howie back in the mid-1980s when they hit a bad patch in their relationship. Thinking about it all now, he felt ashamed at having encouraged Timm to leave Howie. He had always envied Timm's body, hoping that maybe one day they would have sex together again. How could he have been so selfish?

The morning after he hugged his pillows all night, he saw Howie in a different light. Howie was methodical, always seeing each project through. Nick thought that was one reason why Timm had loved him so. He would be the kind of lover who always made sure the other guy had achieved an orgasm first. He would be the kind of man who could handle all sorts of sexual positions. When Howie took a phone call, he put down his pencil and looked at the bulletin board next to his desk. He didn't multi-task. He was probably the kind of lover who would not be distracted by idle thoughts.

That night Nick went online to look at furry naked men. He realized that they were an acquired taste. He decided that he'd have to stop thinking about Howie. He grabbed his pillows and tried to sleep. He rubbed his face in the pillows, imagining that it was someone's back. He was surprised when he felt his own tears smudge against the pillowcases. Why the hell was he crying? He wasn't thinking about anything or anybody in particular.

He signed on anonymously on a gay forum online and asked what others thought.

One person said bluntly, "You've never had intimacy."

That hit him hard. He had thought the word "intimacy" quite meaningless. What was it supposed to mean anyway? Holding hands and staring deep into each other's eyes and cooing baby words at each other? He felt the word gnaw at him. He had never felt this lonely. His cock had enabled him to keep company with anyone who wanted sex with him. All these years of fucking around had taught him absolutely nothing beyond the fact that he was an accomplished sexual acrobat. Intimacy was what kept people together. Intimacy was the one apple a day that kept the doctor of loneliness away.

He felt a growing disgust with himself when he saw how he'd written his profiles. It was all sex, sex, sex. Nothing about him as a person. He realized only now, at the ripe old age of 59, why some guys said they weren't interested in hooking up and merely listed their non-sexual interests and hobbies. He winced from recalling how he had put some of them down online when they mentioned being interested in having a monogamous relationship. He had declared them as losers, and worse. As it turned out, he himself was the real loser. He had squandered the best years of his body on men he'd never see again. Eventually, he started to notice that some of the LTR-minded guys updated their profiles to say that they were now happily taken. He felt sick to the stomach. They had been honest to themselves and gotten what they truly deserved. Would they attack him if he changed his profile to "looking for dates and an eventual LTR only"? God, he felt like an asshole.

He wanted to share his observations with Howie the next day. The more he thought about it, the more he realized that Howie was his closest friend. He was a great listener. He rarely showed a flicker of shock whenever Nick detailed a kinky situation he'd had participated in the night before. He realized only now why he'd told Howie such things; he had to emphasize the moral superiority of sleeping around with anyone because, hey, everybody cheats sooner or later, right? He knew that if he shared his newfound understanding of intimacy with Howie, it would be an act of true humility. He just couldn't embarrass himself. No, not in front of Howie. He was a *man*, right?

He went out to the Eagle and took his usual spot by the counter. He knew a lot of the regulars, so several of them chatted with him over beers and checked out the few new faces in their midst. They were mostly out-of-towners on business trips. As Nick talked with his buddies, he felt an intense longing start to mix with an equally intense self-loathing. What was wrong with him? He had always felt comfortable in bars. Why not? He had a high tolerance for alcohol, and feeling that buzz kick in made him feel good even if he never got to invite that cute guy standing by the railing back to his condo. Now? He felt utterly lost. What the hell was he supposed to do now? Go up to a handsome stranger and say, "I need to cuddle tonight"? The word "cuddle" was definitely another dirty word for impotence. Using it implied a failure in bed. One cuddled because one couldn't fuck, or be fucked. No, he couldn't be a wuss. He had nurtured a reputation of being a superstud. He couldn't bear to tell anyone that he was finding that he needed to use more of those blue pills to stay erect, or that he was lonelier than ever.

He left the bar early. He lied to everyone that he had a hot play date later that night. He walked to his condo and sat outside on its terrace even though it was cold out. He liked having a view of Loring Park and the sunset even though it scarcely resembled the Loring Park of his youth. It was there that he'd befriended Timm after they had sex behind some shrubs. He'd hoped for another round of sex with Timm, but it never happened. He wasn't sure why. Maybe Timm didn't do encore sex with friends. He looked down at the few street lamps that lit spots of the park along the paved paths and shimmered off the big pond. A few couples walked hand in hand, and a few men walked their dogs. The park was almost a sterile place now. The promise of meeting a handsome stranger and giving in to the mad impulse of lust had died a long time ago.

The next night he removed the nude pictures from his profiles and posted a face picture of himself. He wrote, "I want to say sorry to guys on here who were looking for monogamous LTRs and stuff like that. I didn't understand what intimacy meant until now." The instant messages bombarded him with a mix of hatred from those who'd remembered his putdowns and encouragement from those who had never seen his face before. It hurt when he saw people questioning his sincerity since he had once proudly called himself Mr. Anti-Monogamy. This was what he was afraid of.

Thinking about all of this didn't help him sleep.

He asked Dr. Benz for sleeping pills. Those helped.

At work, when Nick wasn't busy filling out orders in the cooler rooms or coordinating orders with his customers on the phone, he felt an acute listlessness. Nobody seemed to believe that he was serious about dating. He couldn't pay much attention to anything. Sometimes he needed to reread his emails to double-check things he normally remembered.

"Hey. You all right?"

Surprised to see Howie standing next to his cubicle, Nick felt something catch in his throat. Did Howie know just how handsome he was with that concerned gaze?

Howie walked over and put a hand on Nick's shoulder. "Want some water or something?"

Nick shook his head. "Can we talk in your office?"

"Sure."

In the privacy of his office, Nick sat opposite Howie. Nick blubbered everything; well, almost everything. He didn't mention his desire to snuggle up to Howie.

Howie sat there, not saying a word. He was almost like a statue.

Nick finally ran out of steam.

Howie handed him a tissue.

"Sorry if I made you feel uncomfortable."

"No, it's okay. Just surprised, is all."

Nick reached to touch Howie's forearm.

"I'm sorry, but ..."

"Right." Nick pulled away.

They never talked about Nick's outburst again. In a way, Nick felt relieved. It was much better this way when life went on as before. Aside from the usual frustrations of getting customers to pay on time, work was predictable. Yet Nick began to feel more and more depressed, so in the spring of 2008, he went on antidepressants. He was no longer able to get aroused. That was another humiliation that he couldn't share with anyone. He had tried being fucked a few times when he was younger, and he hated the sensation. It didn't feel comfortable or pleasurable at all, so he was always amazed at how his bottoms had kept begging him to do it harder. How they were able to find so much pleasure, he couldn't imagine, but he knew he liked penetrating them.

But now? How was he supposed to advertise himself online? He was a *top*, for Christ's sake. He felt as if he was withering away on the vine of life. No one was going to find him attractive, not once they found out he couldn't do anything with his cock. He couldn't say that he was into oral sex only, because that was another dead giveaway to his impotence. Besides, oral sex was for sissies.

Then Timm died.

He was shocked, but he was more surprised when everyone found out that Mr. Taft had taken a funeral leave for his partner. People said, "He's gay? I had no idea!" The business suit had worked well as a façade. That was how little Howie had shared of himself with others at the office. Of course, colleagues knew Nick was gay, but no one ever talked about that part of his life. It was totally off-limits. Everyone contributed twenty dollars each to Mr. Taft. It was clear that even though they didn't know Mr. Taft well, they liked the way he treated them with the utmost respect. He was almost like an artifact from a time when manners meant *something*. Many of his single female colleagues often asked Nick if he had a girlfriend or a wife. "Ask him yourself," he said. As it turned out, no one had the nerve to ask him.

Once Timm died, Nick couldn't stop thinking about Howie and how difficult everything must be for him. Then he heard about the upcoming memorial service for Timm. He didn't want to wear a dress, but he'd do it for Howie. He called him and asked if he wanted a ride to the cathedral. He was disappointed to hear Howie say no.

Over the years, Nick attended many memorial services for friends and acquaintances who'd died young. He remembered choking back his tears at some of the recollections shared, but the service held in Timm's memory was far and away the best one he had ever been to. He laughed and cried in the darkness. In spite of his legend, Timm was a far more amazing guy than he'd realized. It was easy to understand why Howie wasn't interested in having sex with other men. How could you not love someone like Timm? But he had never cried as hard in his whole life when the drag queens lip-synced that Connie Francis song as those dorky men came out onstage. He wanted to sweep all those clumsy guys off and sing that song straight to Howie!

At the reception afterwards, Howie broke into a laugh when he saw how Nick had tried to dress up like Joan Crawford from *What Ever Happened to Baby Jane?* "Oh, you look just great! Thank you for coming."

"Oh, I'm so sorry. Is there anything I could do?"

"No."

"Really?" Nick extended his arms for a hug. He wasn't sure if Howie would feel comfortable doing that, but he was surprised when Howie held him. In that embrace, he felt the warmth of someone full of sweat and sighs. Howie would not be just another trick. Nick wanted to kiss him, but he didn't. "I'll see you at work."

"Yeah. Thank you for coming."

Later that night, he prayed to Timm's spirit for forgiveness and guidance. He fell asleep for the first time in many months without having to use a sleeping pill. Surely Howie would be ready for someone new at some point. It was only a matter of time before Howie would look at him with fresh eyes and reconsider.

7
Betsy

When Betsy picked up her cell phone on June 15, 2008, and saw that the caller was Howie, she knew what he was going to say before she even said, "Hello." She was not surprised to hear a lack of emotion in his voice when he mentioned Timm's passing. But it wasn't the first call she'd gotten about death. More than twenty years before, she had gotten many calls about friends and acquaintances who died from a disease with the meanest acronym possible: AIDS. What was "aiding" all these gay men to die? Couldn't someone have come up with something more respectful?

Like so many of her gay friends throughout the 1980s and early 1990s, she endured many nights of gut-wrenching helplessness. She didn't know what else to do but to host one fundraiser after another all over the Twin Cities. But that didn't compare to the feeling that she had on the worst night of her life. One night in the spring of 1982, Betsy joined a group of gay friends at the Plymouth Congregational Church and listened to Dr. John Whyte, who later became a founder of the Minnesota AIDS Project, and Michael Osterholm, the state epidemiologist at the time, warning them of this disease that was striking down gay men in cities everywhere. There was no cure, no answers. All the doctors knew was that if you got night sweats, chest-wracking coughs, and purplish lesions, you were certain to wither away and die. Nothing in the world could save you. When she first heard that, everyone turned silent. The nonstop partying that had made the 1970s so wonderful was indeed ending. Her friends had long made fun of the fact that she wasn't interested in sleeping with anyone. She wasn't even interested in blowjobs or hanging out in the hot tub up in the Locker Room. She never told anyone, but she had horrific dreams in which she castrated herself with a butcher's knife and became whole as a woman. She hated the two-inch thing between her legs. It didn't belong to her.

That repulsively dangling thing between her legs had brought her from Long Island to Minneapolis. First christened as William James Todd, Betsy had grown up in a funeral home, and it was expected that she would follow in her father's footsteps. She went to mortuary school and hated every minute of its two years. She was competent. She didn't enjoy talking shop with her father at the dinner table when she came home on weekends. She was only doing it because she had nothing else to do with her life. For as long as she could remember, she hated her life. Everything draped over her like oversized clothes or squeezed her two sizes too small. She knew that here were her parents and sister. She knew that there was their house with its ample backyard off a cul-de-sac. She knew that there was the church they attended every Sunday. But even later, when she moved into a one-bedroom apartment halfway between her father's funeral home and the Nassau Boulevard train station, she felt she was just drifting through life.

She loved the pop songs on the radio, and often sang with the girl groups. Then at 15, she heard Judy sing "The Man That Got Away" on her Carnegie Hall live album. She was stunned. She knew who Judy was, but she thought of her as the eternally young Dorothy in *The Wizard of Oz*. She ended up buying all of Judy Garland's records and playing them over and over again. She experimented with her falsetto, pushing it upward in the higher registers without turning hoarse, as she dueted with Judy. She eventually mastered nine of her songs. Then, one afternoon when she was seventeen, she stole away from her high school to see Judy sing at the Palace in Manhattan. As everyone waited for Judy to come onstage, Betsy noticed that there was something peculiar about all these men in all the best seats. They behaved differently from the men she had seen elsewhere. She didn't know what they were, but they seemed so friendly that she liked seeing them. They were always brushing shoulders with each other. She stole glances at them whenever Judy sang. She couldn't believe just how entranced these men were. The love on their faces was transcendent. Then she caught two men holding hands as if they were lovers.

She was stunned. Of course, that was what she was! Even though she was a man at the time, she was into *men*, not girls!

She fixated her eyes on Judy. She couldn't believe how tiny she was, yet her voice filled the entire theater. She knew that Judy would never leave her body; that was how physical her voice was.

She breezed giddily out of the buzzing crowds as they pushed their way out of the theater. She had seen something real, something that might fit her like a glove. On the train home that night, she was in a dreamland inspired by all the songs she'd heard. That night she'd finally understood that there wasn't anything wrong with her. It was the world itself.

When Judy died at the age of 47 on June 22, 1969, Betsy was utterly aghast. She herself was only 21 years old. When she heard about the glass-enclosed coffin containing Judy's body, she knew she had to join the meandering multitudes and pay her respects. So, on June 27, she called in sick, took the first morning train to Manhattan, and trooped out to the Frank E. Campbell Funeral Home on East 81st Street. She didn't mind the long hours waiting. Just being there with all those people who loved Judy as much as she did was more than enough. She didn't talk with anyone, but she didn't feel alone. She was stunned by how waif-like Judy was up close, but she shook her head as she zeroed in on the makeup on her face. She'd have done a better job and made it more subtle. She reined in her tears, though.

Once outside, she didn't know where she was supposed to go. She stood and glanced around. She overheard two men talking about dressing up as ladies for some club in Greenwich Village. Men actually dressed up like women, and it wasn't Halloween? She took the subway down to Broadway and 8th Street, and walked west. She observed a trio of men who moved a little differently than the others walking toward Fifth Avenue. She followed them and watched how they talked with each other. Sometimes she backed off a bit, but she caught wisps of words and exclamations. Judy's name came up again. She heard backstage stories about her drug addictions and one of her husbands, who used to date one of the men. A man could date another? She thought it peculiar that a man would call another "darling." The trio dawdled for a long time. Then they separated at Sixth Avenue.

Where to go? Which one to follow?

She chose to continue with the man who crossed over to Christopher Street. She had never seen a neighborhood like Greenwich Village. She had heard a bit about it, but this was a very different world. It wasn't particularly fancy, but it had a lot of character. She wasn't sure what kind of character it was, but she liked it. The Village was nothing like the bland suburban tracts of her childhood. The man disappeared into a tenement building on Christopher and Bleecker Streets. Hungry, she walked around the neighborhood and its crooked streets, trying to decide where to eat. Then she ate a very late lunch at the Silver Dollar Restaurant, a slightly greasy place at the corner of Christopher and Washington Streets. She rested by the window as she sipped her iced tea and swirled its melting ice cubes. The oppressive heat all day showed no signs of abating.

She watched the neighborhood change its tempo from afternoon to evening. Men were often paired together. She knew they had to live around here. There were so many of them. She wanted so much to talk to someone about this ... *feeling*. They had to understand. But who would talk to a gawky stranger from Long Island?

Still not feeling quite ready to go home, she walked to the West Side Highway. There was a long row of trucks and vans parked. Silhouettes of men disappeared among the trucks and then slipped into sight minutes later. It was so mysterious. What was going on over there? Then she saw two policemen stroll by the trucks. She hurried away and stayed close to her side of the street. She intuited that she had to be more masculine.

She wandered in and out of one coffeehouse after another. Most of them looked a bit seedy, unkempt. Patrons gave her a bored once-over and returned to their drinks. Why did they give her looks like that? She sat outside on a stoop on Perry Street and watched people pass by. She knew she had to move here. This was where she truly belonged.

She resumed walking around the brownstones and tenements, wondering about the kind of apartment she'd find. She surveyed bulletin boards advertising rooms for rent. She observed people walking in and out of lobbies and front doors. They had lives, and she had nothing. She walked up and down Seventh Avenue and then turned the corner east on Christopher Street. She looked up and saw the vertical sign: STONEWALL INN. There was something slightly sinister about the way the heavy doors looked, but she saw two men nod at a bouncer before entering. Maybe they were like those men who were into Judy.

Her heart palpitating, she nodded nervously at the bouncer.

"Look at me," he said. His eyes pierced hers. "You're new."

She wasn't sure why, but her hands were trembling.

"You're one of them. Get in."

The bar's admission fee of three dollars struck her as rather high, but she paid anyway. In exchange, she got tickets for two free drinks. When the guestbook was presented to her, she didn't know what to say. She decided to sign herself as "Francis Gumm," a twist on Judy's birth name, and went straight for her drinks. She saw what a dump the bar was. On her left were plywood propped up with two-by-fours against the front glass windows; this was clearly designed to prevent anyone from smashing his way inside. The bar counter stretched down on the right, and music was blaring from the jukebox. The song wasn't by Judy or any of those girl groups; it was one of those hard rock songs that she disliked hearing. Seeing that others were drinking from bottles, she asked for one of vodka. As she'd always liked the sound of the word "vodka," but never having tasted it in her life, she hesitated about looking into the bartender's eyes. She leaned against the counter's end facing the dance floor and tried to look jaded as she sipped her very first vodka. She didn't like the bitter taste, but as long as she sipped a little at a time, she'd get her money's worth. Might as well stick around. She had no idea that the Mafia, which owned the bar, had watered down their liquor and labeled their bottles for customers instead of using name-brand liquor as a loophole against the cops who were always raiding gay bars. Stonewall Inn was a private club.

Not knowing any of this, she sipped and kept her eyes averted from everyone's; she didn't dare move from her post. She watched men dance together. Then she noticed the women. They didn't look quite like women at all. They kept their hair trimmed short and seemed to have permanent frowns. She didn't like their menacing toughness. Did this mean that they wanted to look like men? But why? That didn't make sense.

Then she noticed some gangly street kids around her age enter the bar. Their pimply faces were scarred with bitterness. They nodded to people they knew, and approached their friends. Because the music was so loud, she couldn't hear what they were saying. The more she watched the young patrons carry on, the more confused she became. They were nothing like these clean-shaven men she'd seen at Judy's concert at the Palace. They looked a bit rowdy with a streak of furtiveness. What were they doing here? She had never been in a place where she saw seedy people up close. Even though there had to be at least a hundred patrons in the place, she didn't feel safe with them around. They reeked of trouble, a stink worse than cigarettes. Some of them went to the other dance floor facing the wide-angle of the bar, but it looked dangerous. There was a narrow doorway, so you couldn't circulate freely between the dance floors.

After an hour, she finally felt able to relax her shoulders a bit. She asked for a beer. The music was better now—Motown songs. More people kept coming in, usually alone, but occasionally in pairs. She noticed something quite disturbing. A tall man was dressed as a woman. At first, when she first saw him, she kept thinking: I've never seen a woman that tall. And when the woman opened her mouth to say something to the bartender, whom she clearly knew, she was startled to hear a man's voice. Why did he have to dress up like that? Wasn't that a bit unnatural? And with so much makeup? Most women never wore all that pancake makeup. He didn't look attractive at all.

She checked her watch. It was already 1:15 in the morning. She realized just how tired her feet were. It was time to go home.

She left her bottle on the counter and walked to the front door. As she pushed the door open and stepped out on Christopher Street, she noticed four men in suits and ties and two policemen about to cross the street. Something was wrong.

She pretended not to notice them as she turned left on the sidewalk and was about to continue east past a parked police car. It was then that she heard the most unearthly shriek behind her. It wasn't a man. It wasn't a woman. It was *something else*. It was *that* something inside her shrieking, but she wasn't shrieking. She turned and crossed the street over to Christopher Park to watch. The jukebox inside the bar had stopped.

A few bystanders also stopped and stood next to her. No one said anything. The police car in front said everything that they needed to know. She couldn't stop thanking her lucky stars for having left the bar when she had.

Minutes passed.

More people clustered on her side of the park. There was a murmur among themselves as they awaited the cops to come out with their arrests. The word "gay" jumped out at her. Was it the word that described these patrons? How could there be one word if they were all so different from each other?

Patrons, released, filtered out the doors. They joined the people across the street.

Then a paddy wagon arrived and parked against the traffic.

The crowd turned quiet.

Finally, the cops opened the doors and brought out their first arrests, now in handcuffs.

By then, more had gathered up their boos, which escalated once the police brought out some Italian-looking men to the paddy wagon. Could they be the Mafioso? She started to remember reading about their activities in the *New York Times* and felt sick to the stomach.

The crowd soon numbered over 200. She felt more and more pushed to the front, so she slid toward the back against the iron fence surrounding Christopher Park. Two men stood on the stoop on the west side of the bar, and one of them yelled, "Gay Power!"

Then came a few men. She recognized two of them as the bar's employees.

Suddenly the crowd began singing "We Shall Overcome," but it petered out.

Then came three more arrests. They were obviously men in women's dresses. She was stunned when she watched a cop shove one of them, only to get smacked on the head with his purse. But she was horrified when the cop clubbed him back.

The crowd unleashed a deafening boo.

The paddy wagon began rocking. People were pushing against it.

The crowd flung pennies at the cops' heads. That had to hurt. More people spilled out on both sides of Christopher Park. The electricity was palpable even in the heat.

Then three cops struggled to pull a tall and stout woman in pants from the bar. In spite of her handcuffs, she was cursing, kicking, and fighting like a caged panther. It took a fourth cop to get her into the police car. Yet when she was inside the car, she managed to push herself out and fought her way back to the bar's entrance.

The crowd screamed, "Let her go! Let her go!"

The cops dragged her back to the car.

The woman slid out of the car and kicked and cursed and swung at the cops back to the entrance. The fury in her was beyond words. She had never seen anyone like that.

The cops struggled to contain her as they brought her to the car.

She pushed herself out and tried to walk away.

But a beefy cop picked her up and pushed her right into the car.

People booed and whistled and shouted, "Pigs!" She thought she would go deaf.

She tried to back away from their uncontainable fury, but she was trapped. She pushed through the crowd, nearly tripping on the curb. She fell into the arms of a tall man-as-woman.

"Sorry!"

"Are you for us or against us?"

"I don't know."

The man-as-woman handed a cobblestone to her. "You're for us. Throw!"

Without paying attention to exactly where she should throw the stone, she flung it toward the police car. Instead, it hit a cop on the shoulder, causing him to fall forward.

If the crowd hadn't been berserk before, they were now.

"Oh, my God," she said. She slipped past the angry mob spilling all over the street and hurried around the park on West 4th Street. She had to get away from here. *Now!*

On the train home, she was completely rattled. She had hit a cop. A *cop*. What if she had killed him? At home, she listened to the news on the radio for any mention of the riots taking place in Greenwich Village. It was curiously silent on the subject. Then she scanned the newspapers for a mention. Nothing there.

She couldn't sleep that night. She was now a murderer, a cop killer. They would surely converge on her the second they figured who had done it.

That morning she walked to the bank down the block and withdrew her entire savings. Then she fitted what few clothes she had into a suitcase and took the train back to New York. She wasn't sure where she should go, but she knew she couldn't stay on Long Island. She had to go somewhere. Maybe she was meant to be a man-as-woman.

At the Grand Central Terminal, she saw a few cops standing close together. They seemed to be making casual talk, but their eyes were constantly roving across the crowds. She wasn't sure who they were looking for, but they were probably looking for her. She slipped through the crowds and went straight to the ticket counter.

"Where would you like to go to?"

Behind the teller was a list of cities.

"Sir, where are you headed?"

"Uh, St. Paul, Minnesota."

He checked his watch. "Boarding in ten minutes."

"I'm ready."

A few minutes later, she scurried through the milling crowds and leaped onto the train. She was afraid to glance back and catch those cops chasing her. She took a window seat away from the platform and felt skittish as the train groaned and then clanked away. She had no idea that she wouldn't see New York again.

Three days later, she arrived in St. Paul. The morning was hot and sweltering. By then, she had made friends with a Minneapolis native on the train so she had a better sense of where to go. She took a Minneapolis-bound bus from the train station. She checked into Hotel Andrews at the corner of Fifth Street and Hennepin Avenue, and then walked along the few sleazy blocks west of the hotel. She caught sight of a tall clean-shaven man who was immaculately dressed walking toward her. She recognized him as that kind of person who'd have hung around in Greenwich Village.

As he passed her, she said, "Hi. I was wondering where I could get a nice dress. Um, for my girlfriend."

The man looked horrified. "Shh! You don't ask strangers on the street those kinds of questions. You're a *man*, remember."

"Sorry." She started to move away.

"Wait, wait. Come here."

She glanced around them. No one was walking nearby.

"You're gay, right?"

"Is that what we're called?"

He nodded. "Come with me."

Erwin lived alone in a studio in the Stevens Square neighborhood, which was a bit run-down. He sold socks on the second floor of Dayton's, the most renowned department store in town. Most evenings, he went over to Bella Smith's mansion, where everyone wore dresses and sang songs around a grand piano. That night she helped carry Erwin's suitcase. Bella lived on the northwest corner of Eliot Square, which was within walking distance of Stevens Square. The minute she saw all these drag queens flutter about and laugh with each other, she knew she had found her home. She eventually chose to be called Queen Betsy in honor of the fact that she shared the same birthday as Queen Elizabeth II.

It didn't take long for her to find a job embalming dead bodies at a funeral home on Plymouth Avenue in North Minneapolis. It wasn't what she wanted, but she needed a job. She now had a compelling reason to do the work. She was sure that no one would find her now. Who would've escaped to a city in the Midwest? She knew that had to be a brilliant stroke of luck. It wasn't until Minneapolis was about to hold its first Gay Freedom March in June 1972 that she realized she'd witnessed the *actual* Stonewall Riots, its anniversary being the inspiration for the yearly marches! But she knew she could never tell anyone, not even her very best friend Timm, that she had been there.

While hanging out with those gloriously knocked-out drag queens at Bella's, she discovered that she had a natural knack for emceeing. She managed to come up with the perfect bon mot for each awkward moment around the piano, so when the Gay 90s needed an emcee for their first drag show in 1976, everyone pointed at Queen Betsy. She liked the feeling of camaraderie among people who'd understood and appreciated the art of dressing up in wigs and gowns. She loved the entire process of remaking herself into a woman, starting with her vanity mirror and an enviable makeup kit that she'd pulled together from the mortuary. Weekends she prowled garage sales and thrift shops. She bought a sewing machine and learned how to stitch. After learning how to sew pieces of fabric together from Butterick patterns, she began designing her own gowns and began a New Year's Eve tradition: Her newest gown became the centerpiece of her New Year's Eve shows. She had to make herself dazzling and unforgettable, and that she did.

As for dating, the beautiful men came and went. Almost all of them broke her heart. They wanted to penetrate her like a woman, but being fucked back there *hurt*. It didn't matter how stoned she was, or whether she sniffed poppers to make herself horny. She hated the looks on their faces when they realized how under-endowed she was. She gave up on the idea of dating anyone ever again. Then a friend lent her a copy of *Second Serve*, the autobiography of Renée Richards, the male tennis champion who underwent a sex change operation. She wept the entire time while reading the autobiography. *Of course*. That was what she had been all along: a transsexual. Once she discovered that beautiful word, all her horrific dreams of self-castration disappeared. They were replaced with visions of paradise. She would be all woman. She worked harder and more efficiently at her day job to save up for her surgery. She also promoted her shows more aggressively because the more people came to see her, the more she could justify her request for better pay from the Gay 90s. She began paying closer attention to the private parts of the dead women she worked on, especially those around her age. What would her own vagina look like? She had dreams about it.

Then she heard about a new psychiatrist and surgeon working together at the University of Minnesota, where they specialized in working with people who had feelings of gender confusion. Within ten minutes of meeting her in his cramped office, Dr. Schmitt said, "You know, you're a cookie-cutter transsexual." The doctor was the first man she felt capable of loving completely and utterly. He was so quiet and attentive. He was married with four children. He admitted to a fascination with those inner feelings and the reality of one's physical genitals, but he never made her feel like a freak show.

Still, even with her savings, she was afraid of the risks associated with such a radical procedure. She decided to wait.

By the time the late 1990s rolled around, she knew she was ready. Along with her legal name change to Elizabeth Ann York, she needed something special to celebrate her 40th birthday; she had already begun hormone treatments to enable her transition. She was amazed when her boss took her intent to become a woman in stride. Maybe it was because they both worked with bodies all day long. He did, however, ask her pointed questions about how her genitals would be transformed, even going so far as to compare a dead man's penis against a dead woman's vagina in the preparation room. He did stumble a few times when he accidentally dead-named her, but he learned to call her

Betsy. At the Gay 90s, though, patrons and drag queens still called her by her stage name.

Dr. Schmitt delayed his retirement date by one more week to operate on her. She had never felt so loved as in that moment when he smiled quietly, and then fell quickly into a sleep of no-more-man's-land. When she woke up, she had no idea that the level of pain between her legs could be so much. She imagined that it was like childbirth, except that she was giving birth to a new *her*self. Even though she was feeling woozy, she was overjoyed to see that her ladies-in-waiting were packed into her room.

Dr. Schmitt, white-browed and gruff, chortled when he saw them. "Betsy, how are you feeling?"

"Shit."

He chuckled, "Told ya. Hang in there."

She was really touched when Timm, wearing a natty T-shirt and jeans, and Howie, in his impeccable suit and tie, showed up with four vases of orchids.

"You didn't have to do that!"

"Darling," Timm said. "You're my favorite pussy in the whole world. Imagine saying that in front of your own husband!"

Everyone laughed so hard that some ended up crying.

Betsy was an emotional mess. She had waited all her life, and now this fucking pain?! Everyone was a kaleidoscope of voices and faces and colors. Still, through that first hazy hour of waking up as a woman, she saw how quiet and anchored Howie was in the middle of the spectacle. He simply sat to the side while everyone carried on. Howie seemed slightly uncomfortable. In that moment, she realized that was the kind of man she truly needed. She had more than enough drama backstage, and onstage when she emceed. She was tired of feeling practically nothing when she showed up to prepare another body for burial.

She wanted more than anything to have someone like Howie hold her hand and say nothing. She wanted silence. She wanted the comfort of a man's strong hand. She couldn't stay awake and didn't give a flying fuck once her eyelids drooped. She was too woozy. In her return to woman's land, she saw Howie standing quietly there as Timm said goodbye. Why weren't there more men like Howie?

In all the years she'd known him, she rarely talked with Howie. To do so, she felt, was almost like cheating of the worst kind. She didn't judge others for having all sorts of relationships. But she felt that being a proper woman meant not trying to steal her best friend's husband. She always said a cordial hello to him, and she felt good when he smiled quietly back at her. Maybe it was the lemon Madeleine cookies she always served when they visited her apartment. She felt more like a woman than ever when she saw how Howie ate those. He seemed very happy.

When Timm called her that morning in April 2008 to tell her that he was dying, she felt her heart drop in a clutch. "Please don't cry for me, Queen Argentina," Timm said. "You've done dozens of memorial services, so I want you to put on a show that will put everyone to shame." Betsy was surprised by Timm's suggestion that the service focus on Howie. "I'm worried about him. He needs a husband more than anyone I know."

Three nights before he died, Betsy came to his house. Howie happened to be out, picking up groceries, so they had a few minutes alone. "I have to tell you something."

"Darling, you can always tell me anything. You know that."

She held his hand. "I hope you don't hate me, but I've always been in love with your husband."

"I'm not surprised," he said. "If only he was bisexual."

"You're not mad at me?"

"No! He needs to know that people love him. Not enough people care about him."

"He's not very ..."

"No, he's not an emotional guy. I know. But that's one of the reasons why I love him so much. We should learn to love what is so difficult about a person because ... God, I'm going to miss him." They heard the front door click open downstairs. "He believes that I'm gonna beat this," he whispered as he wiped away his tears. "Please be there for him when I go."

She nodded.

"I'll tell all our friends you said hello."

They both looked up at the ceiling and waved their hands. It was one of their many inside jokes. They often talked about how their dead friends must be watching their moves, guiding them on toward a Greater Fabulousness.

Howie entered the bedroom with a glass of blueberry-pomegranate juice. "Timm. I got your favorite."

Betsy felt like an invader when she saw how focused Howie was on Timm, almost not noticing that she was there in the room. She left quietly. On her walk home, she knew that Howie was the real thing. Maybe he would be happy to settle for mere companionship. She wouldn't insist on having sex with him.

She would take care of him the way Howie had taken care of Timm. She would learn how to cook his favorite recipes, and he would kiss her on the cheek in thanks. They would cuddle to sleep.

Timm's memorial service turned her into a wreck afterwards. Up until then, she had maintained her cool. All those details—the calling, the emails, the favors—made it easy to forget that she was doing it not for just another person who died, but for her best friend. It was Timm this, Timm that, but it was never Timm is dead. She knew she had to honor his request that the service be a *real* party filled with dance music and frothy pop songs. "No more sad songs," he insisted. "And lots of queens with revolting taste."

When she saw that night how Howie had dressed up as a matron with pearls, she thought he was the most beautiful man she'd ever seen. Nothing looked right on him, but that wasn't the point. He had managed to put on a dress instead of a suit. He was not the kind of guy to do that for anyone, so her heart melted like butter. But she had a show to take care of, so her 32 years of working onstage had steeled her against losing her resolve. She was so proud of the way things had turned out, but she had kept her eye on Howie the whole time when she wasn't addressing the audience. She felt like a mother hen toward him, but she knew that if she pestered him, he would push her away. She had to keep her distance. Maybe he would warm up once he was used to the idea of being without Timm.

She dropped by at Howie's house every week. At first, they didn't talk much about anything beyond the paperwork details that Howie had to take care of. She could see how exhausted he was even when he lied that he was fine. She offered to drive him up north for a weekend at a friend's cabin off the famous North Shore overlooking Lake Superior, but he declined. He had a lot of tidying up to do first. Then he said he needed to be left alone for a while.

Being ten years older than him, she knew she might be too old, but couldn't an old gal always dream? She'd failed so miserably in love, but she knew she would take good care of him and make Timm proud of her.

8
Howie

A week before Timm died, he turned to Howie. "Promise me that if I suddenly drop dead, you'll get rid of all my shit. Sell everything. You need an empty house. No one's gonna want to move in with a guy and his dead lover."

In that first month alone, he knew Timm was right, but he felt better sitting where he was, right there in the living room. The house was full of shadowy laughter. He was sure that Timm was hiding like a cat somewhere in the house. He would pop up out of nowhere and start talking about a particular customer at work who in turn reminded him of a certain B-movie star who in turn reminded him of an unmarried dyke teacher at school who in turn reminded him of a hot high school quarterback he'd lusted after who in turn reminded him of a neighbor woman who looked exactly like that customer who'd showed up with her brassy voice and demanded that she get another two-percent discount off her bill because she had been coming to his floral shop for 21 years. When Howie first heard how Timm talked in such a circuitous way, it frustrated him. But Timm told one story after another, often with broad brushstrokes, that he learned to sit back and relax. Timm was a great storyteller who inserted sharp stabs of acerbity into the meat of his anecdotes.

He asked Timm once why he had to bring home so much *junk*.

"They're not junk. They're reminders."

"Reminders of what?"

"I'm a full-rounded personality."

Howie chortled. "You don't need *things*. You fill up every single room no matter where you go."

It was true. Even if he could strip away all the florid wallpaper and get rid of every little trinket, the house would still feel full of Timm. Sometimes Howie would move this or that box around the house, but he couldn't bring himself to call his friends and ask for help. It was so much easier to sit in the living room and look up at the wall where only one thing was left hanging: a framed album cover featuring Jayne Mansfield in a fur stole, as if caught unawares by the busts of Shakespeare and Tchaikovsky. He wasn't sure if the autograph was authentic, but he loved how Timm laughed and howled with helpless laughter while listening to Jayne read poetry set to Tchaikovsky's music. He had played the vinyl record so much that it was pretty worn out. Howie had sought out a CD of it, but the vinyl record had become a major collector's item. Timm had found it at Steeple People, a thrift shop at the corner of Lyndale and Franklin. He thought the cover hilarious, and the inane recording was priceless. But it was not something that Howie would've chosen for himself.

That summer Howie wandered listlessly around his own house. There was so much *stuff*. He couldn't even remember where most of it came from. These were some of the things Timm left behind and the things Howie remembered of the occasion, usually at a garage sale in formerly respectable neighborhoods: A dusty porcelain lamp with red fringes that used to belong in a madam's house before the place was razed to make way for a new apartment building ("Oh, my God, I gotta have this—I've always wanted to be a harlot!"), a painted mirror from the 1940s advertising the virtues of smoking Marlboro ("I don't care for smoking, but look at his jaw—isn't he hot as fuck or what?"), a horsehair-backed fainting couch that needed new upholstery ("This would be so perfect for the sun room!"), an excruciatingly bad acrylic painting of a flabby-assed man looking at a curvaceous woman in a polka-dot bikini sunning on a beach in the distance ("I'm sorry, but this—this is dreadful. Excuse me? You say it's only three dollars? Why, I'll take it!"), a pair of gray floor urns ("If I brush the gunk outta the ridges over here, I can sell them at my shop."), an oval coffee table with a glass top and antique photographs placed under the glass ("I don't know who these people are, but they look nice, don't they?"), and a retouched poster that showed an oversized black-and-white picture of Anita Bryant with the nipples of bright oranges pasted onto her breasts and I'M SO FULL OF TIT below her pearly whites. That poster made Howie laugh. It'd been so long since he'd thought of her.

In the first few months after Timm died, Howie had no interest in sex. He didn't want anyone in the house with him. He was secretly hoping that Timm would come into the living room and say, "There you are! Howard Dwight Taft, where have you been hiding all this time?" He looked at pictures of naked men online, but he didn't feel like stroking. These men might as well be wearing clothes. Eventually, he forced himself not to think about Timm so much and achieved an intense orgasm. He couldn't remember what he'd fantasized about, but it wasn't Timm. Even though Timm had encouraged him to explore his own fantasies, whatever they may be, he still felt guilty. How do you honor someone who's loved you for thirty years? He just couldn't do what Timm always did, which was to have sex with almost anyone and not require an emotional connection. The more he browsed hookup ads on Craigslist, the more depressed he became. Was there truly a place in the world for guys like Howie who was old-fashioned at heart? Why did gay men have to obsess on sex? Didn't anyone care about having an emotional connection anymore? Sometimes he felt as if the gay community would laugh at his unrealistic hopes for a monogamous relationship. As much as he'd loved Timm, he'd never felt entirely comfortable with open relationships. Yes, Timm had clearly loved him, but Howie had sometimes felt neglected. So no more open relationships.

And so that first summer without Timm passed as if it had been some feverish dream. Howie woke up one early September morning and found his pillow completely soaked. His first thought was, I've just had night sweats. His second thought was, I must've been crying all night. His third thought was, I need to fuck somebody.

It was Saturday morning. He went online and scanned Craigslist's local personals for anyone who wanted to get fucked that morning. He didn't care who the guy was as long as he didn't mind being fucked without mercy. He read one by a guy who listed himself as "42 yo, 5'8", 252, always horny" and from the Whittier neighborhood, which was next door to his own. The guy didn't post a picture of himself. Howie included a picture that Nick had taken of him at work and said that he hadn't had sex in a few months. The guy responded a few minutes later with his phone number. Not even a face picture. Just a number.

Howie felt a bit skittish about calling a faceless stranger for sex. In a way, he felt like he was asking to set up a transaction with a hooker. It wasn't a good feeling, but it had been so long since—

"Hello?"

"Hi, this is Howie. You gave me your number—"

"Oh, yeah, great. You ready to come over?"

"Uh, sure. What's the address?"

Howie grabbed a pen and paper, and wrote it down. As it turned out, he lived in an apartment at the corner of Grand and 24th Street, only five blocks away from his house. "I'll be there in 15."

He checked himself in the foyer mirror one more time before he went out. He was wearing a long-sleeved shirt, a pair of jeans, and sneakers. Even though it was balmy weather, he still covered himself up. He hated the looks he always got when he exposed his forearms. He'd overheard things on the street and in stores like, "Where's the rest of your sweater? Look at that gorilla! Hey, you just escaped the zoo or what?"

Howie walked east on 22nd Street and made a right on Grand Avenue. It felt as if his erection was leading the way. He was definitely going to pound ass. He pressed the buzzer for Apartment 4 and climbed the stairs quickly. He felt almost in a swoon, but he righted himself on the railing. He hadn't felt this horny in so long!

He adjusted himself in the one minute it took the guy to answer the knock.

"Hi there."

Howie didn't know what to expect, but surely not this sandy-haired guy in a well-worn bathrobe. The clean-shaven guy was everything he'd advertised himself as, but he seemed a lot heavier than 252 pounds. He had dark circles under his eyes. His teeth were crooked and ragged. Behind him was a studio apartment where the walls were covered with oversized pictures of muscular men sporting erections, already fading from years in the sun. Porn was playing on the TV. The bed was front and center. The sheets looked slightly old.

"Something the matter?"

"Uh, no."

"You don't have to stay here, if you don't wanna."

"No, it's okay."

"I'm losing weight. Seriously."

"Great, great."

The guy approached Howie and groped him. "Wow. You got a major stiffy there."

He gasped from the way the guy kneaded him. It was if his cock was being handled like velvet. He pushed the bathrobe off the guy and knelt before him with the intention of giving him a blow job. But he was stunned by the flagrant stretch marks around his love handles and the stringy folds of skin that roped around his inner thighs. A vertical scar ran from his belly button down to his pubes. He'd always been used to Timm's lithe body—no stretch marks, no overhanging belly, no anything. Howie suddenly felt conscious about his own body. Of course, he had been trying to lose some weight for quite a while, but seeing the scars of fatness up close made him wonder what his body must look like to another guy. He wanted to get up and hurry home and not come out for days. Why did he agree to come over without seeing a picture of him? How could he have been so stupid? This was the sort of guy he'd pass over in a second online.

"Hey, I lost 89 pounds in six months."

"Well ..."

"Stand up." The guy turned around and bent over. "Fuck me. I'm already lubed." His asscheeks were pocked with cellulite.

"I'm sorry, I ..." Howie got up to his feet. "I've never hooked up before."

The guy turned around. "You on the down low?"

"Sorry?"

"Married but play on the side."

"No. My husband died last June."

"I get it. You're one of those romantic types. Lemme tell you something. Love's a fantasy made up to hurt more people. The more you believe in this ... love fantasy," he waved at the air as he said the phrase, "the more you're gonna get hurt. Just get over it, and let's fuck." He turned around and bent over. "You can fuck me raw if you want."

"I'm sorry. I just can't ..."

"Oh, man. You don't like my fat ass? Boo-boo. Get outta here. Bitch."

As Howie hurried out of the building, he felt a wave of relief and grief hit him like a tsunami. He leaned against the brick wall next to the front doors until his tears finally ebbed away. What the fuck did that asshole think he was? Why was it so hard to be a single gay man now? Presumably, over time, society would have less and less of an issue with the existence of gay people, but it seemed as if gay men themselves had a built-in death wish when it came to intimacy. It was all about the fuck. Hell, that asshole didn't even offer his first name, and he didn't care if he'd gotten fucked without a condom! What did That Asshole think he was?

Finally, inside the safety of his own bathroom, Howie took off his clothes and drew his fingertips lightly across his ass. He needed to confirm whether he was packing cellulite back there, but the problem was that he had so much fur. It was hard to detect. Then he used a self-timer on his digital camera on himself in the bedroom. He stood, turned, and paused after each flash and hum of the camera. On his computer monitor, he looked at the pictures of his naked flesh in the most unflattering light possible. At first he didn't want to examine them closely. Visions of that guy's folds of flab were like neon imprinted on his brain. He couldn't look like that himself, could he? He was stocky, but he was damned if he was going to let his body go to seed like that!

His body looked almost the same from all angles. His dark fur, already graying, covered whatever flaws his body might have. This wasn't enough. In the bathroom, he took out his beard trimmer and bent over in front of his mirror. He guided the trimmer carefully around his ass, which now felt like two mounds of short porcupine needles. He applied some shaving lotion to his ass and slid a razor, shaking it under the faucet's running water. It was hard going. The fur was far too thick. Thirty minutes later after the shave and shower, he returned to his bedroom and stood in front of his self-timing camera on a low tripod. He stood a foot away from the camera and tilted his ass slightly for each shot. Done, he sat in front of the computer and watched each new picture pop up on the screen while it was being imported onto the hard drive.

He gasped at the white smoothness of his ass compared to his furry backside. His ass wasn't as big as he'd thought, so that was good news. Then he saw the closeups. The flash and the half-shadow made his cellulite, which had begun creeping out of nowhere, plain as day. He pounded his desk and shouted, "Fuuuuuck!" He stifled his own sobs and stared at these pictures. Timm was indeed lying when he said Howie was the most beautiful man in the world. He didn't want to hear that shit about how beautiful one could be inside. Most guys never cared about what was inside a stranger unless he was hot enough to fuck in the first place. He knew that he had to start dieting *immediately*.

In his usual methodical way, he researched online the most effective tips and strategies for losing weight. No fast food. No high-fructose corn syrup. Less red meat and dairy products. Fewer carbs. Less caffeine. No diet sodas. No artificial sweeteners. More salads. Fewer desserts. No microwave-ready frozen entrees. No meals after 7 o'clock in the evening. And of course, lots of exercise. A few suggested that dieters cook their own meals because it was the most reliable way to be sure of what they were actually eating.

As long as he thought of That Asshole on Grand Avenue, he found it a bit easier to push himself to lose weight. He still ate takeout from the Wedge Natural Foods Co-op, but in smaller portions. He checked the weight of each container of the same takeout dish until he found the lightest one, as in choosing .6 lbs over .61 lbs. He walked more briskly in the morning and in the evening. He was going to look far better than That Asshole, so he disciplined himself to eat a bit less. Eventually his body didn't seem to crave as much. By then the fur on his ass had grown back to its normal length.

By then he'd thought a lot about That Asshole. How could someone like him turn out to be so full of dismissive hatred? The answer—because he'd probably never felt loved in return—made Howie feel a bit of sympathy for That Asshole. He was angry at the world and he took it out in spades. His body was the first victim of his self-hatred, and he'd never forgiven his own body for turning against him. Howie had many conversations with That Asshole in his mind, all of which were pointless. The most important thing was the inedible image of That Asshole's saggy thighs.

Then Howie ran into That Asshole at the Wedge two months later. Of course, that was expected to happen sooner or later given that they were sort of neighbors. Howie had just walked two miles that evening so he was feeling a bit more hungry than usual. He picked up a cold orzo pasta salad cooked with Kalamata olives, red pepper, and capers. He would steam some vegetables, which he already had, as a side. As he waited in the Express Checkout (10 Items Or Fewer) lane, he was contemplating what he should drink with his meal. He heard someone push a cart behind him in line. The cart was filled with a few bags of chips, a few six-packs of sodas, and a pile of microwavable entrees. He had clearly more than ten items in his cart. Howie glanced up at the man behind the cart and stopped. Somehow, the layers of clothing worn against the oncoming winter season made That Asshole look more jowly.

That Asshole gave him a "What do you want?" look. It was clear that he hadn't recognized Howie at all.

Howie turned around, faced the windows overlooking Lyndale Avenue, and paid for his takeout quite happily when his turn came. He felt content in knowing that he was indeed losing weight, but he had to be careful not to turn into a bitter old queen.

As the days wore on with its autumnal numbness, Howie wondered what the house would look like once it was all cleared of Timm's stuff. Maybe he would have that florid wallpaper taken out and repaint the walls in neutral colors. The dining room's hardwood floor needed to be resanded and varnished. The carpet on the stairs had worn thin in spots. The leaky tub faucet in the guest bathroom needed to be replaced. And so on. But nothing major.

One night, when he found himself unable to sleep, he wandered aimlessly throughout the house as if in a maze. It gradually dawned on him that if he took everything that belonged to Timm, there was really nothing much of his own stuff left. He had allowed Timm to fill that empty vessel of loneliness, and now he was a nobody. He didn't own things that made him colorful like a flame that attracted moth-like friends. He was the dour-faced husband that everyone merely greeted before carrying on with Timm for the rest of the evening. He didn't mind that so much because once they all left, Timm focused completely on him, cooking him insanely delicious meals and making love to him, even after so many years. Howie had never felt the need to hook up online or hang out at the Gay 90s. He knew he was a homebody, but Timm had never made him feel bad about it. "That's just you, and I love you for it."

As Timm's friends appeared less and less frequently at his house when they realized that Howie wasn't going to give away those expensive antiques for free, Howie began to nurture the sneaking suspicion, long kept at bay by the drama and flurry that surrounded Timm, that he himself was boring. He was an uninteresting man. He had nothing to offer anyone. They all had wanted Timm, and not him. Howie liked to watch the news, and when the elections came around, he became a politics junkie. Even though Timm was obsessed with classics that aired on the Turner Movie Channel, he never insisted that Howie turn the channel away from Rachel Maddow and others. On election days, Timm and Howie always took the day off to volunteer their time at the polls. They insisted on not serving in their own neighborhood as they wanted to be more impartial in the electoral process.

That night Timm always served steak and potatoes with red wine. Nothing special about the meal except that the cooking was first-rate. The steak had a sprinkle of sea salt. The potatoes, once boiled, had marinated for ten minutes in rosemary- and thyme-infused olive oil before being sautéed in the steak's pan juices. They sat in front of the TV and watched the election results come in.

Timm was the one who'd taught him the value of paying close attention to politics. After all, Timm was the one who made a point over the years of refusing to take sides between gay activists and legislators like Jack Baker, Steve "Weebee" Endean, Thom Higgins, Allan Spear, Tim Campbell, and Brian Coyle. They all had clashing opinions over the best approach to secure their rights within a heterosexual majority. Some of them *hated* each other, but they never advertised their feuds. They simply avoided each other whenever they could. Yet they all knew that Timm was a friend of everyone's, so they didn't object when he and Howie wrote out checks in equal amounts for each candidate and said, "Whatever works as long as we get our rights." Some of Timm's friends were surprised when Timm encouraged Tim Campbell to make a run for mayor even though it was clear he wouldn't win. "Doesn't matter, darling. People need to see all *kinds* of gay politicians out there. There's no straight way to win gay."

Sometimes Timm cooked private gourmet meals for some of these people, but he was always careful not to invite the guest of honor's enemies who happened to be friends of his. On such occasions he served the food and wore clothes instead of being *au naturel.* When these politicians and activists sat down in the dining room, Howie felt curiously alive listening to their passionate discussions on this or that pending legislative bill and the dirt swept under the rug in the Capitol building in St. Paul. While Timm socialized in bars and encouraged everyone to vote, Howie ended up volunteering by making phone calls on the behalf of the state senator Allan Spear and other gay political organizations as well as some Democrat-Farmer-Labor candidates. He never told Jack Baker and Mike McConnell just how much they inspired him with their dedicated drive for the legal recognition of gay marriage. They had actually gotten married legally in Mankato, Minnesota, when no other county seat in the state would marry same-sex couples back in 1970. He admired these two men because they were willing to do something about what was legally due them. Eventually, some years after Tim Campbell moved back to Houston to be closer to his biological family in the late 1990s, Howie kept tabs on Tim's blog on gay marriage. Jack and Mike were always featured. And then the Republicans made it a decisive election issue. It wasn't just Jack and Mike or a few isolated cases anymore.

But this year Howie couldn't focus on any of the talking heads on the TV. All he knew was that Barack Obama, in spite of his flaws and inexperience, had to win. That was all he cared about, and there he was, with his wife and daughters, onstage in the Midland Park. He snapped out of his reverie when he heard President-Elect Obama use the phrase "gays and lesbians" in his victory speech. He knew that ever since Timm died, he was supposed to cry as part of the grieving process, but strangely enough he hadn't felt an acute need to do so. Yet when Obama said that phrase, Howie wept. His body wracked with gut-ripping spasms. He fell down to the carpet and blubbered out tears. He heard on TV people cheering and clapping from Chicago, and in his own neighborhood, people whooped and cheered. Timm would've held his hand and wept incoherently like an old lady. This was the sort of thing he had waited all his life to see. Howie knew how proud Timm would have been to see Obama win. He would've cried happily nonstop. He hated racism as much as homophobia.

The morning after Howie woke up to hear a TV newscaster announce that Obama had already hit the ground running with his transition team. He wasn't going to stand around and savor the bitter fruits of his victory. Howie looked up at the TV and felt that he, too, had to find a way to be as strong as Obama facing the many insurmountable challenges ahead. He called in sick, and stood in the living room.

All this silence. He really should clean out the rest of the house. Start anew. He remembered the first day when he brought Timm to their house for the first time. Timm was aflutter at how roomy their new house was, but it didn't take him very long to fill it up. Timm browsed garage sales because most sellers never knew the true value of what they had, and he could get some good things for literally pennies. Howie never objected.

Then the living room was no longer a living room. It was packed with glass display stands that Timm had gotten for almost nothing from a store that went under, and in them went his coveted Walt Disney collectibles. "Timm!"

Timm turned. Howie had never raised his voice in the twenty-two years they were together. "What's wrong?"

"We don't have a living room anymore." He pointed to the display cases. "This has got to go. Sell all of this!"

"I can't!" Timm tried to embrace Howie, but he wasn't having any of it. He went upstairs to their bedroom and picked up the *Star Tribune* to read.

A week later, Howie came home to find the living room practically empty. He almost didn't recognize the velvet sofa he'd bought for Timm as a birthday present years before. He sat down on the sofa and sighed happily. How nice it was to have a room that looked like a real *room* instead of a storage room. Now he could *see* the TV, unobstructed. About time.

Later that night, Timm returned.

"How did you—?"

"I rented a storage unit in Bloomington."

"Damn," Howie said upon reflection. Which storage facility? It was yet another detail to worry about.

He began uploading pictures of the various items he wanted to sell online. Gradually the dining room walls revealed permanent shadows of furniture and *objets d'art*. The dining room set was all that was left. Then he moved on to the parlor room. He gave away its ferns and busts. There was an antique bicycle. Howie had completely forgotten about it. He had taken it from his parents' house when they passed away. It had been a gift from a neighbor man who was horrified to learn that his own parents were too miserly to buy him a bike. Years later he realized that he was probably in love with Mr. Raynais, but certainly not in a sexual way. Why it was put in the house instead of the garage, he couldn't recall.

On the few days when he got tired of cleaning objects, photographing, measuring, uploading, writing descriptions for sale online, and selling, he thought about trying to cook. He had to learn how if he wanted to lose more weight. There was no way he could cook like Timm. Trying to read a recipe intimidated him. He knew a recipe was only a list of ingredients and instructions. Timm had made it look so easy; it was as if he never had to look at anything! In the pantry were ten shelves packed with cookbooks. Dust jackets had a slight film of grease on its spines. He took one out. The book had no pictures so he had no idea how a dish was supposed to look like. He put it back and took out another one. It had more pictures but the instructions were set in chunks of dense prose. He just couldn't take out another cookbook. Why did cooking have to be so difficult? He ended up buying organic takeout from the Wedge, just around the block. The food was great, but of course, nothing could beat Timm's cooking. He thought about taking a cooking class at the Wedge or uptown at the Kitchen Window. Maybe later.

One evening at the Wedge, he spotted a tattooed tall man stocking bags and he blanched. Being bearded with a thick untrimmed mustache was one thing, but he stretched his earring holes with wooden spools as big as nickels. He wore wooden horns that seemed to shoot right out of his nostrils. His eyebrows were thick with consternation. His neck was tattooed with what looked like a devil's tail brandishing about. His forearms were covered with splashes of orange, red, and smoke.

Howie was amazed that anyone would hire him looking like *that*. Sure, he had the heft and hands to do the job. He didn't know what his name was until the stranger walked past him and flashed a great smile. Howie caught sight of his name badge: BILLY.

On the way home Howie wondered about why anyone would tattoo so much of themselves. Wasn't it supposed to be painful with those needles piercing the skin? Was it a sexual thing? Or were they looking for attention? Or advertising to the world just how "different" they were? Now that Timm was gone, he had noticed more and more young people with tattoos and piercings that no one would have foreseen a decade earlier. He did see them before, but he had never dwelled on *why* they would do such things to themselves.

Even though he knew he should watch a few cooking DVDs, he shopped at the Wedge every day after work. Some evenings Billy was around; sometimes not. He clearly didn't care about looking fashionable unlike the yuppie customers who frequented the Wedge. Howie would've felt the same way except that Timm had made a point of buying the best simple clothes for him: suit jackets, ties, shirts, polo shirts, and socks. It was something of a joke when Timm brandished a brand-new tie for Howie every Christmas morning.

"Aww, just what I need. A new tie!" he exclaimed.

They both laughed. Howie had at least thirty ties immaculately organized and hung in the closet upstairs. The ties ran the gamut of Looney Tunes characters to paisley swirls to Ellsworth Kelly-like stripes.

Once, Howie asked, "Why do you have to give me ties every year?"

"You don't like them?"

"Oh, no, I love them!"

"Then what are you complaining about?"

"I have too many."

"You need lots of color in your life."

"Oh, but you're my favorite color."

Timm beamed. "That's one of the nicest things anyone's ever said to me."

He knew that his first Christmas alone would be hard. No one would give him a new tie. He counted his 47 ties. By his mental calculations, it would take him approximately every nine weeks to rotate all of them. He would make sure to think of Timm every morning when he put the tie on for another day at the office. He was grateful now to have gotten so many ties. They made him feel that much more special. Maybe that was why Billy had to tattoo himself so much. He couldn't feel special otherwise.

The next time he saw Billy, he was standing behind the register. "Good afternoon, sir. How are you today?"

Howie was surprised at the sound of his mellifluous voice. He didn't know what a man like Billy would sound like, but certainly not like that. "I'm good." He watched Billy's hand lift each item and hold it across the glass scanner. His hands were nothing like Timm's. They were not pretty. They had a wart and a few nicks. His fingernails were not trimmed perfectly.

"Sir? Thirteen dollars and eight cents."

"Oh!" Howie took out his wallet and gave him a twenty.

"Thanks."

Howie was a bit disconcerted by Billy's gaze. He didn't know how to decode him. It had been so long since anyone looked at him like that. What could a bearded punk possibly see in him?

Each time he visited the Wedge, he looked for Billy. He was always laughing and joking with his colleagues. They don't seem to be bothered by his appearance. His neck had more tattoos than he'd realized. All of this made Billy look more intense. It was different from looking at a drag queen, who was usually more of a caricature than a real person, but Billy had no artifice. He actually modified his own body with tattoos and piercings. They were not removable like wigs and makeup.

One Saturday morning, Howie hid his own gasp when he caught sight of the few strands of hair just above his ass crack when Billy bent down to pick up a pen off the floor in the Wedge. He thought he saw some ink there, but he couldn't tell. It had been so fast. Later, he went online and looked at naked men showing off their tattoos. Most of them, he thought, were unattractive. Maybe it was just bad lighting. But still, why did they have to make their bodies look worse? They had been fine before. He liked looking at smooth chests, so tattoos were a distraction.

The next time Billy smiled at the register. Howie was holding a half-pound container of the Wedge's famous garlic lovers pasta salad.

"What?"

"I think I got you figured out," Billy said.

"What?" He was relieved that there wasn't anyone else behind him.

"You don't know how to cook."

"What makes you say that?"

"You buy nothing but takeout."

Howie started to stammer.

"Hey. It's cool." Billy handed him a copy of the Wedge newsletter with the course listings.

Humiliated, Howie forced himself to stand before Timm's beloved cookbooks in the pantry and chose a cookbook that looked easy enough. Each evening he focused on cooking something new, which turned out to be so time-consuming that he had to wonder how Timm had managed to cook so quickly. He saw that it was all about planning, prepping, and timing. Sometimes the dish worked; sometimes it came out undercooked and inedible. With the dishes that tasted good, he took the leftovers to work. He knew he wasn't a good cook, but he would have to keep trying. Somehow, without him realizing it, his dishes improved. He could cook a lot more quickly once he realized that many recipes had room for error. He didn't need to be precise with his measurements. Recipes no longer intimidated him. By the time he had made his first lemon soufflé, the guest bedroom had been emptied.

There was so much emptiness everywhere, so he chose the most pungent dishes to help fill up the house.

Even Billy took notice when he saw the leeks and potatoes, and rang them up on the register. "Making soup tonight?"

"Of course."

"Killer." Billy said this with a grin.

That Billy noticed Howie wasn't buying takeout anymore pleased him. Maybe he could ask Billy out to dinner at his house. He dreamed of having someone like Billy stand there in the kitchen and cook. Billy would chatter away all the shadows from the kitchen, and it would be like before. But the more he thought about the idea, though, the more he decided against it. He didn't have a single tattoo on his body. And as far as he could tell, Billy was not gay. He was somewhat relieved when Billy stopped working at the Wedge a few days later. Why bother, right?

9
Howie

Even though Betsy gave him a lovely call, that Christmas morning alone was hard. Howie tried not to think about the presents they'd given each other over the years. They were rarely extravagant, but Timm always insisted on spending the day alone with his husband. What did they usually do? They sat together on the sofa and watched sappy holiday films. That was something he couldn't do alone on that day. He had to go out walking, so he put on his coat and hat.

He walked west to the Lake of the Isles. There, in the bright sun, were couples and trios skating together on the frozen lake. Neighborhood boys played a makeshift hockey game using road construction cones for goalposts. People walked by with their dogs. He saw no one else walking alone, and this depressed him even more.

When he returned to his house, he changed his mind about going in. He decided to walk along Franklin Avenue to the Plymouth Congregational Church instead. It had been a good many years since he and Timm had volunteered to help with their soup kitchen. Timm cooked, and Howie was all too happy to help clean up. He liked the feeling of good cheer and camaraderie among the men and women mopping the floors and wiping the counters after the homeless had left. It had broken his heart when Howie saw the desolation in their eyes. Maybe they'd let him in as a volunteer even though he hadn't signed up.

At the soup kitchen's entrance, the homeless seemed miffed when he walked past them inside. He glanced around and recognized Nancy Minnes, who was much older and heavier since the last time he'd seen her. "Nancy?" She was shuttling back and forth with piles of clean plates from the dishwasher and putting them on the first table.

"Do I know you?"

"I'm Howie Taft. I volunteered here years ago."

"You were with this guy named Timm. Um, Timm Johnson?"

"Yes. That was me."

She glanced around. "Where's he?"

"He died last June."

"Oh! I'm so sorry. We're kinda short here—"

"I can help."

"Would you?" She turned to the servers. "We got another volunteer here." She turned to Howie. "You can help with the stuffing."

Within minutes he put on a white plastic apron and picked up the huge spoon. He scooped up the bread stuffing onto their plates and forced a smile when the homeless said thanks and moved on down the line. This was a lot better than moping alone in his living room. A lot better.

As he scooped up more stuffing onto another waiting plate before him, he looked up and saw who was holding the plate. "Billy?"

"Shit."

"It's okay. Where have you been?"

"Got kicked out. Long story."

"Right." Howie shook the spoon one more time to ensure that Billy got every bit of stuffing. He was not supposed to give too much stuffing to any one person. This occasion felt a bit festive; change was definitely in the air now that an African American President was going to move into the White House next month. "Where are you staying?"

"You don't wanna know."

"You don't have a place to stay?"

He shook his head no.

"You can stay at my house for a while." Howie stopped. Had he actually said that?

"Really?"

"Yes."

"You sure?"

Howie nodded.

"Thanks. I can wait. I'll be over there."

As the number of people in the church basement dwindled, Howie liked the feeling he got whenever he saw Billy sitting quietly by himself. Billy looked up at him from time to time. He was reading a yellowed mass market paperback.

Eventually, Billy was asked to leave.

"Hey. I'm gonna wait outside, okay?"

"Sure."

Nancy turned to him. "How well do you know that guy?"

"He used to work at the Wedge Food Co-op."

"Okay, if you say so."

"Why?"

"He doesn't seem like the kind of friend you'd have."

"It's Christmas, okay?"

An hour later, when the kitchen and the basement were deemed clean, Howie bounced up the steps. Somehow hearing the banter between the volunteers had lightened his mood. He found Billy standing across the street. He was wearing a thick battered leather jacket. He tucked his hands into his jeans.

"Hey. Over here." Howie waved at him.

They walked together past snowbanks plowed against the curb. Howie was struck again by how tall Billy was. Maybe the salt-seared boots had given his height an extra inch or so.

On the way to Howie's house, Billy shared his life story.

He had been born near the northwestern corner of Iowa, about 90 miles south of Luverne. He was a farm boy, number nine in a family of sons and no daughters. His mother died of cancer when he was fourteen. His father often drank at night, and if, for some reason, he felt that his sons weren't doing their chores right, he whipped them in the barn. One night his father swore that Billy had been shirking his duties. He wasn't doing enough. Didn't matter that he was still sixteen or that he was a good student. Billy was nonplussed. He got up at five every morning to milk the cows, let out the horses, shovel out the manure, take a quick shower, and grab breakfast before catching the bus for school six miles away. His brothers had other tasks, too, so it wasn't as if Billy was the only one. He envied his older brothers because when they married, they moved away to their wives' family farms. Their absences escalated their father's drinking.

Nevertheless, it was time for Billy to take a whipping. His father hadn't anticipated that Billy had dipped the whip in gasoline the week before. He had watched how his father whipped his older brother Ethan. Billy wanted to stop the whipping, but he knew if he did, his father would whip him too. Ever since that realization, he thought about the gasoline having soaked into the leather weave and carried around a lighter in his pocket even though that was against school regulations. When no one was looking, he practiced flicking the lighter on. It got so that he could do it without looking and not feel the flame scorch his skin. Out in the woods, he practiced whipping a stump. At first, it was hard because he couldn't get the whip to hit a specific spot, so he tied a neon orange plastic ribbon to the top. It took him a good hour to finally hit the ribbon. It was a matter of patience and technique. He wasn't sure when his father would demand the whip, but he had to be ready no matter what happened. On that night, lit by a few lonely light bulbs, his brothers stood by to watch. The ritual was the same. Dad would ask a son to take the whip off the wall and hand it to him. Billy usually did this task.

"Take off your shirt."

The crisp November air, creeping through the cracks from outside, swirled around Billy's exposed back.

Dad said to Ethan. "Gimme the whip."

Billy turned around. "I'll get it."

"No."

Billy shot a look of *don't* at Ethan and went up to the wall. His hands were shaking. It wouldn't be easy to finesse this. He inhaled a wordless prayer as he tried to be subtle about tightening the whip's coil and pulled out his lighter. He kept his back to his father and brothers. He saw the lonely barren fields through a side window. Maybe he'd have to run out there and escape.

All was silent.

Then as Billy coughed, he flicked the lighter.

"Turn around, boy."

He faced his father. The whip had a lovely flame flickering on its tail end.

"What the hell are you doin'?"

Billy didn't say a word as he let the whip's tail end dangle. The flame crept upward.

"Stop that now. Right now."

Then Billy brought up his arm and cracked the whip. The flame scorched his father's shoulder. Perfect.

Dad fell to his knees. "You're the fucking Devil," he gasped.

"No more whipping," Billy said as his brothers watched the flame consume the rest of the whip, like a snake vanishing into smoke.

Then Billy cracked the whip. This time ashes flew apart all around their father.

Things were never the same after that. His brothers refused to do their chores the next morning. One by one, they defected, no longer caring what the neighbors thought of them for abandoning their father. Billy, left behind, took care of all the animals. Eventually, Dad complained of bruises and bleeding, and the local clinic said he had cirrhosis. He died a month before Billy graduated from high school.

Billy had stopped feeling anything for his father since that night. He thought it was very telling when he saw how his brothers didn't want to drink the night after he was buried. No one argued when Billy suggested to their lawyer that they sell the farm and divide the proceeds nine ways. By then, Billy had met a girl named Mandy, and he'd run off with her to Denver. They broke up after two months, but by then, he'd made friends with some gay guys who ran a tattoo shop. The whole process—creating mimeographs in reverse, sterilizing needles, and observing how the colors poured out of the tip into the skin—fascinated him. The first time he had a small tat made—a tiny match lit on his ankle—it hurt but, at the same time, he felt strangely sexy. It was something like feeling the sear of pain that came from being whipped; the difference was, he had *chosen* to be tattooed. He knew what his next tattoo would be like, so he did a lot of research about the various incarnations of devils through the ages. He thought a long time about how he would cover his body with the Devil's whip-like tail, almost like a snake uncoiling and rising before its attack.

As an apprentice, Billy didn't mind the long hours. He used the time to pay close attention to Ed and Biff's craftsmanship in the shop. These guys were so meticulous about keeping everything clean and sterile. If there was any doubt that a needle wasn't sterile enough, they made Billy sterilize it all over again. He pored through their portfolios containing photographs of their handiwork. He practiced colorings on bananas, oranges, and other fruits to see how the ink interacted with the fruit's skin.

Three months later, Billy wielded the needle on a muscular man who wanted a link of chains on his left arm. "Why that arm?"

"I thought you knew."

"What?"

"The left arm means that I'm a top."

"Oh."

The more he hung out with Ed and Biff in the leather community, the more fascinated he became with body piercings. He was agog at how some men could wear thick rings in their nipples, and stretch the holes in their earlobes to accommodate thick grommets. He didn't think of them as beautiful or sexy. Somehow, he liked the idea that modifying one's own body was a statement of self-empowerment, of willful choice. Even though his first tattoo had been a bit painful, it didn't scare him. In fact, he often thought about how good it felt, but he never masturbated to the memory of the experience.

Eventually, he met women who were into the BDSM lifestyle. They were surprised that he was straight because they'd assumed that because Ed and Biff were his friends, he had to be gay too. He slept with them, discovering to his amazement the many places on a woman's body that could be pierced and tattooed. Over time, though, he asked his bosses to tattoo his body. He loved talking in detail with Ed and Biff about the process, which ink, which colors, and so on. Biff had said it best: "Each person that comes in through that door is a walking totem pole. The best tattoos have stories behind them."

Ed and Biff became the first people he'd ever told the story of how he whipped his father when Billy showed them the designs for his body. They suggested other sources where he could find better images of the Devil. They measured his arms, thighs, chest, and back. For some reason, he hadn't felt bothered by standing naked in front of gay men, or that they were measuring the space between his nipples, and the proximity of his belly button and pubic hairs as well as the height from his shoulders down to the top of his ass crack. Then they measured his body again when he lay down on the table. They wanted to see how much the musculature of his body adjusted. As their hands touched him with their tape measures, he felt safe. He knew that they'd never hurt him. He didn't feel attracted to them, but he nevertheless began to sport an erection. Ed and Biff chuckled, but they didn't touch it. The tattooing of the Devil dervishing around his body took eight months to complete; he needed four to six weeks to recover from each session that lasted anywhere from eight to twelve hours. The pain was unbelievable here and there on his body, but he felt *alive*.

He dated one woman after another, but nothing felt right. Then he met a customer named Vic at the parlor. A longtime friend of Ed and Biff's, he was proud of how his massive pecs showed off a beautifully colored tiger pouncing with bared claws. Vic was a hardcore BDSM daddy who enjoyed mentoring novices in the joys of being flogged. Billy felt angry at first when the topic was brought up; that sort of thing was supposed to be kept *private*. Ed and Biff said that they understood the fine line between pain and pleasure. So when they proposed that Vic, being the very best at flogging, do the honors, Billy wasn't sure if he'd like that, but much to his surprise, Vic's precision right down to the tender ferocity and pressure felt astonishingly good even though it stung now and then. Afterwards, Billy was surprised that Vic wasn't expecting anything sexually from him. "Some guys don't want sex. They just want the pain. I think you're one of them. Doesn't matter if it's a guy or a woman to you. Ed and Biff were right about you."

Then he met an older dominatrix who happened to be visiting from Minneapolis. He wasn't into older women, but the way Mistress Heloise inflicted sweet flicks of pain to his body blew his mind. He fell in love with her, but she insisted that he didn't love her. He was only in lust with her. She said, "I don't do boyfriends. I'm a very free woman." That was fine by him, as long as she could be with him again from time to time once the welts on his back healed. With an impressive portfolio in hand, he followed her to Minneapolis and found a part-time job at a tattoo parlor and a part-time job at the Wedge Food Co-op.

By the time Billy had finished telling his story to Howie, it was already late. He had followed Howie upstairs to the guest bedroom. "You can sleep with me."

"What?" Howie was surprised.

"I don't mean sexually. Just ... we could hold each other."

"I don't understand."

"I don't understand it myself either. Sometimes I think I'm straight, or bisexual, or gay. Hell, I think I'm asexual!"

"I thought you wanted ..." Howie just couldn't finish the thought.

Billy leaned forward and kissed Howie on the lips. "Is this what you were hoping for?"

"Uh, yes." But the kiss had been dry. He knew this wasn't going to work. "I think I'll go sleep in my room."

"You can look."

"What?"

Billy took off the rest of his clothes and stood there. He slowly turned around to show his backside.

Howie stared. The tattoo of the Devil wrapped around his smooth was indeed a work of art. Oranges, reds, and smoky white and grays stormed around those beady eyes piercing from Billy's shoulder blade. Then there were thick rings in his nipples, just above his belly button, and through the tip of his penis. The Prince Albert was the one thing he couldn't wrap his mind around; in fact, it was a sexual turn-off. Why would anyone want to pierce *that*? It made the penis look ugly. "Well, good night."

"Thank you again for letting me stay here. You're a good man."

On the other side of the bedroom wall, Howie listened to the sound of Billy sleeping. He felt uncomfortable with the idea of someone being sexually ambivalent. He wasn't bisexual; just ... he also didn't like the feeling that if Billy stroked him to a climax, it would be out of pity. If he were going to have sex, it had to be with someone who had the hots for him. Yet Howie felt an intense pang of loneliness. He had never stayed the night with another man since he met Timm in the fall of 1978. Thirty years.

He entered the guest bedroom and slipped into bed beside Billy.

He was surprised when he felt Billy's arms surround him. No kisses or anything. Somehow, he was able to fall asleep.

10
Howie

Howie was not entirely surprised when Billy disappeared in the morning. He walked around the house and spot-checked to see if anything was stolen. Nothing.

Still, he wondered what he had done to drive Billy away. He had wanted to roam his hands all over Billy's body, rather like how he traced the outline of a map in an atlas. He knew that tattoos didn't leave tactile marks, but he still wanted to explore how a traced drawing could leave such a permanent image in one's skin. He had enjoyed listening to Billy describe what being a licensed tattoo artist involved, and how a person could get tattooed.

Howie looked at himself in the mirror. He had thought often about shaving his chest and having his back waxed. He hated being hairy, period. His shoulders had thickened along with his biceps. He didn't like the way some fat had gathered on his sides just below his upper arms, but it didn't seem too bad when he lifted his arms and put his hands behind his head. That pose made him look like he had a real V-shaped chest like a strongman. He turned sideways to the mirror and flexed his bicep. Okay, not bad. He dropped his arm and rubbed his other arm, trying to imagine a tattoo there. He didn't know what it would look like, but if that was what it would take to get Billy interested in him, he would've been fine with that. It wasn't as if he'd be the only middle-aged man with a tattoo. Maybe wearing a tattoo would make him look a bit more butch, but he wasn't the kind of guy who went shirtless. Heck, wearing a short-sleeved shirt made him nervous.

Later that night, he took out a blank legal pad and doodled. He had the strangest urge to draw, something that he hadn't done since high school. First, he drew circles. He got bored with spirals. Then he tried all sorts of random shapes. Nothing. He tried faces. He was a terrible artist. He put the pad aside and went to bed.

As he was about to nod off, it came to him. Would it be possible to use a picture of Timm for a tattoo? He wasn't sure which one, as there had been so many taken over the years, but he liked the idea of having Timm's face tattooed on his body.

The next day Howie returned to the soup kitchen and asked after Billy. No, he didn't come in all that often. No one knew his schedule or where he stayed. He was apparently homeless. He wondered if Billy had a cell phone and wished to have thought to ask for his number. Wouldn't a homeless person want a night in his heated house? He also didn't have a Christmas tree up, so maybe that would've been a detail that a homeless person would appreciate. Who wanted to be reminded of the things one doesn't have in the holiday season?

Having Billy there, even if it was for only one night, was a godsend. Howie hadn't wanted to notice that none of Timm's friends showed up or called him to see how he was doing over the holidays. Not even a single email. Just a phone call from Betsy. It was as if all the attention he'd gotten at Timm's memorial service was all for naught. He had downloaded that Madonna song onto his iPod, which he rarely used anyway, and found himself unable to listen to it all the way through. He deleted it even though he'd paid for it.

Howie glanced around his house, which was practically empty and forlorn. It had taken him a while to sell things online, but he felt good about it. He even got rid of the tall filing cabinets from the basement; they had contained every single piece of important paperwork dating from the day Timm had bought Antonio out. People online had left angry and disappointed comments when *Lavender* announced the unexpected sale of The Fairy Florists to a local horticultural chain, who said that they would continue to respect the reputation and traditions of the legendary shop. Yet when they posted signs announcing the liquidation of the Fairy Florists' assets by mid-December, it became apparent that the chain had wanted a tax write-off that year. That spurred a more passionate round of comments online, but nothing else happened. In a way, Howie was relieved. He didn't want to have to go past the shop and know that Timm wasn't there anymore. The money made from the sale wasn't too shabby, so that went toward Howie's retirement savings. Timm always teased him, "Are you sure you're gay? Because you're so much like a straight dad."

Years before, when Timm first saw how Howie suited up for work, he told him to relax. "Smith & Keeler isn't Wall Street." He tried to unravel Howie's tie, but Howie brushed him away. "You're like an old man, and you're not even twenty!" Back in their old apartment on Bryant Avenue, they were in the tiny bathroom where there was a full-length mirror behind the door.

"I just like it this way."

"Darling, I like you better without the suit and tie."

"Well, it doesn't feel right to go to work without this."

"No one's going to care if you showed up in a T-shirt and shorts. I go there every week to pick up my flowers. You can't be formal in there." Timm whirled Howie around to face him and began unbuttoning his vest. "Lose this."

"No!" he glared at Timm. "I don't pick on you or your clothes. I'd never walk around in a dress and call myself the 'Fairy Florist,' but I didn't stop you."

A few days later, Timm gave him an orange-and-blue Hawaiian shirt as a suggestion for weekend wear.

"You want me to wear *this*? Why?"

"You should have a little more color."

"I don't need to scream for attention."

"No, you don't understand. You need to look like a fun person."

"Why are you so worried about what others think about me? You don't worry about what other people think of you." He thrust the garish shirt back into Timm's hands and left the bedroom.

Howie hated how people wondered out loud within earshot whether he was a closet conservative, or even worse, a Republican. These acquaintances and strangers were always careful not to say it in front of him, but they weren't as discreet when they saw Timm nearby. It was their way of admonishing Timm for not being more fashion-stringent when it came to his husband. He knew how they didn't like the way Howie wore a pair of ironed slacks and shirt. Informal meant no tie. It didn't matter how much the fur on his body had turned Timm on beyond belief. It was a big deal if Howie wore a pair of shorts, and even then, it was only if they were alone in a car traveling to an antiques meet a few hours away. The fur on his legs was so dark and thick that no one noticed how pale his skin was.

Timm tried to explain that for some men, hirsuteness was a highly desirable virtue. It was a fetish for some, just like dick size.

Howie wouldn't hear any of it. Howie didn't want gawkers. He had enough of them in high school.

Over the years, though, a few of his friends whispered to Timm. "Does he have a hairy back?"

"Why do you ask?"

"The fur on his fingers is so sexy."

"Ask him yourself."

Timm knew full well what his answer would be. He was happily married. He never told them the real reason why. He hated his own body. When the bear community exploded by the early 1990s, Timm brought home a pornographic bear magazine from A Brother's Touch, a gay bookstore near the Fairy Florist.

"Why are you giving me this?"

"Just look at them."

He opened the magazine to its centerfold. A heavyset man, covered with fur and a beard, proudly showed off his wares while leaving his flannel shirt open. "And?"

"Don't you get it? You're a *hot* man. You always were!"

"You should talk with my friend Glen. He's a bear. He says that you're a walking wet dream."

"Me?" Howie burst out laughing. "That's so funny."

"No. He meant every word of it. He saw your legs once. You know what he said later that night? He called me to say that he finally understood why I married you."

"Why do guys have to be so shallow?" He rifled through the magazine. Men of a certain age showed off their bellies and erections. Almost all of them wore a combination of baseball caps, flannel shirts, jockstraps, jeans, and boots. "They all look the same."

"Some people say that California blonds look the same."

"No, they don't. They're all different."

"See?"

"But I'm not a bear."

"Howie, you should grow a beard. Just try it once and see what happens."

"I don't think it'd look good on me."

"You'd be surprised. Just don't shave your face for a month."

More out of curiosity than anything else, Howie decided to let his weekend stubble grow. That Monday morning, when he suited up and caught himself in the mirror, he felt weird. Could a nascent beard look good with a suit? No. Too scruffy with patches of gray. He took off his suit, shirt, tie, and undershirt, and leaned forward over the bathroom sink as he lathered his neck and face. He shaved only his neck and the upper half of his cheeks. Suited up again, he regarded himself in the mirror. Much better. He wasn't sure if he liked the graying part of his face. That was the sole advantage of being clean-shaven. He could look much younger.

At the office, Howie said nothing about his stubble, but everyone raised their eyebrows. This was not typically him. What was going on? Still, they said nothing. Even though Joe felt the stubble framed Howie's face well, he didn't dare comment. He didn't want to make Howie feel more self-conscious. He would have to ask Timm later.

A week later, Timm was already in the kitchen when Howie arrived from work.

"You're home early," Howie said.

"I wasn't short-staffed today, so I got a lot of stuff done. I decided to make some flageolet bean soup. Come here." Timm beckoned Howie closer. "Wow. Look at you!" Timm caressed his husband's thickening beard. "It's growing out nicely. I love the way it looks on you. You're so sexy in that suit!" Before Howie knew it, Timm was kneeling before his husband and demanding that he open his own trousers. "You're so hot!"

Later that month, Timm took him to Trikkx, a bear-friendly bar in downtown St. Paul. He hadn't warned Howie that it was their monthly bear bar night. They entered the cavernous club. Bears of all shapes and sizes stood around and chatted with each other amidst dark lighting and loud trance music. No one was dancing. It was a hot summer night. Howie wore a polo shirt, which had been a major decision, and jeans.

"Your friends—where are they?" Howie practically shouted into Timm's ear. They were supposed to meet Steven and Eric, a couple they vaguely knew.

At the bar counter, they ordered drinks. Howie didn't notice how the lights from above recast the fur on his forearms, almost like shadows.

A few men soon clustered around Howie.

"Woof!"

"What?" Howie turned to the trio.

"It means you're hot."

"I'm a dog?"

"No. Just a big woof!"

Without being asked first, Howie found these men, wearing sleeveless flannel shirts and tank tops, caressing his forearms and squeezing them. "What are you doing?"

"Oh, my God. Look at this!"

Then one brushed his hand against the front of his taut polo shirt where his nipples stood out. "They're like pencil erasers!"

"Would you mind?" Howie glanced around for Timm. Where the hell did he go?

"Sorry."

He scowled, took his drink, and waited for his eyes to adjust to the dimness. He sipped a bit and walked slowly around the place. It was so unlike Timm to disappear so completely. The more he couldn't find him, the angrier he became. If Timm was hoping he'd fall in with the bear community, it wasn't going to happen. He didn't appreciate being touched without his permission, and by strangers at that. His short sleeves turned out to be a mistake.

The bar had two different dance floors, so Howie went to the other one and scanned the crowd. There, in the distance, was Timm gabbering with Nick.

"Hi, Nick." Howie shook hands with him. Even though they had known each other for years, Howie still had a certain reticence when it came to affection.

"You enjoying yourself?"

"No." He turned to Timm. "What the hell were you thinking?" Howie downed the rest of his drink and set it down on the counter. He left.

Outside the bar, it was still a bit light out. Howie was standing by their car on Roberts Street as he knew Timm would follow. "Well?"

"Darling. You need some friends."

"Did you hear me complain? No. I don't like it when you decide to fix me as if I'm broken. If I have a problem, I'll let you know."

Timm sighed. "Steven and Eric haven't arrived yet."

"They can give you a ride home."

"I know how sensitive you are about your body. I just thought you'd feel good to be appreciated as you are. You're perfect as you are."

"Then stop trying to change me!"

In that moment, Timm had the strongest urge to say, "This is not working." He had a delicious vision of saying, "Fuck off, you stubborn asshole. You're not gonna have any friends the way you operate!" He would watch Howie drive off in a fit of hurt and rage, and he himself would join Steven and Eric in a hot threesome as a way of letting off steam. He wouldn't go home that night. Howie would fret like a concerned father but screw him. He didn't have to be so damn pigheaded about everything, because he wasn't always right.

Yet, in the same split second, he remembered the fact that they had been together for fourteen years. He was a wonderful and patient companion who took care of the house when he was too busy with his business. He was also a great listener. He laughed at most of his jokes. And even though they had been together a long time, they still had great sex at least once a month. He liked the familiarity of Howie's body. There was something incredibly comforting about him that he couldn't get from any of his tricks. Did he really want to give up all that?

He looked at Howie and quavered.

Without thinking, Timm got into the car. "Take me away before I change my mind."

They held hands and didn't say a word the whole time as Howie navigated the freeway from St. Paul to Minneapolis. In the foyer, once the door was closed, Howie turned to Timm. "Please don't leave me. If you do, you might as well shoot me dead."

Timm was startled to see a few tears in his husband's eyes.

That night their lovemaking was surreal. It had passion, to be sure, but it was full of tenderness and forgiveness. Timm had never experienced anything like it.

Afterwards, he rested his head on Howie's shoulder. "I was lying to myself when I said you were perfect. But I was telling you the truth. You *are* perfect."

He felt Howie's big arms envelop him. "Apology accepted." Timm never asked Howie to change any of his ways again. Every time he got annoyed with Howie over anything, he only had to remind himself of that awful night at Trikkx. If Timm was going to be a better husband, he needed to learn how to accept Howie as he was, not as what he'd hoped Howie would become. It was a hard lesson, but once he understood that, he was surprised by how much more he felt even more loved and appreciated. In the mornings, Howie sometimes left a card with a gift certificate to Patina, one of his favorite local shops, or some other small gift on his placemat. But Timm's favorite gift of all time had to be the few dandelions plucked from their front yard with a note that Howie wrote: "You make these weeds look beautiful. H." Timm had meant to frame that note with a trio of preserved dandelions, but he never got around to it.

Howie was thinking of that particular morning after he opened another dust-covered box from the guest bedroom closet. There, in a shoebox, were the carefully flattened dandelions and the note. He opened it and smiled. He wasn't a bad romantic after all, was he? This was not something he'd give up. He had decided early on that he wasn't going to throw out photographs and certain souvenirs from their many road trips together. The rest could go. But that note—well, he had felt so proud of coming up with something so original. He hadn't really seen himself as a romantic guy, but Timm being Timm had made it a lot easier for him. The dandelions had lost their bright yellowness, but that didn't matter. He could still see that spring morning when the impulse to gather up a few dandelions hit him in that moment of stepping out to take the car for work. He didn't think what he would say, but the radiant yellow color spoke to him in a way he couldn't articulate until he took out a blank note card and scribbled without thinking. He left everything on Timm's placemat and went straight to work.

At the office, there was already a message from home. He called Timm back.

"Darling, that note was the most beautiful present I've ever gotten. You are truly a world-class act." His voice was thick with emotion, which meant he must've shed a few tears.

"Anytime."

"I love you."

Howie didn't know what to say. He knew he was supposed to say those three words, but he didn't feel comfortable saying them. He felt like a fraud if he did say them. He did love Timm, no question about it, but he had never felt the need to say those three words. Besides, these three words had been overused. It was time to put them on a moratorium, and demonstrate how one loved another with *action*, not words. That was how Howie saw it. "I do too," he said at last.

Howie ended up keeping his beard.

11
Nick

During the entire holiday season, it seemed like everyone in the world wanted flowers, so the entire staff worked overtime to fill orders. In comparison, the days between Christmas and New Year's weren't too bad. Everything came to a standstill of sorts, even though, for the company it was the end of one fiscal year and the beginning of the next. Nick hated the work that involved year-end accounting and receipts and invoices and ...

"Hey," Howie said. "What do you need?"

"The receipts for the month of June for Jillian's Floral Shop in Eau Claire. I need to double-check."

Howie would point to the filing cabinets room without glancing up. "Third drawer in the green cabinet."

Nick was always agog at how Howie seemed to remember the location of every little piece of paper. It was downright scary.

Whenever Nick asked about his Christmas plans, Howie said, "I'm good." Nick usually flew to his friend's condo in Fort Lauderdale on the morning of New Year's Eve and stayed there for a week, but this year, he decided not to go. The large older gay community in Fort Lauderdale was yet small enough in which everyone seemed to know each other, and he had something of a reputation to maintain. Everyone there knew that Nick was a total top, which typically proved to his advantage. Of the hundreds of gay out-of-town visitors, the bottoms seemed to outnumber the tops. For each hookup site he used online, he maintained two separate profiles—one for Minneapolis and another for Fort Lauderdale. He liked the idea of having two different identities by using different pictures of himself. For Minneapolis, he posted a few face pictures so his buddies could chat with him now and then, and for Fort Lauderdale, he posted a few pictures of his erection. Those pictures were admittedly more than a few years old, but so far no one had called him out on them. But now? He was afraid of disappointing anyone who showed up at his door in Fort Lauderdale. He didn't want to be one of those limp guys. He was still hot, dammit! Besides, he had to keep an eye on Howie, waiting for a change in his demeanor that said: *I'm lonely too.* But Howie wore his mask very well. He rarely talked about Timm. It was almost as if he had never been partnered.

Since Nick stayed until four o'clock while Howie went home at three, Nick usually took Hennepin Avenue for his route home. The traffic wasn't too bad at that hour, but this time he drove past Loring Park and detoured off Lyndale Avenue to make a right on Franklin Avenue and head south on Aldrich Avenue.

He had to check up on Howie's house. Was he dating someone? Was his driveway shoveled clear of snow? Were the lights on? Most of the time, it was just a flicker of television off to the side. That was enough for Nick, and then he would go home. He felt strange that he wasn't in Fort Lauderdale walking alongside the scenic A1A highway on his beloved beach overlooking the balmy Atlantic at this time of year, but he didn't mind. He wasn't up for hooking up as he usually did in the past. How could he explain himself these days? That he was in love with his own colleague, so much so that he had learned not to think of Howie as chubby? Still, he chatted online with one man after another, but none of them struck him as nearly as stable and reliable as Howie. They simply wanted sex on their first dates. They wanted to know if he was a top or a bottom. They wanted to know if he was STD-free. They didn't ask about his life, nor did they volunteer any tidbits about their own backgrounds. Everything had become sterilized. There wasn't much feeling to be found anywhere, and this depressed Nick even more. He knew that being out and about in Fort Lauderdale would have made things worse. All those beautiful men walking around—in years past, he thought nothing about approaching them for a fuck. Now? It was so humiliating to try timing himself with the blue pill so that he could fondle a guy and make out with him long enough before he was truly erect. He couldn't do quickies anymore. He wanted to tell Howie about all of this. Maybe Howie would understand and love him anyway.

Earlier one night in November, he met a stocky bear online. A businessman from Cleveland, he wasn't looking for sex. Nevertheless, Nick invited him over since his hotel was only two blocks away. The guy said he was just over six feet tall and weighed 307 pounds. He said that he was quite hairy, but again, he wasn't looking for sex. He wanted companionship more than anything else. Nick almost laughed at seeing how the man wore a T-shirt and sweat pants underneath his jacket. That outfit was almost *de rigueur* for tricks. The first words out of Drew's mouth upon entering the condo were, "I didn't think you were that skinny!"

Nick laughed. He didn't feel insulted.

They talked for hours about all sorts of things. He was truly great company.

Drew said he didn't have to be anywhere until one o'clock the next day.

Nick inhaled and said, "I can't get hard."

"So?"

"That's not a problem?"

"No! I'm not that shallow. My favorite thing in sex? Cuddling." He opened his arms wide. "Daddy's here."

"But you're younger than me."

"You're such a silly boy. Age has got nothing to do with it."

Nick hesitated.

Drew leaned forward, pulled Nick off his sofa, and brought him close to his body. "Just you take it easy."

Nick didn't struggle. He closed his eyes and tried to imagine it was Howie's hands rubbing all over his backside. His face was squished between Drew's manboobs. The heat from Drew's body soaked through Drew's T-shirt. He became aware of an intense odor. It was more than sweat. He couldn't pinpoint what it was. He struggled to break free.

"You okay, boy?"

Nick paused, "No."

Drew let go, and Nick stepped back.

"Did I do something wrong?"

"No. Just ..."

"Am I too fat for you?"

Nick couldn't look him in the eye.

"I get it. I'll go."

Nick wanted to apologize, but he knew he couldn't take it back. He watched Drew push himself off the sofa and walk out the door. Not even the customary lie of "I'll be in touch."

As Nick locked the door, he rested his face against the cold metal. He couldn't be this desperate to want someone like Howie. He wasn't a bear chaser. He had to do far better than that.

Later that night, on his favorite hookup site, he was surprised to see what he was most afraid of finding: Howie's new profile. There it was—a picture of him standing in his suit and smiling a bit dorkily with his glasses. Nick recognized the picture; he had taken that shot in the hallway outside their office the year before. "Just looking around" was all he wrote below his picture. He wanted to tell Howie that suits were a turn-off for many people. He should be a lot more descriptive. He should list his stats. He should have a picture that showed off a sexy side of himself. His beard alone would surely attract pogonophiles. More casual and approachable. At least Howie seemed to be ready for someone new. Good news, indeed.

He thought about sharing his ideas at work but changed his mind. He updated his profile to say that he was a "hard worker," "realize that dicks aren't everything," and "looking for someone stable, hairy guys ok." Maybe Howie would read that and get the hint. He favorited Howie so he could see whenever Howie logged on. In the weeks ahead, Nick saw how often Howie went online, which meant that he was probably getting a ton of instant messages. He was fresh meat.

At work, Nick felt vastly disappointed when Howie never mentioned seeing his profile. There seemed to be no change in his demeanor. He was the same old Howie who had worked with him for nearly thirty years. Howie had been a stocky but tall man. He was height-and-weight proportional. He was a bit dorky, but he had a nice smile.

In past years, Nick had never noticed Howie's weight. Then, some years later, he noticed that all that time Howie spent sitting behind his desk was causing him to gain weight in some unflattering places. Nick hadn't quite noticed that before; he had been too busy working out and turning tricks. But the weight had made Howie seem like an old man even though he wasn't quite 30! Hadn't Timm noticed? Was he embarrassed to be seen with an overweight man?

Nick called Timm later that night. "What kind of food have you been feeding him?"

"Why do you ask?"

"He's fat!"

"Ssh."

Then he overheard Howie's voice in the background. "Who's that?"

"Nick."

"What does he want?"

"It's not work-related."

A moment.

"Look, I'll do what I can."

The next day he watched Howie sit unhappily with his lunch at his desk.

"What's wrong?"

"This. Veggies and a dip."

"Looks good."

He picked up a celery stick and munched on it. "Timm says I'm fat."

"Well, maybe you should take an hour off for lunch. Just get outside and walk."

"There's nothing but parking lots out here. Nothing to see."

"How about joining a gym?"

Howie shook his head no. He focused instead on eating all of his veggies and licking the small bowl of dip when he was done. He looked angry at the fact that he had to drink water, not a can of soda.

Nick watched him all that afternoon. He felt sorry for him, but it was truly for his own good. When Howie left for the day, Nick dialed Timm's work number.

"Your husband was not happy with his lunch."

"I'm not surprised. He does love to eat."

"Maybe you should go out on walks with him."

"Say, that's an idea."

Timm gave Howie, being keen on history, a locally published guidebook about the various mansions and houses in the Kenwood neighborhood on the other side of Hennepin. Howie took to walking around the neighborhood, checking off each house and wondering what it must look like inside now. He returned with observations that he was too happy to share while Timm prepared their dinners. If he noticed how Timm had substituted certain ingredients with less fattening ones or chose healthier recipes, he didn't let on. As an eater, Howie was very easy to please.

Every day Howie walked. He seemed happier. Nick was relieved to see that. Howie was still chunky, but at least his slacks didn't swell to reveal the bumps of his cellulite.

Nick was afraid to ask how much weight he had lost. It had to be up to Howie to say something. He wasn't the type of guy to share much background information about anything. Nick nearly had a heart attack one morning when Howie whispered, "In case you were wondering, I've lost 74 pounds."

Nick sputtered, "Well, that's so fantastic!"

Howie went to his office and disappeared for the day. He didn't talk about his diet or exercise. That was just him. Nick later learned from Timm that Howie was now in the habit of walking for an hour in the morning and again in the afternoon before Timm came home.

Now that Timm was gone, Nick realized that if he was going to pull Howie closer to him, he needed to be more quiet. Trying to keep quiet, he knew, might be as bad as those withdrawal symptoms he'd experienced when he finally quit smoking cold turkey. His body kept craving that gentle high. He missed the feeling of something in his mouth. He felt jittery. He couldn't sleep. His body kept crying for release. He couldn't stop walking long distances around his neighborhood. He walked around Loring Park a few times before he felt sufficiently tired to fall asleep, only to find himself reaching for his lighter on his bedside table and then realizing that there wasn't a cigarette anywhere in his condo. His dreams were disjointed. He fought those sharp hunger pangs. He wasn't going to be one of those people who gained 50 pounds just because he quit smoking. He was going to ride this one out. He controlled the precise amount of what he ate. Sometimes he felt as if he was going to pass out from wanting more in his mouth, but he held on. Soon he no longer craved cigarettes.

He watched Howie crunch on some baby carrots as he ate a sandwich. Nick was eating a half-sandwich and a half-cup of soup from the diner across the street. Then the creak of his chair as Howie swiveled and got off for the bathroom. Howie returned and continued as before.

Finally, Nick couldn't take it anymore. "Do you ever want to talk to me?"

"About what?"

"Anything."

"Why? I don't have anything new to say."

"But don't you like talking?"

"Sometimes."

That stopped Nick dead in his tracks. "Why?"

"No offense, but I think too many people babble for nothing."

"So you're saying I babble."

"Well, you do like to talk. I like to listen, so it's not a problem."

"I want to know you better."

"Why? I've been here since '79."

"You know what I mean."

"No, I don't."

Nick pushed his chair closer to Howie's desk. "I saw your profile."

"So?"

"Did you see mine?"

"Of course."

"I thought we were good friends, Howie."

"We are."

"Then you should say something about my profile."

"'Good luck with your hunt'?"

Nick swallowed. "Oh." He got up and went to the bathroom. He wanted to pummel Howie with his fists, but he also felt a wave of grief overtake him. Grief for what? He couldn't articulate what he'd lost. Was it Howie? Or was it something else deeper? He slid down to the floor next to the toilet in his stall. He wanted to cry, but tears weren't forthcoming.

Then the door clicked open. "Nick?" It was Howie.

"I'll be out."

"Get up."

"Don't tell me what to do."

"Sorry."

The door closed.

Nick felt angrier with himself. Fuck, he shouldn't have said *that*.

A minute later, the door opened. "Sorry, but I really have to take a piss."

Nick watched Howie's feet amble to the urinal on the other side of the stall and listened to the sound of urine hitting the porcelain. Then Howie moved away to the sink, where he washed his hands and wiped them on paper towels.

Nick felt worse when Howie left and closed the door. What now? How could he face him now? Maybe he should keep quiet like Howie, and they would end up an odd couple where no one spoke or quarreled. Maybe Nick would die a lonely man.

He looked at the toilet bowl and wished he could vomit. That would've provided a legitimate excuse for leaving work early.

He got up and left the bathroom.

Howie, with his arms crossed, was waiting outside the bathroom. "Let's talk in my office."

"I don't feel so good." Nick leaned against the bathroom's doorframe.

"Then go home. We can talk about this when you come back."

"I can't believe you're talking like this."

"I'm certainly capable of talking when I want to."

"I'm so embarrassed."

"It's okay."

Howie returned to his desk and resumed his work on the computer. He didn't close his office door.

Nick stared at him.

"What's wrong?"

"You don't get it, do you?"

"What's there to get?" Howie asked.

"I have *feelings*. For you."

"Oh." Howie seemed genuinely surprised. "I didn't see that one coming."

"I can explain."

"You work here. It's not professional."

"I want you."

"Me? Why?"

"Because you'd make a great husband."

"Is that all I am to you?"

"Well, you're more than that. Of course."

"I don't want to be a 'husband.' I want a lover too."

"I can be your lover."

Howie shook his head no. "Sorry."

"Why not?"

"Just ..." He closed his spreadsheet program. "You know what? I think I'm gonna go home. This is getting too weird for me." He picked up his jacket and cap off the hook and left. He didn't even button himself up completely the way he usually did.

In that moment, Nick thought about killing himself. Ever since he found himself unable to get erect on command, the idea had floated through his mind now and then. Who was going to want him now? No one wants a guy with a flaccid dick. Then he thought about how that would affect Howie. He changed his mind. Losing Timm was bad enough. The worst part, he knew, was that not many people would show up at Howie's memorial service. He wasn't hated, but he wasn't loved either. Howie was a just-there guy. The thought of having not many people show up at Howie's service saddened him. Howie had to improve his ability to make new friends and spend more time with them.

But how? He was so set in his ways. Nick wasn't sure if Howie still walked around his neighborhood twice a day. He knew that Howie was teaching himself how to cook, but he never mentioned whether he made meals for other people. He had hoped to be invited to taste Howie's cooking, but that was out of the question now. He had weirded Howie out too much.

He looked at his cell, wondering whom he should call. Then he knew. He scrolled down his contacts and found Queen Betsy's number.

"Hello. Who's this?"

"Hi, it's Nick Clayton. We met a couple of times at fundraisers. I was one of Timm's friends. I think I need your help with Howie."

12
Howie

As Howie drove home in the drifting snow, he still felt freaked out by the idea of Nick being attracted to him. He truly had no idea! He'd never even thought of him in that way. Nick was a highly talkative fellow who was a bit flighty but committed to his job. Howie wasn't bothered by how Nick talked about the men he'd tricked with, or how he worked out to maintain a certain weight and body mass. Nick just wasn't for him.

After Billy's disappearance, he had felt lonely again. The men that he liked online didn't seem interested in him. If anyone instant-messaged him, he usually wanted to know if Howie had nude pictures to trade or how big his cock was. Those he blocked immediately. He wasn't a beauty, and he wasn't Timm. When he began to clean out Timm's hard drive, he found quite a few pictures that someone had taken of Timm's erection from a variety of angles. He couldn't make out the fuzzy background, but he was pretty sure that it wasn't taken at their house. He looked at the pictures on the monitor and remembered the first time when he saw Timm's gigantic penis. They were in Timm's apartment on Bryant and Franklin. They had been making out on the bed.

Howie had been horrified. He couldn't believe that anyone could be that large. He was afraid that he'd get raped with that thing. He slipped off the bed.

"Where are you going?"

"Home. It's too big."

"Darling. I'm not going to fuck you."

"Still." He whispered, "I like the rest of you better."

Timm raised his eyebrows. "Come here." He patted the space beside him on his bed. "I want to take care of you."

Howie reluctantly returned to the bed.

"Take off your clothes."

"You're going to laugh."

"At what?"

"No, I won't."

Howie turned around, pulled off the rest of his clothes, and faced him.

"Darling, let me tell you something. Having a huge dick like this is so overrated. They see this, and they don't see your face anymore. I want to see your face all the time." Timm reached forward and pulled Howie onto the bed. "And your fur is so much better than this!" He gripped himself.

Their lovemaking that first night together was just extraordinary, with Timm explaining the mechanics of gay sex and guiding Howie through his first sexual positions with another man. It wasn't long before Howie turned around on Timm and made passionate love. After Howie's third orgasm in the space of an hour, Timm had to beg Howie for a break. His ass was feeling sore. He never bottomed for anyone, but this guy was truly special. He was almost a souvenir from back home when men were men and women were women, except that he was totally into Timm. Howie turned out to be completely insatiable. He always got instant erections, whereas Timm occasionally had to work himself to stiffness.

As they grew older as a couple, and as they fretted about whether one of them would come down with AIDS, Howie entertained fantasies about having sex with others. Watching porn was such a relief, and he appreciated having Timm there with him because sooner or later they'd turn to each other and forget about the white snow flickering at the end of the VHS tape on their bedroom VCR. Their lovemaking was not as passionate as before; it was tinged with the fear of getting *it*. Each kiss was a plea for forgiveness in case one did get infected. They knew that their bodies were not as limber as before, but they never talked about how different their slowly aging bodies felt. They still saw themselves as young, but their mirrors revealed slight stretches of skin and a loosening in other places. Timm and Howie didn't worry about such things because as long as their cocks worked, that was all that ultimately mattered.

The more Howie traveled online, the more he had to wonder: Why this obsession with sizes? He knew that according to Wikipedia, which he often browsed during his lunch break, the average cock size was six inches, with 95% of men falling below that. Knowing that, what did "hung" mean anyway? At home, when he got tired of taking pictures of things he had to sell, he went online and read profiles. He didn't approach anyone. A few instant messages popped up now and then, but they all wanted to know if he wanted to hook up.

He declined. He just wasn't in the mood for *sex*. He wasn't sure what he wanted, and he knew it wasn't love. He had that with Timm. No one else could give him that. Yet he definitely wanted something more.

Eventually a few things about those profiles became transparent. Anyone who called himself "VGL," as in "very good looking," was not for him. Calling himself "hung" was actually a deal breaker, because no one could be as hung as Timm was. It also revealed an arrogance that because he was hung, he had to be a bit better and therefore more desirable than you. He had gone through that crap with Timm, so no thanks. Timm had a spectacular cock, the stuff that porn stars dreamed of having, but Howie was eternally grateful that he had no interest in doing porn. Timm had a number of porn filmmakers call him up and ask if he was interested in doing a gig or two in San Fernando Valley. Somewhere in L.A. All expenses paid plus two thousand dollars. He didn't need to send in a picture of himself. That was how legendary his appendage had become. He didn't mind the thing between Timm's legs so much; he had often wished it shorter. Yet, to Howie, anyone who called himself an "average Joe" online demonstrated a lack of confidence in himself. If a guy offered only pictures of his private parts, Howie passed on those. If that was the best part of himself that he could offer online, he was not interested. What more could the guy possibly offer?

Over time, he began to realize a few other things. Some men approached him because he was a big guy. They thought he was a bear. This depressed him because he didn't care for the bear community at all. He was a big guy, but he didn't fit in anywhere. He decided to omit his height and weight for a while to see what would happen. Most instant messages revealed the assumption that he must be terribly overweight, and therefore hotter to these men who saw extreme obesity as a sexual attribute. This grossed him out. He reposted his weight and height online.

He read up on the tried-and-true strategies for weight loss, and realized that he had to watch what he ate. He sought out healthy cookbooks and tried a few recipes. Most didn't taste very good, but it had to be about the calories. He still craved a little flavor. Then he read a cookbook author remarking that fat equaled flavor, and that some dishes needed just a little fat to taste edible. Of course, that made sense. Why did all those healthy cookbooks understand that? *Just a little.* That's all! He decided to try using very tiny drops of sour cream on every fifth bite after he'd steamed a plateful of vegetables. That was a revelation, so he took along a vegetarian cookbook to work. The more he perused the recipes, the more grateful he was to have a store like the Wedge so close by. Over the years he had gone there, he always rolled his eyes when Timm said things like, "Ooh! Fresh eggplant." He hadn't cared about what he ate as long as Timm made it. "I'll pay for it as long as you cook it," he always said. When he walked around the store's produce section now, the more he missed Timm. He was only starting to see what could be done with this or that ingredient. Cooking didn't have to be rocket science. Timm would've been agog at how Howie caressed this or that vegetable, checking for firmness; he'd given up a long time before of ever asking Howie to pick out the best vegetables from a bin. Howie never checked; he blindly threw the potatoes into a bag and weighed it. Later that night, Howie was horrified to see a few truly old potatoes on his counter. But now? He felt pangs of remorse for not appreciating the level of obsession that Timm brought to his cooking. Little things did make a huge difference. Just like those dabs of sour cream.

When he was finished cooking, he sat down to eat. Initially, when he was so excited about making his first potato au gratin, he set the dining room table for two out of habit. He had always set the table while Timm cooked, but when he went into the empty kitchen that night, he realized that no one else was going to eat his first potato dish. It was good, but the loneliness had made it taste okay. He was sure that Timm would've raved about it. He felt a pang of sorrow when he realized he'd never once cooked a meal for Timm in their three decades together. How could he have been so selfish, so demanding? Timm never complained. The more he thought about food and cooking, the more he missed his husband terribly. He would've been too happy to be Timm's *sous chef*, chopping and mincing, instead of sitting there in the living room and watching the news as Timm prepared their dinner.

He updated his online profile to say that he was exploring how to cook better. The instant messages were finally less about sexual come-ons and more about what kind of cuisines they liked. He put some of these guys on his pal list. He enjoyed chatting with them very much. There was something reassuring about typing things and not having to use his own voice, or being seen while chatting. Almost all of these chatbuds were far away, so it wasn't as if they'd show up at his house. He felt safe.

But tonight he wasn't in the mood to sit around and wait for someone to come online. He got up and saw through his front window that it was nice out. He logged off to put on his jacket and cap. The brisk nip in the air was just right. He never understood why people everywhere went, "Oh, Minnesota is so cold!" when North Dakota and other northern states bordering Canada could be just as cold, if not colder. He remembered winters when he was younger how he filled a cup with water and set it by his bedroom window. The water would be almost frozen by the time he woke up. He found that so fascinating. It was almost like magic. The cold never bothered him. It was just part of life. He didn't see it as something to complain about. It just was. The more weight he gained as he grew older, the more he preferred winter to summer. Everything was crisp. The sharpness of air was far more invigorating than the balm of heat, and yet forced everyone to slow down.

Unlike most people, he didn't mind the snow at all. He understood why people hated shoveling the snow, but he didn't mind the chore. After the first major snowfall of 2008, he took out his gas snowblower. He liked how the snow spewed out of the orange chute and left behind jagged mountain-like ridges along the sidewalk and driveway. Then he suddenly thought of Timm. He stopped and turned off the ignition. He was afraid that neighbors and passersby would catch him in a fit of sobbing. He had always loved shoveling the snow because he knew Timm would be heating up milk and stirring in some dark chocolate powder so that it would be ready and at the right temperature when he clomped into the foyer and took off his thick boots. Timm usually made sure that the fireplace had a fire going, so they could sit together and watch the fire while they talked in low voices. Now Timm wasn't checking up on Howie's progress through the window while monitoring the milk on their gas stove. "Fuck," he whispered.

Betsy was right. She had warned him that it would take a year to lose someone after you've lost him. At first that didn't make sense. How could anyone *lose* someone after he's already gone? But he saw exactly what she'd meant. He himself had to *lose* Timm. This was precisely why Timm had insisted that his possessions be sold and given away. This was his way of forcing Howie to give up his dead husband. He sniffled and wiped away his nose with his sleeve before he resumed the snowblowing. It seemed to take much longer to clear the driveway. He forced himself not to check that window every so often. He liked waving back to Timm in the window. That night, when he put away his snowblower in the garage, he missed that smell of hot cocoa wafting from the kitchen. He went there and took out a small paring knife. He looked at his thick wrists. He couldn't take any more of this. Fuck Connie Francis.

Then he heard the front door knock. He was startled. Who could it be at this hour?

He set down the knife, hurried to the door, and looked out. There was no one around.

Maybe the sound had been a figment of his imagination. But he was quite sure that he had heard *something*. He went back to the kitchen and put away the knife. He looked for the cocoa powder and read its instructions. Water? He was supposed to use water? He remembered the hot chocolate to be quite creamy. *Of course*. It all came to him now. Timm had mentioned that he used whole milk with a dollop of heavy cream when he heated up the chocolate. No, he couldn't do that to his waist now. He put the powder back.

He kept thinking about that noise, which happened again. He returned to the foyer and jiggled the knob. Was it just a forceful gust of wind that rattled the door? The door was very solid. It'd take more than wind to make a noise. He peered out the side window and caught sight of someone walking down the sidewalk. He opened the door and peered into the darkness. "Hey! You."

The apparition stopped and turned.

It was Billy wearing an army pea jacket. His eyes looked slightly manic.

"Hey. You shouldn't be out there." Howie waved him in and saw how thin and gaunt he had become. His veins were almost blue. He closed the door.

"Thank you," he whispered. His teeth were chattering.

"Come this way." Howie guided Billy to his chair. He switch-opened the fireplace's flue, piled newspapers on top of a few logs, struck a match, and waited for the logs to catch fire. He stoked the flames a bit more until the heat flickered all over their faces. "Give me a few minutes."

He went into the kitchen and heated up a mixture of milk and heavy cream. That boy could use some fattening. He dumped spoonfuls of cocoa and stirred. He dipped a finger into the cup and licked it. Tastes about right, he thought. He set the mug beside Billy. "I'll go get some blankets and slippers for you."

He hurried upstairs and grabbed what he could.

Billy didn't resist when Howie pulled the jacket off and wrapped the blankets around him. Howie took off his boots and tried to hide his reaction to the unusually pungent stench of his socks. He massaged Billy's feet. They were almost like bones. When his toes finally wriggled, Howie put the slippers on. "There you go."

"Thank you."

"Oh, it's no problem at all. You need to wash your feet later."

Billy nodded.

"I'm sorry that I don't have marshmallows, but that should keep you warm. I can heat up some soup if you want."

"Please."

By the time he returned to the living room with a tray of microwaved soup and a bowl of crackers, Billy was gulping down the hot cocoa. He set down the tray on the coffee table. "Eat."

"Yes, sir!"

They both broke out in laughter.

As Howie watched Billy eat, he felt strangely content. He was curious about where Billy had been, but he didn't ask questions. He was here, now and safer than wherever he was. Howie returned with a sandwich, which Billy consumed in mere minutes. He set the plate aside and took Billy's hands into his. They were still a bit cold. Howie looked into Billy's eyes.

"I'm not gay."

"I wasn't asking if you were."

"I'm such a fuckup," Billy mumbled.

"Shh. Tonight you'll sleep in your bed, but you can't disappear whenever you feel like it."

"I just couldn't stay here. Just couldn't. Sorry."

"We'll talk more tomorrow morning, but when you're ready to move around, you're going to take a shower. I'll put an electric heater in your room so you can stay warm."

"You're not sleeping with me, right?"

"No. Did you want me to?"

"I'm not gay."

"Just answer my question. Do you want me to sleep next to you?"

Billy nodded.

As he escorted Billy up the stairs, he was surprised by how much thinner Billy had become. He was almost a skeleton.

In the bathroom Billy hesitated as Howie turned on the water. "What?"

"I can do this."

"Okay. But you seem awfully weak."

"Well, I can take care of myself."

"I've seen you naked."

"Oh, right. Right."

"I'm not going to do anything you don't want me to." He checked the water's temperature. "Kinda hot, but see for yourself."

Billy stuck his hand into the shower, stripped, and stepped inside.

As Howie prepared the guest bed, he couldn't shake how surreal his back tattoos looked against the deepened ridges of his chest cage. He didn't have much of an ass now. When he heard the shower stop, he hurried back to the bathroom and picked up a towel. "Let me dry you."

"You don't have to."

"I insist."

Billy lifted his arms and closed his eyes.

Howie didn't touch his body at all. Just rubbed the towel everywhere he could until he saw no more water beads on Billy's body. He gave him his own bathrobe even though it was way too large. "For now."

In the bedroom, he took the bathrobe off Billy and lifted the bed sheets for him.

"Fuck. This is cold."

"If you don't move for a few minutes, you'll be hot. Trust me."

When Howie returned from locking the house and cleaning up the kitchen, he found Billy sound asleep. He gazed at the young man. Billy was actually more handsome than he'd realized. Howie took off his clothes and slipped into bed. He took Billy into his arms and kissed him on the forehead. "You're safe with me now," he whispered. He was surprised when he saw how Billy snuggled up to him.

Howie didn't sleep that night, watching how the young man wouldn't let him go. He was filled with all sorts of thoughts, memories, dreams, and questions. Exactly what the hell was he doing in bed with a young tattooed man who said he wasn't gay? There was no future in this.

Exhausted yet unable to sleep, Howie called in sick by leaving a message on his boss Elaine's answering machine the next morning.

Billy was still asleep when Howie returned from the bathroom. It was already ten o'clock. He had slept thirteen hours.

Howie went downstairs and prepared a bowl of oatmeal, topped with dried berries. He brought it up with a glass of juice to the guest room. He nudged Billy. "Hey, sleepyhead." When he saw how Billy struggled to awaken and then smiled once he realized where he was, Howie knew he could easily fall in love with him.

13
Betsy

When Betsy got the call from Nick, she was a bit confused at first. Usually very good with faces and names, she tried to place his face. Nick Clayton? What did he look like? Maybe Timm had mentioned something about Howie's friend. If he had, she couldn't remember anything. Sensing the panic in his voice, she agreed to meet him at Dunn Bros Coffee on West 15th overlooking Loring Park an hour later. She wore a blouse, slacks, and a faux fur jacket; she wore her long hair tight in a bun. Even though she wasn't as slender as the actress Diana Rigg, she loved the way she carried herself. She made sure that the bright red lacquer hadn't chipped off her fingernails before she ordered a stiff espresso. She was due to show up at the Gay 90s in an hour. It wouldn't take long to change. Besides, those drag shows always started notoriously late. The bar certainly didn't seem to mind because it meant more drinks would be sold to the waiting customers.

She sat down in a plush chair next to the fireplace on the front patio and sipped. A woman tapped on her wireless laptop a few chairs away.

A gray-haired short man wearing a thick coat and earmuffs strode in. He took off his leather gloves. "Queen Betsy?"

"Oh, yes."

He bowed before her and shook her hand. "Your Majesty."

She glanced around. "This isn't a gay bar. I'm a woman."

"Sorry." He glanced at her espresso. "I'll go get something to drink." He left for the counter up the steps in the back.

She thought about how Nick had greeted her and felt a slight churn in her stomach. At first, when she called herself Queen Betsy, she thought it a fitting one at the time. Now? Her name and legend had decreed that people meeting her must bow before her as if she was royalty. The problem was, she wasn't even a drag queen. She was a heterosexual woman who could dress up to the hilt with the best of them; she only happened to have been a man in a former lifetime. She loved every queen who strutted across the tiny stage on the third floor of the Gay 90s every weekend. It didn't matter if the queen couldn't lip-sync perfectly to the recording or not. Many of them weren't all that great, but it still didn't matter. What was important was the act of dressing up to be something they were inside. A few were trans, but most of them were gay men who loved to, in the words of a friend, "drag it up." A few of them were straight with understanding wives.

Ever since the pain between her legs subsided after the surgery, she worked hard on sublimating the little telltale details of being a woman into herself. She worked with a speech pathologist who specialized in working on voice and pitch with transitioning transgender individuals. She was puzzled at first when she began attending voice and speech therapy sessions. She could alter the pitch of her voice, so what was the big deal? Then Dr. Huston played a few recordings. "Male or female?"

"Male." Another. "Female." One more. "Female."

Dr. Huston smiled. "You guessed wrong on all three counts."

"What?"

He explained how people pronounce words not only based on local influence but also based on gender. People could also sound quite different at higher or lower pitches. More so with different inflections. Betsy recalled how she'd taken phone calls from clients in the preparation room only to be thrown off when she learned she had been talking to a man—or a woman—when it was the other way around. One could be equally fooled into thinking someone was completely female not only by the appearance but also by the sound of her voice. She was agog at the discovery and insisted that recordings be made of her own voice. Listening to herself with Dr. Huston liberated her. She knew that gender, and its baggage of assumptions, was inseparable from the fabric of life, but here she had gained another tool to be more like the woman she knew she was destined to be. Out there in the world, when she did her shopping, she didn't overdo her makeup. She was proud of how unobtrusive she looked as a woman. She didn't want to be gawked at. Walking in slacks and low pumps made her feel more feminine when she browsed through ladies' undergarments. Sometimes, when she had to walk through the home improvement section in the larger chain stores, she felt like a foreigner in a country she once knew. She had never cared for power drills, hammers, and the like. She only cared for the tools she used to embalm the dead and the few vibrators she kept in her bedside drawer. Learning to speak more naturally as a woman gave her so much more confidence. Did people really think about how they treated a person differently because of their gender? She knew the answer to that question, but she was always amazed by the answer. People were far more judgmental than they admitted, even to themselves.

She tried to go out on dates with straight men.

Nothing worked.

She couldn't figure out what was going wrong. She hadn't even told any of them that she was trans!

Then Timm pointed out something. "You tell jokes like a drag queen. Just shut up and listen. That'll make the guy feel you're into him."

Betsy's next blind date was arranged through a friend who had no idea about her past life. She agreed to meet a man named Walter at Rudolph's, a neighborhood landmark restaurant two blocks down the hill from her apartment. She dressed simply and chose to wear only earrings. Walter turned out to be rather tall and four-eyed with his thick glasses.

They sat down by a window.

Walter was a divorced physicist who did research and taught at the University of Minnesota. He spoke in fits and starts. He seemed afraid to look her in the eye. She watched how he fumbled with the barbecued ribs. His hands were trembling.

She put her hand on his. "Are you nervous? Don't be."

He looked quietly into her face. "You're really beautiful."

"Really?"

"Yes. Hasn't anyone told you that?"

Yes, she wanted to tell him, but they were all drag queens who couldn't stop marveling at her ability to pass for straight.

"Not many," she said.

"Why not?" He took her hands into his. "Whoever let you go was a fool. All of them!"

She was careful with how she spoke with him. No risqué jokes that she'd picked up at the Gay 90s. No slices of bitchy humor. No double entendres, even though she was a proven master of triple entendres.

"You embalm bodies?" he said when she told him what she did for a living.

"Yes." She braced herself for a barrage of prurient questions.

"That's got to be interesting."

"It has its moments, but you get used to it."

"Right." He took her hand and lifted it to his lips. "I'm so glad that you're alive."

She burst out laughing. "You're so sweet."

"Didn't our friend Marcia tell you? I'm a romantic guy."

After dinner, she was surprised by how nice a man's kiss could be. She had kissed men in the days when she thought she was gay, but they were always filled with a sexual urgency. But the way Walter leaned forward and kissed her squarely on the lips was different. He wasn't insistent. He was stating a fact with the tender weight of his kiss: *I like you.*

She melted on the spot. She wanted to spend the night with him, but she didn't ask. She was a woman, not a slut.

They agreed to meet again the following Thursday, but this time at Murray's in downtown Minneapolis. The steakhouse had candles and round tables. Soft jazz played in the background. They linked hands as they ate and listened attentively to each other. She didn't mind the fact that he was so interested in physics and astronomy, or that he didn't seem to know much else about anything else. He was myopic in conversation, but his eyes were intense. Desire and ache lit like stars in them.

All that week before their second date, when she prepared one dead body after another, she felt euphoric. A man with absolutely no connection with the gay community was interested in *her* as her. She didn't have to say anything about her body, or the journey she had taken from Long Island to Minneapolis. She wanted to tell someone about Walter, but she was afraid to jinx her chances. She thought about telling Timm, but she changed her mind. No one needed to know, not yet. Each time she thought of Walter, she felt her body get all tingly. She was horny. She longed to show him what a real woman she was, and she would. She liked how he called her almost every night to talk. There was something so endearing about the sound of his flat Midwestern voice.

After dinner, they walked hand-in-hand on the desolate streets of downtown and talked. They mostly looked at each other's reflections in the huge glass windows and smiled. She loved how he squeezed her hand at particular times as if he was trying to tell her things he couldn't articulate. She wanted to invite him home that night.

"How about tomorrow night? That way we could spend the weekend together."

She thought of how proud she'd been of the fact that she had never once missed emceeing the twice-nightly shows every weekend at the Gay 90s. Who could take over for her? Those ladies who bickered and backstabbed each other backstage weren't leaders. They all needed guidance, and she always gave it to them. Some of them called her "Momma Betsy," but she always said, "Can it. I ain't old yet." If she became a no-show tomorrow night, she'd never be able to live it down. She had been doing it for over ten years. People would ask her if there was something wrong. If there weren't, they'd want to know why. Eventually, she'd give in and say that she had a date. They'd ask why he hadn't come to her show. No. Her friends would gawk at him, dressed in such geeky garb, as if he were from outer space. "Can't. I have plans. How about Sunday?"

He tried to hide his disappointment. "That'd be good. Actually, great."

When she went home that night, she pondered the question of her successor. If she did end up having a relationship with Walter, she wouldn't have qualms about quitting the Gay 90s altogether. She loved her friends there but noticed how exhausted she felt the mornings after. She needed the rest of the day, particularly on Saturdays, to decompress. It was odd because once she was on stage, it didn't feel like too much effort. But once she got into her apartment, she wanted nothing more than to take off her makeup and go straight to sleep.

That Friday night, she chose an outfit she hadn't worn in a few years; she'd debuted it on one of her New Year's Eves. It was made of gold lamé, which matched the color of her wig, earrings, and pumps. At twenty past nine, she strode onstage amidst applause. "Good evening, ladies" —which she always delivered with a glance of rolling eyes backstage—"and gentlemen," to which she always opened her arms to the audience. "We're running a little late with our nylon stockings, but a scratch in the right spot will never hurt you, is always what I say. Right, ladies? I feel your itch too." She made a few playful scratches on her body. "Now, some of you may know me as Queen Betsy, but I insist that all of you call me Miss Queen Butter ... Krugerass." As she delivered the pun to peals of laughter, she caught sight of a mortified Walter sitting at a side table. She had to think fast. "But tonight, I'm going to be a class act. No more four-letter words tonight, or someone is going to get spanked!"

Someone in the audience yelled, "Whooo!"

"Would you like to get up here and get spanked?" She paused for dramatic effect. "I thought so. All of you spankees are in the closet." She clapped twice, her cue to the first lady waiting offstage. "We have here a woman who has more hair, more glitter, and more lip gloss than all of you combined. You all know who she is, and for the rest of you who don't—well, you are not fit to kiss her pinky finger. Ladies and gentlemen, please welcome Miz Izzie Pique!"

As the Brothers Johnson song "Get the Funk Out Ma Face" played, Miz Izzie Pique strutted onstage in an outfit festooned with blinking Christmas lights. Miz Izzie lip-synced the lyrics while she grooved and played with her lights as if they were all nipples. She was like a whirling Christmas tree on a pair of feet that looked like boxed gifts. She wore a bright yellow star on top of her head. The crowd went wild.

But Betsy wasn't looking at her. She had hurried offstage and crouched low as she crossed over to where Walter was sitting.

His chair was empty.

She glanced around and hurried down the stairs.

But he was gone. She nearly lost her temper when a few people recognized her. "Queen Betsy! I haven't seen you in ages!"

"Sorry, but I'm looking for someone." She knew the song upstairs would end soon. The steps up were the hardest for her. She had been used to walking in high pumps, but ... *Walt.* She should've told him about herself upfront. Some of her trans friends had talked at great length about the crucial timing of disclosure. They weren't interested in dating tranny chasers.

Betsy hurried back and took the microphone once the song ended. "I don't know about you, but I wouldn't want you to get the funk outta my face!"

It was hard going. She wanted to keep the jokes flowing, but she knew it wasn't working. They weren't laughing as much.

"Hey, Queen Betsy!" an older man called from the back tables. "You okay?" It was George Carlos, a long-time fan and a straight man who liked crossdressers.

She stared at him a moment before she said, "No."

"Do tell us about it, Queen Betsy. We all love you!"

She looked about herself, and she beckoned the DJ from behind the window. The audience murmured among themselves as they watched her whisper into his ear. He nodded, Gotcha. She went backstage and grabbed a stool.

"I don't want to divulge too much about my private life, but I think this song will explain everything you need to know." She walked to the stage's center. Judy's live version of "The Man That Got Away" began playing. Betsy sat on the stool and dueted with her voice, like she used to when she was a young man: "The night is bitter, the stars have lost their glitter ..." She kept looking at the empty chair the whole time. She didn't care whether her voice was on pitch or not. This song wasn't for the audience, it was for her. She had to *feel* this inside her. It wasn't until that moment she came to appreciate Judy's depth of emotion and artistry. Judy had given so much, and still, she continued to *give*. She had been so selfless! Betsy felt as if she was in a dream from long ago in the living room of her first apartment near the train station on Long Island. She had been the man who got away the second she realized what she'd done with that chunk of concrete, and what was she now? She was a *woman*. If she wanted a straight man, she had no business hanging out with these high-maintenance gay friends of hers.

As the crowd's applause melted into the recorded applause for Judy, Betsy stood up, wiped her tears, and faced her audience. "Thank you." She paused. "I quit." She set down the microphone on the stool and walked from the stage into the stunned silence. She didn't look back when friends and acquaintances called after her. She sobbed in her parked car for a good ten minutes before she felt clear-headed enough to drive home.

She called Walter the minute she got into her apartment. All she got was his answering machine. She wasn't sure how long it could record her message, so she decided to speed up what she had to say. "Walter, I'm sorry you had to find out the way you did tonight, but I want you to know that I quit. I'm a real woman in every way. I don't have a penis. I miss you more than you'll ever know. Please call me. I'll be here all weekend."

She hung up and poured herself a shot of whiskey. She rarely drank, but she was so full of nerves. She sat on the sofa and kicked off her pumps. She didn't care how she flung her wig away or kicked off her dress. She was going to get *drunk*. She fucking deserved it.

He never called back that night.

At three o'clock in the morning, she walked the two blocks over to Timm and Howie's house and knocked. She knew she should call ahead, but she couldn't just sit still.

Howie, wearing a bathrobe, opened the front door. "Betsy! You all right?"

"I need to talk to Timm."

"I'll go get him."

"Oh, no, not yet." She flung herself into Howie's arms and sobbed all over again. She never had the peculiar experience of having her face against a man's *hairy* chest. She inhaled his body odor and wished it were Walt holding her instead. "Sorry," she said as she finally pushed herself away.

"It's all right. What happened?"

"Darling!"

They turned to find Timm standing naked on the stairs. She had been used to what he'd called his "hardcore nudity."

"I heard you bawling like a baby, so why don't you come in the kitchen?"

She was touched when Howie followed them. She told Timm and Howie everything about her dating troubles and Walt.

Timm continued to stroke her forearm while she drank herbal tea and carried on.

Howie leaned against the counter and drank water. He said nothing.

She noticed how handsome he truly was. He was all man, standing there in a bathrobe that exposed his incredible chest fur.

After she'd run out of steam and felt empty, Timm said, "Why don't you sleep in our guest room tonight?"

"I'll go change the sheets," Howie said and went upstairs.

She looked after him.

"You have such a good husband."

"Thank you. Tomorrow, when you get up, I'll cook you a fabulous brunch."

She had a horrible hangover the next day.

Timm accompanied her to her apartment. "Let's check your machine." There were messages of concern from friends and fans at the Gay 90s, but nothing from Walt.

She plopped down on the sofa and looked at Timm. "Now what?"

"Walt came alone, right?"

"I suppose so."

"Maybe he has a thing for trannies."

"Oh God, no. Not another tranny chaser."

She spent that weekend alone in her apartment. She forced herself to wash dishes, vacuum, and do laundry. She checked her answering machine, but Walt never called.

The manager of Gay 90s showed up at her apartment that Sunday afternoon and offered to pay her double what she had always gotten. "The show last night was horrible. We need you. You're our guiding spirit." He slipped a hundred into her hands. "Make yourself a new dress. That should cheer you up." As he was about to leave, he stopped and turned. "One more thing. You have a wonderful voice. You should pick a song and sing at the end of each show."

Each day when she went to the preparation room in the basement and worked on the bodies, she imagined that each woman's body had belonged to Walt. He was in the habit of breaking their hearts only to see them commit suicide. She felt a kinship with each woman she dressed. It didn't matter how old they were. She was a woman, too.

She went back onstage that Friday. The house was SRO, and all of the ladies backstage were actually ready. *On time.* That was practically unheard of! "Good evening, ladies—" that infamous glance— "and gentlemen. Contrary to what you might've heard, I won't be the woman that got away." She felt warm when everyone cheered. She chose to sing to a karaoke version of Gloria Gaynor's "I Will Survive," which brought down the house. Just before she bowed again, she caught sight of Timm's tears and hands clapping, and Howie's quiet smile. He was such a good trooper! She knew that Howie had little interest in drag shows, but he tagged along with Timm.

Eventually, she met some men who wanted to date her. She resisted at first, but the more she thought about it, she liked the idea that she didn't have to pretend. She was a woman, period. If they didn't like it, it was their problem, not hers. The sex was different with men. When she was a man, she had found more pleasure when she imagined herself as a woman with a man, not as a man with another man. But now, she was a woman with a vagina. She was amazed at how the men begged to lick her down there and fuck her. When she wrapped her legs around them, she felt more complete. She was not a man anymore. But in the end, it turned out to be more about the novelty of dating a transwoman. Those dates never went anywhere. Worse yet, none of the men were interested in the art of romancing. Betsy wanted more than just sex; she wanted to be *wooed.* Whatever happened to candlelit dinners in a restaurant? A bouquet of flowers? A simple walk while holding hands? She missed Walt more than ever.

When Timm showed her the love note that Howie had written to go with a small handful of dandelions ("You make these weeds look beautiful"), she fought the urge to cry. She still missed Walt. She envied Timm more than ever. He had everything a man could want—a highly successful business, a reliable and romantic husband, a fantastic house, and a great body. Every time she visited Timm and Howie, she rarely got to talk with Howie. He was more like a shadow that nodded hello. She often dreamed of that moment when her face was pressed against his furry chest. He was really like a big teddy bear.

So, when Nick Clayton called her, she had been thinking long and hard about quitting the Gay 90s. It was time for a new generation to take over. Hell, she was almost 60! She needed to be a woman, and nothing more. She didn't need to wear outrageous wigs and dresses for self-fulfillment. She needed to find her place in the world of men and women, not in the world of gender ambiguity. She needed to spend time among straight women and learn their ways better. More importantly, she needed a husband more than ever. She was, for all legal purposes, a woman. She could marry a man if she wanted to. She felt sad that wasn't the case—yet!—for her gay friends. She knew that she wouldn't turn her back on doing fundraisers for all those important causes, but she had to stop doing those weekend shows. She hadn't told anyone about her plans yet, so when Nick called her about Howie, she agreed. Maybe she would learn something about him.

Nick returned with a chai latte and sat in the chair next to Betsy. "Sorry. They were short-staffed tonight."

"Oh, it's no problem." As Betsy said those words, she realized that she was still speaking in that queer way rather than as a straight woman; she was speaking as if she was still in the Gay 90s. It was odd that just her knowing whether a person was gay could instantly change the way she spoke. This was another reason why she had to get out of the Gay 90s altogether. She was becoming too queer for straight men. "So what seems to be the problem with Howie?"

"I know it sounds kinda funny, and I've never told this to anyone, but I'm in love with Howie."

Her eyes widened. "Is he in love with you too?"

"That's the problem." He recounted his problems with intimacy, admitting that he had been Mr. Anti-Monogamy online, and realizing that he was growing older and needed a husband like Howie.

She sat and sipped quietly. The more she listened to Nick ramble on, the more she did not like him. Of course, she shouldn't judge anyone, but he exuded an air of desperation that was most unappealing.

"What should I tell him?"

"I'm sorry?"

"Tomorrow morning he's going to come into work. What do I tell him?"

"Let him take the lead. If he wants to talk about it, he will. If he doesn't, let it be. It takes most people at least one year to get over losing someone." She looked at him with a frown. "You need to be patient."

"But I can't just sit around and wait."

"Then go find someone else to date. Surely you know lots of people."

"You don't understand. No one dates to date a guy who can't …" He showed his index finger going straight up, then dropping down.

"Can I be frank here?"

"Sure."

"For someone who's slept around as much as you have, you've shown an incredible lack of imagination. You don't have to fuck like straight people do. You could fuck … differently."

He looked like he was about to cry. "I thought maybe you could help me. I love him so much!"

"What do you want me to do?"

"Tell him that I'd be a great guy to date. You were Timm's best friend. He'll listen to you."

"Howie's a big boy. He can figure out things for himself." She checked her watch. "I'm sorry, but I have to go."

"Oh, right. Right. Thank you for coming."

As she walked to her car, it hit her. Timm had said that the axiom about the way to a man's heart was through his stomach was utterly true of Howie. Anyone could tell that he loved to eat. Nick didn't seem to be much of a cook. He was a workout nut who probably fretted over every single calorie. *Yes*. That's what she would do. She'd invite Howie over for dinner.

14
Howie

Earlier that day, Howie felt a sigh of relief when he saw how Billy was warm enough to move around. He had taken a hot shower, and by then, Howie had washed his clothes. He even found some winter clothes that Timm used to wear, so he gave them to Billy. He had been meaning to clean out that last closet anyway.

Billy was so happy to have a new winter jacket that he hugged Howie. "Thank you. This is so killer!" He kept unzipping and zipping up his ski jacket; it was a Bill Blass limited edition. "This is gonna keep me warm."

"You know all this comes with a price."

There was a slight shift of weight in Billy's feet. "You want me to blow you?"

"No. Just call me and let me know where you are okay. I want to make sure you're all right."

"Yes, Dad."

"Don't call me that, but you know what I mean."

They went to the living room and watched television. Nothing gripping was on, but during commercials and lackluster snippets, they talked in fits and starts over a few hours.

"So, where were you?"

"I tried to hitchhike back home. Southwestern Minnesota. Didn't work out."

"Want some tea?"

"Nah. Thanks anyway."

"What did you do for money?"

"Sucked cock here and there. Sometimes tattooed a guy while some guy fucked him." He bit nonchalantly into a celery stick. "Sometimes I stole food."

"Billy."

"Didn't get caught. I'm just bein' honest here."

"Can't you go back to your job at the Wedge? Everyone liked you there."

He chortled. "Not everyone. I got fired."

"Why?"

"You know the area when you can scoop peanut butter out into your own containers? Well, someone had accidentally dropped a glass container and it broke into sticky pieces, so I had to go mop it up. Then not even a minute later, this lady brings her baby and tilts him over like this—" he demonstrated with his hands holding the baby over the shoulder, "and the baby proceeded to vomit right on this area that I'd just mopped. She wiped this baby's mouth, and you know what she said to me? 'Sorry, but I knew Gene was going to throw up so I thought since you had the mop there, I thought maybe you could, you know.' I told her to fuck off. My boss overheard that." Billy used his finger to gesture slitting his throat and made the sound *kccch*. "The fucking bitch."

"Maybe you can go back to tattooing professionally."

"My portfolio book got stolen. Or lost. Whatever. I don't care."

"How good are you?"

"At tattooing? Pretty good."

"Got your tools and stuff?"

He shrugged. "Had to sell 'em for food."

"I can buy them for you. So you can start again."

Billy took the TV remote and turned it off.

"Why are you so nice to me? What's in it for you?"

"I just want to help you," Howie stammered. "Is that so wrong?"

"If you're in love with me, snap out of it. I love pussy, okay?"

"Well, I'm versatile."

Billy stood up. "I don't fucking believe this. I thought you were concerned about my health and stuff, but no, you just want me to fuck you 'cause tattoos get you all hot and bothered. Well, just because I look freaky doesn't mean that I get freaky in bed. You queer guys just don't get it. What's so bad about your own people that you don't want to have each other? You know what? I should go. Thanks for everything."

Howie didn't turn to watch. He listened to the sounds of Billy walking upstairs. The crinkle of a plastic bag being stuffed with his own clothes. The clomp of his boots down the steps. The zipping up of his new jacket. The clicking of the front door being shut. Howie leaned forward, picked up the remote, and turned the TV back on. He pushed the volume button up high and told himself that he was not going to shed tears over a tattooed straight fuckwad. Billy was just not worth it.

After thirty minutes of echoed commercials and canned laughter, Howie abruptly shut the TV off. He got up and looked out the front window. Billy was indeed gone. He walked to the kitchen and opened the fridge. Maybe he could eat something. Then he thought about wanting to lose more weight, so he shut the fridge. He glanced around. There had to be something he could do. Something productive, something demanding that would make him forget all about Billy. There had been moments over the years when something bad happened to Timm where Howie wished he could be more comfortable about drinking as a way of relieving stress, but he didn't really have a high alcohol tolerance like Timm's. He wanted to get drunk, but he had given away the liquor to Betsy early on after Timm died. "Timm would want you to have this."

Her eyes widened. "Really? This is so expensive."

"I don't drink. I'm boring."

"No, Howie, you're not boring. You're just ... quiet."

"That's another way of saying 'boring.'"

She gave a nervous laugh. "Well, thank you."

When he heard her laugh like that, he knew then that she was yet another "friend" who had promised to be there for him but wouldn't deliver. She was too busy with her friends, her day job, and the shows at the Gay 90s. He followed her out of his house and carried two bags of liquor while she cradled a huge bag of clinking bottles.

As they went up Franklin and made a right on Bryant, he thought about how many years had passed since he and Timm moved out of her apartment building. It was an old building, but he had a lot of affection for the old place. It was where he had sex with a man for the first time. It was also where he'd married Timm. It was also where he'd first lived with his husband. Every time he went by the building, he always gave it a quick glance of remembrance, even more so now that Timm was gone. They had lived on the third floor on the north side, where they could see a partial glimpse of the downtown skyline and the gateway to Loring Park.

He climbed the four flights of stairs to her apartment.

She turned the key and pushed against the door. "Sorry."

He put the bags on her kitchen table and entered the living room. The hardwood floors, once covered with a ratty wall-to-wall carpet, gleamed gold and tan in the afternoon sunlight. The curtains were gauzy. The walls had been repainted a dull bronze. "Wow. This place looks so different."

"You like it?"

"Well, it's not like before."

"I got tired of being in a drag queen's apartment, so I decided to grow up."

"I like it."

"Really?"

"Yes."

"You're the only person who said that. All my friends think I've become dullsville with this place."

"So? You're the one who lives here, not them." He looked out the window. He couldn't see the downtown skyline because branches were in the way.

"How are you feeling?"

"Okay."

"I meant, about Timm."

"Well. He's gone. I can't do anything about that."

"It's okay to cry."

"Am I supposed to cry to feel better? You're not me."

"Sorry. Do you want some water before you go?"

"I'm good." He gave her a perfunctory hug and left.

As he walked back to his house, he felt that flare of anger rise up in his guts. He hated how people thought it was their right to pry into the state of his heart and had an implied intimacy because they knew he had lost his husband. He hated how they insinuated that he hadn't appropriately grieved and should do so through tears. He wasn't a crying man. Why couldn't anyone understand that? There were plenty of ways to cry, and tears had nothing to do with them. He cried every single time he thought of Timm, or came across a memento from a road trip somewhere, or wondered what Timm would think if he gave up on his backyard gardening for just one summer. Right now, it was important that he honor Timm's wishes by selling off practically everything.

On his daily walks, neighbors smiled. Sometimes they said hello and told him that if he needed their help with anything, he should let them know at any time. He was touched when he heard that. Some of them were straight with kids. Thirty years ago, when he first moved to Minneapolis, it would've been unheard of to be neighborly with known homosexuals and have them know your children. Many enlightened straight people had figured out that gay people weren't sexually interested in kids at all. So much had changed in this neighborhood.

Sometimes he sat on his favorite bench overlooking the Lake of the Isles and watched the sun pull its luxurious goodbye across the waves. The bench was situated on a big rectangle of grass between two paths. Bicyclists sped on the path near the parkway behind him, and dogs and their walkers waddled in front of him close to the lake. He liked to blank himself out when he sat there. Sometimes he brought along his iPod and listened to the music he liked from the 70s, but that made him feel dorky. He wouldn't admit this to anyone even though it seemed as if disco had never entirely gone away. Remixes made by the deejays had given some of these songs a new life in the clubs. But these days he just couldn't listen to his iPod. The music reminded him of a younger and freer time when he didn't think too much about the future. What mattered in those days was that he had a *husband*. He knew he was an odd bird when he confided in Timm how much he loved having a husband, someone to come home to at the end of the workday.

"Darling, you're so old-fashioned. But I love that about you."

At the time, the more he thought about what being a husband meant, the more he fell into wanting to keep their cluttered apartment clean. He sprinkled Comet all over their brown-ringed tub and scrubbed it until its white porcelain gleamed. He gathered up their dirty clothes and hauled them to the laundromat nearby on Lyndale Avenue. He folded their dried clothes and put them away in their dressers. He didn't mind doing any of these chores at all. It was something that a husband should do for his partner. In such moments when he reflected on this, he thought about his parents. As stern-faced as they were, they did not complain about the tasks around the house. Taking care of these chores was how they expressed love for each other. That nothing was ever out of place while he was growing up was a measure of how much they cared for each other. They rarely raised their voices. He sometimes missed them in the sense that they had come from a world that no longer existed. Their world was set forth in black and white. Either you lied, or you didn't. Either you stole, or you didn't. Either you cheated, or you didn't.

Sometimes it was challenging to be a husband with Timm because, as far as he was concerned, the entire world was a gray area. If Timm had sex with another man, it couldn't be called cheating because he had been upfront about the possibility since the night they'd met. If Timm was late for a meeting because he just made out with a client's boyfriend, it couldn't be called lying because he had a business to run. And so on. Each bump sometimes bothered him, but he rarely raised his voice. Timm had always told him everything, and Howie always shared everything with him.

Well, almost everything.

It had been many years since he thought about Pete Olsson. He was a scrawny boy who had moved south from Duluth to the Twin Cities. They had met, quite by accident at an AIDS fundraiser that Timm had sponsored with Betsy hosting the show. It was a benefit for the Minnesota AIDS Project back in the mid-1980s. Howie had been sitting by himself; everyone else from Timm and Betsy's table had gone up to mingle in the back where the drinks were. Miss Thinga Ming was lip-syncing to the Diana Ross and the Supremes's hit, "Someday We'll Be Together," but not many people were paying attention. No one truly knew what the hell was going on with AIDS, so it was a very scary time. Timm and Howie were still having sex, but only sporadically. Howie said very little in those days when Timm wept and raged on after hanging up the phone. "Guess what?" He'd then announce who had just died.

He never told Timm this, but he had come to respect Betsy much more in those days. She was like a saint who shone a light. Every time she and Timm got together, they flitted from one topic to another, but when it came to their dead friends, they were quiet and methodical. Betsy had boiled it down to a science. She knew just who among the dead man's friends would be good for this or that spot in the memorial service. She ran everything like a show, but it never felt like a show. That was the one thing he'd always admired about Betsy, so that was another reason why he was a bit put off by how she'd run Timm's memorial service. Still, who else could do his husband justice?

That night, while Diana Ross cooed her farewell notes, he glanced around the bar. He hated the feeling of sitting alone when everyone seemed to have friends nearby. It made him look unwanted, unloved, and unpopular. He sipped some ginger ale and contemplated getting up and joining Timm, who was carrying on with one funny story after another. Timm was always the life of any party he attended. He set down his glass when he heard someone say, "Hello? Is this seat taken?"

Howie turned to those guileless blue eyes. He had never seen him before. "Oh. Sure. Be my guest."

The young man sat beside him. He wore a purple shirt that opened to his smooth chest. "I just want to thank you for helping out with this."

"This? Oh, no. It's all Timm and Queen Betsy's work."

"Timm tells me otherwise. He said he wouldn't be where he is if it wasn't for you."

"Well, he's being very generous."

"I don't think so." He extended his hand. "I'm Pete Olsson."

"Nice to meet you, Pete."

Then a tired applause broke out to Miss Thinga Ming's performance. Queen Betsy took the microphone and urged the audience to part with one more Ben Franklin in memory of those who'd died.

Howie turned away and looked at the young man. He was stunned when he flashed a grin. "So are you a volunteer here?"

"Yeah." His eyes lingered on Howie's. "I know you're taken, but I gotta say this. Timm's so lucky. You're hot."

"Me?" he barely whispered.

"I like older guys. You got meat on your bones."

"That's Timm's fault. I'll eat anything he cooks."

"It looks good on you."

"Well, thank you."

Pete caught a flicker of movement behind Howie. "Look, I gotta go. They need me over there. Talk later, okay?" He squeezed Howie's hand and whispered into his ear. "The fur on your fingers makes me wanna cum."

Howie was relieved that the tablecloth draped so much over the edge, hiding his instant erection. He wasn't used to such directness from a handsome stranger. Later that night, he ravaged Timm. He couldn't stop thinking of how Pete had said that line about his fingers. He was insatiable. Even Timm had to beg him to stop.

Pete Olsson turned out to be the first secret he'd keep from Timm. How could he explain something like Pete? There was no way he'd have sex with Pete, not when no one was sure who was going to get *it* next. Still, in the privacy of the men's room at work, he often masturbated, just like he used to when he was a teenager in Luverne. He wanted that boy so bad. People so rarely even said hello to him.

He kept looking out for Pete at each gay event he and Timm attended. No sign of him.

Six months later, though, he made an impulse stop at Sebastian Joe's, a legendary ice cream parlor not too far from his house. He would buy a pint of raspberry chocolate chip, Timm's favorite, and surprise him. When he walked in, he caught sight of Pete licking a cone of vanilla ice cream while laughing and talking with an older man in a suit. They were alone at a table. Howie felt a flare of jealousy at the older man. Howie knew he had met the older man, but he couldn't place his name at the moment. He was one of Timm's friends who gave generously to AIDS-related local causes. The man was balding and had a few liver spots on the back of his hands. He had to be in his 60s. He had never thought of gay men as *old* until that moment. Of course, he had seen older gay men sitting and talking among themselves when they watched go-go boys prance about on the bar counter at the Gay 90s, but he never saw them as possibly sexual beings until that moment when he saw the man touch Pete's hand ever so casually. He wanted to tell Pete not to bother with that man; he was far too old for him!

As he walked by, he was disappointed when Pete didn't look up.

He joined the line and looked at the wall above the array of sorbets and ice creams. Yes, raspberry chocolate was still available. He turned to Pete and the old man.

Pete said something to the old man and got up. As he headed toward the bathroom behind the line, his eyes widened at the sight of Howie. "Come with me," he whispered as he softly rubbed Howie's belly.

Everyone around them were too fixated on the ice cream flavors listed on the wall to pay any attention to their intimacy.

He entered the bathroom after Pete.

With the door locked, Pete pulled Howie into an embrace. He fished out Howie's tongue with his own. Pete's hands roamed underneath Howie's shirt. "Fuck, fuck, fuck," he kept moaning. "All this hair. Fuck."

Howie ground his hips against Pete. It had been so long since he was with anyone else. *Oh, man.* He erupted inside his boxers. He couldn't control himself. "Shit."

Pete looked down and giggled.

"What?"

He took one of Howie's hands and rubbed his face all over the back of his fingers, and took his other hand down on himself. "Squeeze it."

The second Howie fondled him, he felt the distinct throbs of ejaculation inside Pete's shorts.

Pete moaned. "You're so hot. You know that, right?"

He gave Pete his work number. In those days, no one had email or cell phones.

The young man left.

Howie splashed cold water on his face. Did he really have sex with a near-stranger in a public restroom, or was it one of those gray areas that Timm had been so comfortable with? What about that French kiss? He decided not to buy that pint after all. Timm might detect a change in his bearing and surmise that the pint was an admission of guilt.

In the privacy of his office, Howie was able to talk on the phone often with Pete for a good hour. He learned a great deal about Pete. The son of respected shop owners who sold furniture in downtown Duluth, Pete was a junior at Hamline University. He wanted to study law and become a lawyer. He had come out the year before. His parents were initially upset, but they told him to keep it quiet when he visited home. They didn't want their customers to know. Then Pete told him just how old he was.

Howie felt strange to think that he had become considered "older" because he was 15 years Pete's senior. He felt like a cradle robber. He had known of older men who liked younger men, but he had never noticed a younger man who deliberately wanted an older man. Why would anyone want an older man? He found the idea rather preposterous, but damn, that boy was definitely hot. They whispered hoarsely about what they would do once they were naked, but nothing came of it. Pete was always too busy with his studies. He didn't have his own car. He had to take the bus up to Duluth on some weekends.

Howie came to realize that because of the difficulties and because of what was going on with AIDS in the gay community, sex with Pete would never happen. The realization of this was triggered when Timm called him to tell him Robbie Smeth ("that's an e, not an i" was his trademark saying whenever he became acquainted with someone) had died that morning. The news shocked Howie. He hadn't a clue that Robbie had come down with *it*. He had always liked Robbie. He was one of the few people who spent more time with Howie than with Timm, perhaps because Robbie loved to talk about the latest world events. He was always good company.

Howie was more than usually quiet that evening when he came home.

Timm noticed. "I'm so sorry about Robbie."

He sighed. Howie knew he couldn't afford the risk of exposure to *it* with Pete. Who knew how many older men Pete might've slept with? That night, he pulled Timm close and cuddled. Howie knew he had made the right decision by staying monogamous.

Still, he looked out for Pete over the years. Sometimes he was around; sometimes not. It was odd how cold Pete had become. He did not acknowledge Howie's presence. That hurt. He knew that it was impossible to explain Pete to

Timm. It would hurt Timm so much, especially when he had made himself out to be a very monogamous creature. Sometimes it was better to say nothing.

Now he wasn't sure why he was thinking about Pete all of a sudden. It had been so long. He checked his watch. It was time to go. He got up and walked through Kenwood along West 22nd Street. He nodded hello to familiar strangers whose names he didn't know. That night he couldn't stop thinking about Pete. Had he become a lawyer? He had to be one by now. He went online and searched for him, but nothing conclusive came up. Was his real name Peter? And just how was his last name spelled? With one "s" or two? His name was generic enough to generate dozens of results. Not knowing Pete's middle name didn't help any.

A few weeks later, Nick tossed him a copy of *Lavender*, the local LGBTQ magazine. "Something for you to read for lunch."

Howie browsed through the pages and stopped when he saw a black-and-white ad featuring a picture of Pete. He was advertising his services as an attorney who specialized in issues facing the LGBTQ community: PETE OLSSON, AN ATTORNEY WHO UNDERSTANDS. Pete looked nothing like the young man he remembered. The smile was there, but it wasn't as devilish. His hair had thinned considerably. Howie wondered what the hell happened to the cherubic quality of that face. It had to have been caused by something else other than aging itself. He contemplated sending him an email, or even calling him, but decided not to. What good would it do? He wasn't interested in Pete as a prospective husband. He didn't want anyone who made a game out of ignoring him.

And now Billy had just done the same thing. What was it about Howie that made him so expendable? Did he look that desperate and lonely? Should he have been a lot less trusting? A lot meaner? What? What kind of a guy was he supposed to be in this day and age? It was clear what he had to do next.

He'd go online and meet someone better. He'd actually go out on dates. *Real* dates with *real* guys. This lonesomeness had to stop.

15
Nick

All that Sunday morning, Nick thought about Betsy. She didn't seem all that interested in helping him. Surely, she had to understand that Howie was an LTR-oriented guy and that he deserved a second chance at love. Didn't she allow those drag queens to lip-sync that Connie Francis song to Howie? He wasn't surprised when Howie didn't show too much emotion. That was just the way he was.

Nick had dreams in which Howie would be completely unfettered with his emotions. Howie would laugh and cry and scream and squeal and giggle. That would be quite something to see. He was sure that Timm had seen that side of Howie many times over their thirty years together. Why else would Timm, a man with a legendary cock, stay with Howie? Timm didn't have to stick around. Everyone in town knew about Timm's tool, and they often had a chance to feel it for themselves.

He wondered how Howie must've felt about all of that. Surely, he must have felt humiliated by the attention that Timm got.

Once Nick said to him in one of his ramblings: "Don't you ever feel jealous of Timm?"

"No. Why should I?"

"He's got a big one."

Howie looked right through him. "So you had him too. Figures."

The shadow that flickered across his face was enough to stop Nick from questioning further.

Nick often thought about what it felt like to have something so large. He fantasized about how he'd have his way with one man after another. He'd have a play date at least once a day. Heck, he'd be a porn star! He'd buff up even more and pose for nude stills that would be reshared all over the Internet. Men would flock to him in bars, give him free drinks, and fondle him in the dark. That was how people had treated Timm in any bar he went in. Whenever he stood next to Timm, he saw how some of them looked pissed at Nick for standing in the way. That's how he'd first heard the term "cock block."

He overheard things said to Timm like, "Is it true you have a partner?"

"Yes. My husband's home."

"So does he allow you to play around?"

"Well, yes."

"Maybe you and I could ... you know."

Most of the time, though, Timm said he didn't have the time to travel to their places. He just wanted to hang out with his friends.

Nick felt envious of the ease with how Timm was able to say no. Some of these guys were hot beyond belief. They worked out at least five times a week and walked around shirtless. Their waists were slender, and their muscles sculpted of stone. Nick would never have turned any of them away.

But now? He'd be afraid to go to bed with any of them. They would try not to laugh at how soft his cock was when they were perfectly hard. They would roll their eyes with disappointment when they learned that he didn't like being fucked. They would stand up, put on their 501s, and leave. Word would spread among their friends what a lousy fuck Nick was, just like how word about Timm's cock had traveled among so many people.

He had to stop hanging out at the Eagle. It was always good to see his buddies, but would they want to understand what he was going through? No. They were there to check out the men and have a good time. Every Saturday night, he put on his jeans and leather chaps along with a tight-fitting white undershirt with its sleeves rolled up to showcase his biceps. He always got looks, and someone from his stable of fuck buddies usually showed up and asked for a night of fun at his condo. His buddies, typically older and heavier with white-tinged beards, shook their heads at how Nick was always so lucky.

He wasn't even sixty years old. He wasn't ready to be a senior citizen, or one of those losers who couldn't get laid. The most important thing was attitude. As long as he was careful not to give anyone a look of distain, he could feed off the flame of hope flickering in the eyes of men interested in him. He had to think of himself as someone with a lot of time ahead of himself. As long as he convinced himself that he wasn't approaching sixty, he was still young at heart. He knew that there were signs of wrinkles all over his body, but in those days before he began to feel himself inadequate, he was grateful for the way the shadows, so plentiful in bars, masked the true damage of aging.

But nothing could hide the problem between his legs. Guys wanting to go home with him usually made out with him and fondled him. Now? His body wouldn't lie. He was soft. If he wanted to pop in a blue pill, he'd have to drink something non-alcoholic. That would announce to everyone that he needed some medical assistance. He was known for drinking beer. He was never drunk, so no one would think that he was in recovery. Damn, he hated how bars everywhere belittled people who chose not to drink alcohol by giving him plastic cups instead of regular glasses. Drinkers with plastic cups in their hands were sissies.

When Betsy left him at the coffee shop the evening before, he felt more confused than ever. He just couldn't wait for Howie to make the first move because Howie would probably never say anything. He thought about standing behind Howie and stroking those massive shoulders without saying a word. Maybe Howie was as lonely, if not more, as he was. Howie would sigh at being touched after so long. Nick had no idea if Howie had hooked up with anyone online, but surely, he must've by now. All he had to do was to post a chest picture on any bear-oriented website. He knew Howie didn't care for the bear community, but that was where the action was for guys like him.

Finishing up his chai latte, Nick zipped up his jacket and decided to take the long way home around the larger pond on Loring Park. The path had been plowed. It hadn't dropped below zero lately, so there was little chance of slipping on a patch of ice. He walked down the sharp incline from West 15th Street and went west. The pond had been frozen over a few weeks before, but the ice didn't seem thick enough to withstand people walking across it. The snow-capped lamps looked sad and lonely.

He had always loved this park. When he was younger, he knew all of its best places for anonymous encounters. It was so easy to hook a guy with a look, and just as easy to make out and unload. Sometimes it was better than going to the baths because there was a real chance of getting caught. He was still proud of the fact that he had never been. But now, with those favorite hiding places stripped away many years before, the park looked desolate in white. God, how he used to love hanging out here on lazy summer nights! He really enjoyed the feeling of casually roaming and looking for his next prey. Those days of men cruising on the street and going somewhere secluded for a quickie were truly gone.

When Nick got into his condo, he logged online. Howie's profile was unchanged. Not that Howie was in the habit of updating. Nick was hoping for another between-the-lines clue there, but none was forthcoming. Instead, he talked with some chat buddies about nothing much in particular. They wanted to know how he was doing, but they didn't seem all that interested in listening. He sometimes felt as if they were only asking him how he was doing as a way of killing time until one of their favorited guys came online. It was almost no different from how some of his bar buddies talked with him. For years, he hadn't minded it at all because, after all, he was also on the prowl for fresh meat.

The more he perused the profiles of local men, the more depressed he felt. They specified whether they were tops or bottoms or versatile. What about guys like Nick? Did he really want to broadcast to the world that he was neither? He remembered an online conversation that he had with a guy from Anchorage, Alaska. The guy was actually a top, but had chosen not to say so. He felt that it was unfair to so many men because, for eight months after the death of his partner of two decades, he had to take antidepressants. For those eight months, he was unable to have an erection. He felt worse about that, so once he started to feel more focused, he eventually weaned himself off the meds. He said that made him realize how unfairly limiting those sexual designations were, so by not saying anything, he felt he was making a statement. If people wanted to know, they should ask. Nick felt a warm kinship with the guy who had been rather understanding of his situation, but damn, he was so far away in Alaska! He didn't want to live in a place where winters lasted longer than Minnesota's. Why were all the good and understanding guys so far away? Worse yet, most of them weren't interested in relocating to Minnesota. It wasn't a bad state to live in, but its reputation for harsh winters was becoming more and more undeserved because of global warming. Winters were becoming actually milder.

He looked at Howie's profile again. Who would contact him? What kind of guys would they be? Would they recognize him as Timm's partner? What would they talk about? Would their conversations be short? Or would they talk at length about documentaries? Cooking? Sex? Or would he just sit there and let the other guy ramble on? He wondered again about how Howie thought of him now that he knew Nick wasn't quite the stud anymore. Maybe Howie had erectile difficulties too and didn't want to talk about it. Much too humiliating. He couldn't imagine Howie talking easily about his own penis. He was rather strait-laced for someone who used to live with a militant nudist.

Maybe he should bake a batch of pot brownies and give some to Howie at the office. That would relax him. Howie never cared for recreational drugs, but what he didn't know couldn't hurt him, right? Nick hadn't baked marijuana brownies in years. He had some weed stashed away, so he went online to find the best recipe. After he printed it out, he saw how late it was. He'd have to go to the store and pick up some chocolate.

He decided to go to SuperTarget in Richfield. Each visit always meant a case of mild shock. He always forgot how gigantic the store was compared to the smaller shops downtown and in the Wedge neighborhood. He had to walk almost a block to the grocery section and hunt down the chocolate. There they were. The price wasn't too bad, considering that New Year's Eve was coming up shortly. He carried the bags toward the checkout line.

Up ahead was a tattooed man with a beard waiting his turn in line. He was wearing an expensive down ski jacket when the rest of him was saggy jeans and old boots. He was holding a new rolled up sleeping bag. Something about him didn't jibe. There was something familiar about his look, but he couldn't quite place him. He had seen him somewhere, but where? He wanted to ask him, but the stranger didn't seem like a member of the family. He stood behind the stranger. "Excuse me?"

The stranger turned.

Nick recognized those ear spools and the tusks in his nose. He remembered where he'd seen him before. "I haven't seen you in a long time."

"Um, do I know you?"

"You worked at the Wedge, right?"

"Oh, yes. I'm working over at the Seward Food Co-op. Much better now."

"I know this sounds weird, but your jacket ... where did you get it?"

"A friend gave it to me."

"Just like that?"

"Well, I had this other jacket that was falling apart, so he gave it to me."

"I've seen this jacket before. I just can't place where, though."

"A friend of mine had a partner who died recently so he gave it to me. Said he didn't need it."

Nick stared at him. "Would your friend's name happen to be Howie?"

"How did you know?"

"I know him very well. I work with him."

"Oh, gee. Small world, hey." He extended his hand. "Nice to meet you."

"I'm Nick. You are?"

"Billy." He turned to the salesclerk. "How much?"

"Sixty-two dollars and twenty-one cents."

Billy dug into his pocket and pulled out some grimy dollar bills and coins. "No bag."

"Thank you."

Nick looked at Billy. "Um, can you wait a minute? I have some questions for you."

"Sorry, but I gotta go. My friend's waiting for me in his car."

On the way home, Nick couldn't stop thinking about Billy. What else wasn't Howie telling him? Had Howie found someone new and didn't tell anyone? If he were in love, shouldn't he be whistling happily? Smiling more? Laughing a little bit more? What was he doing online, then? And what the hell was Howie thinking when he gave away Timm's favorite winter jacket? That alone had to cost at least half a thousand dollars!

He thought about driving over to Howie and having a word with him. Walk straight up to that front door and knock like he meant business. Howie had no right to throw away Timm's memory on a seedy and tattooed stock boy like— what's his name again? Ah, yes. Billy. Howie couldn't possibly be in love with such a lowdown guy like that. The only way it could work was because Howie had been too lonely and too ashamed to admit it to anyone. He wondered if they had sex. It was strange because Billy never blipped on his gaydar, so if Billy was indeed gay, or at least bisexual, that would be a shock. Nick had always been proud of his gaydar's accuracy. He had never been wrong—not ever.

Then it occurred to him that maybe Howie was one of those gay men who got off on servicing straight men. The more he thought about it, though, the more disgusted he felt. What if he himself had to resort to blowing guys and not having anyone touch him? He had seen ads online where gay men advertised "blow-and-go." He never wondered about these men, but now he had to. Were they that way because they had the same problem he had? Were they too ashamed to admit it? Did they ever want intimacy at all, or was that strictly for sissies?

He navigated the slow traffic along Lyndale Avenue and finally made a left on West 24th Street. He turned right on Aldrich Avenue, coasting carefully over the speed bumps. Off the corner of Aldrich and West 22nd Street, he saw that Howie's main window was lit. One upstairs window was lit. His sidewalk and driveway were, of course, neatly shoveled.

Up ahead was an empty parking spot. He couldn't believe his luck. The problem with Howie's neighborhood was the serious lack of parking spaces. He swerved into place and got out. He put on his gloves and walked to the house.

On the porch, Nick was about to press the doorbell. Then it struck him. Exactly what was he going to say? How would he say it? He thought about what Betsy had advised. What if she was right after all? Maybe Nick shouldn't rush things after all. Maybe Billy was just a fling, a rebound affair? If so, Nick would look possessive on top of how much he'd told Howie the day before. Who wants to date a demanding and desperate guy? He glanced around himself. The street was quiet. A light snow was starting to fall again.

He turned around and went back to his car. Yes, Betsy might be right, but he would ask Howie first thing the next morning.

16
Howie

Earlier that day, Howie went online and changed what he was looking for in his profile. The gay website allowed its members to highlight their preferred choice: CHAT, SEX, FRIENDS, or LOVE. He wasn't looking for CHAT anymore. He was now officially looking for LOVE. Some months before, when he had signed up to be a member, he browsed hundreds of profiles. He never said hello to anyone. He felt safe looking at their pictures and reading what they'd shared. He didn't have to hide his own reactions in the privacy of his study on the second floor. Many he didn't care for, but quite a few surprised him. How was it possible that these good-looking ones were still looking for an LTR? That didn't make sense at all.

He was pragmatic enough to realize that compared to these handsome men of a certain age, and yet proud enough of their bodies to show them off, he looked like a dork. Every day, after he showered, he put on a white undershirt and a long-sleeved shirt that hid his fur as much as possible. If there were too much tuft at the base of his throat, Howie pulled down the front of his undershirt and trimmed them just so that no one could see his chest fur once he let go of his collar. He knew he wasn't as in shape as these hot guys. He had a belly, but like some overweight guys said upfront after mentioning their weight in their profiles, he was working on losing. He still walked twice a day. This gave him an excuse to hurry through the loneliness of morning. At the buzz of his alarm clock, he got up, donned old clothes, and went out the door. He liked being outside at dawn when everyone was still asleep. He usually walked west and around the Lake of the Isles and then back home. Sometimes he went in the opposite direction and headed to Eliot Square, which faced the Minneapolis Institute of Art, but that wasn't very often. There was something about lakes that constantly pulled him back. He also enjoyed observing how winter could transform a lake. First, it was a dull and scary gray, and then when a spell of subzero temperatures held steady for a few days, the water seemed to stop moving. He wondered about how trapped the fish must feel under that first layer when the ice was still translucent. Then came another round of snowfall and more brittle temperatures. Layer by layer, the lake became stiff, paralyzed. Its expanse was brushed every which way by sharp winds. Then the holiday season meant the first tentative stab of stick against the ice off the shore, where it was weakest. Then came a day when someone's foot, light at first then rough to gauge the ice's thickness, would lead the way for everyone else. Neighborhood boys would bring their push-shovels and clear a large area and play hockey. Mothers watched their toddlers waddle and fall down on thin mats of snow, only to push themselves up again. To avoid slipping, couples held hands as they walked from one shore to another, hardly believing the miracle of ice under their boots.

Once, long before anyone was driving their cars around on the parkway, Howie decided to walk across the lake and back. He knew it was dangerous to do when no one was around, but he had been feeling too lonely that morning. Howie wasn't thinking of suicide on that particular morning, but he wouldn't have objected if the ice suddenly broke and swallowed him whole. Having no one sleeping beside him was worse than death; it was all that he had thought the night before. At first, he was a bit scared, but he was astonished how the ice didn't bend under his weight. He walked toward one of the small islands in the middle of the lake, where people were off-limits. These islands were wildlife sanctuaries.

It felt surreal to be out there amidst so much white. He walked around the island's periphery. It was nothing more than a cluster of hills and rocks, and a morass of trees and crooked tall grasses that still poked through the snow. He listened for signs of life there, but all was quiet. He turned to look up at the sun making its tired march over housetops and treetops. It was going to be an overcast day with the glare of sun, a white glow through the clouds. He wondered what it would feel like to lie right there on the lake, as if he was floating on his back, and feel the sun warm his body. It was such a wild and crazy idea that after a quick glance around, Howie lay down. He felt the kiss of snow trickle along the back of his exposed neck, but he adjusted his cap and looked up at the skies. This was quite nice, actually. No one was bothering him. He imagined again what it might feel like to be dead, with no blood or warmth inside. Everyone knew how a dead human body decomposed in the ground, eventually dismantling its teeth and bones after centuries, but no one knew what happened to the unquantifiable quality of spirit that transformed a human body into a person rather than just another animal who looked almost identical to its offspring. Where was Timm's spirit? Where did he go? Was he already having a party with all those friends who'd died too young? Were they all watching the living as if life was a movie without end? He was sure that they would come up with some wisecracks to which everyone would laugh, but they'd never interfere with the lives of the living they'd left behind. They were no longer actors; they had become the audience. At least that was one of Howie's pet theories about life after death, but Timm had never talked about heaven and hell, or any of that religious stuff. He regretted not asking Timm about it.

He closed his eyes and breathed more slowly. Heaven would feel like this: a fog rising like steam off the water to reveal a bright day dawning. This lake, just like Lake Superior a few hours north, would go on forever, like an ocean. Timm was the reason why he'd come to adore winter, because once the holiday season ended, he had Timm pretty much to himself. He liked how Timm cuddled up to him under their heavy quilts. That morning he'd found himself clutching onto a pair of pillows. He wanted so much to fuck Timm, and pillows just couldn't cut it. And he had gotten tired of using his right hand.

He knew he was already late for work that morning, but what the hell. Being a few more minutes late wasn't going to hurt anything. Customers could always leave a message on the answering machine, and he'd take care of them all when he came into the office. He felt so peaceful lying there. He was breathing a dream. He was there on the lake, and yet he wasn't. He was drifting in a land of ether that had no discernible landmark anywhere. It was neither cloud nor sky or ocean. He felt as if he could go on floating forever. Maybe this was heaven after all. It wouldn't be such a bad place. He wondered if that was where Timm had gone. Suddenly freed of his body and its physical needs, he would be at peace. No more worries. Everything was all right because he didn't need to ask for anything else. Howie ached to see Timm appear out of nowhere and take his hand—

"Hey! You okay?!"

A young woman in a ski hat and a parka was throttling him.

"Uh." He blinked his eyes. The clouds had cleared up some, so the sun was brighter. He couldn't see her face very well. Puffs of air shot up all over her face as she continued talking.

"I thought you were dead or something!"

"No, no. I'm fine."

A split second later, they heard the distinct sound of an ambulance approaching.

"Fuck," he said.

He ended up two hours late for work. Nick thought the incident was quite funny. It had reminded him of an incident in his boyhood. He'd seen a neighbor lie face down, straight down with his arms flat against his side, on the grass. He hadn't known that it was a yoga move, so he ran down to his house, but no one was home. He phoned the operator and said that Mr. Davidson was dead, face down in his yard. The ambulance and the police car arrived only to find Mr. Davidson cussing out Nick. After that incident, Mr. Davidson always scowled at Nick when he saw him. It wasn't until Mr. Davidson died and his parents took him to the wake that he saw him smiling for the first time.

After changing CHAT to LOVE on his profile, Howie looked at his own photograph. It showed him in a suit and tie. He thought it was a nice one because he didn't look shy. He hated having his own picture taken, which explained why there had been so many photographs of Timm and so few of him in those shoeboxes. He knew where they were, and he knew that he could never bear looking at them again. It was far better that these pictures collected dust. He had plenty of memories, and they would serve him well. Maybe far too well. He got up from his desk and went to the bathroom. He looked in the mirror and tried to smile. He felt dishonest in smiling. A smile should be earned, much like a frown of sorrow. He had seen many pictures of guys who held up their cell phones and digital cameras, snapping shots of themselves in bathroom mirrors. Some of them were shirtless, or even naked. He wouldn't go that far in exposing himself like that. He stood sideways to gauge how fat he looked. The hem of his T-shirt hung over his waist like a dress, so he flattened his stomach. The hem now touched his crotch. Much better. He let out a sigh and pulled out his cell phone. He held in his stomach again and snapped a self-portrait in the mirror.

On the computer, his body didn't look too bad, but his face revealed nothing. Not even a flicker of a smile, or even a hopeful glance. Was he really that obtuse? Maybe that was why no one wanted him. Great. Not only was he fat and furry, but emotionally vacant as well. That would explain why no one wanted to date him, and those who did were hundreds of miles away. "The curse of the Internet," they always said with asterisks around the word "sighs." He went back to the bathroom and snapped shots of him trying on various expressions. He hated the feeling that he was lying to himself on camera when he smiled, both by showing his teeth and not showing. He tilted his head a bit this way and that for effect.

After uploading the pictures off his cell phone, he cringed. They didn't look like him at all. He looked worse. Those facial expressions had made him look dorkier. All he needed was a plastic pocket and pen stuck in his T-shirt pocket to make him a complete dork! He decided to stick with the one he had been using all along.

He began searching for local guys who were also looking for LOVE. He was surprised by how many good-looking young men were also looking for an LTR. How was that possible? He remembered the good old days when handsome young men were constantly having boyfriends and breaking up with them before moving on to the next. The pall of AIDS would soon change all of that, of course, and many of his friends became coupled. They still were, but so many of them had open relationships. He was surprised to see a few of his friends being open about wanting a boyfriend on the side while being committed to their partners. What did that mean, to love another person while still married? What about their hearts? Wasn't that the same thing as cheating? But how would that constitute cheating if the couple said they either played separately or together? What about the third guy? Where did this arrangement leave him? Of course, he wasn't going to be judgmental of anyone. Timm had taught him that much, but he was now gone. Howie wasn't sure if he could go through that cycle of feeling those pangs of jealousy and hurt whenever he was passed over for his sexier husband all over again.

In the middle of his browsing, an instant message from TUGS&HUGS popped up. *hey there how you doing*

Howie checked his profile quickly. TUGS&HUGS had a nice shot of himself in a tank top, tattooed forearms crossed in front, and he was smiling with a thick cigar in his mouth. He had a thick goatee colored with a gnarl of sand and gray. It looked like it had been snapped in the back patio of the Eagle. TUGS&HUGS was looking for "DATES ONLY. NOT LOOKING FOR HOOKUPS." At 45 years old, he stood 5'10" tall and weighed 234 pounds. He had something of a belly, but that didn't bother Howie any. Heck, he himself had one too!

im ok how about you?

It wasn't long before they asked about who each other's friends were. Dan had been living in the Twin Cities for eight years now, but he'd never hung around the Gay 90s. He was partial to the Eagle and its leather community. He was also very partial to stocky men.

They exchanged phone numbers.

Howie was pleasantly surprised when he heard his cell ring. He felt butterflies in his stomach when he heard Dan's voice for the first time. It was deep and sure, and sounded nothing like Timm.

Dan made jokes, and Howie laughed.

Howie was surprised. It wasn't always easy to make him laugh. This was a good sign.

An hour later, they agreed to meet nearby at Sebastian Joe's for ice cream. That it was a freezing night in December didn't matter. Howie shaved, showered, and fretted over what he should wear for his first date in … well, he never had a proper date with anyone! Even he and Timm never went out on dates. They had lots of sex and dinners in Timm's apartment, and they had married each other before coming out to their friends as a couple. Timm said, "If my friends don't like you, they're not my friends." Howie loved him even more. Timm was so strong and courageous in ways that he could never be. But how the hell does a middle-aged man go about on his very first date? Should they sleep together on their first date afterward? Or were they supposed to hold out longer than that if they were serious about having an LTR? Howie decided on wearing a pair of jeans, which he rarely wore. Jeans weren't his style, but he saw how everyone wore them. He supposed that he should do so as well, and besides, he had to show that he could be a bit hip. He chose a solid color shirt and buttoned himself up. He didn't like how blatant the tufts showed up, so he went back and put on a black T-shirt underneath his Eddie Bauer shirt. Much better. He trimmed his nails and buffed its edges.

He walked the three blocks to Sebastian Joe's. His palms were sweating inside his gloves. What would they talk about? Would they just sit there and eat their ice cream quietly? He couldn't bear the idea. Maybe he should turn around and go straight back home, but he knew he couldn't. He was the type of man who honored all his obligations no matter what. He had promised Dan that he would be there at seven o'clock. He arrived there nine minutes early. The parlor was almost empty. He checked the flavors available on the wall. He was happy to see that they were serving blueberry ice cream among the flavors. They changed and rotated their flavors. Everything was handmade in small batches, so it wasn't just the kind of ice cream one could buy in a store.

Howie decided to stand outside. He needed to cool off. He wanted so much to take off his jacket, but he was afraid of sweating so much inside the parlor. He berated himself for having forgotten to use a deodorant. Maybe Dan wouldn't notice. He glanced about until he saw a man in a leather jacket and boots approach him. He wore a neon orange hat that fitted like a skull cap.

"Howie?"

"Yes!" He felt embarrassed at almost yelling. He made a mental note to himself that he should keep his voice low at all times, which he usually did.

They shook hands.

Howie noted how firm Dan's handshake was. He was so unlike Timm, who was far more gentle whenever he met a new person.

They went into the parlor and ordered their bowls of ice cream. They sat next to each other and looked at each other.

Howie needed a few minutes to decide whether Dan was handsome. He was a few years younger, yes, but he began to realize that he preferred guys to be younger than Dan. How much younger? He wasn't sure. "What? What's so funny?"

"You're better looking than your picture," Dan said.

"Me?"

"Yes. You. I can take pictures if you want." He reached over and lifted Howie's hand. "Just how hairy are you?"

He blushed.

"Man. Don't you know how many guys have a thing for fur?"

"I'm not a bear."

"Get used to it. You *are* a bear."

"Well, I'm not."

"Okay, if you say so."

Howie asked him about his background.

Dan had grown up in a suburb south of Minneapolis, but he went to the University of Wisconsin in Madison for a degree in business administration. He worked in the sales division at 3M, and had been there for fifteen years. He wanted to quit and move on to something different, but with the economy being the way it was, he couldn't afford the risk. Besides, he had a mortgage on a fixer-upper in North Minneapolis.

Howie shared his background, carefully avoiding a mention of Timm. He was surprised by how persistently Dan asked him about money. What kind of a house did he own? Just where did he live? What kind of a job did he have? What kinds of things did he have to sell? What kind of money was he getting for them? And so on. Howie hedged his answers carefully. He wasn't used to being grilled on his personal finances. He never saw himself as rich or anything. Yes, it was true that his inheritance from his parents enabled him to put down a substantial down payment on his house, but he was always conservative with his money. His parents had taught him that much. He was grateful for that lesson because, over the years, it had held him and Timm steadily through the economic ups and downs over the years. Especially when supermarkets began selling ready-made bouquets. That really ate into the profits at the Fairy

Florists. So when times were hard, Howie and Timm scrimped, but strangely enough, it never felt difficult. Maybe it was because Timm was such a good cook, even with cheaper ingredients. When he finished the last of his blueberry ice cream, he looked at Dan. "Why are you asking me all those questions? You're not a private detective, are you?"

He glanced around them even though there was no one in their end of the parlor. "I'm in Debtors Anonymous," he whispered.

"Oh. How much do you owe?"

"Don't ask."

"You expect me to tell you everything about my money, and you can't tell me anything?"

"Please. I'm in recovery."

"Just don't talk about money, okay? It's disgusting."

As it turned out, Dan too enjoyed watching documentaries and movies. He sometimes hung out at bars, but that was only because of his friends. He hated hooking up because he found himself feeling so empty afterwards. He couldn't imagine how some guys could do open relationships when it was so hard to find the right guy in the first place.

Howie began to feel better about him. "Maybe that's how they can tolerate the wrong guys because they already have the right guys to go back home to."

Dan looked at him. "You know, you could be right."

Outside the parlor, they looked at each other.

"Well, what do we do now?"

Howie tried to gauge whether he should ask Dan to stay the night. Maybe not. He'd need to explain Timm, and tonight was not the time to do it. "I really enjoyed meeting you. Can we meet again?"

"Sure. When?"

"Friday evening at D'amico's? It's one block over there on Hennepin."

They agreed on the time.

Then Dan leaned forward and kissed him on the lips.

Howie was surprised. The kiss felt genuine. It was different from that boy Pete Olsson's kiss. Come to think of it, he had met Pete there too!

"Thank you," Dan said.

"For what?"

"You seem like a nice guy."

"Me?"

"Yes. You."

"Well, thank you."

"Can you do something for me next time? Don't wear long sleeves."

Howie nodded and walked home.

In the bathroom, he took off his long-sleeved shirt. The graying fur on his arms was excessive. He didn't like how the hairs seemed to puff out his arms. Maybe he should get his body waxed even though Timm had begged him not to every time Howie brought up the subject. "Why? You're every inch a man. You make me look like a woman."

"You? A woman? With that thing of yours? Oh, come on."

In the end Howie always relented because it turned Timm on so much to rub his face all over his body.

After he took off his shirt and put on his bathrobe, Howie went to the computer. He found an instant message from Dan thanking him for a grand time. Then he found a small number of instant messages from local men who were also looking for LOVE. This gave him hope, even though he didn't like most of their profiles. A few of them had posted nude pictures of themselves, which sent out the mixed message of looking for sex *and* looking for love.

Even though he liked Dan, he still felt the need to meet other guys. He made dates with Rick (TOPPER60) and Lawrence (ORCHIDPIG). Rick would get together with him for dinner the next night, and Lawrence would meet him on Tuesday at Christo's, a famed Greek restaurant on Nicollet Avenue, otherwise known as Eat Street. Howie honestly didn't care who he was eating with as long as he was meeting new guys. He had to stop moping over Billy and get out more often.

That night he tore the bed sheets off where Billy had slept and crumpled them into the laundry bin. He liked how stripped the guest bed looked. Content, he quickly fell asleep in his own bed and dreamed of the day when he would have a husband of his own.

17
Betsy

At her job, Betsy was used to seeing all sorts of bodies mangled from accidents. It didn't matter too much what the cause was or where it happened: car, factory, or even lawnmower. Sometimes it was a gun wound. A stabbing. An overdose. It was all the same to her, but there were heart-stopping moments when she had to look at faces so damaged beyond comparison to the photographs she was given for her restoration work. She often wondered if she could somehow transform the face back into the ghost of what the person must've looked like. She usually had three bodies going on at the same time in the preparation room, but after more than two decades on the job, she knew how to time things just so. She embalmed the bodies, and her expertise in makeup was often what enabled her to mask some of the bruises. She had told her boss a long time before that she had no interest in talking directly with the bereaved. Having grown up in the shadow of a funeral home, she knew what clients were like, and what kinds of games they would play with her boss. It wasn't too bad if the bereaved came alone, but next to impossible when there was more than one, and even worse if they had unresolved issues between them. They squabbled and sobbed. Even trying to decide on the right color for the casket, even if both choices were available for the same price, set off nuclear family wars.

The irony was that dead people had no control over how their bodies were disposed of. They had lived years in the bodies they were given, and then they died. That was life in a nutshell. Driving on the highway, she had often seen roadkill flattened and strewn about. Aside from her concern that the dead animal might cause accidents, seeing them did not upset her. Human corpses were mannequins in need of touch-ups. Their bodies didn't always convey the quality of their lives gone by. She wasn't interested. Dwelling on such matters would make her less efficient and impact her pay. If there weren't any bodies to be dressed, she was paid by the hour but also received additional compensation based on the number of bodies she processed. The more bodies that came in, the more she got paid because she had to work a few extra hours. That was quite all right because she didn't have to do weeknight shows at the Gay 90s. Over the years, she and her boss had seen many assistant embalmers come and go. They both agreed that, together, they worked more efficiently and did not need the extra help.

Most of the time, she worked alone, which was how she preferred it. She often played jazz and standards from the Great American Songbook when she worked. Sometimes, when her boss was gone from the building, she turned up the CD player and sang along with Nina Simone, Diana Krall, and others. Even though she wasn't as talented and flexible as these singers, she liked the challenges that their singing styles presented. It relieved the drudgery of making a lifeless face look somehow alive. That was always challenging. But she knew it would've been more disconcerting had she known the person when they were alive.

The 1980s were very hard. For a period of two years, when there was much hysteria, and not much understanding about the AIDS epidemic, the funeral home where she worked was known to be the only place in town that was willing to take care of those men who'd died. Even her boss refused to dress those men and insisted that she give the embalming room a complete cleaning at the end of each day. He was that paranoid. He was also upset that she hadn't first checked with him about accepting these bodies, but she insisted. Those were hard times when other people, hearing that they handled corpses with AIDS, chose to go elsewhere with their dead beloved. Her boss was quite angry and threatened to fire her. In the end, he realized that it was too late. He decided to stick it out. If the business failed, he'd find work at another funeral home. He stayed upstairs the whole time and tried not to focus on these teary-eyed men being *homosexuals*.

When she first saw their skeletons and those purple splotches, she wept. She had long been used to the idea of death as part of life. She wasn't scared by it at all. Her father had explained that death was nothing to be afraid of, so he showed her around at a young age. Yet she never thought that she'd grow up to be a mortician because it was the last thing she wanted. She was always embarrassed when classmates talked about her father and made remarks behind her back. But she went to mortuary school in deference to her father. She wasn't really interested in college. It seemed so expensive, and she had gotten a full-time scholarship, so it all worked out in her favor.

Even then, it took her a long time before she felt completely comfortable in working alone with dead bodies. She had never felt creeped out, but something else had been bothering her. She couldn't pinpoint what for a long while until she allowed herself to relax long enough to look at their private parts without revulsion or shame. At first, when she thought herself gay, she looked at their shriveled penises and bodies. Doing so had taught her a great deal about the male anatomy. She had never cared to look at her own body in the mirror because she didn't really like what she had between her legs. A penis. She sometimes didn't know what to do with it when she made out with a man. Eventually, she allowed herself to be anally penetrated, but she didn't like the discomfort it caused. Poppers, which were supposed to help her relax and become much more sexually excited, were worthless. She tried pot, and that didn't work. She got headaches.

She looked at the vaginas and wondered how it felt to be fucked. Did these women truly enjoy the experience? Or did they just tolerate it as a way of keeping their men? She began to fantasize about what it would be like to have a vagina instead of a penis. Instead of encircling herself in the old way, she began rubbing the top of her penis downward. She found it more satisfying. She stopped having sex with men and going to the baths altogether.

The more she worked on the dead bodies, the more she thought about her own body. She had never thought long and hard about what it meant to have the body given her. She had been born male, a given. She did what people expected of her, and that was to behave like a boy. She sometimes felt that she didn't know her lines in the script of being a boy, but that was quite all right. She knew children her age were supposed to learn, so she would be forgiven for not being that interested in picking up that baseball bat or hanging out with the boys and talking about girls. Yet the more she overheard her male classmates talking about girls, the more she wondered about them. She saw them as strange creatures. She couldn't pinpoint why she was so interested in them. She didn't get excited or hard like some of her male classmates said when they saw a sexy girl strut down the hallway by their lockers. She saw how she was growing hair on her chest, and down there. She didn't know what to make of such hormonal changes. She didn't feel quite right. She knew she wasn't supposed to want to be a woman, so when she befriended all those drag queens, Betsy thought she had found a home. But the body, both dead and alive, was her livelihood: reducing the awful blunt of death through artful makeup and embalming fluids was her job, and amplifying her own femaleness—her own human beingness, actually—was her true livelihood.

She couldn't stop thinking about the vaginas she saw. Young and old and in-between: They were all so different. Even though she knew it was highly unnatural, she imagined what it would feel like to have one of her own. She imagined posing in a bikini, showing an absence of the penis that never truly belonged to her. And the breasts too. She liked looking at them, but not once did she want to touch them that way. She rarely touched their cold skin with her bare fingers; by law, she had to wear latex gloves. Besides, their breasts hardened almost like stone, so it wasn't as if they looked sexual. Hardly. There was another reason why she never told anyone, except Timm and a select few friends, about her job. Strangers often asked if she'd heard anything about people having sex with corpses. She gave them dirty looks. "Why are you asking? It's so disgusting." She wasn't interested in talking about ghosts, cemeteries, and the afterlife. Death was just a job. Unlike touching a living person's body, a corpse's body had no "give." Death weighted their bodies like lead and made them difficult to transport from gurney to table to casket. Death made gravity a relentless force. She did not envy the pallbearers who distributed the casket's weight among themselves when they carried it into the church.

She stopped denying that she was indeed female when she started her estrogen treatments. Recognizing that she'd eventually need to undergo the surgery that would make her complete as a woman, she envied the surgeons and doctors who could go inside her body. They worked daily with bodies that had a lot of give. There was still warmth inside them. It didn't matter that the organs inside were gross to look at, or that these bodies might be stitched up and scarred here and there after recovery. They did not have to meditate on the larger question of what happened after death. They were there to help improve and extend life with less pain. Even though she knew it was weird and something she couldn't explain to her friends, she loved being in the hospital. Bodies were everywhere, and they were *alive*. They were hooked up to machines. They were talking. Reading. Complaining. Napping. And they often had visitors in their rooms. These warm bodies weren't alone. On her 40th birthday, she was only too happy to lie on the gurney, and partake in the warmth of friends and staff attending to her. The nurses and the anesthesiology talked and nodded and smiled when Dr. Schmitt came into the room for a light chat before she would go under. She loved how nonjudgmental he looked at her as if she was just another patient, not as someone who was about to undergo a genuinely life-changing procedure. When she signed the paperwork earlier, she knew in her heart that if she did die accidentally, it wouldn't be a bad way to go. Regardless of what happened to her body that day, she would have become a true woman in heaven. Her old male self would die like that caterpillar who had walked a lifetime around, dazedly, in that cocoon of confusion, but she would awaken into a butterfly.

Even the pain she endured from the operation made her grateful. It hurt like hell, unimaginably so, but it meant that she was *alive*. She wasn't going to be just another corpse in a funeral home's assembly line somewhere. She felt loved when she saw her friends gather around her and ask if she was all right. Those orchids from Timm made her birthday that much more special. She was able to hang in there for ten minutes or so until she felt the pain to be unbearable. She needed more morphine. She fell asleep in a cocoon of fantasy and flashback. She often wondered about how her parents would feel about having another daughter, but she knew from late-night conversations in her apartment with her trans friends that it was very hard on the parents. Very few of them ever accepted the change. People hadn't truly realized the extent to which gender was woven into anyone's expectations, let alone parental dreams for their child. Being with Timm and her friends was much better than her own family. Even though some of her friends had a bit of difficulty comprehending why she would want to give up her perfectly functional penis, they were honest and loving with their questions.

This was why she could still feel strong and supported, especially with her trans friends, when she shared her dating woes with men who didn't quite understand her. Too many of them were into the novel aspect of having sex with a transgender person when she wanted more than anything to be treated as a woman in every way. It didn't matter that her vagina was not as biologically natural as a cisgender woman's, but she did have a vagina that gave her a great deal of pleasure. She liked the feeling she got when she stroked herself. Of course, she couldn't ejaculate, but she nevertheless had intense orgasms. Feeling fully female made it easy for her to achieve one dry orgasm after another. After the vaginal pain eventually wore away, she looked at the vaginas of dead women more closely. She had asked Dr. Schmitt to take pictures once hers healed. They sat together and looked at photographs of vaginas he'd done. They appeared virtually indistinguishable from the real thing. He was most proud of this fact.

When she allowed one of her dates to bed her, she only admitted that she had occasional difficulty generating natural lubrication. The man, usually erect and more than ready to have a go, didn't think much of it. She felt happy and complete in those all-too-brief moments, but so many of them didn't seem to want something more lasting. A few of them said, "You shittin' me? You a tranny? You sure had me fooled!" She realized that was their way of saying, "I'm not gonna do freaky shit now." They never returned her calls.

There were days when she had to remind herself how lucky she was to have a boss who didn't care if she was a man or a woman. To him, it was just a body thing. He didn't want to know anything more, but it did take him a few years to get used to calling her Betsy instead of her old name. Nevertheless, she tried to count her blessings every day. She had her own group of friends. And because she had passed so well once the extra estrogen took full effect, she didn't feel discriminated at all when she shopped. She felt lucky not to be tall because that would've made it tougher for her to pass. The operation had changed her in another way she didn't expect: She came to love her job even more. It was all about the body by day, and about what the body looked like at night. She liked the idea of striking such a balance in her life. Timm was one of the few people who understood exactly how she felt, and why she continued to embalm. After all, he dealt with propping up flowers that died not too long after they were cut and put in vases. He preferred houseplants to flowers because they didn't bloom and wither. He often wondered out loud to her that placing dead flowers in bouquets at the wake was an odd tradition. Shouldn't they be using potted plants instead? After all, these plants would continue to live. She saw his point.

Still, she wondered about Walt from time to time. A few years back, when she finally bought a laptop and signed up for Internet access, she searched for Walter Kreitzman on the University of Minnesota's website. He was apparently still working there, but there wasn't a picture of him. It listed only his curriculum vitae and office contact information. She'd never admit it to anyone, but he was the only man who had made her feel tingly and whole. He was kind and romantic. He was tall and considerate. He was handsome and reliable. How many straight men could be like that? She didn't send him an email, though. What good would it have done, anyway? Surely he'd be remarried by now.

She thought again about Howie. Sure, he was gay, but she would be happy to have him as her husband. He could sleep with anyone he wanted for all she cared. She could see herself cooking meals for him and sitting with him. He was a teddy bear who could keep her warm on those bitter winter nights. They would talk about all sorts of things and about the many friends they had in common. He would understand her second job at the Gay 90s, and he would wait up for her. He wasn't a tranny chaser, and that was the most important quality she sought in a man.

She considered what meal she should cook for Howie. Maybe they could eat together on the night before New Year's Eve. Even though Timm admitted that Howie would eat almost anything, she wished more than ever that Timm were there to advise her on his favorite dishes. It had to be a special meal, but what?

But this morning there was no body in the preparation room. That was quite a rare occurrence, so she decided to take the opportunity to relocate all the paperwork for 2008 from the office upstairs to the back room, where there was an empty filing cabinet. Might as well do that since 2008 was almost over.

She strapped piles of files onto a gurney and went down the elevator. Once in the backroom, she unbuckled the first strap. As she did so, the first pile popped up and scattered all over the floor. "Oh, crap!"

She checked the name of the deceased on the paperwork against the folio's tab. The names meant nothing to her. After having prepared so many bodies, she knew she couldn't possibly remember. When she left the preparation room for the day, that was it. She preferred not to dwell on the gruesomeness of her job because it wasn't about the dead. Embalming was to appease the living, not the dead.

Then she picked up another folio and checked its name tab: MURIEL ELEANOR KREITZMAN.

Could this woman be related in any way to Walt? Most Jews used their own Jewish funeral homes, and of course, Jews are never embalmed, but once in a great while, they used her preparation room to perform the traditional ritual of *tahara*. A small group of Jewish women, known as *Chevra Kadisha*, would come into the preparation room as long as there was no other body there, and wash the body before its burial a few hours later. She never told anyone this, but she truly liked how the *Chevra Kadisha* cleansed the body and put it in a shroud of white muslin before placing it in an all-wooden coffin. No byproducts—not even a metal nail—were ever used in the burial of a Jew. She thought it was a powerful statement about returning the body to the earth. She knew she had to write up her will and state her wishes: No embalming.

Betsy scanned the floor for the paper for Ms. Kreitzman. There it was. She picked it up and read the name of the contact person underneath hers: WALTER D. KREITZMAN. How was it possible? She'd have been there that day. Of course, she wouldn't dare stay in the same room as the *Chevra Kadisha*; she'd have taken care of something mundane as checking inventory in the other room and making sure that she had what she needed for the next few months. She checked the bottom of the form. Ah. Her boss had signed off on it. Ms. Kreitzman had died on December 31, 2007, and she was buried the next day. Of course, she hadn't been there that day. She never went to work on New Year's Eve.

She set the file aside and gathered up the rest for the filing cabinet. There.

Even though she knew it was morally questionable, she copied down Walter's street address, phone number, and email address. She had no plans to contact him, but just knowing where he lived was more than enough to stoke that dormant hope. Maybe she should wait on Howie.

18
Nick

Nick suddenly woke up in his bed. He glanced up at the clock on his nightstand. Its red digits showed 5:13. That early in the morning? How was that possible? But then again he was thinking a great deal about the good old days when his cock had worked without fail. When he was younger and starting out, Nick scrimped and saved to pay for trips to New York, Los Angeles, and San Francisco. He had friends in those cities, so when he visited them, they always went out to the bars, the clubs, and the baths. It was all about the unlimited sex, which was something that Minneapolis, due to its relatively small size, could never hope to match. He envied his friends who lived in gay neighborhoods like Greenwich Village, West Hollywood, and the Castro—places where men could hold each other's hands. Sometimes they made out in public! But all those gay neighborhoods had become more run-of-the-mill.

He wouldn't have minded the disappearance of all the gay strongholds in cities around America so much if gay people were allowed to make out with each other in the same way that straight couples did. He remembered one time when he was walking with Timm through Loring Park toward his condo when all the shrubs and bushes had been stripped away to stop men from having sex. This happened in 1988. Timm lamented when he caught sight of the brutal forlornness left in place of his favorite spots. "Why? Oh, why did they have to do that? It's not as if we're going around stabbing people in the dark."

They came across a young man and woman on a bench, making out with their tongues snaking around each other. Even though the woman was wearing tight jeans, she was straddling her boyfriend's groin. They were both zipped up.

Timm stopped. "Hey."

The couple didn't respond.

Timm came closer and looked at them. He was about two feet away.

The couple was still lost in their passion.

Timm looked at his can of soda and then flung its liquid at their faces.

"HEY!"

"Serves you two right. I'm sick and tired of straight people acting like they fucking own this world. You two disgust me."

The woman got off and said, "Fuck you, homo!"

"No, fuck *you*. I got something that your man doesn't have."

The man chortled. "A bigger pussy?"

Timm glanced around, unzipped himself, and flopped his cock out.

"Holy fuck!" the man said.

"You should see it when it's like a flagpole." Timm zipped himself up. "Have a nice day." He turned to her. "Cunt." Timm whirled around and turned on his swish. When he walked normally, he never swished. Timm held out his arms like a helpless faggot and swished by, crossing one foot over the other one in a straight line. Timm could be one mean queen.

Nick, speechless, followed Timm.

When they got into his condo, Nick finally sputtered out: "That took balls."

"Darling," Timm laughed. "That's the best thing I've heard all day. I can now tell the world I have balls."

That was why people still needed their own ghettos. They needed to be able to be themselves without being judged. How else could they gain their self-confidence and inner strength before they went back out in the real world? They needed to be completely queer and unapologetic about it. If straight people could be unapologetic about being themselves in their own world, why couldn't gay people? Timm had understood this, and that's why Nick had admired him so.

Nick thought that the disappearance of distinctly gay neighborhoods was a real problem in America. Gay men weren't special anymore. They didn't have their own enclaves like they had before. Too many had died. And with them gone, other faces had taken their places and became more outspoken in their memory. Touching, yes, but at what price? They had lost these beautiful men *and* the idea of a neighborhood all their own. They had not been ashamed of themselves in restaurants, bookstores, and other gathering places. They never thought twice about holding hands. That was a huge reason why Nick usually stayed in Fort Lauderdale for a whole week after New Year's. The city, a good half-hour's drive north of Miami, had at least 30 gay bars, many clothing-optional resorts, and a few bathhouses. Its mayor was openly gay. He loved being there because it was so full of *men*.

He closed his eyes and tried to sleep. He knew that his days of visiting Fort Lauderdale had to end. He couldn't hang out in the baths, not when he couldn't count on his body to perform like before. Of course, he could revel in the anonymity of all these out-of-town visitors, and risk embarrassment. He thought about the kind of men who lived there year-round, and they were mostly retired. In other words, they were *old*. They packed gay restaurants like Tropics and Rosie's, and they floated around the baths. When he was younger, he found them repulsive. They had sagging pectorals, bloated stomachs, and thinning hair. Somehow age had made their eyes look more lecherous than before. He couldn't bear being touched by these men when he went up and down the corridors, scoping out the more attractive men for his next conquest. But he himself was nearing sixty! How did that happen? He never thought of himself as an old man, and he still refused to think that way. He would continue to work out and stay buff.

For a long time, he had thought about retiring to Fort Lauderdale, where he could tan himself and be proud of not having a tan line. Having a place near the ocean would make him quite popular with friends, particularly those who were tired of the long Minnesota winters and needed a break. Every time he visited Fort Lauderdale, he scoured the local papers for its real estate listings. He often thought about making a down payment and having someone rent it from him to help cover its mortgage, but the national foreclosure crisis of 2008 that fall nipped that idea.

He opened his eyes. He couldn't stop thinking about Billy. And Howie. And the idea of Howie having sex with a tattooed bearded freak. Even though his body still felt tired, he was mentally wide awake. He never cared for reading books, but this was an occasion when having a book on hand would've proven useful. Reading a textbook out loud would've lulled him back to slumber, and he thought about getting a secondhand book from Magers & Quinn. Unfortunately, he always forgot about going to a bookstore in the first place. So he never had a book in the house when he needed it.

What the hell, he thought. Might as well go online.

Nick started his coffee machine and spotted his bags of chocolate chips that he'd bought the night before. Of course: He could bake his hash brownies. That would be something to do. He rubbed his eyes as he reread the printed recipe. Yes, he had everything he needed on hand, so he measured out the marijuana. He greased the baking sheets and spread the batter until it touched the edges.

He set the timer and went online. So few local men were online at this godforsaken hour. No one had sent him an email or an instant message.

He browsed idly through the same old profiles. He had known some of these people from the Eagle and some from idle chats. There were a few new ones, though. They were mostly in their 20s. He'd never minded their youth because they were so overly enthusiastic, they often came quickly and excused that disaster by claiming that they could ejaculate again. "Oh, yeah? Prove it," Nick usually said with a smile. He couldn't very well say that now.

He pulled down the front of his briefs and fondled himself. He felt a faint stirring of hardness, but he didn't get erect. He looked at himself. He was truly, *truly* an old man. He remembered how, in his younger days when he was able to achieve multiple orgasms over the course of a single day, he'd occasionally agreed to let an older man service him. These men, having had a lifetime of experience, knew just how to bring him to the edge and pull back just in time before giving him the sweetest torture that led to mind-blowing orgasms. He had found it peculiar that these men didn't get hard, but they always said, "Thank you." He thought that was their way of saying, "Thank you for letting this old geezer touch you." Only in recent days did he begin wondering if such servitude was their way of allowing them to fantasize about having the kind of erections they used to have.

He switched to a different website where porn was featured. He stroked himself as he clicked on a clip of young men engaged in a threesome in a warehouse, but nothing happened down there. Truly, this didn't make sense. Mentally and emotionally, he felt himself to be as horny as ever, but his body wasn't cooperating. It had to! There was no way he was going to end up like these desperate-looking geezers who haunted the baths. He'd need to find a boyfriend who didn't mind his condition and stay monogamous. No one needed to know that he was unable to fuck, and he'd maintain his pride and standing among his buddies at the Eagle.

The timer buzzed.

Nick hurried to the kitchen, plucked a toothpick from the table, and pulled out the pan. Yes, the toothpick came out clean. The brownies were ready. As they cooled off on a cookie rack, Nick bent down to the counter and sniffed. Nope. No one could tell that they had pot in them. The smell of freshly baked chocolate was overwhelming and wonderful.

Nick checked the clock on his microwave oven: 6:23. He was sure that around this time, Howie was taking his daily morning walk around the Lake of the Isles before taking his quick shower and driving to work. Nick went back to his computer and found an instant message from TWINSMIKE78 awaiting him. Nick clicked on his profile and saw the red-haired young man smiling a bit impishly at the camera. Cute. His profile said, *just checking this site out. Chat me up guys!*

hi there think youre hot

Nick beamed to himself. Considering how crappy he had been feeling lately, any compliment would be most welcome!

thanks u r cute what r u doing

bored horny waiting for the day to start

me too but i dont start work until 8

Their conversation was pleasant enough with surprisingly no talk about the usual statistics and favorite sexual positions. Nick learned that Mike worked downtown, where he ran the Information Technology department. *IT means nothing IT means computers that break down all the time or get hit with viruses,* Mike explained. *boring stuff for me but everyone turns into a drama queen when their computers go kaput big whoopee* Mike liked to read sci-fi and fantasy novels, and went to all the home games for the Minnesota Twins, his favorite baseball team in the whole world. He collected Twins paraphernalia and memorabilia, and was hoping to share that with someone special. Mike was a scooter fanatic and an anime junkie. He played videogames like World of Warcraft and Dungeons & Dragons. The son of professors, Mike had grown up in Iowa, but he moved to Minneapolis because of the Twins. Mike was quite a chatty Cathy, but since Nick wasn't really in the mood to chat so early in the morning, he didn't mind.

Nick kept clicking back to Mike's profile. He was really a handsome boy. The second he thought that, he stopped. Did he just think of a 30-year-old man as a "boy"? He couldn't be old. No. They were still men. Of course, there were kids out there, but he couldn't be old enough to start thinking of men as "boys" and "kids." What was wrong with him? He wasn't supposed to discriminate against a hot man based on his age.

got a question 4 u u know how old i am???

yeah so?

im 59 i am 30 years older than u old enuf to be ur dad He didn't want to mention that he would turn 60 next month.

so?? youre still hot

Nick felt a giddy warmth overtake his body. His age didn't matter to this handsome young man? He couldn't believe his luck. *wanna meet up sometime*

sure

Details were arranged. Mike thought it a hoot that he could meet Nick for dinner at Nick's Garage off the north side of Loring Park that evening. It was one of Mike's favorite restaurants.

In the shower, Nick soaped up happily. Afterwards, in the fogged mirror, he regarded his body. His pecs weren't drooping. His biceps had definition. He still had his abs. Hell, he had one hell of a body for someone who was 59! The thought added a little bounce to his step as he sliced the brownies into squares, put them on a plate, and covered them with plastic wrap before bringing it to his car.

On the way there, he decided not to ask Howie about Billy. He'd just leave the brownies on Howie's desk and wait for them to work their magic. No one else at the office would know about his brownies; he'd hide them in a bag from his co-workers when he came into work. He also decided not to say anything about Mike in case tonight didn't work out. He didn't want Howie to think that he was a flake when it came to matters of the heart. Best to keep it quiet.

When Nick came in, Howie was dumping some freshly ground coffee into the coffee machine. Seeing him there, even in his suit and tie, heartened him. He was so predictable, and so faithful. "Guess what I made?" He held the plate in front of Howie and pulled off its plastic wrap.

"Ooh." Howie immediately snatched one. "Mmm. Very good. Thank you."

"You're welcome." He left the plate on Howie's desk.

Nick wasn't surprised that Howie would devour the entire plate by noon, but he was a bit disappointed to see that Howie didn't change his demeanor. Not even a loosening of his tie. He debated asking him point-blank about Billy, but the mood between them was easy and relaxed. Nick hesitated. He didn't want to break that spell. It almost felt as if they were lovers the morning after the first time they had sex.

"Have you ever had a tattoo done?"

Nick shot up a look at Howie. "Why?"

"Oh, was just thinking, that's all."

"What kind of tattoo?"

"I don't know. Maybe a picture of Timm."

"Where would you put it?"

"That's the problem. I have too much hair. If I have it here—" he pointed to his upper arm— "no one can see it."

Nick softened. "I thought you didn't want people to see your body."

"Well, it's just for me. Nobody else."

"Nobody else?"

"What did you mean by that?"

Nick stared at him for a long moment. "I ran into Billy last night."

"Where?"

"At Targay in Richfield."

"He's working there now?"

"No. He was buying a sleeping bag."

"Sleeping bag? He can't be homeless again."

"Wait a minute. He was homeless?"

"Yes. How did he look?"

"Alive. Why do you care? He looks ... freakish. He's not for you."

"Wait a minute. You're not my daddy. You're someone I work with. That's all." He took a tissue from its box and wiped his forehead.

"You okay?"

"I feel funny. In the head, you know?"

"I've got some aspirin."

"It's not a headache. It's something else." He checked his watch. "Maybe I should go home early."

"Let's talk about Billy. Was he your boyfriend?"

"No."

"Then why did you give him Timm's favorite jacket?"

"Oh, he was wearing it?" He chuckled in spite of himself. "At least it's not collecting dust in the closet."

"You shouldn't give those things away. Think of how Timm must feel!"

"Timm told me to sell everything and give the rest away. He said that I had to clear out our house to make room for someone new. I can't believe this!" Howie stood up. "You sleep around like a slut, and now I'm supposed to apologize for giving away a fucking jacket to a friend who needed to keep warm? Jesus." He started to wobble a little, so he sat down at his desk. "I don't feel so good."

"Maybe you should go home."

"Yes, but I feel kinda woozy in the head. What shit did you put in those brownies?"

Nick tried to hide his reaction, but it was too late.

"Fuck. You. Go. Home."

"What about you?"

"I'll sit and wait this out. Fuck. This is not good."

"I'm sorry, but I—"

"Just get the hell outta here." Howie placed his elbows in front of his keyboard and rested his head in his hands. He looked broad and as brutal as an ox.

Nick closed the door to Howie's office and told his own boss that he wasn't feeling good. He needed to go home. Outside, a light snow was falling. Even though he was all zipped up, he felt as if his heart had turned ice cold inside. He had no chance with Howie now. He was sure that Howie wouldn't trust any food he brought in from now on.

Besides, he had a *real* date tonight. A handsome boy—no, a handsome young man. He realized that with a pang of despair, he'd actually used the word "young." He was now officially an older man. The minute a man uses that adjective to describe another adult, it means that he is now older, or at least middle-aged. The thought saddened him, but only for a moment. Mike knew how old he was, and he hadn't cared. How many handsome men were like that? How refreshing. Maybe there was hope for Nick after all.

19
Howie

In his office, Howie wiped his forehead again. He hadn't felt this hot or woozy before. What the fuck was Nick thinking? Had he really put pot in the brownies? He tried to stand up, but when he glanced at the floor, he felt as if he had vertigo. He closed his eyes, felt along the edge of his desk, and pulled the chair up. He looked at his computer monitor, but the numbers on the screen seemed to be leapfrogging each other. Damn.

Howie had tried pot only once in the early days of his relationship with Timm. He didn't like the smell, and he didn't like the way the smoke filled his lungs like sandpaper. But once he stopped coughing, he felt a lightheaded wooziness. He just sat there giggling with Timm. Then he discovered that he had lost his erection, so no more pot for him. When he first allowed himself to be fucked, Timm gave him some amyl nitrate to inhale. The hit of relaxation circulated through his body almost instantly, so when Timm fucked him for the first time, he felt great. He couldn't believe that his body didn't feel pain from something that huge. Eventually, Howie stopped using poppers when Timm found it too difficult and time-consuming to get stiff enough for penetration. That was the problem with oversized dicks when one got older. Sometimes Timm said in the middle of their lovemaking, "Fuck. I wish my cock was shorter like yours. All it does is flop around like a wet noodle." In those moments, Howie didn't feel so envious of Timm.

As he waited for the wooziness to pass, he realized that he needed to drink water. The water cooler was just outside in the hallway. He stood up again and felt a surge of vertigo. He sat down. Would he have to sit there, thirsty as all hell, until this passed? He tried to focus his eyes on his watch. It looked to be about 2:36. How could that be? Why did he think it was much later in the day?

"Darling."

He looked up.

There he was again, standing completely naked beside Nick's desk. "One thing I could always count on you is that you always looked sexy in a suit and tie. Funny thing was, I used to think that businessmen were so unsexy, but you—" Timm walked with a swagger toward Howie's desk— "yes, you, Howard Dwight, made me see the light."

"Timm?" he finally croaked. His throat was so parched it almost hurt to talk. He saw the things about Timm's body that he'd totally forgotten: the mole on his left shoulder, the stomach scar from his emergency hernia surgery, and the dark pink birthmark on one side of his chest.

"Darling, I've learned a lot since I went away. None of us are ever alone. We think we are, but we never are. Have you ever felt that someone was watching you even though you were crystal-sure you were absolutely alone? That's your guardian telling you not to be afraid. He's been with you from the moment you were born, and he'll be with you long after you've died. There's no greater love than you can get from a guardian. Not even mothers come close. Oh, you're so lucky."

"Why?"

"All my friends are so jealous of you."

"Me? Why?"

"Darling, you don't have just one guardian. You have *three* standing watch."

"Am I that bad? I'm not on suicide watch."

"You see, it's a mark of honor to love someone who doesn't feel loved. They teach you more about love than anyone else."

"Oh, gee. Thanks."

"You don't believe me. Well, I did something awful. I fired all of your guardians. They weren't doing a good enough job because you didn't feel loved enough, so I'm your guardian. I chose to stay with you instead of gallivanting with my friends in heaven. They can party all night if they want. You're my husband, dammit. While you sleep, I review the movie of your life from beginning to end. Sometimes I let your dream-self see bits and pieces because they're my favorite moments. Selfish, I know, but I just had to share them with you. Darling, you know me. Always had to share stuff with you first!"

Howie tried not to cry.

"Oh, my dear man. Don't cry." Timm's eyes turned dreamy. "Heaven's the most magical place. It's so full of light and warmth and forgiveness. I don't know why people are so afraid of death. My darling, I'll be waiting, and I'll be the first to tell you that anyone who didn't take the time to understand you are the biggest fools. Because they fucking are!"

Timm started to fade.

"Wait!"

"I'll always love you no matter what ..." Then he was gone.

Howie woke up with a start. His face had been pressed against the keyboard, which left squarish indentations across his cheek. There had been a bit of drool from his mouth on the desk itself. He found the right side of his neck and his right shoulder stiff. He blew his nose. What was *that* about? He never cared for religious shit, so the idea of having a guardian following you all your life was a bit rich.

He checked his watch. It was 4:41. He realized that he didn't feel so woozy. He stood up and looked at the floor. No more vertigo. He took Nick's empty plate and wiped it clean of crumbs. He stepped outside and drank some water from the cooler. Man, that tasted so good. He guzzled some more. Then he pulled rubbers onto his shoes and put on his long coat.

Colleagues were surprised to see him still there; they'd assumed he'd left early like Nick had. Howie mumbled, "Happy New Year," and stepped outside. The snow was falling a bit harder than it had that morning. As he walked to his car, he did an involuntary glance back. Of course, there was no Timm. What was he thinking? He glanced across the snow-caked cars to East Hennepin, and vehicles had slowed down. As he took out his keys, he looked up. There were faceless figures—no, more like shadows but not quite—hovering above cars. Then he saw a figure sitting next to a woman driving her SUV past on her way out of the parking lot. This was freaky. No, way too freaky. He had to be feeling the side effects of those damn brownies still.

He got into his car and resolved to think no more about guardians. At least he could focus on his driving. He had a date at six tonight. Rick. He had never met him, but he remembered his stats: 48, 5'3", 184 lbs., 36w, 7.5c. A stout man with a walrus mustache, he worked as a baggage thrower at the airport near the Mall of America. He had posted pictures of his impressive biceps and bragged that he never needed to work out. He was one of those guys who wore ear protectors and goggles while lugging suitcases onto the carrel. He also liked drinking beer and shooting the breeze with his buddies. He wasn't interested in drama queens or show tunes. He preferred his men to be masculine. That word always stopped him when he came across that in a profile. What the hell did "masculine" mean? Built with muscles? Redneck interests like demolition derby races? Baseball caps? Tattoos? Cigar smoking? Boots and jeans? What?

Howie never understood why anyone had to use that word. Wasn't being a man enough? It didn't matter if he was a bit on the effeminate side. Timm was very obvious, but that never bothered Howie. He was masculine where it mattered, so why the obsession over that word? He'd never seen himself as masculine. Timm had often told him that he was "a *real* man." He looked at himself in the mirror and couldn't see just how he was a real man. He was just Howie. A real man wouldn't care about what he looked like, and Howie was definitely not that. He cared.

Considering the snow, the commute home turned out to be surprisingly quick. He checked his computer to see if Rick had left a message. There wasn't any. Howie took a quick shower, chose a solid color shirt with his khakis, and drove the short distance to Uptown where Lucia's was located. He had suggested Lucia's only because it was Timm's favorite restaurant. He wore his long overcoat, which he fiddled with as he waited. He looked discreetly at his reflection in the restaurant's window. Should he open up his lapels, or should he flatten his scarf? Did it look too much like an ascot? Then he wondered if he was masculine enough. The snow falling wasn't as heavy as before.

Almost as if by magic, Rick strode up to Howie. "Hi."

"Oh! There you are." He'd forgotten how short Rick was supposed to be. "Nice to meet you."

They shook hands.

"You hungry?"

"Yeah."

They sat down at a table in the corner. Customers nearby were well-groomed with expensive clothes.

Rick glanced around. "This is, um, a fancy restaurant."

"The food's great."

"This is not ..."

In that instant, Howie realized he shouldn't have invited Rick to this place. Lucia's was big on using organic and natural ingredients, and locally grown whenever possible; its menu changed weekly depending on the seasonal availability of ingredients. Howie realized he should've invited Rick instead to the Uptown Diner five blocks away, where they served obscenely large and fattening portions. Howie loved that place too, but he had to think about his weight. He'd figured that Rick was the same way.

Howie tried to hide his cringe when he saw how bewildered Rick looked as he surveyed the menu. "Where are the burgers?"

"I don't think they have any."

"This is overpriced hooey."

"Well, try something different. You might like it."

"So many vegetable dishes here. Are you a vegetarian?"

"No. They have meat dishes near the bottom."

"Wow." Rick's eyes opened at the prices.

"Look, I can pay for this."

"Well, how big are the, you know ..." Rick gestured with his hands.

"Ask the waitress."

By the time Rick had ordered his beef tenderloin, Howie knew that they weren't clicking. Rick wasn't a flexible person. Did being "masculine" have to include being demanding and inflexible? Howie missed Timm more than ever because he was so flexible. If one wanted to try something new in a restaurant, the other wanted something else, because, in the end, they always sampled each other's dishes. He really loved eating out with Timm.

Howie considered himself a patient man. He had spent hours waiting for Timm to finish dragging out his long good-byes at fundraisers and parties, and he hadn't minded. He was *the* husband that Timm went home with, and everyone knew this. Sometimes a friend would nudge Timm and say, "I think your husband's waiting."

"Oh!"

Timm always found ways to make it up to Howie, and he loved him for it. Sometimes Timm would apologize for making him wait so long the night before that he had to come home early and put together a Pear Napoleon, one of his favorite desserts, but rarely made because it was so time-consuming and intricate to make. Or sometimes Timm would insist on trying to make Howie cum a second time. Whatever. But *something*.

But trying to make conversation with Rick was excruciating. It was clear on Rick's face that Lucia's wasn't masculine enough. He knew what Timm would've said about Rick: "He's so butch he's afraid of his own shadow." It didn't matter that Rick was indeed a virile man; veins throbbed in his thick forearms. His nails weren't evenly trimmed. For someone who wasn't interested in drama queens, he was surprisingly one in ways he didn't think he was. He didn't want to share a carafe of wine. He wanted some Tabasco sauce on his well-done tenderloin. He complained about the portion size of their appetizers. "For this much money, I should be getting a lot more food! Heck, we should be eating at McDonald's and save our money for beer at the Eagle."

Howie gave him the coldest stare he'd ever given anyone. He didn't blink his eyes. He was going to stare down this asshole who didn't even appreciate the effort that went into making this scrumptious meal! Cooking could take a lot of work.

"Whoa. You're scaring me."

Howie measured out his words slowly; any faster, he'd have lost his temper. "You've been complaining about everything. Rick, you *are* the biggest drama queen I've ever met."

"Well, you're the biggest fat fuck snob I ever met." He picked up his jacket. "Since you're paying, I'm going."

Howie averted his eyes from everyone's as Rick made a loud rustle with his motorcycle leather jacket. He kept his eyes on his plate and finished the rest of his meal. He longed more than anything to have someone sitting there, facing him and carrying on a conversation. He didn't want to show the world that he was lonely as hell, sitting there all by himself in a favorite restaurant. He would not cry. He paid the bill and took his car home.

In his bedroom, he pulled down his pants and lay there on his bed. As he watched an old porn DVD, he found himself not in the mood for arousal. He realized he hadn't been to a bathhouse since that night he caught someone going down on Timm in the Locker Room, and he longed to be lost in a bathhouse somewhere and not worry about what others thought of him when he had nonstop sex. He'd fuck one man after another and show that scumbag what a real man he was. He'd make that scumbag his bitch and make him choke on the word "masculine." But nothing felt right or satisfying.

He needed to get out of the house, but where? He thought again about Rick and decided that he would cook something elaborate tomorrow night. Maybe he would invite Betsy over for dinner. He was sure she wouldn't say no. But what should he make? He wasn't surprised to find a copy of Beth Dooley and Lucia Watson's cookbook, *Savoring the Seasons*, on the pantry shelf. It was one of those things Timm would've insisted on owning. He flipped through the pages, came across Ellen Ostman's pasty recipe, and scanned its list of ingredients. Even though he ate almost everything, he had a pronounced dislike for turnips, but he could replace them with rutabaga. He wrote down what he needed and walked over to the Wedge.

They had everything but rutabaga. A stockboy said to try the Seward Food Coop.

Howie had heard about the new Seward Co-op, which had to be open. They had given up their old building and built a brand-new LEED-certified building some blocks away. So this was a good excuse as any to check it out. He drove along Franklin Street and eventually caught sight of its green exterior. The old Seward Coop was indeed no more. He parked, found rutabaga almost immediately in the produce section, and wandered its aisles. It was much better than the old space. Timm would've been so thrilled with this place.

As he entered the last of its aisles, he nearly stopped. Up ahead was Billy, who was rotating cans and jars of soup on one of the shelves. He was now wearing overalls and a long-sleeved thermal shirt. His head was shaved. He debated saying something, but he decided not to. Billy wasn't paying attention to anything except his task at hand.

Howie walked quietly past Billy. His tattoos hadn't changed. The whiteness of his bald scalp made him look almost alien. Why would anyone shave off his hair in the middle of winter? Everyone knew that at least 60% of a person's body heat escaped through the scalp. Staying bald in winter made absolutely no sense.

"Hey."

Howie fought that urge to turn and look into those beautiful brown eyes of his, but he had to go. Go, go, *go.*

"Hey there!"

Keeping his face away from Billy, he walked straight to the checkout lanes.

When he finally parked his car in the garage, he found his hands trembling.

20
Betsy

That afternoon Betsy felt like a dirty little criminal.

Of course, she had previously committed little crimes that she never told anyone about. Even though she had been given a generous weekly allowance while growing up, she developed a weird compulsion. She had to steal the latest 45 records by girl groups like the Ronettes and the Shangri-Las by slipping them into a newspaper under her arm. In those days, no one seemed to think it odd that a teenager would carry around a folded newspaper. She sometimes ended up buying the whole album if she discovered how much she liked a B-side song. Later, when rock and roll turned psychedelic with Jefferson Airplane and heavy with Jimi Hendrix, she lost interest. She didn't like the voice of protest growing stronger on the radio; that was how she discovered Judy Garland. She hated the new popular music that aired grievances and complaints because that was an impossible luxury for her. She was a young mortician, and the last thing she needed to hear, even if she never interacted directly with the aggrieved, was how lamentable life was. If one was going to be sad, one might as well put a glorious harmony on it. She couldn't stop playing that Shangri-Las song, the one about walking in the sand, over and over again. It was two minutes and twenty seconds of pure confection filled with so much ache that she often had to play it again on her hi-fi record player. She had been so proud of that record player because it was the first major purchase she ever made after graduating from mortuary school. Her father had given her a check for $300 as a graduation gift, so off she went and bought a brand-new Sony stereo system. She took great care of it. She felt so grown up when she saw how it anchored her living room. She didn't own a TV in those days. She had no need for it because the news was so full of Vietnam, and then those MLK and RFK assassinations. She saw the unrest explicated in the pages of the *New York Times*, so that was enough. She needed to lose herself in the cocoon of those girl group songs. All she had to do was to listen to their voices and forget the disappointment of her day job. Sometimes she thought about those days when she was in the habit of shoplifting. Why did she ever do that? Had she wanted to be caught? Yes, and no. Yes, she wanted to be caught because she had felt she was somehow a criminal for feeling out of sorts and needed to be punished.

Now, with Walter's address in hand, she parked two houses away on Huntington Avenue north of Cedar Lake Avenue. The house was a pale brown with white trimming; there was a ramp that led straight up to the side door. The driveway was filled with a van and two cars. Perhaps Walter had siblings to deal with at the house.

She knew that marriage to Walter had been long out of the question, but she liked to dream of such things. In the years since she last saw him at the Gay 90s, she often thought about what he must be doing at that moment. Today he would talk about the Hubble Telescope in a bored voice now that the improvements the astronomers had made were surely old hat. Today he would be dressed up in a medieval costume at the Minnesota Renaissance Fair down in Shakopee. Today he would be eating Chinese takeout and watching Lesley Stahl on *60 Minutes*. Today he would be walking with his new wife at yet another estate sale. But she knew that such unrequited love was a habit worse than nicotine, so she forced herself to quit him cold turkey. But it wasn't easy. Too many men after him turned out to be turkeys.

After she finished putting away the client files for 2008 earlier that morning, she left in a hurry. The air was crisp as a knife. The snow on lawns was still white. The streets were lined with salty slush that was packed like sorbet. She had known vaguely where Ms. Kreitzman's house was; she had been through St. Louis Park many times. It was known to have a strong Jewish enclave. That was another thing she liked about Walt. He reminded her of home, back home on Long Island, where so many of her classmates were Jewish. She couldn't define the essential qualities of what made a Jew a Jew, but she had sensed it the minute she met Walt. She liked his strong nose. She liked how educated he was. All those years on Long Island came rushing back when she thought about the Jewish kids she'd known. She had always envied them because they acted as if they were part of a club. She'd never be invited into their world, so having so many of them in her classes amplified her aching silence. It was strange that even though she worked with dead bodies for a living, she couldn't stomach watching historical footage of naked bodies dumped into a massive pit during the Holocaust. Seeing that made her sick. How could such evil-minded men dispose of strangers like that? Didn't they care that these people had lives and families of their own? Then she talked with a friend who had gone to the Holocaust Museum in Washington, DC. Her friend, who saw slasher flicks as blood-infested comedies, said that she couldn't last five minutes without crying. The difference was that it was *real*. It wasn't fiction. It didn't matter if the fuzzy pictures were still in black and white. These were ordinary drab-looking people, not beautiful-looking actors artfully made up with fake blood ready to curdle in screams. Betsy understood when her friend said, "I had to leave. So I gave them another twenty. It's so important. Because it could be *us*." She reminded her friend that the Nazis had rounded up gay people and made them wear pink triangles in the concentration camps, the same way the Jews were marked with the yellow Star of David badge. That was the most upsetting thing about the Holocaust. That anyone could decide to try wiping out a whole group of people so systematically. What had the Jews and other groups done to hurt the Nazis? Nothing, really. Adolf Hitler just happened to decide that they had to be scapegoats for Germany's problems.

An hour of silence in her car. Still no movement from within Ms. Kreitzman's house, or visitors coming and going. She checked her watch. It wasn't even four o'clock. She wished she had a better cell phone where she could check her email and go online, but she was a cheap Luddite. She wondered what the time of sundown was. Winter meant shorter days, but it didn't always get dark fast. It all depended on whether the day had been overcast. Maybe she shouldn't be doing this. Walter might think she was a stalker.

She checked the house one more time before she turned the ignition and went home. She had to finish the seams on her new gown anyway. It was her tradition to debut a whole new gown for New Year's Eve, which was two nights from now, so she'd thought all year long about how she could top her previous efforts. This time, though, she needed to make an absolutely killer gown to end all of her gowns. She really missed having Timm around because he was the one who knew just how to make her hesitant ideas outrageous and full of life. Now that Timm was gone, whom could she rely on for ideas now? So many of those drag queens were clever, but their costumes weren't really statements. She had thought that dressing elegantly but more naturally would be a statement to all her friends that she was a *woman*, foremost of all. She wasn't a drag queen. But no one had seemed to notice that about her. The only person to notice was Howie, who said, "Wow. I didn't think you'd dress down. You look good." Apparently, for everyone else at Timm's memorial service, seeing all those drag queens dressed to the nines and strutting in a cathedral was a rare and dazzling spectacle.

So what should she wear to say goodbye to 2008 and hello to 2009? Ever since Timm had died, she felt bereft of inspiration. Maybe she should dress simply and elegantly, something like what Jackie Kennedy would've worn when she lived in the White House, but then again, people wouldn't remember her.

If she was going to leave for good, she had to exit in style. Then she heard about how the guys had to repair the spinning mirror ball on the first floor of the Gay 90s. Somehow she imagined the mirror ball sliced in half like a hardboiled egg. Yes! The bottom half of her gown would be the top half of a mirror ball, and the top half of her gown would be the other half of the mirror-ball turned upside down. Designing it was not easy, but on slow days at work, she drew the trapeze shapes on cardboard and cut them out. Adjustment after another, she finally measured the exact dimensions for each piece of Mylar to be cut out. Then came the wire skeleton onto which she sewed swaths of gray Lycra. For her upper half, she added Mylar on both sides so lights would bounce off all over her chest. She decided that a simple gray short-sleeved top with no decoration would be most effective; she'd wear gray suspenders to hold up her gown. She could wear the mirror ball earrings that Timm had given her eons ago; he would've loved that touch. She needed to finish the zipper seam now that she had found a zipper with the right shade of gray and the right length for her back at her favorite fabric store.

All this was on her mind when she entered her apartment. The sewing machine was waiting for her. She put away her jacket. She sat down and whistled, knowing full well that it would be her last gown. Betsy didn't know where she'd celebrate New Year's Eve next year, but she knew she had to be anywhere but the Gay 90s. Satisfied with how the seam looked, she lifted the halves of her dress and beamed. Everyone would be so blown away.

But she reflected on what gave her the final shove to quit. Two weeks before, she had gone to the Gay 90s with the intent to wear an orange taffeta dress with neon yellow lipstick and crack jokes about construction men and ROAD WORK AHEAD signs. She'd get a lot of mileage out of replacing the word "road" with "slow," "zippy," and so on, depending on who was coming onstage next. Once inside the bar, she waved hello to everyone she knew on the first floor before she hauled her oversized bag up the stairs. Other than the men eating dinner near the go-go boys dancing on the counter, the bar was fairly quiet in spite of echoing with dance music. She passed a thin man who was limping up the stairs; he must've had a sore knee.

A pair of college-aged women, wearing tight jeans and imitation Ugg boots, slowed down on the stairs when they saw the man struggling to go up. They traded glances and tried to hide their titters as they passed him.

There was a sudden lull between songs, so she distinctly heard their stage whisper: "Look at that fag swishing!"

She turned and gave them a Medusa stare.

They broke into a gaggle of laughter and skittered down the stairs.

She turned to the man. "Sorry about that."

But he didn't respond.

"Hello?"

He was completely focused on moving himself up to the next step.

She waited for him to come up to the landing.

"I'm so sorry about those two girls—"

It was then she noticed his hearing aids.

The man said, "What?"

"Never mind. Sorry."

When she got to the top floor, she knew she had to quit. It used to be that drag queens were the fuck-you embodiment of self-empowerment, but apparently, straight people had begun to feel comfortable enough to enter gay bars just to mock them. This wasn't right. Before she went into her dressing room, she went up to the manager. "I know you've heard this from me before, but I want to retire on New Year's Eve. I can't take it anymore." She walked away.

"Betsy! Please!"

She turned. "How about this? Make New Year's Eve *my* retirement party? I have a new gown that would make grown men cry."

All that night, she couldn't stop thinking about that deaf man. She didn't see him anywhere, so she wondered if she had a sign language interpreter, he might've stayed and felt welcomed here. How much did he hear? Had he chosen not to hear? She had seen a number of deaf people come and go in the bars over the years, but she never gave much thought about them. Like most people, she enjoyed watching the sign language interpreters, especially when she hosted the day-long program of drag performers at the Pride Festival on Loring Park. She never understood their signing, but there was something powerful about these hands saying *something* meaningful to a group of people who didn't feel otherwise included. Sometimes she wanted to cry when she thought about how hard it must be for deaf people. In fact, she wanted to have a deaf drag queen in her show, but no one came forth. Maybe it was her lack of sign language skills. She should've learned it a long time ago. Maybe she should take classes in sign language.

At the end of her show that night, she cleared her voice and said, "I have something to share with you. No, I'm not going to come out and say that I need a jackhammer between my legs tonight ..." she waited for the laughter to die down before she continued, "but many of you know that every New Year's Eve here is always special. I must tell you that as much as I love you all, I need to retire. My last show will be on New Year's Eve. I hope all of you can come and celebrate my 32 years onstage. Thank you all for coming."

There was a moment of stunned silence before the audience remembered to clap.

She bowed. The weird thing was, she didn't feel a tear. This was clearly the right thing to do.

Afterwards, fans and friends came up to her, expressing shock and kind wishes. In the dressing room, everyone backstage had to give her a double-hug and a double-air kiss.

That night she easily fell asleep.

Instead of sleeping in late, as she usually did on Saturdays, she made a list of songs as she went through her scrapbooks. She reflected on her favorite moments over the years. It was really so easy to come up with the songs. The girls would love them. The problem was, what song should *she* sing? She needed a perfect swan song. She couldn't repeat that impromptu performance of "The Man That Got Away" the night Walter left her, or Gloria Gaynor's "I Will Survive." It had been so long ago.

She picked up her cell phone and speed-dialed Howie.

"Hey."

"It's me, Betsy."

"Hey. How're you doing?"

"I'm awake, for one thing. Listen, what are you doing on New Year's Eve?"

"Nothing."

"Would you like to be my date that night?"

"Uh, sure."

"You don't have to come if you don't want to."

"No, no, I'll come."

"One more thing. I'm retiring from the stage for good, so it should be a great show."

"You're quitting?"

"Honey, I've been doing it for 32 years. I need to give my feet a rest and let someone else take over."

"Wow," he finally said.

"I've been meaning to quit for a long time." She paused. "Well. I'll call you later and we can figure out the time of pickup."

"Sure."

There. Betsy knew that at least one man wouldn't run away when he saw her decked out like a splintered mirror ball. She couldn't wait to see the expression on his face. He would understand that she wanted to slow down and be a homebody like him. She had to forget about Walt. Again.

21
Nick

At 6:45 p.m., it was time. It wouldn't take Nick a full quarter-hour to walk from his condo to Nick's Garage. He had shaven off his faint stubble of white, which made him look older. He tucked a tiny envelope containing his blue pill into his key pocket. He put on a black T-shirt and jeans. He wrapped a black scarf around himself and zipped up his aviator jacket. He wore his army boots, just in case Mike liked that sort of thing.

The streetlamps were on, glowing only the way they do in the winter air. He inhaled the briskness of chilled air and descended the steps out of his building. He thought about Howie again and hoped that the effects of his hash brownies had worn off by now. He had called his office number a few times, but Howie didn't pick up the phone. Then he tried calling him on his cell phone. No answer there either. He was sure that Howie had caller ID on his phone. He had thought about driving back to the office and checking up on him. Maybe he could give Howie a ride home and let him ride out those side effects. He knew that he'd never serve hash brownies again. He even had worrisome visions of Howie announcing his intent to quit his job.

He avoided the shortcut through Loring Park itself. He couldn't tell if the paths had been snowplowed or not. He took the slightly longer route by going north toward the Minneapolis Community Technical College campus and walking past it to the restaurant. He noticed a heavyset man, wearing a grizzly beard, walking toward him. For a split second, he thought it was Howie, angry, storming toward him with the intent to choke him to death. Then he saw, to much relief, that it wasn't. It was someone else. The stranger nodded acknowledgement and continued past him. Where was he going? Sometimes Nick wondered about where all those strangers on the street were going and what kind of lives they led. Did they have happier lives than his? Did they constantly worry about their children? Did they max out their credit cards?

Would they change their lives if given the chance? He never asked anyone these questions, but he couldn't help but wonder. Perhaps, he thought, the answers would enable him to find a happier life of his own.

Maybe this young man Mike would become his first *real* boyfriend. Not someone who was more like a friend with benefits or a fuck buddy, but someone who'd be proud enough to be called Nick's partner. It had been a long while since he had good sex, so he couldn't afford to risk this date. Not tonight!

Nick was pleased to see Mike standing outside. He wore glasses, a Twins baseball cap, and a navy blue down-quilted jacket that matched his cap. He broke into a smile and said, "Nick?"

"Mike! Good to meet you." Nick made sure to be firm with his handshake. He had to prove that he was a man. As he followed Mike inside the restaurant, he liked the way Mike carried himself. He was shorter and slender, yes, but he didn't carry himself like a queen. Mike took off his jacket and scarf, but he didn't remove his cap. His hair was redder than in his profile picture.

"I know that you're thinking, but I warned ya. I'm a hardcore Twins man."

"That's quite all right," Nick said with a smile. "It looks good on you." He noted how assured Mike was when he scanned the menu. He didn't hesitate. He ordered a glass of lemonade with extra slices of lemon on the side, a plate of fried mozzarella sticks, and a large salad with no onions.

"No hamburger?" Nick asked.

"Nah. I'm trying to eat meat only once a day. I had a burger for lunch, so."

"Always good to balance your diet."

"Yeah." Mike leaned forward to sip his lemonade. "So ... here we are."

Nick chuckled. "Here we are." He liked the warm light in Mike's eyes. "So why did you choose to meet me?"

"You're handsome. Yeah, sue me for being shallow."

"Oh, no. I'm flattered. Thank you."

Mike beamed. "So are you from around here?"

Nick shared his growing up years in the Whittier neighborhood and his job at Rex Hardware Store on Lyndale Avenue and West 26th Street. Then he snagged a better-paying job at Smith & Keeler. "How about yourself?"

"I think I told you a lot online. I'm still close to my parents. I came out to them when I was 13."

"Wow. Did they freak out?"

"Nope. My dad asked me if I needed condoms. He gave me this brochure that showed how to put one on. He didn't want me to get AIDS."

Nick was impressed. "I wish I had an understanding dad. What about your mom?"

"She teaches sex ed in school, so she wasn't upset at all. They've met my boyfriends." He laughed to himself. "My parents freaked out when they met my last one."

"Why?"

"He was almost as old as they were."

Nick turned silent. Did Mike understand how amazing his parents were? He had been truly blessed. Times had truly changed from the days when he came out in the early 1970s. Maybe not having a gay neighborhood was a good thing after all.

"It didn't work out because he didn't like to feel old."

"Old?"

"Old as my parents."

The more Nick listened to Mike while he ate his burger and fries, the more he began to feel that fear rise up inside him. Nick knew the day would come when he would have to stop pretending he was younger than he was. He'd have to live with the label of "old" and get used to it for the rest of his ever-shrinking life. He had noticed how some of his friends talked about joining AARP, buying cheaper shoes, and wondering when would be a good time to retire. He still couldn't get over the prospect of retirement. What did sixty mean? Was it just a number in the incessant march of time, or was it something else?

The question was something he'd always avoided every morning when he woke up. He stretched before getting out of bed. He was afraid that if he didn't do that and didn't eat a few cherries every morning, he'd develop arthritis. But his body felt the same as before; he was just slightly less limber than before. He didn't mind that so much because he wasn't a bottom. What was important was the fact that his knees didn't hurt at all when he mounted someone from behind on the bed. Every time he thought about this made him feel a whiff of bitterness. He couldn't fuck even if he wanted to. He wondered if Mike was versatile, but he wasn't sure when was a good time to ask. Maybe he'd have to wing it. He debated when to pop in his blue pill.

The waitress gave Nick the bill. "Thank you."

This was something else different. The waitress usually placed the check squarely between him and his friends of a similar age, but this time, she assumed that because he was older, he'd be the one to pay.

"Tell me how much to pay," Mike said. "I got money."

A few minutes later, they stood outside and looked up at the skies.

"The stars are out tonight," Nick said. "Nice."

"Yeah." Then came the inevitable and awkward moment of reckoning. "Um, I really enjoyed meeting you tonight."

"So did I. Well, I live that way over there. Want to come in for a drink or something?"

"Sure."

Mike wanted to know more about the history of Loring Park, so Nick obliged him. He had done some research about the park when he bought his condo, so he told him about how the west side of the park used to be lined with mansions before they were torn down to make way for the freeway that began right between the Minneapolis Sculpture Garden and the park itself.

In the condo, Mike hung up his jacket and took off his boots.

Nick saw how small Mike truly was. For some reason, he'd seen him as a bigger guy, but a lack of shadows in the foyer made him look slender.

"Come this way." Nick showed him the one thing that had sold him on this place: the condo-wide window. He could see the entire expanse of the park below. "Every day there's always something different."

"Yeah. I can see that."

"What'll you have for a drink? I have vodka, whiskey, gin, and ... I don't know what else I have on hand, so what'll you have?"

"I don't drink that much, to be honest. Do you have beer?"

"Sure. Rolling Rock good for you?"

"Yeah!"

Nick knew he shouldn't mix alcohol with the blue pill. He decided to make a tonic for himself, squeezing some limes into his glass, and popped the pill discreetly into his mouth.

Mike was sitting comfortably on the sofa when Nick returned with a bottle of beer and his own glass of tonic.

"Cheers," Nick said before they each took a sip.

"Your place's really nice. How long have you been living here?"

"Oh, gee. I moved here in, oh, 1985. Yes, '85."

"That's 23 years. I've never lived in a place for that long."

Nick tried not to wince. The problem with youth was that they had no concept of time, and they were constantly reminding him. "One day you will."

He sipped. He wanted to touch himself and see if it was on its way to arousal, but it would've been too obvious. He had to play this cool. He'd intuited that as an older man, he was to be the one with experience and therefore had to take the lead.

"What's that?" Mike pointed to a huge poster print of Mondigliani's *Little Servant Girl*.

"Oh, it's this painting at the Minneapolis Institute of Art. Have you been there?"

"No. Can you believe that? I'm so embarrassed. I know, I know—people tell me it's free and all that, but I'm not an art freak. I like it, but you know."

Nick felt the stirring of blood slowly building into his cock and set down his drink. "Art freak or not, I like you." He put his hand on Mike's thigh.

Mike leaned forward for a kiss.

They rolled over on the sofa and continued making out.

Nick felt hornier, even ready to show off, when he felt his cock growing harder by the minute. "Let's go to the bedroom," he rasped. His body was overheating again, but now was not the time to worry.

Mike followed.

Nick took off his shirt and jeans.

Mike took off his shirt and undershirt, and unbuckled himself. He looked like a boy in boxers.

Nick went to the bed and put his hands behind his head. "Suck." Man, it felt good to be in charge again!

Mike dove to the bed, pulled down Nick's CK briefs, and began licking.

Nick nearly burst with pride when he saw how erect his cock was. He was still a man, dammit. Thank God for those blue pills; he simply had to use them for special occasions only. They had to be the best thing since sliced bread. He moaned at Mike's eagerness to please. He began thrusting upward.

Then, inexplicably, his cock lost its firmness in Mike's mouth, but Mike didn't change his pace.

Bless his heart, Nick thought. Yet the more he watched Mike's oral ministrations, the more he realized that his cock wasn't going to get hard again. In fact, his cock was shriveling, no matter how good Mike was.

Mike looked up at Nick.

"It's okay. It's not you."

"Did you lie about your age?"

"Me? No. I'm 59. I can show you my driver's license if you want."

"Did you take one of those pills?"

"Yes, but ..."

"What can I do to make you feel better?"

"Oh, you were great. It's this ... problem. Nothing to do with you." He caught the slight start of hesitation in Mike's body. "Look, I can blow you."

"You don't understand. I like to please older guys. I get off on that."

"Why don't you lie over here? I wanna make you cum."

"Gee, thanks. You make me sound like a pity suck." Mike got off the bed. "I think I should go anyway."

"I'd love to see you again."

"Well, I'm going to be honest here. I don't think so."

"Why not?"

"I like getting fucked."

"We can use toys."

"It's not the same thing."

"Please."

Mike had already zipped up his pants and tugged on his shirt. "Sorry."

"Just wait till you're my age. Then you'll feel differently."

"I've had sex with guys older than you, and they had no problem getting hard." He sighed. "Sorry, but this isn't working for me. Let's just be friends, okay?"

Mike left the bedroom.

Nick had no heart left to get up and lock the front door behind him. He didn't want to listen to Mike zipping up his jacket and clomping outside in his boots, and that door clicking shut with the unmistakable sound of finality. He looked down at his limpid cock. He should've suggested that they cuddle together for the night. No sex required. Maybe Mike might've reacted differently.

He closed his eyes and fell into a half-sleep. He saw Mike in his 60s. Of course, Mike would be spry and full of life, and there he was, naked with a big grin. He was waiting for a young man not unlike Mike now to go down on him. Mike turned to Nick and said, "Who needs pills? Thirty years from now doctors will have perfected the age-old problem of male pleasure. Ninety year-old guys will be fucking young guys all the time." He turned to the young man between his legs. "Oh, yeah. Do it just like that, yeah."

Nick woke up with a startle. Why did youth have to be so cruel? He knew the dream was true in one sense. One day ED wouldn't be so complicated. The future couldn't come fast enough. He went to his computer and posted an ad, listing his age and stats, on Craigslist:

tonight my blue pill didn't work for me am i too old for love? i don't think im gonna get hard again want to meet local guys who have the same problem maybe a date looking for a ltr only no more hookups no more games

He put on his bathrobe and went to the living room window. The streetlamps below twinkled as he watched two men approach each other on the path, turning to look back after a few seconds. They changed direction and shook hands. He felt colder inside than ever when the two men walked together through the park. They were going to have sex in a matter of minutes, and it wasn't going to be a problem for them.

Damn. This was more than enough to make him want to jump out the window. Who'd want him now? He was old, old, *old*! Worthless! He knew that the gay community was extremely youth-oriented, but why couldn't these young *kids* understand that they would grow into croak-voiced geezers too? He thought about how they'd party all weekend, and how they insisted on NSA sex online. They weren't interested in intimacy at all. He wanted to tell them that they were looking for the wrong things. They needed to grow up, or it'd be too late for them to grow up. Nick wanted so much to redo his life and look for a husband like Howie. Well, not Howie now, obviously, but someone solid and loyal.

No, he'd get drunk tonight. It wasn't as if he was going to drive anyway. He took a swig of whiskey, which burned his throat something fierce. He coughed, and he gulped some more. He had been such a good boy about drinking all these years. It wasn't until this moment of pain in his entire body that he finally understood why so many gay men drank. They didn't feel wanted. They didn't feel sexy. They didn't like how they'd come to hate themselves. Society had told them over and over again that they shouldn't exist, and then to be told they weren't desired by their own kind was worse, almost suicidal. Alcohol was a pure palliative for their pain.

Thinking about some of his friends who were in recovery made him feel sick to his stomach. He thought he'd understood what they were going through, but he had been so wrong about them. They were in *pain*. He felt so inadequate now, knowing that he'd failed in embracing them no matter what. He shouldn't have given them such glances of attitude in the bar when they tentatively expressed desire for him. He should've said, "Oh, I'd love to go out on a date with you," instead of acting like he had better things to do. These men needed love and understanding far more than he had. He looked at his half-empty bottle of whiskey and set it on the coffee table. No. He couldn't afford to start drinking.

He felt a clamor of fever spread across his forehead. Was he about to die? No. Without thinking about what he was doing next, he knelt before the toilet and upchucked his dinner. He felt clammy and shivery. He deserved all this. Tonight God had sent Mike to teach him a lesson about what it meant to be an old fag, and boy, was he learning it hard. *Hard,* he winced at the unintended irony of his thought.

He turned on the hot water in his shower. He stood there, letting his tears merge into the water below his feet. He was so lonely that he had to waste ten minutes of hot water just to delude himself into thinking that he was feeling a man's arms enclosing him.

Now dried and in a bathrobe closed all the way up to his neck, he walked around his condo. It was too cold for a walk at this hour, and besides, he wasn't sure if he still had a fever. His forehead felt better, but he wasn't about to take chances. He hated this feeling of restlessness, which was ironic, because that feeling was another reason why he'd chosen this condo. It was central enough so that he could cruise nearby or take a walk to the gay bars on Hennepin. But not tonight.

He sat in front of his computer and checked his email. He was surprised to see a few already in response to his ad. They were far more honest than he was, going so far to include face pics of themselves. They weren't always handsome, at least not in the way he liked his men, but he knew that beggars couldn't be choosers. He had had enough of begging. He would meet them all, no matter how old or fat or ugly they were.

He wrote back to each of them, but not with a face picture of himself. He wasn't quite ready to announce to the world that he was impotent. He was afraid that given his turbulent online notoriety as Mr. Anti-Monogamy, his picture would be broadcast all over the Internet with a note that he couldn't get a stiffy.

The one that got him the most had said: *People think I'm an asshole. What they don't know is that I hate my dick. I work out 5 times a week. I never shower there because guys hit on me all the time. I don't go with them because I can't get hard.* Nick couldn't stop rereading this man's note. He had no idea what this man looked like, as he didn't include a snapshot, a phone number, or even a real name next to his email address, but he knew he could easily fall in love with this man. He felt like taking this man, whoever he was, into his arms and making love to him. He would tell him over and over that he was still hot and beautiful, and that he'd still love him no matter if he got hard or not. He deserved to be loved.

Nick decided to be just as bold and wrote exactly these thoughts, and clicked on SEND.

22
Howie

With each brutal chop of onion, rutabaga, and carrot on the butcher block stand, Howie felt slightly better. Tonight he was making Cornish pasties, an immigrant dish closely associated with Michigan's Upper Peninsula. He wasn't going to sit there in the living room and watch TV idly like he had done earlier that summer. He would do *something*. He had made the dough, from scratch which initially intimidated him. Rolling the pin across the dough was an unexpected pleasure. Who cared if flour was getting into the fur of his forearms and fingers? He liked pushing down and watching the dough flatten and become large as continents. He traced perfect circles out of them by using an inverted pie shell. That way, he could fill its middle with vegetables and bits of ground chuck before he folded them in half and baked them.

Making the pasties took him two hours. He was sure it would've taken him less time had he needed to chop up all those vegetables. Still, as he slid the second rack containing two baking sheets back into the oven, he felt good. He now had a total of eight pasties in there. He wouldn't have to worry about lunch for the coming week. He set the timer and went to his computer.

No emails, no instant messages. Everyone must be offline. He checked his watch. He had two more hours before his date with Lawrence at Christo's. He always liked the Greek restaurant, where they provided excellent service in elegant but comfortable surroundings, so he was looking forward to eating there again. He'd last eaten there with Timm. He tried to remember what they ate there. Timm would've told him exactly what they ate. He had that kind of memory for food.

Still, he knew he had to stop remembering Timm so much. When he found piles of newspaper clippings about Timm stuffed into folders, it hit him again how much he missed his husband. Timm had talked about piecing together a series of scrapbooks, but he never did. He thought about tossing all of the clippings into the fireplace, but a call to the Jean-Nickolaus Tretter Collection at the University of Minnesota Library took care of everything. He was only too happy to see these young students haul those boxes out. He thought it was so peculiar how much times had changed. In the 1970s, no major university would've wanted the remains of a gay man's collection, but now? Howie was surprised by the estimated value listed on the donation letter.

While waiting for the pasties to bake, Howie vacuumed and swept the dust bunnies from under the furniture all over the house. It was something to do, and it needed to be done anyway. He changed the sheets on his bed. Maybe, if things felt right, he'd invite Lawrence for the night. He went to the computer and checked out Lawrence's profile again. He was a clean-shaven blond with a vivacious smile. There was a hint of acne scar just under his cheekbones. He suspected that it might've come from taking HIV medications, but Lawrence never said anything about his status. Would he go to bed with someone who had HIV? Aside from the fear of having Timm get infected by one of his tricks, Howie never thought much about the possibility. Some of his acquaintances told him they were "poz," but they were otherwise very healthy. It took him a while to figure out how to spot someone who was taking those toxic meds. Their cheeks looked sunken, almost ravaged, and they developed weirdly bloated stomachs. But Lawrence had posted other pictures of himself, and he didn't have that bloat. Howie saw photos of openly poz men who were still buff as ever. They showed perfect washboard abs. It was as if nothing had ever ravaged their bodies. If he was going to have sex with anyone, he'd have to play it safe. He wasn't going to be one of those freaky guys who wanted to get infected with HIV by having poz men bareback them, or asking online to be fucked raw. Those were the kinds of men who made the gay community look very screwed up. And what about other STDs?

Howie read Lawrence's profile again. He was 49, 5'9", 219 lbs, 8" uncut. Interests included films, fair trade coffee, eating out, music, and art museums and galleries. He taught painting classes at the Atelier. He was an artist who specialized in erotic paintings, mostly of male orgies, which he shared in his profile. Not being much of an art connoisseur, Howie didn't have a strong feeling one way or another about these paintings. Naked bodies were usually in an elaborate tumble, with certain body parts enlarged just out of proportion. They looked almost like photographs that had more than one optical focus.

The timer in the kitchen went off. The pasties, cooling off on the counter, smelled incredible. Somehow it was as if Timm was nearby.

Suddenly the front buzzer rang.

He tiptoed to the foyer and tried to see who it was through a side window. He slowly positioned himself to look through the peephole. Billy, wearing Timm's jacket, was stamping his feet lightly and glancing around.

Howie unlocked the door and opened it. "What's up?"

"Hey. Calm down."

"You come here when it's only convenient for you. Fuck you."

"Whoa. Can we, uh, talk inside?"

"Five minutes."

Billy looked quietly at him. "What's come over you, man?"

Howie stood in the way. He had no intention of letting Billy enter the rest of his house. "You walked all over me, and you left. If I didn't care for you so much, I wouldn't have let you inside."

Billy sniffed. "What's that?"

"I made some pasties."

"Killer."

"Get to the point."

"Okay. Okay." He gave a nervous sigh. "Well, seeing the way you are now, I know the answer to my question."

"Then don't ask."

"Wow. What's come over you? You used to be so nice."

"Nobody sees me for *me*. People see me for the things they can get from me, but they don't visit me for *me*. Nobody wants to talk with me."

"Well, maybe if you lightened up some ..."

"Oh? Maybe you shouldn't have so many tattoos."

Billy became silent.

"What were you going to ask me about?"

"Well, I got kicked out—"

"Again?"

"Hey. It's not what you think it is. I just need a place to crash for a while."

"See what I mean? You see me only when you want *something* from me. I'm not a fucking flophouse."

"I can blow you if you want."

"You don't get it, do you?"

"Yeah, I do. You're in love with me, and you want to fuck me."

"But you're not attracted to me. I don't want to be with someone who tolerates me. I want to be with someone who *loves* me for *me*."

"Right. Right." Billy took off his jacket and put it in Howie's hands. "I shouldn't take this."

"Why? I don't need it anymore."

"Someone recognized it as your ... lover's jacket."

"I don't care about that. Take it. I insist."

Billy put the jacket back on. "Where do I go now?"

"You still have a job, right?"

"Yeah."

"There's a rooming house up the hill from here. Bryant and 22nd. My husband lived there when he first moved to Minneapolis. I have no idea how much they charge."

"I don't make enough to cover my bills."

"Then find a part-time job. I don't know what else to tell you."

"Could I borrow some money?"

"'Borrow'?"

"Sorry."

"Just don't come knocking on my door again, okay?"

"Right." Billy stepped outside. "Well. Happy New Year."

"Wait right here. Be right back." Howie hurried to the kitchen, grabbed two sheets of aluminum foil, and wrapped one of the pasties in them. "Billy?"

He turned to find the pasty steaming. "For me?"

Howie nodded. "Miners in the Upper Peninsula used to carry it in their coats early in the morning way down underground and then eat it for lunch. Gave them a lot of energy and nourishment. I think you'll need it."

Billy took the pasty and nearly dropped it. "Shit. It's hot!"

"Put it inside your jacket. Keep it warm that way."

"Yes, sir." Billy unzipped it and tried to keep the pasty upright, almost like a papoose. "Wow. I'm fucking sweatin' already."

Howie smiled in spite of himself.

"I promise I'll never bother you again, but I wanna say one more thing before I go. The women in my life haven't treated me very well, but you—you make me wish I was into guys. You're everything I'd want in a woman, but I can't—I don't feel right about having sex with guys. It's just not my style, you know? I know this is gonna sound weird, but I'll be so fucking jealous of that guy who becomes your husband. He's going to be so lucky." Billy wiped away his tears. "Well. I should go. Thanks for everything—" he pointed to the pasty hidden in his jacket— "again."

Howie watched Billy turn the corner for the rooming house up the hill before finally closing the door.

At seven o'clock, Howie showed up in the waiting area inside Christo's. The place hadn't changed at all. He found that very comforting.

"Howie?"

He turned to find Lawrence smiling. "Oh, hi there." He looked a bit squatter and older than he'd expected.

They shook hands and made small talk.

At their table, they regarded each other as they perused their menus.

"You look better than your picture," Lawrence said at last.

"Thank you." He wasn't sure what else to say. The man didn't look as good as in his picture. He wanted to ask how old the photos were or if they had been retouched. The scars on his face were far more pronounced. There were a lot more wrinkles around his eyes. He saw how slender Lawrence's wrists were. He couldn't be 49 at all. He had to be older. A *lot* older. "What are you having?"

"Not sure yet."

"I'm going to have the dip sampler as appetizer. That's practically my favorite dish here. After that, I'll have some spanakopita."

"Oh, that's a good idea. I'll have that too."

Over dinner, they shared hopes for President-Elect Obama's first term. Howie mentioned that he was planning to take January 20th, the day of Obama's inauguration, off from work to stay home and watch television all day. He didn't mention that Timm always joined him on those occasions, and he didn't want to think about the fact that he might be alone all that day. Timm had seen each inauguration day as an excuse to make elaborate meals that took all day to cook.

"Oh, I was planning to do that, too!" Lawrence placed his hand over Howie's. "It's so wonderful to meet someone who cares about the future of America."

"Yes. What year did you graduate from high school?"

"Uh," he seemed lost for a second. "196—no, 1978."

Howie looked askance at Lawrence.

"What?"

"Are you really 49?"

Howie wondered if anyone had ever pointed out the problem with Internet dating. So many guys were single for reasons one understood once they met in person, and this Lawrence was no different. All those Internet dating sites were filled with losers. He thought about finding dates the old way before the Internet came along: gay events, parties, and gatherings at friends' houses. It had worked for many guys of his generation, so there was no reason it couldn't these days. Maybe he should delete his profile altogether and take his chances out there.

"All right. I admit it. I'm 64. I lied because so many guys don't want to date anyone—quote 'old' unquote." People forget that they will grow old, too. You're 48, right?"

"Well, yes."

"That makes you middle-aged already."

Howie wanted to say something, maybe a barbed comeback, but he could only look at Lawrence. He wanted to see a younger face there, someone to love, someone to make love to, something like that picture Lawrence had posted online, but Lawrence was right. Howie had seen people older than himself as *older*, but that never bothered him. It had somehow never occurred to him that in spite of the thirty birthdays he had celebrated with Timm, he, too, could be seen as old. How was that possible? He had never seen himself as old. Yes, he had the beginnings of crow's feet around his eyes, and his chest fur had already sprouted curls of white here and there. The grays in his beard were becoming more prominent, but he always took the pains to trim those out. He had initially thought about dyeing his beard black, but the obviousness would emphasize the fact that he was getting older. Did he want to be one of those older men in the bars and at fundraisers who dyed their hair, wore toupees, underwent facelifts, and ogled the go-go dancers at the Gay 90s? He didn't want to be a cliché. He wanted to be just Howie Taft.

"Howie?"

"Sorry." He looked about himself and the plate in front of him.

"Howie, look at me. It's okay if you're not interested in me—"

"No, no, no. It's just that I'm so lonely. My husband of 30 years died last June. I miss having a best friend, and I ..." Without warning, a tsunami of tears rose up like lava from the volcano of his being. He burst into waves of sobs that quaked his entire body, so much that he felt like he would fall off his chair and curl up in a fetal position under the table, where he belonged. Each wrack of sob felt as if a two-by-four was hitting him on the inside, and without mercy. He knew grief could be painful, but he never knew just how much it could *hurt*. His shoulders tensed up. He wanted so much to have Timm massage the stiffness out of his weary bones; Timm's hands would've targeted the points of tension, and not pull at his fur while massaging. He didn't want to be old, certainly not like this blubbering mess in front of a date in a nice restaurant. He wanted to be young again. It would be so much easier to attract a man then. *Timm Timm Timm*, his body kept begging. *Come back*. His sobs began to subside. He began to feel hollowed out. Didn't he have any feelings left? He didn't hear the murmurs of concern from the waitress who came to the table or that Lawrence whispered something to her. He grabbed a napkin from his lap and blew his nose hard. Without looking at Lawrence, he drank from his glass of water. "Sorry about that." He was now a spectacle, a fool. He couldn't bear to look directly at Lawrence.

"Don't be sorry. I lost my partner five years ago. If I'm not careful, it can still feel like yesterday."

"I've never cried like that in my whole life. I'm so embarrassed!"

"Please don't be. It means you did really love someone, and that's a wonderful thing. It's nothing to be ashamed about." A pause. "Look at me. Please."

When Howie lifted his face, he saw that Lawrence had tears in his eyes. "Believe me, I do understand what you're going through. It's hard. Very hard. I'd like it if we could be friends."

Somehow hearing that made Howie smile a little. "Okay."

"Now, let's talk about TCM."

"Turner Classic Movies? I'm a subscriber."

"Fantastic!"

From there, their conversation drifted among the many Hollywood classics they loved to watch repeatedly to the history of art and painting, and then to Lawrence's amusing travel anecdotes. It was the easiest conversation Howie had with a near-stranger. Lawrence wasn't really his type, but he enjoyed listening to Lawrence hold forth about art. Some of his comments made him curious about going back to the Minneapolis Institute of Art. Maybe he should renew his membership after all.

When the check came, Howie grabbed it. "It's on me."

"Oh, thank you."

"Sorry about my ... you know." He gesticulated with his hands.

"Oh, don't worry about it. You're going through a rough time."

"But I did have a wonderful time."

"Me too. I think we could become good friends."

Howie nodded. "I'm still learning, but maybe I could cook you something sometime?"

"I'd like that very much."

They exchanged phone numbers and email addresses.

Howie stepped into his car parked on Nicollet Avenue but he didn't feel ready to turn on the ignition. Had he sobbed that much in front of a near stranger, and in a restaurant no less? He had never thought himself capable of such a torrent. He felt empty, but he wasn't ready to go home. He needed to be with *someone*, as in fucking. He needed to touch a naked man. He wanted to explore a new man's body and revel in it. Like his favorite Olivia Newton-John song, he needed to get *physical*.

Maybe he should go down to the Eagle and try to pick up someone. On second thought, he rarely had anyone hit on him. Who'd want him? He wasn't going to humiliate himself by becoming one of those guys who stood by the sidelines and got ignored all night. Besides, he was sure that Nick would be there with his buddies, and he wasn't interested in seeing him again anytime soon, not after the stunt he'd pulled with the brownies. He thought about taking a walk somewhere, but where? There wasn't a gay bar in the neighborhood. Then he thought of Sebastian Joe's. It had been a long time since he had a cone of ice cream. He was still feeling full, but fuck it. He wasn't in the mood to sit and watch a movie or look at his computer.

He felt a bit better once he stood in line for his ice cream at Sebastian Joe's. Tonight, he'd forget about dieting. He had his eye on a scoop of coconut cream pie ice cream and raspberry chocolate, but as a minor concession to his weight, he decided to go with a paper cup instead of a chocolate-dipped cone. He walked to the back of the parlor. Glancing around for an empty seat, he spotted someone familiar sitting with an older man.

The stranger, flashing a smile, waved him over. "Howie, right?"

He walked closer. "Pete? Pete Olsson? Oh, my God."

Pete stood up and held him tightly. "It's so good to see you."

This was getting too surreal for words. Pete was balding, and his face was lined with wrinkles. Whatever effervescent youth he had was gone.

"Yeah. Mind if I sit here?"

"Oh, please." Pete moved a chair out for him. "John, this is Howie. We used to know each other back in the 80s. I used to volunteer a lot for Pride Alive, and we met at a fundraiser. Howie, John's my partner."

Howie shook hands with John. He had a slight stoop to his shoulders, but otherwise, he had piercing bright blue eyes. He looked Norwegian, or at least Scandinavian, like so many Minnesota natives.

"The ice cream here's great," Pete said. "What brings you here tonight? Waiting for a date?"

"No. Just felt like some ice cream."

"You still live in the neighborhood, right?"

"Yep. What about you two?"

"Oh, we live over on Lincoln Avenue. One block away."

John smiled and touched Howie's hand. "I'm so sorry about your husband. He gave so much to this world, and he's told me how much he adored you. He said he couldn't ask for a better husband."

"Thank you. That's the first time someone else used the word that Timm always insisted on using. I swear it was his second favorite word after 'darling'." Howie took in a spoonful from his cup of ice cream.

"It's a beautiful word, isn't it? Strength and dignity and honor all wrapped up in one word. Straight people can't have it all to themselves when they keep dirtying it with divorce."

"Well, yes," Howie laughed.

"I'm not sure if you know this, but John's one of the lawyers who's handled gay marriage cases. Lambda Legal has him on tap as an advisor."

"So are you two married?"

Pete smiled. "We've gotten married in four states so far. I don't know many straight people who are seriously committed to marrying like we are!"

"How long have you been together?"

"Eighteen years," Pete said.

"Mind if I ask how many years apart are you two?"

"Twenty-seven years."

"Wow."

"And believe it or not, we still have great sex. He's still my daddy."

"Oh."

John chuckled. "It used to bother me a great deal, but I realize it's just another word of affection. Sounds a lot better than 'old man.' You can use as many labels as you want, but it all boils down to the same thing." He pointed to his own heart. "Just don't judge, and you'll be fine. I mean, when I first met Pete, I wasn't interested in him because he was so young!" He smiled at Pete. "But he sort of grew on me. Here we are, eighteen years later."

Howie sat at the table and listened to the two of them carry on. He missed Timm more than anything. He and Timm had talked to each other all the time, with an occasional burst of laughter, and they always held hands at the table when they ate. Seeing how Pete and John talked made him feel more lonesome than ever. And these two had met in the Saloon, a bar on Hennepin! Who would've thought? But then he had to remind himself: He had met Timm in Loring Park! There was absolutely no logic to how people, destined for each other, met. No more online dating for him.

After they exchanged email addresses and phone numbers, John said, "I want to invite you over for dinner. I can introduce you to some of my friends. They're looking too."

"That'd be great."

Instead of heading straight home, Howie strolled through Kenwood, the neighborhood where Pete and John lived. The well-kept houses, usually lined with bricks, were big, but they all looked more than just houses. Its lit windows made them look filled with family and love. What did he have back home? Just a collection of emptied rooms. It didn't feel like *home* anymore. It was just a place where he spent time waiting for something to happen, or maybe he was waiting to die so he could join Timm. Even though he could produce the deed that showed him as the rightful owner of his house, he felt homeless. He needed someone to anchor him, to give him a reason to wake up every morning with a smile.

When he turned on the lights in his house, he saw the empty rooms as if for the first time: so much loneliness everywhere. Even memories seemed to have moved out. It was so different from the first time when he brought Timm here. The hope of a life together filled each room in a way that mere things couldn't. Maybe he should just sell the fucking house and move. But where?

23
Betsy

Even though she'd gone to bed four hours earlier, Betsy woke up at 6:37. It was New Year's Eve. Her mind was abuzz with the details she'd have to take care of. Moments after she'd announced her intent to retire, she had an epiphany backstage. What was she going to do with all those gowns she'd never wear again? She immediately wrapped her measuring tape around all her girls, wrote down their measurements, and told them not to worry about their costumes. She thought about how much work it'd take to make the adjustments, but then she remembered that she always took the few last days of the old year off.

Sipping her coffee, she went through her gowns and instinctively plucked out the ones that would work. For a few years during the 1990s, she had gained weight around her middle. Even though it wasn't her style to engorge on food while depressed, she did anyway. She didn't want to become an alcoholic, so she went for the next best thing. Of course, she knew she could've handled her depression over Walter differently, but doubts about her body had risen to the surface again. She knew she was a woman, all right, but she hated the feeling that no matter how realistic her vagina looked, she'd never be seen as a natural woman. Walter's silence needed to be filled, and she stuffed it with food. She didn't care. Even Timm pestered her about losing weight. It wasn't long before she ballooned, and she had to adjust her gown designs to reflect the body that she now hated. But Timm, bless his heart, kept calling her every morning. "Let's walk." "Let's go swimming." "Let's work out." And finally: "Stop eating that shit."

She couldn't articulate why she'd felt so down. It wasn't just Walter; it was everything. She'd been so disappointed by how no one seemed interested in dating her. She felt like she was going nowhere with her job. She was stuck in the same two-bedroom apartment that she'd begun renting back in 1969. 1969! Thirty-nine years! She was never interested in buying a house because all her friends talked about nothing else but how expensive it was to maintain their homes. She decided it was better to rent, and as long as her measly rent didn't go up much, she was fine. She also thought about what Howie had told her. Timm had ordered him to clean out their house of his junk so that his house could be more open to having a new life with someone else. Every time she thought about that, she missed Timm even more. Why weren't there more friends like him? Despite all his slutting around and outrageousness, he was so incredibly wise. That's how it occurred to her that she, too, would need to give away her gowns. That part of her life was over, and if she wanted it back, she had dozens of shoeboxes filled with photographs.

She went straight to work at her sewing machine. With each gown, she laughed and remembered. A particularly long train made of loose chains attached to a wedding dress inspired by the robot girl in Fritz Lang's silent film *Metropolis* had made her trip onstage. "That's a sign for you everyone. When you're married, you're automatically in chains." The audience roared and cheered when she got up and tried to whiplash the stage with a link of chains. "Wanna get *linky* with me?" The audience hooted and whistled. Yes, she'd give her *Metropolis* dress to the tallest girl of the bunch. Even though it was so heavy, she knew Josie Bosie could wear it well. Then there were all those dresses inspired by Marlene Dietrich in those Josef von Sternberg films. Damn, she thought. I'm an excellent designer.

She double-checked the new measurements on her list and adjusted the seams accordingly. She pinned the names of each girl to the appropriate gowns and hung them on a rack. By the time she decided to take a break, it was already 11:30. She peeked outside to see what the weather was like. Bright and clear. No new snow had fallen. Yes, she'd go out to Lakewood Cemetery to visit Timm's tombstone for the first time, and then on to the Minneapolis Jewish Cemetery. She'd called the Jewish cemetery for Ms. Kreitzman's plot location. It had been many years since she visited a cemetery. Even she couldn't bear to be there for Timm's burial. After dealing with death all the time at work, it had proven too hard for her. She simply left a message on Howie's cell. "I hope you understand. I loved him so much, and I miss him, and I just can't go there. I'm— I'm in pieces." Thinking about Howie these past few months made her regret not attending it with him. He would've stood there, strong and stony-faced, and wrapped his arm around her as she went to pieces at the first toss of soil on top of his casket. He was solid as an oak tree. So many people would've been there.

She found a withered synthetic corsage that Timm had given her the previous New Year's Eve. It was a bizarre gift considering that he could've given her a live corsage from his shop as he always did every year, but he said, "You need something more permanent. See? I'm wearing one too." He showed off his bright pink lily on his lapel and pointed to Howie, who was wearing a white marigold. "He's too butch for flowers." She knew she couldn't wear it this year. It would clash with her mirror-ball gown, but she knew he'd understand. She put it in her purse and set out.

Then she remembered she was to place a few rocks on Ms. Kreitzman's tombstone. She remembered the one gift that Walter had given her: a worry stone made of malachite. During their last walk together in downtown Minneapolis, she caught him holding something in his hand. "What's that?"

"Oh, nothing." He put it away in his pocket.

"Please. Let me see."

"Well, if you say so." He took out a worry stone. Its thumb impression was deep.

"Wow. This is so beautiful."

"You can have it."

"What?"

"I don't know why I was rubbing it. Just habit, I suppose."

"I couldn't possibly take it."

"Please. I want you to have it. I feel like I don't have to worry anymore."

Over the years, she touched it when she felt the need to pray for guidance, but only in her apartment. She was afraid of taking it with her to the Gay 90s and losing it in the middle of backstage pandemonium. But it was really time to give it up.

At the very end of Hennepin Avenue South, Lakewood Cemetery was open. Even though she hadn't been there in years, she knew where Timm's tombstone was. She had seen its plot location on the cemetery map when Howie showed her. It was in the southeast quadrant behind the main building. She drove slowly down the road and got out. She immediately recognized it from a distance: Carved out of pink marble, the vase had been shaped in such a way that it had flowers drooping in a way that suggested semen dribbling out of an erection. Timm had shown her a drawing and told her that Howie hadn't seen it. She was surprised that Howie allowed it to be carved like that, but he apparently wanted to honor all his wishes to the letter. She plodded through the snow and looked at the engraving.

TIMM GAY JOHNSON
Loving Fairy and Devoted Husband
to Howard Dwight Taft
21 May 1958 – 15 June 2008

She gasped. Had Timm actually asked to put "Fairy" there? She looked up at the vase again. Once she saw it as an erection in its moment of orgasm, it was impossible to think of it as otherwise. Timm was a truly unrepentant homosexual right to the end. Thank God for that, she thought. Too many tombstones here were starting to look the same, like cars made in the last twenty years. She took out her corsage and placed it at the base.

"Oh, Timm," she said at last. "I wish you could be with me for New Year's. I'm taking Howie with me this year, you know. I hope you don't mind. He's such a fine man. I hope he's doing all right. I worry about him all the time. I'm going to cook him a nice meal later this week. I know I don't cook as well as you, but who can?" She glanced around and saw squirrels skitter around the tombstones and up the trees. "I know this sounds selfish, but I want to borrow Howie until he goes. Then I'll hand him back to you and he can join you here." She looked at the empty plot next to Timm's. "I promise to take real good care of him. Happy New Year." She kissed her fingertips and placed them on the tombstone. She knew she'd need to come back here more often. Somehow the obscene vase had made it feel less depressing. It was so Timm.

She turned back for her car and drove south on Penn Avenue to the Minneapolis Jewish Cemetery in Richfield. Unlike the hilly Lakewood Cemetery, this cemetery was flat and austere in perfect rows. The tombstones were huddled next to each other. She was struck by how neatly the roads were maintained in spite of the snow. She checked her notes from the call for the location again. Ah, there it was. Three tombstones away from the road. She found it a bit peculiar that practically all of the tombstones had the deceased's last name engraved on the back, but there was almost always a Hebrew engraving in front with the years of birth and death. Ms. Kreitzman's snow-capped tombstone, which was a bit wide, was polished and simple.

KREITZMAN

CARL DAVID & MURIEL ELEANOR

1926 – 2001   1931 – 2007

פ'נ

חיים דוד בן שמואל גרסון ומרים דבורה בת אברהם יעקב
תנצב'ה

She stood a moment, looking at the tombstone. There were so many things she'd have liked to say to Ms. Kreitzman, which was odd. She had never met her, but she knew she needed to say at least this much out loud to someone, even if it was to his dead mother. "I love Walt," she whispered. "I'll always love him to the day I die." She took out Walt's worry stone and placed it on the top of Ms. Kreitzman's tombstone. Betsy imagined her standing proudly in a beautiful blue dress and a simple pearl necklace, welcoming her with open arms when Walt introduced her. They would have a lovely brunch somewhere, and she'd sit there, awed and delighted by all the stories about her son that Ms. Kreitzman was sure to share. She'd take Betsy's hand and whisper behind Walter's back in a conspiratorial tone: "I like you." Of course, when Walt asked for her hand in marriage, she'd agree to convert to Judaism. She'd learn the traditions and ways of being Jewish, and reconnect to something of her past in Long Island. They would live together happily as husband and wife, and no one need know that she used to be a man.

The sound of a van door getting shut snapped her out of her reverie. She turned to look. A mustached man, wearing a hat and black overcoat, was pushing himself in a wheelchair. She blinked her eyes to believe what she was seeing. That couldn't be Walt himself. No, no. Not Walter. He couldn't be a fucking cripple. She wanted to run and hide, but she was out there in the open. He had to have seen her already. Maybe he wouldn't recognize her. She saw that the ground and the snow between the road and the tombstone had deep indentations from his wheelchair.

She was careful not to look into his eyes when she passed him.

"Wait."

She held her breath and tried not to look into those eyes she'd missed so much.

"Do I know you?"

She shook her head no.

"You look so familiar. How did you know my mother?"

No. She had to run. As she turned for her car, she felt his hand grab her arm. She saw how fingerless his battered gloves were. He must've been disabled for a long time now. The wheelchair had a lot of wear and tear all over it.

"Betsy? Please."

She kept her face away from his. How could she face him now? She had always dreamed of him standing tall above her and looking down into her face before they kissed again—just like that summer night when they walked around downtown Minneapolis. But he looked so short and almost ungainly. How many years had it been? Sixteen years?

"Please. Look at me."

She felt him take off one of her gloves and kiss the back of her hand. Startled, she looked down at his head. Walter had a growing bald spot. His gray hair was a lot thinner.

"I'm so sorry."

"Sorry for what?"

His eyes met hers.

"I didn't mean to run away like that. I freaked out because I didn't think you were really one of those people. I mean, I sort of knew you were different, and then a friend of mine told me that you did those shows. I had to see for myself, and then ... there you were. I was so angry that I'd fallen for a guy. A *guy*."

"I'm not a guy—"

"Let me finish. I read that newspaper interview you did."

She nodded. The interview she'd done with *Star Tribune* was a local media breakthrough back in the mid-1990s. She talked about living as a transgender woman, so it was a big deal for a straight newspaper to have an incredibly sympathetic viewpoint. She had also shared her dating problems, hoping that the reporter would include it in the article so maybe—just maybe!—Walt would come across it and understand. Hoping to reach out to Walt in this way was the only reason why she'd bothered to do the interview. Instead, it attracted so many more people to her shows.

"Then I did a lot of reading. I had no idea. Honestly."

"It's okay. You're not the only one."

"No. I'm not done yet. I tried to call you, but you were disconnected. I figured you had gotten a cell phone like everyone else." His voice turned monotone. "Then I had this accident. A woman was driving and shouting at her kid on her cell phone, and she didn't brake in time. Thanks to her stupid phone, I can't walk again."

"Oh, my God."

"Don't say 'sorry.' Please. It doesn't make me feel better."

Gripping the arms of his chair, she brought herself down to make herself level with his face. "Then tell me what to do. Anything."

He gazed quietly into her eyes. It was as if he wanted to stop time for a minute.

She was stunned by how different his face had become. He must've been made fun of. Kicked around. Pushed aside. All because he didn't look like everyone else. He had become steely-faced from years of rejection and loneliness. It was the same look on many of her trans friends once they began transitioning, so she understood. There was no need for explanation. But those beautiful eyes, still so full of soul. They had been the very reason she couldn't stop aching for him all those years, and for way too long.

"Can we pick up where we left off?"

She smiled. She brought her ungloved hand to his face. She nearly keeled to the side when he suddenly gripped her hand on his face and kissed it again. "In case you were wondering, I can still ... you know." He pointed to his groin. "I'm not a complete cripple."

"Doesn't matter. I'm not a complete woman."

"No, that's not true! I don't want to hear *that* from you. You're more woman than anyone I've ever met. You've gone through so much. You're a real woman, period."

"Honey," she whispered. "I don't care about this—*this*—your wheelchair or your legs. You're still a man to me." She leaned forward to kiss him.

The unexpected tickle of his mustache on her lips made her giggle. "Sorry." She kissed him a bit forcefully, and he responded right back.

They took a quick breath and looked nakedly into each other's faces.

"Oh, honey," she whimpered. She knelt forward, wrapped her arms around him, and placed her head on his shoulder. "Just don't run away again."

"I can't, but I can certainly roll away."

She looked up at him.

"Sorry. Bad joke." He pulled her back to his chest and kissed her on the forehead. "I'm not very good with jokes. You're the funny one. You always made me laugh."

Even though it was starting to get cold again, they didn't let go of each other. She didn't care that her knees were beginning to feel sore and chilled, or that her feet were starting to feel pins and needles. It felt so right to keep him in her arms as they talked. She told him about her farewell party at the Gay 90s and invited him as her honorary guest. "The bar has a freight elevator in the back, so I'll tell them the show won't start until you're right at my table. You'll sit front and center, and I'm going to tell you all about my magnificent girls and their outfits. Oh, the stories I'll have to tell you, and only to you. Everyone'll just have to listen in, that's all. Remember, I'm *the* Queen Betsy." In that moment, she knew what her farewell song would be: The Teddy Bears' "To Know Him Is To Love Him." It was the first song she'd lip-synced to in public when she started out at Bella Smith's mansion back in 1969, and this time she would sing it to him.

He laughed.

She closed her eyes and rested her ear against his chest. She loved the sound of his voice, no longer without feeling, explaining how different it was to live in a wheelchair. How humiliating it was at first to sit in front of his students and give a lecture. How often he had to ask for someone to take down something from a higher shelf when shopping. How he hated the look in everyone's eyes as if he was totally helpless and therefore worthless. Why did people have to be so ignorant and cruel? Being disabled was really no different from being trans.

"Walter, people don't want us around because we make them feel uncomfortable. We must stare back into their faces and make them feel squirm because how else are they going to learn how to deal with anyone who's different? Just like how gay folks came out decades ago. People have got to stop judging everyone else."

"Yes. That's why I'm so grateful for my crip friends. They've really helped me get over my shame. I hope you can meet them."

"I'd really love that."

"Seriously?"

"Sure. Why not? A human being is still a human being."

"Betsy, did anyone ever tell you how amazing you are?"

"Me?"

He kissed her hand. "Am I allowed to romance the most perfect woman in the world?"

She laughed. "Only if we have candle-lit dinners." She stopped. "Shit. My apartment building doesn't have an elevator. Oh, I'm so sorry about that. I really want to cook you something special."

"Well. That's very easy to fix. I have a kitchen, you know."

She chuckled, and then stared deeply into his eyes. "Looks like we have a date."

Walt took her hand and kissed it again. "Yes, my queen, we do."

24
Nick

Sunday mornings, Nick usually went down to the Eagle, where they served cheap brunch. The food wasn't always something to rave about, but he liked sitting with his buddies and shooting the breeze. The music wasn't so loud either. The bar looked lonely in the stark sunlight, but that suited his mood just fine. The men who showed up were the ones who didn't get laid the night before. No one ever pointed this out; it was understood, and not to be talked about. Then there were the older guys who never hung out evenings at the Eagle but sat down for Sunday brunch. He recognized them from the days when everyone went to the Locker Room. Some he had sex with; some he couldn't remember whether he had or not. No matter: He was one of them. He knew who they'd slept with, had their hearts broken, and then set their sights on the next object of desire. He was surprised at how these men seemed to recognize this cycle. Didn't they want to get off the rollercoaster and settle down with one guy? What could be so bad about that?

Today most of the guys were getting together for a special New Year's Eve brunch. After he checked his email and saw nothing from that workout guy, he walked all the way from Loring Park to the Eagle on Washington Avenue South. The skies were spectacularly blue. He zigzagged his way through downtown to the bar. He liked it when the city was quiet like this. Everything felt monolithic. The winds were fiercer when they squeezed between the buildings and swept the streets. Still, he longed to be back in Fort Lauderdale. He couldn't see himself growing old and freezing to death. Maybe he could winter in Florida and summer in Minnesota, but he wasn't sure if he could afford a second home.

He waved to everyone, kissing each buddy lightly on the lips, and sat down near the end of the tables cobbled together. He ordered a Bloody Mary and listened. The big news of the morning was Queen Betsy's farewell party that night. She was really leaving the stage after 32 years. He was surprised to hear that. She'd never said anything about that when they met for coffee. Yes, he'd heard rumors and stories about her quitting now and then, but this seemed definite. One of his buddies handed him the photocopied flier.

Nick looked at the picture of Queen Betsy in one of her more outrageous poses. She had deliberately made herself up to be an overweight Marilyn Monroe over a sidewalk grill, just like she'd done to promote *The Seven Year Itch*, but only with a bad case of the itches down there in front of the Gay 90s. It was an old photograph from years ago that never ceased to make people laugh. This party was definitely not to be missed. He wondered if Howie knew about this, as Queen Betsy and Timm had been best friends.

For several years he had felt jealous of Betsy because he wanted to make Timm his own best friend. He knew he wasn't as witty and biting as Timm, but he loved the way he felt whenever he was around Timm. He was so full of life and come-hither. Of course, truth be told, he wanted another look at Timm's cock. He never forgot the one time they had sex together at the Locker Room. Fantasizing about being well-hung was one thing, but it was a whole other thing to feel the girth and heft in your own hands. After they shot all over the mattress in Timm's room, Timm pulled Nick to himself. "Let's rest together." The music pounded out Donna Summer's new hit "I Feel Love."

Nick draped his arm across Timm's body and closed his eyes. Somehow Donna Summer's voice made the coldness of everything else warmer. When the song ended only to be replaced by Village People's "San Francisco (You've Got Me)," he asked, "What's your name?"

"Timm Gay Johnson."

Nick was surprised that a stranger would give out his full name like that. "I'm Nick Clayton." He extended his hand.

Timm brushed his hand away, laughing. "Darling, we just had sex."

They made small talk: their hometowns, families, jobs.

Timm suddenly put a finger to his lips and craned his head to listen.

Nick tried to hear, but the Village People were a bit louder.

Timm tried not to laugh.

"What?"

"They're fucking their brains out, and they're screaming at the top of their lungs. Shh."

Nick heard. It was as if they *needed* to be heard above the music. He caught the look of delight on Timm's face. "What's so funny?"

"It's so beautiful. If only more people were honest about fucking."

Nick smiled and kissed Timm on the lips. "Can I be honest here? I'd like to see you again."

"Are you asking me out on a date?"

"Unh, yeah."

"I just moved here. All I want right now is cock, and lots of different ones."

Nick smiled.

"It's not the end of the world. You can have cocks too."

"But ..."

"We can be friends. I work over at Antonio's Florist Shop. Hennepin between 24th and 25th Streets. It's on the way to Uptown."

When the Village People song ended, Timm got up and picked up his towel. "You can have this room."

Two days later, he found Timm in the greenhouse attached to the florist shop. Nick had no idea what sort of clothes Timm would wear because he had first seen him in a white towel, which didn't stay on for a full minute when they met. He was wearing a T-shirt and cut-off shorts—this was before he started dressing up in a tiara and gown as the Fairy Florist. He looked a bit more effeminate than he'd realized. They went across the street for lunch and got together fairly often after that. But they never had sex again.

Nick hadn't stopped hoping, though. He saw how he wasn't the only one who wanted an encore. Men were like moths chasing the flame between Timm's legs. It wasn't long before Timm allowed himself to be the center of impromptu orgies here and there in the Locker Room. Everyone wanted his turn. When that happened, Nick felt queasy at the prospect of joining their line. He didn't want to be just another mouth to Timm. Yet, when Timm declared a time-out after yet another orgasm, he was secretly pleased that Timm often chose to sit downstairs in the lobby and talk with him about all sorts of things. It felt no different from their lunch get-togethers, except they had only towels around their waists. It wasn't long, though, before men congregated near the doorway, waiting for Timm to return to their fold. When Nick saw the hunger in their eyes, he wished he too were the object of their lust. He felt bitterness burble up in his throat when they parted to let Timm through and followed.

He didn't know what to do with this feeling, practically choking him, so the next guy who offered him his ass, he took. He fucked the poor guy's butt without mercy. He imagined his erection like a knife stabbing at all those hot men who didn't want him. When he was done, he was surprised to hear: "Oh, man. That was the best fuck of my life!" In the back of his mind, he thought he'd become a rapist and felt remorse.

"Really?"

"Yes. The way you fucked ... it was like you're a *real* man."

He was more surprised when the guy knelt before him. "I need you in my hole again."

So that was how some men began coming to him. They'd heard his grunts and the bottom's screams of ecstasy through the thin paneled walls of the corridors. By then, he'd figured out how to keep men interested in him. When he pulled out, and before he opened the door to their cubicle, he masturbated himself to another erection. He put his towel around his neck and opened the door to reveal the bottom, completely exhausted. There was no mistaking what had just happened. It didn't matter that he wasn't as well hung as Timm; what mattered was that he was a true stallion. A *real* top.

"Sir?"

Nick snapped out of his reverie and saw a tall glass of Bloody Mary in front of him.

"Would you like to order something else?"

He looked up at the waiter. His face showed that he couldn't be older than 22, but his arms were covered with tattoos. He wore tight jeans and boots.

"Uh, sure. Two eggs, scrambled medium. Sausages. Whole wheat toast."

"Thank you, sir."

He turned to the men talking among themselves. The morning sunlight fell across their faces, accentuating their wrinkles. The more he listened to them talk about Queen Betsy and the shows she'd put on over the years, the more he saw that they weren't old men. They were just old boys who'd refused to grow up. That was why they hung out in places like these. Sure, they dressed their age, but they were still boys who'd seen friends die and who'd chosen to deny that dark chapter of their lives by limiting comments about people they used to know: "He's dead now." End of discussion. They seemed to believe that still having sex was proof enough that they weren't dead yet. But what about love and intimacy?

"You know, I have a question."

Everyone turned in Nick's direction.

"How many of you can't get hard?"

He had never seen men get so uncomfortable all at once. They put food in their mouths and averted their eyes from everyone else's.

"Sorry if I'm a party pooper, but I just had to ask."

"Why?" Rick, the baggage thrower who worked at the local airport, turned to him. "You're a top who can't get hard? Pop a pill. Big fucking deal."

"What about the guys I've met online? Some of them can't get hard."

"It's not our problem."

Nick glared at Rick. "Oh, because you get hard means you're not a fag?"

"Hey, hey now," Steve, an older bear in his mid-50s and a notorious bottom, patted Nick's forearm. "You don't want to talk about this."

"Why not? We're the *other* gay community. We don't have bodies like those circuit boys. We don't dance all night long. We don't play musical chairs with boyfriends. Why the hell are we wasting time in bars where it's so loud we can't really talk? We're going nowhere, and we're still pretending this shit doesn't happen. All right, I'll tell you. Everybody knows I'm 110% top, but you know what? I can't get it up anymore, no matter how many milligrams of blue I take. My body's quit on me, but I want *it* more than ever. Last night I tried to hook up with a hot young man, and I couldn't get hard. That hurts. What about you, and you, and *you*? I know you take antidepressants. That's got to do a number on you down there. Why do we have to feel ashamed about this? I hate this feeling that without cock, we're nothing. Can't we ever have a community that's not based on sex?" He scanned their faces and saw fear aflame in their eyes. "I thought you were my friends. Can't you give me some moral support? No? Then why the hell am I wasting my time on the gay community if no one's willing to support each other? Huh? We're *all* getting old."

"Please," Steve said. "Don't you have a therapist?"

He stood up, pulled out a ten from his billfold, and left it on his placemat. "I thought you were my friends all these years. What kind of people are you? I mean, really."

Outside he hurried home. The coldness of the wind made the streaks of tears feel like touches of ice on his face. He didn't want to dwell on the fact that he'd made a laughingstock out of himself. Now that the cat was out of the bag, everyone would walk away because he wasn't a complete man anymore. It didn't matter that he looked every bit healthy and fit as men half his age. What he had between his legs didn't work, and that, more than anything else, stamped him as damaged goods. Who'd want him now? He couldn't hide anymore. It was the sort of thing that people would whisper among themselves. Maybe he should sell his condo, retire early, and buy a small place in Fort Lauderdale. That way so many visitors from out of town would be coming and going all the time that he'd never run the risk of being found out.

By the time he got home, he knew exactly what he had to do. He'd learn how to set up an email group where gay men could talk about this problem and date each other. He wasn't sure what to call the new group, but that was the least of his worries. He sat down in front of his computer and saw that the workout guy had sent him an email. Yes, there was a photograph attached to it. He did a double-take. No, it couldn't be. Rick? That guy who'd just told him off by telling him to go take a pill? He couldn't get it up either? What the fuck?

He turned to what Rick had to say.

Wow. You scared me with your words but in a good way. You have no idea how good you made me feel. I tell people I'm a top because I don't like to get fucked cuz if you're a top, people think you're a stud, right? Anyway, I'm 48, 5'3", 184 lbs., 36w, 7.5c. Please send me a face pic. Would love to talk to you and maybe meet. Thanx.

Nick wanted to kick the computer's tower on the floor under his desk. What a fucking asshole! Rick didn't have to say anything, but he did, and when he did, he wasn't empathetic at all. He was no better than Roy Cohn, a closeted homosexual who exposed other closeted gay men back in the 1950s as part of the McCarthy witch hunts, turning in his own people for the sake of fame and his own career. The prick.

He walked away from the computer and looked out at Loring Park. What should he do? He had all the email addresses of their buddies at the Eagle in his address book. Maybe he should forward Rick's first and second emails to them, showing his picture, with a carbon copy to Rick himself. Nick wouldn't have to say a word. That would serve that hypocrite right.

His cell phone rang. Nick picked it up. "Hello?"

"Hey. Nick? It's Steve."

"Yeah. What do you want?"

"That was a very brave thing you did."

"If you're tired of being lonely all the time, bravery means nothing."

"Well," Steve said and cleared his throat. "I have this problem too. That's why I don't want a boyfriend."

"Wow. That explains all the questions I always had about you. How could a handsome man like you *not* have a boyfriend?"

"Gee, thanks."

"Do you want to come over and talk?"

"Uh, no. I have a therapist and a psychiatrist helping me out, so ..."

"Okay. Don't worry—I won't tell anyone."

"Good. Look, I gotta hand it to you. Everyone looked scared as shit after you left. Nobody could just talk and carry on like before. You gotta remember, everyone always thought of you as Mr. Stud. This came at them right outta the left field, you know?"

"So no one talked about what I said?"

"Nope. Everyone left early. They all had excuses. Hell, even *I* had an excuse."

"Wow," Nick whispered. Steve was notorious for staying the longest of anyone in the group. Friends had always joked that the word "good-bye" didn't exist in his vocabulary. "Can I ask you something?"

"Sure. What?"

"Have you ever heard of Trimix?"

"Yeah. Have you ever used it?"

"No. I'm just ... you know."

"Don't be scared of the needle. I've known guys to use it, and it worked out great for them. If you wanted to try it out and use my hole for a test drive, I'd be up for that." Steve gasped to himself. "Sorry. I didn't mean to—"

"Don't be sorry." Nick took a deep breath. "You've always been so nice to me all those years."

"That's because I've always wanted you."

"Really?"

"Yes."

"What if I can't get it up?"

"Doesn't matter to me." Steve's voice took on a stronger resolve. "I don't care if you're soft or hard. I've wanted you for years."

"Me?" Nick inhaled and fought back his tears. "Wow," he finally spoke softly.

"Sorry if I've scared you off—"

"No, no. It's great. I'm just not used to doing the boyfriend thing."

"I'm not asking you to be my boyfriend, although I'd be very happy if you were. What you did back at the Eagle today has made you a better man. And, yeah, hotter, if I must say so."

"Oh, Steve."

"Oooh, I like the way you said my name. Such a sexy sigh right there at the end."

They burst out laughing together.

"Well, Nick, are you coming to Queen Betsy's farewell party?"

"Yeah. Come to think of it, I think I'll walk over there to buy a ticket right now."

"Can you get me one? Please? I'll pay you back."

"Nah. It's a date."

"You sure? I mean, I don't have a great body like yours—"

"My body isn't perfect either. Steve, I got to say one more thing before we hang up. Thank you."

"For what?"

"You've made me feel so good today."

"Really? I have some ideas how I can improve on that. Mmm. It involves a fair amount of nudity."

Nick chuckled. "Bye."

He turned off his cell phone. Steve Aaronson? *Him?* How could Nick have overlooked him all these years? Maybe he needed to learn to be less judgmental of others and their bodies. Steve was a chunky guy who always wore a black leather vest, his western button shirt, and a pair of Wranglers, but he had always carried himself well.

Nick knew what he should do about Rick's email. He sat down and attached a face picture of himself, and clicked on SEND. No words needed. He laughed out loud at the vision of Rick's reaction to seeing his picture. He put his jacket, hat, and boots on, and went out to Hennepin Avenue toward the Gay 90s. He couldn't stop chuckling. He hoped that Rick would stop hanging out with him and his buddies at the Eagle next week. He hadn't felt this great in so long!

Better yet, he couldn't stop smiling at the thrilling prospect of inviting Steve over to his bedroom long past midnight in the new year. They'd lie next to each other. Their hands and arms and tongues and faces would feel a rush of nervousness and relaxation as they explored each other's bodies in the half-lit darkness. They wouldn't take their eyes off each other's cock, as if they were hoping that they'd get hard. They wouldn't stop touching this or that body part. They couldn't believe how sexy the other man's body was. They wouldn't stop kissing. Minutes would turn into an hour, and then another. Sometimes they'd pause and hold each other, listening to the sound of their own breathing, before they resumed touching each other with light caresses. Such skin hunger was somehow better than an orgasm. Afterwards, they'd snuggle together, arms tightly around each other. Nothing else would truly matter.

25
Howie

Even though he hadn't set the alarm, Howie woke up at the same time he usually did during the week. He glanced at the red digits on his clock and grumbled. Damn. It's only the last day of 2008, possibly the worst year of his life. He had dreamed about Pete and John, but it was a weird one that made sense while it happened but didn't when he thought about it. In the dream, Howie had become John, sitting there with Pete in Sebastian Joe's and talking about nothing in particular. Howie looked like himself, except that he wasn't his age. He was John's age, older, and a good deal fatter than he was now. But, for some reason, that didn't bother him. Then they saw a younger John at Howie's age, coming in with a bowl of coconut cream pie ice cream.

Their conversation was surreal.

Pete said, "Oh, you remember John? We used to fuck all the time at my house when you and I were dating."

Howie said, "Oh, yes. Did you two have a good time?"

John said, "Yeah. But he said you were a much better lay so that's why he chose you. No hard feelings, though."

Pete giggled. "I've always wanted to be a man of quality and taste."

John smiled. "That you are. Tell me what was the difference between Howie and me?"

"He said the three words that you never did."

"What three words?"

"'I love you.'"

"Are you saying that men like me are fools?"

"Yes. Have less sex and love more."

Howie beamed. "That's why he's my boy."

Then he woke up. Nothing about the dream made any sense. It was completely pointless. Why would he be so much older than he was now? Why would he want to be with Pete? He had no desire whatsoever left for him. Pete was just a reminder of the worst guilt that he'd ever experienced. Howie thought it was the start of a great love affair, but it wasn't even love. It hurt to understand that reality when Pete called less and less.

Howie poured himself a glass of orange juice and sat in front of his computer. There were a few instant messages from strangers, both local and national, and they all said the same thing. *wanna fuck? you are so hot. damn, wish you weren't so far away. got any hot pix?* Nothing about wanting to know each other better, and he hadn't posted a picture of himself shirtless like so many online had. If he had, he was sure that he'd get a barrage of messages begging for sex. But that wasn't what he wanted. He wanted to date only one special guy and marry him, just like he'd married Timm rather unexpectedly. The more he thought about the Internet dating thing, the more he realized he'd truly gotten lucky when he and Timm met that night in Loring Park a lifetime ago. It had been pure chance.

Then an instant message from CIGARPIG popped up: *bet u wanna suck my cock boy?!?*

Howie checked out his profile. It was a tight close-up of his face, partially hidden by the haze of cigar smoke and the shadow from the brim of his leather cap. He looked like a sexy daddy, but the fact that he expected sex upfront counted against him.

Howie messaged back: *no   looking to date for a ltr*

CIGARPIG responded: *get real everyone says they want a ltr but its all sex online*

Howie messaged: *thank you for reminding me*

With that, Howie went to his account settings and clicked on DELETE MY PROFILE.

Then he thought of the other gay dating sites he'd registered with. He went to each one of them, deleting his profile in turn. As he went through the motions to do so, he realized that if he was going to find a husband, he'd have to get out there more often. Maybe he should volunteer at Pride Alive, a local HIV prevention organization. He'd heard about their weekly volunteer nights where strangers got together to talk among themselves and become friends while they stuffed small packets with condoms, lube, and safer sex information to be distributed around town and at presentations. He could do that. Or he could go back and help out with OutFront, his favorite gay political organization. Then he thought about all the other gay groups that must be in need of volunteers. Surely, he could meet someone nice in one of those places. Even if he couldn't find someone to date, he might make a few new friends. That wouldn't be such a bad deal after all, just like he had with Lawrence. Speaking of which, Howie should email Lawrence about doing brunch.

He also went online to search for local cooking classes at the Wedge. Maybe he could meet someone who was as interested in good food as he was. Maybe they could cook a meal together at his house or go out to watch a movie in Uptown. He wondered if there were do-it-yourself home improvement classes. Or maybe he could spend a weekend or two scraping and repainting all those empty rooms. Change the colors of all the walls so that it wouldn't feel like his own house anymore. Maybe he could set up a meeting with a realtor and ask for her advice. On second thought, he knew it'd be a bad idea to sell his house at this point. Far too many foreclosures were happening across the country, and President-Elect Obama hadn't yet taken office. Who knew what sort of legislation he'd push to rectify that situation?

Then he thought about New Year's Eve tonight. It had been a tradition for him to join Timm at Betsy's table. He found the drag performers amusing, but it wasn't honestly his idea of entertainment. He went anyway because Timm had insisted on it. Christmas was to be shared in private, but welcoming a new year was best shared in public. Every time he saw how Timm cheered Betsy every time she returned to the stage, he felt swept up in his passion. Timm wasn't afraid to express his emotions, and he didn't care who saw or heard him. That was another reason why he'd loved Timm so much. Timm was everything he didn't have the guts to be.

He went to the bathroom and stood before the full-length mirror. There in his pajamas, he patted his belly. He knew he needed to lose more weight, but hell, he was *forty-eight*. Most people couldn't possibly expect every middle-aged man to be slim and muscular. He took off his pajama shirt and tried to look at his chest as if he'd never seen it before. Yes, his chest and shoulders were densely packed with fur. He thought about how some men admitted having a huge fur fetish. In fact, Timm had begged him constantly to walk around shirtless in public, especially at the Pride festival. He was so proud of Howie's fur; he couldn't stop roaming his fingers all over. He said, "God gave you this hot body. Why do you have to be so ashamed of it?"

Maybe he should show a bit more of himself. He went to his closet and looked at the business suits, shirts, and ties he'd worn to work for the last 29 years. At the far end of the closet were some T-shirts hanging. He took a blue one out. It was a giveaway shirt from the Eagle when they first opened ten years before. He'd never worn it. He tugged it on and found it slightly tight. His nipples protruded a bit through the fabric. Static electricity caused the fur on his arms to puff out and stand up.

He crossed his arms and saw how his slightly droopy pectorals bundled up. Damn, he thought. Could he be ... *hot*? He lifted his arms like a bodybuilder and flexed his biceps. They weren't well-defined at all, but he had meat on his bones. He dropped his arms and looked at how badly his belly stood out in his shirt. His profile wasn't too bad. Maybe he'd go to work in a T-shirt and Levi's from now on. He chuckled at how Nick and other co-workers might react when he came into the office. They'd probably have a heart attack. Yes, he'd need to lighten up a little if he was going to find a husband. So: No more suits and ties in the new year. No more Internet dating. No more missing Timm.

He knew one other thing for sure: He couldn't go to the Gay 90s for New Year's. It'd remind him too much of Timm and all their New Year's Eves together. He had to be somewhere different this year, a place where Howie hadn't been before. He had no idea where, but he'd have to call Betsy and tell her that she'd need to find someone else to escort her. He felt bad about the prospect, but he knew he couldn't sit there for hours and watch everyone gather around Betsy. It'd be a repeat, the same thing like Timm and his friends, with Howie standing on the sidelines. No, he wasn't going to get overlooked again. He was much more than just Timm's dork of a husband. Dammit, he was Howard Dwight Taft, and he deserved to be *seen*.

Then he thought of something. He pulled off his shirt and imagined walking around shirtless at the Eagle. Maybe that would make everyone gasp and stare, much like how people had stared at Timm's humongous dick. His fur was like a sweater all over his body. He still didn't consider himself a bear, so he wouldn't hang out with those lecherous guys again. But if he was going to go shirtless, it was because he had to remind everyone that he existed. And, of course, once he found a husband, he'd put his shirt back on and stay away from the bars like he always did. He liked the idea of staying home because he felt safe, and because Timm had never ignored him at home. There was no distraction of friends crowding for his attention at home. He knew that not many men were looking to date a homebody, because that didn't sound exciting. Guys were always looking for someone exciting with a perfect body to date, but he'd intuited that a lot of these "exciting" men brought with them a lot of unnecessary drama. Just like that asshole Rick, for instance. Howie was a low-maintenance guy. Didn't anyone want that in a husband? Why was being a little on the boring side such a bad thing? After a number of years together, anyone was sure to seem boring out of sheer familiarity. Even Timm's unrepentant nudity became predictable.

He checked the weather outside. The morning sun was starting to filter through. It was going to be a clear day. He loved winter days when the skies were blue with not a cloud in sight. That always cheered him immeasurably. He might as well go for a walk. He pulled on a pair of sweatpants, a T-shirt, and a pair of boot socks. Fitted with a parka and boots, he set out for a walk along West 22nd Street to the Lake of the Isles. No one was around. He liked how quiet the neighborhood could be. The silence was soothing. Here and there, he spotted puffs of smoke rising from chimneys. Maybe he should light up his fireplace later this afternoon and watch a David Attenborough-narrated documentary on the BBC channel. Maybe he should search online for local gay organizations who might need volunteers and contact a few that interested him.

He walked up the hill and saw that the sign showing ROOM FOR RENT in front had been removed from its front door. He was sure that Billy must've gotten a room there now. Maybe that would teach that boy to stop blaming other people for all his problems. He thought about the idea of having a tattoo made somewhere on his body. Yes, he would do that. Definitely. But a tattoo of what? Certainly not an image of Timm. It would intimidate anyone new into thinking that they'd have to compete with Timm's memory. Not a good idea. He could have one made of an animal on his bicep. A wolf? It didn't matter, really. The fun would be in searching for the right image. He was in no rush. Maybe he would get tattooed by the end of June and walk around shirtless at the Pride Festival in Loring Park. He thought about shaving his head bald, sporting a goatee, and wearing a pair of sunglasses so folks wouldn't recognize him at first. If he could walk around with his new boyfriend and hold his hand while bumping into friends and acquaintances, he would be so happy.

He knew finding a new husband by June 2009 was a tall order. But, as long as he put himself out there meeting new people all the time, he had a better chance of connecting with someone instead of just meeting them online and finding that nothing clicked in person. Trying to connect with someone online was such an incredible waste of time. That seemed so obvious. Why were people still hanging out online when they continued to have such miserable luck? Yes, he had done the right thing by deleting all his profiles. The real world was not online; it was out there among people who walked to work and drove out to malls on errands, and among buildings and places that brought people together. This year he'd go out to the Como Park Conservatory and wander among the plants. He'd miss hearing Timm's ongoing commentary about this or that exotic plant, but that was to be expected. Instead, he'd be on the prowl for that curious glance from a handsome man. Maybe they'd meet and exchange phone numbers, and set up a date. Maybe not. That would be okay too.

He realized that once the Internet came along, it took away the lost art of cruising. People still cruised each other, to be sure, but they seemed to have forgotten *how*. Didn't they ever look up from their laptops and cellphones once in a while? What was so wrong about walking up and down a popular street in a gay neighborhood? He had seen that happen on Eighth Avenue in New York, and on Castro in San Francisco. Seeing such small moments of ache had thrilled him, but he never dwelled on them. He had Timm at his side. He wished he could ask Timm if the hookups he found online felt different from the men he'd spontaneously fallen in with at the baths. He was sure that there had to be. Perhaps he should fly out to Chicago and spend a weekend in a bathhouse, just for the hell of it. Timm would be so shocked at the idea that Howie himself would want this, but he'd have been very supportive. Maybe he'd click big time with a guy there and that would be the end of all his hunting. Maybe he'd sell his house and relocate to Chicago. Would anyone in Minneapolis notice him gone? Probably not.

A few sparrows fluttered from tree to tree. Howie was often amazed at how these tiny birds could survive living out here during winter. They had no feathers to shield their legs and claws from the cold, and yet they bounced from branch to branch after they sought overlooked crumbs on the snow. What kept them going? Did they, like he, have memories of summers past? Was the promise of a warmer season enough to keep them going? Or did they simply live in the now, trying to survive on so little from one minute to the next? Maybe he should get a birdfeeder and hang it outside in his backyard.

Howie looked both ways on Hennepin Avenue before he crossed. He spotted Tao Natural Food and Organic Café on his left and made a mental reminder to himself that he should eat there more often. He liked their food, and it was much healthier than most places. He walked down the hill, noting how well, or how shoddily, each house owner had swept their sidewalks clean of snow. He spotted rabbit footprints and pellets crisscrossing across the yards. Life was still going on with or without Timm, or Howie for that matter. He wondered how animals dealt with death. Did they ever grieve when one of their members was killed by one of their predators? Did they ever pause in a moment's reflection? He was always compelled by the footage of big cats like the cheetah and the panther chasing their prey. Of course, there was drama between predator and prey, but he often wondered how the prey felt when they saw one of their kind consumed alive. Did they all believe that life just was? What if humans behaved the same way? How different would the world be if death were seen the same way as just an incident, say, on the same level as another meal? No one need say the tiresome word "sorry" ever again.

Down the hill was the Lake of the Isles. He contemplated the challenge of walking its entire 2.6-mile periphery, but not today. He'd be too hungry halfway around the lake. He crossed the parkway and sat down on his favorite bench. There was no one on the ice anyway; he shouldn't cross the lake alone. He watched a young man bundled up in a Twins cap, a scarf, and a puffy down jacket dawdling behind his English bulldog wearing a thick vest that covered his body except for his underside. He chuckled when he saw that the dog also had the Twins logo on the sides of his vest. "Cute dog."

He looked up at the young man and saw that he was clean-shaven with hazel eyes. He had a dimpled smile. "You're cuter."

Howie was startled by his directness.

"Sorry if I offended you."

"No. Not at all." He glanced around and gazed at the red-haired young man. "You're *very* cute."

"Really?"

Howie nodded. He stared openly into the stranger's eyes. The more he gazed, the more he liked what he saw. There was something of Timm in his demeanor and height, and something of Pete in his smile, but he didn't remind Howie of either man. Howie found himself never wanting anyone as much as he wanted this boy. Yes, the young man had to be at least 30 years old, which made him technically an adult, but something about him told him that he was a *boy*.

"Wow. I've never had a guy like you stare at me like that."

"I can show you a lot more." Howie whispered, "A lot more, boy."

The man took off his glove and extended his hand. "I'm Mike."

"Howie here. Nice to meet you."

As they shook hands, they didn't let go. It was as if all that cold around them had intensified the heat jumping back and forth in the synapse between their slicked wet palms.

Mike sat next to Howie. "Nice day, isn't it?"

"'Nice'? It's a *great* day." He saw the dog sniffing his boots. "What's his name?"

"Puckett, after Kirby Puckett, the greatest Twins ballplayer who ever lived. I call him Puck for short."

"I see. What's up with your Twins obsession?"

Mike giggled. He explained how he'd fallen in love with baseball as a kid, and later, when his father took Mike to a Twins baseball game at the

Metrodome, he fell in love with the mythology and the reality surrounding his favorite team. He loved the feeling that he was part of a passionate community, more so when they went online to share their thoughts and got together at home games.

Howie laughed at the carefree way Mike chatted. He didn't seem to check his own thoughts. Sometimes he bounced around, but he was delightful to listen to. He wasn't full of himself, but he clearly believed that anything he said had to be interesting as long as he made it sound interesting. The more he listened to the young man babble on about his background, the more Howie couldn't believe his luck. Mike was actually single and liked older men? Did he actually say, "I find so many guys my age flaky, so that's why I prefer daddies"?

"Mike, hold that thought."

"What?"

"You have plans for today?"

"Not really."

"How about coming over to my house for breakfast? I can cook up some eggs and stuff for you."

"What about my dog?"

"My house's practically empty. He can run around."

"Really?"

"Come on." Howie patted Mike's thigh. "Let's go."

"No. Wait." He turned to his dog, who was panting big breaths. "Puck, say hello to Howie. Hello!"

The dog promptly sat down on his hind legs and held up his paw dutifully. His eyes zeroed on one of Mike's coat pockets.

Howie laughed, took off his glove, and shook Puck's paw. "You're a fine gentleman, Mr. Puckett."

Mike and Howie laughed.

Mike took out a treat from his pocket and tossed it to Puck. "Bulldogs can be so stubborn and lazy, but he's the best dog in the whole world. He even eats snow when he gets thirsty. Look at him!"

They laughed at the comical way Puck was crunching on a chunk of snow ice.

Howie stood up and saw that Mike was shorter than he'd initially thought. He smiled.

As they walked east on 22nd Street, he listened to Mike babble on. He laughed now and then. For someone who was barely 30, he had a motherlode of funny stories. He provided tech support for a large corporation downtown, so he was "a self-professed geek."

Howie chuckled at how often Puck had to sniff almost anything that looked like a tree and then lift his leg.

"Oh, he's just checking his peemail."

"You're very funny, Mike."

He liked how Mike seemed to blush in spite of the nip in the air.

"Well, here we are."

Mike followed him to the front door. He looked awed. "Wow. Nice house."

"Thanks."

Inside the foyer, Howie took off his hat, jacket, and boots. He suddenly felt naked when he saw how exposed his furry arms were. Damn. He should've been wearing a long-sleeved shirt!

Mike looked quietly at Howie.

"You okay?"

He found his voice. "Yes."

"Aren't you going to take off your jacket?"

"Oh! Yeah."

"Let your dog off the leash."

They laughed when Puck waddled a beeline for the kitchen straight ahead at the end of the hallway. "He'll be on a sniff-a-thon for a while."

"That's fine." Howie watched Mike take off his jacket and hang it up. "Mike?"

"What?"

"Look, I got to tell you something right off the bat. I'm the kind of guy you never notice in pictures. I don't have a lot of friends, but I'm working on that. I don't do well at dating. I'm trying to lose weight. I want to be a better cook. Well, I think I can be a better cook if I had someone to cook for. I have an okay job. But I always make do with what I have, and I don't complain."

Mike searched Howie's face for a moment.

"Did I say something wrong?"

"No! That's the most honest thing anyone's ever said to me."

"Did I scare you off?"

"No," he said softly. "Not at all."

"Really?"

Mike shook his head. "You had me at those arms of yours. Fuck. That fur!"

Howie looked at his own forearms. "So?"

Mike licked his own lips. He didn't blink.

Howie did something wholly unexpected, something that he'd never dreamed of doing for anyone. He pulled off his T-shirt. Who cared if he hadn't showered that morning? He felt a little weird about the idea of putting his hands behind his head and showing off his dense armpits, but what the hell. He had to have this boy.

Mike's eyes widened at the fur carpeted all over Howie's chest.

The hunger in Mike's eyes turned him on even more. "Pick your jaw off the floor." Howie growled and slapped his own belly. "Get over here, boy." He pulled Mike into his arms and kissed him on the lips forcefully, forcing Mike's hands to roam all over his chest. This time, just like Timm had done with Howie on the night they'd first met, he would show Mike all that he had learned, so much that the boy, already whimpering while he shot helplessly inside his pants, would grow to become the best husband Howie had yearned to have.

About the Author

Raymond Luczak, a native of Michigan's Upper Peninsula, is the author and editor of many books, including *Flannelwood, The Kinda Fella I Am,* and the award-winning Deaf gay novel *Men with Their Hands.* Some LGBTQ titles that he's edited over the years include *QDA: A Queer Disability Anthology* and *Lovejets: Queer Male Poets on 200 Years of Walt Whitman.* His book *once upon a twin: poems* was listed as a Top Ten U.P. Notable Book of the Year for 2021. His most recent title was *A Quiet Foghorn: More Notes from a Deaf Gay Life.* An inaugural Zoeglossia Fellow, he lives in Minneapolis, Minnesota.

9 781955 826310